Frederich held her tightly, awash in emotion,

afraid that Caroline would suddenly remember who he was and pull away. He grazed her cheek with his rough hand, stroked the dark hair he'd been so longing to touch.

"I would do anything for you," he whispered to himself—in German.

He held her, feeling her sorrow and his own, determined to keep her close like this for as long as she would allow it. But the horse pranced nervously, and she abruptly let go of him and slid from his grasp to the ground, hurrying into the house without once looking back.

He sat there completely overwhelmed. He couldn't deny the truth any longer. He cared far more for this exasperating woman than he ever intended, and he wanted her—as a friend, a lover, as a wife...!

Dear Reader,

We are delighted this month at the return of three-time RITA Award winner Cheryl Reavis to Harlequin Historicals. Her heart-wrenching tale, *The Bartered Bride*, is set in Civil War North Carolina. It's the story of a pregnant woman who has little choice but to marry her sister's widower, a man whom she considers heartless, but who, over time, teaches her the healing powers of forgiveness and love.

Abigail Cooprel suddenly comes face-to-face with a man who is the very image of her adopted son in *Abbie's Child*, the second book from talented newcomer Linda Castle, whose first book, *Fearless Hearts,* was released during our annual March Madness promotion in 1995, to loud acclaim.

Multigenre author Merline Lovelace makes history come alive in her new release, *Lady of the Upper Kingdom,* the dramatic story of forbidden love between two strong-willed people separated by the treachery and distrust that exists between their two cultures, the Egyptian and the Greek. And from Catherine Archer comes *Velvet Touch,* the sequel to her previous Medieval, *Velvet Bond,* the bittersweet story of a young nobleman who is sent by his king to arrange a marriage and settle a feud, only to fall in love with the intended bride.

Whatever your taste in reading, we hope you will enjoy all four Harlequin Historicals, available wherever books are sold.

Sincerely,

Tracy Farrell,
Senior Editor

Please address questions and book requests to:
Harlequin Reader Service
U.S.: 3010 Walden Ave., P.O. Box 1325, Buffalo, NY 14269
Canadian: P.O. Box 609, Fort Erie, Ont. L2A 5X3

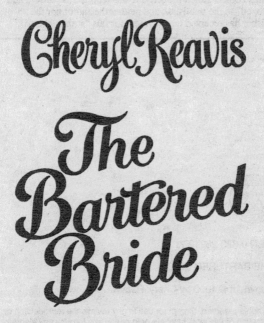

Cheryl Reavis

The Bartered Bride

Harlequin Books

TORONTO • NEW YORK • LONDON
AMSTERDAM • PARIS • SYDNEY • HAMBURG
STOCKHOLM • ATHENS • TOKYO • MILAN
MADRID • WARSAW • BUDAPEST • AUCKLAND

ISBN 0-373-28919-7

THE BARTERED BRIDE

This edition published by arrangement with Harlequin Books S.A.

® and TM are trademarks of the publisher. Trademarks indicated with
® are registered in the United States Patent and Trademark Office, the
Canadian Trade Marks Office and in other countries.

Printed in U.S.A.

Books by Cheryl Reavis

Harlequin Historicals

The Prisoner #126
The Bartered Bride #319

Silhouette Special Edition

A Crime of the Heart #487
Patrick Gallagher's Widow #627
One of Our Own #901

*Family Blessings

CHERYL REAVIS,

public health nurse, short-story author and award-winning romance novelist, says she is a writer of emotions. "I want to feel all the joys and the sorrows and everything in between. Then, with just the right word, the right turn of phrase, I hope to take the reader by the hand and make her feel them, too." Cheryl currently makes her home in North Carolina with her husband and son.

For Josephine, who took me to a Robert E. Lee
lecture *exactly* when I needed to go.

Prologue

North Carolina
December 1861

Someone else was in the church. He stood listening for a moment, certain now that the faint sound had come from the back of the sanctuary.

"Wer ist da?" he called out, not wanting to frighten any of the old women who might have come to polish the candlesticks or put out the hymnals for the Sunday service.

No one answered.

"Who...is it?" he managed in English.

Again there was no reply.

He began to stack the oak logs he'd cut in the wood box near the potbellied stove. He could still hear the girls playing on the front steps by the open door; neither of them had followed him inside. There was much talk among the men these days about the possibility of army deserters or escapees from the new Confederate prison in town, but neither would have been of concern to him—if he had come to the church alone. He didn't care about the politics of this country. He didn't care who won the newly declared war or who escaped from the prisons. He didn't care about anything except the fact that he had Ann's daughters with him and he had given his solemn promise to always keep them out of harm's way.

He took a moment to look around the sanctuary. He saw no one, heard nothing, and he decided that he must have been mistaken. But then the sound came again, a faint whimper he might not have heard if he hadn't already been listening so intently. He turned and walked quietly toward the back of the church, and he saw her almost immediately. She was sitting on the bottom step of the stairs that led to the schoolroom on the second floor.

"Bitte—" he began, but she jumped violently, startling him as well. He moved around so that he could see her better in the dim light, recognizing her now in spite of the fact that she turned sharply away from him. She wiped furtively at her eyes, bringing her feet up under her as if she intended to make herself as small as possible.

He stepped closer.

"Eli," she said, making a great effort to look at him. She attempted a smile, but her mouth trembled and her voice was hardly more than a whisper. She turned away again, telling him something in rapid English he didn't begin to understand.

He stood awkwardly, not knowing what to do. Her hair was coming down and one button at the neck of her bodice hung by a thread. If she had not been Ann's sister and if his promise hadn't included her as well, he would have left her sitting there.

"Caroline? You are...ill?" he said. He had neither the proficiency nor the inclination to ask anything more. Perhaps she'd had another argument with her brother Avery—in which case her current state was to be expected. He knew Avery Holt to be a bully, and he knew from Ann that Caroline did her best to provoke him. He wanted to just go, but for Ann's sake, he stretched out his hand. Surprisingly, Caroline took it, her fingers cold and clinging in his.

"Was haben Sie?" he asked, making her look at him.

"...the children," was all that he understood of her reply.

"*Ja*—yes," he said, looking over his shoulder toward the open door. "Mary Louise is...here. *Und* Lise. Both—here—"

"Eli," she said in alarm, trying to push him in the direction he'd come. "Mary Louise and Lise—please—*bitte!*"

He hesitated, but he understood that her distress was such that she didn't want her nieces to see her.

"*Bitte!*" she said again, her eyes following his glance at the dangling button. She snatched it from its thread and shoved it into her pocket.

He stood up and walked quickly away, glancing back at her when he reached the end of the aisle. She was no longer sitting on the bottom step.

He stepped outside, firmly closing the church door behind him.

Chapter One

March 1862

Caroline Holt had been waiting all afternoon for her brother Avery to return. She kept walking to the window to look out across the fields toward the Graeber farm. That Avery would drop everything to answer a summons from Frederich Graeber was incredible to her. The ground had to be readied for the spring planting, and Avery despised their German brother-in-law.

It was nearly dark when he finally rode into the yard. She went hurriedly back to the churning, a task she'd let take far too long while he'd been gone. She worked the churn hard, determined not to give him the satisfaction of knowing she'd been so curious about his absence that she'd neglected the butter making. He came into the kitchen immediately, leaving the door ajar much longer than was necessary and tracking in mud with no concern at all for the backbreaking effort it took to keep the rough oak floor scrubbed clean. She shivered in the draft of cold air, but she made no comment.

"Frederich Graeber wants to marry you," he said without prelude.

She looked up from the butter churn, but she didn't break the rhythm of the churning. The statement was so ridiculous that her first inclination was to laugh. Her brother was not a humorous man, but still she thought he must be joking. Even if he had somehow guessed how badly she needed marrying, he wouldn't have suggested Frederich Graeber— except as some kind of cruel joke.

"I want you to marry him. I've already answered for you," he said. "They're going to announce it in the German church Sunday— Frederich will make his formal pledge to you then."

She continued to stare at him, realizing now that he was entirely serious and that this marriage plan must account for Frederich's summons and for his willingness of late to bring her nieces here to the house to see her.

Poor Avery, she thought. He had no inkling of the impossibility of his arrangement. For the first time in her life she felt a little sorry for him.

"Why are you looking at me like that?" he said in annoyance. "Did you hear what I said?"

"I heard you, Avery. And I can only suppose that you've lost your mind."

He gave a little smile. "Now why would you *suppose* that?"

"You know I can't marry Frederich Graeber."

"Can't?" he said, coming closer. His hair was sweated to his forehead. Before he had departed for the Graeber farm, he and Frederich's nephew, Eli, had been shoveling horse manure into newly plowed ground all morning. Avery still stank of it, and somewhere along the way he must have lifted a keg of beer—to celebrate the bargain he and Frederich thought they had made.

"It's done, Caroline," he said, his voice still calm because he was used to having his way. Indeed, who ever said no to him? And who else refused to tolerate his arrogance but her? Certainly not their mother when she was alive. And certainly not the women here. Caroline couldn't account for the fact that so many of them preferred the civilian Avery

and his finagled farmer's exemption to the boys who'd gone
for soldiers and were fighting in Virginia—except for the
fact that Avery was *here*, of course. And he was handsome.
But his handsomeness was far surpassed by his fickle nature. The list of widows and maidens who'd aspired and
failed to marry Avery Holt grew longer every day.

"I've already told Frederich you want it," he said, and
she abruptly looked away from him. She felt light-headed
again and she concentrated hard on keeping the rhythm of
the churning by fervently whispering the work poem that
went with the task.

    Come-butter-come

    Come-butter-come

It was only at the last moment that she allowed herself to
acknowledge her anger.

    You-marry-the-German

    This-time-Avery!

But Avery had no use for Germans—unless he needed
manure shoveled or his man's nature satisfied. She had
happened upon how deftly he accomplished the latter at
John Steigermann's corn husking. The drinking and the
dancing and the games on that cold October night had been
incidental to the stripping of a roof-high pile of corn and
John Steigermann's daughter. Avery had bloodied a few
noses to find and keep the first red ear, and Leah Steigermann was supposed to kiss him for it. She lifted her skirts
to him as well—beautiful wine velvet skirts held high for
Avery Holt in a cow stall, and Caroline a witness to it all
because she'd thought to keep her other, too-young brother

from hiding in the barn and sampling Frederich Graeber's famous plum brandy.

Avery slammed his hand down hard on the kitchen table, making her jump. "I'm talking to you, Caroline! I don't know why you think you can pick and choose here. I said you're going to marry Frederich—you owe me, Caroline. You and Ann both owe me!"

"Ann is dead. Whatever you think her debt is, surely you can count it paid now. Just how is it *I* owe you?"

"I sent you to school in town. I stayed here working my tail off and I did without to keep you in ribbons and bread—"

"That was a long time ago. Mother's inheritance paid for most of my schooling and you know it."

"What about the nieces?" he asked, obviously trying a different approach. "What about Ann's girls—you want them raised German?"

"What's wrong with that—if German is good enough for *both* your sisters to marry?"

Avery swore and flung open the pie safe, looking for the fried apple pies left over from breakfast. He had married Ann to Frederich first—more than eight years ago when their mother was still alive but too addled to notice his machinations. He'd gotten the use of an acre of land with a spring out of that arrangement—when *he* should have been the one providing the property for Ann to bring to her marriage. At fourteen, Ann had been too young to marry—a fact that Frederich in his lust and Avery in his greed failed to notice. She endured one pregnancy after another in the effort to get Frederich Graeber a male heir until it killed her. People here pitied Frederich—not because his beautiful young wife had died, but because he had no sons. Caroline gave a wavering sigh. If the announcement was to be made in the German church this Sunday, then they must all know by now where he planned to get *those*.

She abruptly remembered a time last spring when she and Ann had taken the girls on a too-early picnic. The sun had been so bright that day, pinching their eyes shut and warming their faces while their backs stayed winter cold. The robins ran across the ground and the violets poked out from under the dead leaves, and Ann had told her that she was pregnant again.

And Caroline hadn't been able to make her worry.

"Everything will be fine," Ann kept saying.

"But the doctor in town—I thought you weren't supposed to—"

"Life is short, Caroline," she said with a laugh, as if she were the older and wiser sister. "If you ever came out of those books of yours sometime, you'd know that."

Doesn't Frederich care about you at all? Caroline had nearly asked. She had believed even then that he was a cold, indifferent man, their marriage never progressing beyond Avery's mercenary arrangement between two strangers. Ann had never seemed to be anything Frederich considered significant to his well-being—except for *that.*

Don't worry, Caroline. I'm so happy!

But she had worried—and with good reason. Ann had died of the pregnancy that gave her such joy.

Another memory surfaced. Avery had appeared then with his many complaints, disgruntled because she and Ann had picnicked too long and delayed his supper. Ann had done her best to annoy him—she was an old married woman and beyond his command, refusing to speak to him in anything but the German she was suddenly learning, provoking him to swear because he couldn't find out anything about Frederich's latest agricultural successes.

Remembering now, Caroline gave a slight smile, but the smile abruptly faded. She had held Ann's hand while she bled to death from another miscarriage. Nothing the midwife tried and nothing written in the herb book had stopped the flow. Ann was twenty-two years old. She hadn't known where she was, hadn't known her children or Caroline, hadn't asked for Frederich even once.

"I don't understand," she said in those last minutes and nothing more.

Caroline had had to go hunt for Frederich to tell him.

"My sister is dead," she said to him, and he kept chopping wood and never looked at her. Ann had borne him two daughters, died trying to give him his precious son, and Frederich hadn't even looked at her. It was little Lise, who was barely seven, who found the things Caroline needed to ready Ann for burial, not Beata, Frederich's own sister, who should have done it. And it was Eli who lifted Ann into her coffin—Frederich hadn't stopped *chopping*.

Work. Order. Discipline. The Germans believed in nothing else—except perhaps their medieval superstitions. The mirrors had to be covered so that Ann's soul couldn't escape into one. She had to be taken out feetfirst so that she couldn't give the room a "last look." She had to be buried with a lemon under her chin. And what a good thing it was that her baby hadn't lived, Beata said—because Ann's ghost would have come at midnight to suckle it.

And Avery expected her to marry into that.

"You're past your prime, Caroline," he said, startling her because in her reverie she hadn't realized that he had come so close. He suddenly reached out and grabbed the plunger in the churn, stopping it and holding it fast. She tried unsuccessfully to peel his big fingers away. After a moment, he abruptly let go.

"What do you get out of this, Avery?" she asked, picking up the rhythm of the churning again, holding on to it for dear life. Perhaps there had been a reason for Frederich's woodchopping on the day that Ann died after all, she thought. Work could be an anchor, a place to hide, a way to *not* think.

Ah, but to do that, Frederich would have had to be a man capable of feeling in the first place, and she knew better than that.

"I'm the head of the family," Avery said. "It's my duty to see you married."

"What do you get out of this, Avery?" she asked again.

"Nothing I don't already have," he answered obscurely.

"Does William know what you've done?"

"I haven't *done* anything, Caroline, that isn't for your own good—and yes, our little brother knows. He was there when Frederich asked for you."

She abruptly stopped churning; Avery looked up from the pie he was eating and smiled.

"You see?" he said with his mouth full. "You thought it was all my doing. It wasn't, Caroline. The marriage is Frederich's idea, not mine. To tell you the truth, it never even occurred to me."

"I don't believe you."

"Then ask William."

"Beata Graeber won't stand for her brother marrying another Holt, Avery. She despised Ann."

"Since when do you think a man makes his plans according to the whims of some old maid relative?"

"Frederich never went against anything Beata said for Ann's sake. Never. Ann had to live in his house like some kind of poor relation."

"Frederich asked for you. I said yes. So there you are. You're past your prime, Caroline," he said again. "If he wants you, you should be grateful—God knows, *I* am."

"I won't marry my dead sister's husband—"

"Let's see if I've got this right, Caroline. First you 'can't.' Now you 'won't.' You're the one who said it—Ann is dead. And, by God, you *will* marry him. He's got no heir and he's not likely to get one out of you."

She understood then. If Frederich had no sons, then who would be his closest male heir after Eli? Frederich might leave a portion of his land to his inept, non-farmer nephew, but he wouldn't leave the rest of it in the care of his daughters—no man here did if there was any other alternative. His daughters' uncles might be another matter. Avery would be right there waiting, and if not him, then William—which would be the same thing. William was too timid to go against whatever Avery wanted, even if it were to take over an inherited Graeber farm.

But she didn't understand Frederich. He was rich enough to send to Germany for a bride if none of the women here appealed to him. The German men and his sister Beata would have surely pointed out how foolish he was being. The young Holt couldn't breed—nothing but females and dropped litters. And the old one? Why do you want a thirty-year-old wife when you've got no sons? they'd ask him.

Why?

She had no accord with Frederich Graeber. She had hardly spoken a dozen words to him in all the time he and Ann had been married. He'd never made her feel welcome at the Graeber house, never seemed to notice Beata's rudeness to her and Ann both. It couldn't be because she was aunt to Mary Louise and Lise, she thought. Frederich Graeber didn't care in the least for his female children. Or if he did, not enough to marry a woman "past her prime."

Except that she wasn't past her prime, and before long everyone would know it. She had had no monthly bleeding since November; a horrible and unpredictable nausea had taken its place. She couldn't control it, and she'd been frantic that Avery would notice. Clearly, he hadn't.

Oh, God, she thought. *What am I going to do?*

The back door abruptly opened—her younger brother William bringing the cold March wind in with him. She saw immediately that Avery had been telling the truth about him at least. William knew all about her proposed marriage, because he studiously avoided her eyes. He, too, went to the pie safe in a quest for food.

"Is Eli still out there?" Avery asked him.

"He went home," William said, looking again at the bare shelf in the pie safe as if he expected something to just magically appear. He was big for his age, taller than Avery, and he was always hungry.

"You got the horses settled?"

"Eli did it—"

"Damn it, boy, you get back out there and make sure those animals are put up right. Eli doesn't know a damn thing about horses—"

"He does, too," William interrupted in a rare contradiction of one of Avery's pronouncements. "It's farming he don't know nothing about. He can take care of a horse good." He glanced at Caroline, but he wouldn't hold her gaze. He stood awkwardly for a moment. "I...reckon Frederich's got in the habit of marrying Holt women," he offered, still avoiding her eyes.

Why am I arguing with Avery about this? she thought.

It was only out of *her* habit that she sought to defy him. She had no choice about whether a marriage to Frederich Graeber took place, and neither did Avery. It was too late for a deception, even if she'd wanted one, too late for anything but the relentless unraveling of the truth. She was nearly four months pregnant, and no matter how badly she wanted it the secret could not be kept much longer.

"—he don't think much of Kader Gerhardt," William was saying.

"What?" she said, startled by the German schoolmaster's name. Kader Gerhardt was the one man here she had truly respected. He was refined and educated, and she had thought him to be honorable as well. She had earnestly believed that he was somehow different from the rest of the men here. And she had loved him. She had even dared to think that her feelings might be returned, and she had never once perceived what he was really about—when she of all people should have. How could she have Avery for a brother and not have known?

My fault, she thought again. *Mine.*

There was something in her, something she had said or done that had made him think she wanted—

"—the nieces," William said for the second time over his shoulder. And he was still looking for something to eat. He made do with a cold biscuit he found in a pan on the kitchen table. "Maybe Frederich wants you so you can teach them. You got enough schooling to do it as good as Kader Gerhardt. Frederich don't think much of Kader. I heard him tell John Steigermann Kader Gerhardt wasn't fit to teach German children."

"William, you haven't *heard* a damn thing," Avery said. "Since when can you talk German?"

"I can't talk it—but I know what I hear sometimes. You *got* to if you're going to live around here, Avery. You should know that."

"You watch that mouth, boy," Avery said, choosing to take offense.

"None of this matters!" Caroline suddenly cried. This inane discussion had gone on long enough. There was nothing to be done now except to stop the marriage. "I won't marry Frederich Graeber, and you can tell him, Avery, or I will."

"It's *done,* Caroline! Weren't you listening? There's no backing out now!"

She stepped away from the churn and moved to the pegs by the back door, taking down her wool shawl and flinging it over her shoulders.

"Where do you think you're going?"

"You know where I'm going, Avery!"

"Do you think you can just trot yourself over to the Graebers and tell Frederich the wedding is off?" he said incredulously.

"Yes."

"Well, the hell you are. What reason are you going to give him? You're not stupid enough to think you can find somebody with more money and more land than he's got, I hope? I don't see anybody else standing in line for the privilege of marrying you, Caroline!"

She sidestepped him, but he blocked the doorway, grabbing her when she tried to get through. His fingers dug into her shoulders; his eyes held hers. She knew the exact moment he realized that there had to be some reason for her determination. Given his own history, his mind did not have to make a great leap to decide what that reason might be.

"What have you been doing?" he said, giving her a shake. "Who have you been sneaking around with?" He roughly turned her around and put his hands on her belly. "By God, you're already carrying, aren't you? Aren't you! Whose is it!"

"What?" she said, because everything was moving too fast and she was terribly afraid now.

He slapped her hard.

"You're not paying attention, little sister. It's not *what*. It's *who*. Whose is it!"

"Avery, don't!" William cried, bouncing from one foot to the other, but not daring to intervene. "Avery!"

"You stay out of this, William!"

"Don't, Avery—what are you hurting her for?"

"Did you hear that, Caroline?" Avery said, grabbing her by the arm and jerking her around to face him. When she tried to get away, her shawl came off in his hand. He slung it aside and grabbed her arm again, squeezing hard. "William wants to know what I'm hurting you for? Tell him!"

"Avery, please!" she cried, because he *was* hurting her.

"Avery, please? Who else have you been saying *please* to?"

"I won't tell you," she said, forcing herself to stay on her feet, trying not to cry. She had thought herself prepared for the day Avery would know about her condition, but she wasn't prepared for the look in his eyes now or for his bellow of rage.

He hit her with his fist, and he would have hit her again if William hadn't grabbed his arm. William tried vainly to hang on, but Avery yanked free of his grasp. He shoved her hard, and she fell backward. She tried to roll away from him, but Avery came after her in spite of all William could do. She could hear someone gasping, and she realized that the sound must be coming from her. She stayed in a tight ball on the floor, covering her head with her hands, trying to ward off the blows, knowing Avery wouldn't stop.

But he was jerked away from her suddenly, his feet coming up off the floor.

"Mein Gott! You kill the girl!" someone cried.

William knelt beside her, weeping loudly. "Caroline. Caroline!"

Don't cry, William.

She wanted to say it, but no words came. He kept trying to make her sit up, as if he thought that her being upright would somehow negate everything that had gone on before. She tried hard to do what he wanted—he was crying so—but she sagged against him, her fingers digging into his shirt to keep herself from falling. Her hands shook. Her whole body shook.

Another pair of hands reached for her, and she cowered away from them, expecting to be hit again.

"Nein, Fräulein," John Steigermann said gently, wrapping her shawl around her. *"Kommen Sie*—come with me. *Es ist Zeit."*

It's time? she thought, recognizing the German phrase. *For what, John Steigermann?*

"Avery..." she whispered, trying to see where he'd gone.

"You don't worry about your brother. He don't bother you now. Come." He was a big man and he lifted her easily in spite of her protest, carrying her across the kitchen toward the back door.

"What the hell do you think you're doing?" she heard Avery say.

"She goes to my house, Avery Holt," John Steigermann said. "Leah and Frau Steigermann will take care of her. *You* keep yourself and your bad temper here until I send for you."

"This is none of your damn business!"

"I am a Christian man, Avery Holt. It is my business."

They were outside in the cold wind, and she hid her face against John Steigermann's coat, the movement causing her to cry out in pain. He lifted her carefully into the buggy. She closed her eyes tightly as the horse lunged forward, and she let herself be held fast in one of John Steigermann's big arms.

Chapter Two

She was given a hot broth to drink and put to bed in a small upstairs room in the Steigermann house. The bed had been warmed, but she still trembled, and she couldn't stop crying. She had had to have help to undress. Thankfully, it was provided by John Steigermann's quiet wife rather than his daughter, Leah. She couldn't bear the look she saw in Leah's eyes, the profound relief that it was Caroline Holt who had been caught and not Leah Steigermann. Caroline wanted only to be left alone—or to die—but she knew from the whispering that went on around her that neither was likely. Arrangements concerning her were still being made without her knowledge or consent. She had no doubt that John Steigermann was a good man. He had saved her from Avery—but now what was he to do with her?

She slept finally, and she awoke to find that she had completely lost track of time. A cedar wood fire burned low on the hearth. It was daylight, and she seemed to remember being offered things to eat and drink a number of times. The sun had been shining then, too. Was it still the same day? She didn't know.

She made it to the chamber pot and back with difficulty because the nightgown Leah had provided for her was much too long and because every muscle in her body hurt. She climbed painfully back into the narrow bed and closed her eyes. She was far too miserable to take stock of her surroundings, and yet she was surprised to note that she was actually hungry. Even so, she feigned sleep when she heard the door creak open. It was all she could do not to weep. Why were these people being so kind to her? She didn't deserve anyone's kindness. She couldn't stay here—and she had absolutely no place to go.

Someone sniffed loudly, and she opened her eyes. William stood at the foot of the bed.

"Caroline?" he said, his voice tremulous and worried. He had his old felt hat crumpled in his hands, and he was as ill at ease as if he were about to call on a total stranger.

She motioned for him to come closer. Her eyes were badly swollen. She turned her head carefully on the pillow so she could see him out of the slit of vision that remained. She realized how bad she must look by his sharp intake of breath. She could see him better now; tears ran down both his cheeks.

"Don't," she said, reaching for his hand. His hand was chapped and tough from working outdoors, and cold from his walk to the Steigermanns'. "Don't cry."

He gave a halfhearted shrug and tried to do as she asked. "Are you all right, Caroline?" he asked after a moment.

"I'm all right—except that I'm not sure how long I've been here."

"It's almost two days—Caroline, I should have done something. Look at you," he said, tears rolling down his face again. "I should have stopped him—"

"William, don't. Come sit here." She patted the bed beside her.

He did as she asked, sitting down heavily because he was a big, awkward boy. He jarred her painfully and she tried not to wince.

"It ain't right, Caroline," he said, wiping at his eyes with the sleeve of his coat. "How can this be right? I ain't staying in that house with Avery anymore. I'm strong and I know farming. Somebody around here will hire me—maybe I'll go to the army. I could fight the Yankees, I reckon. I can shoot a gun—''

"No!" Caroline said sharply. "William, please. Don't make this any worse for me. I can't worry about you, too. You stay with Avery and you do what he says."

"Caroline—"

"Do it, William. Because I ask you to, if nothing else. Does Avery know you're here?"

"I'm supposed to be plowing."

"William—"

"I couldn't stand not knowing anything, Caroline! I had to come over here."

"I'm...glad you did, but you'd better get the plowing done now. You don't want Avery to find you gone."

"I hate that house with you not there, Caroline," he said, his misery showing plainly on his face. "What's going to happen to you?"

"I...don't know, William. I think Mother had some relatives in Virginia. Maybe I could write to one of them. Maybe they'd let me stay there until" Her voice trailed away. Until what? She hadn't dared think that far ahead. "Go on home now. Go on. I promise I won't do anything or go anywhere without letting you know."

He stood up because she pushed him, but he didn't leave.

"Caroline—"

"I'm sorry, William," she said. "I...didn't mean to be so bad."

"You ain't bad, Caroline! You ain't the first woman this happened to. Don't you go saying you're bad! And nobody else better not say it, either!"

He abruptly bent down to her, giving her an awkward hug, the way he used to when he was a small child. "I'm going to take care of you, Caroline. Don't you worry about that." He stood for a moment longer, then abruptly went out the door, bumping into something in the hall on his way downstairs.

"Little brother," she whispered, trying not to cry. She gave a wavering sigh. She had never felt so bereft in her life. William's love was unconditional and far more than she deserved.

She struggled to sit up on the side of the bed. She had lain in the dark like a wounded animal long enough. She had to get dressed. She had to think. She had to make some kind of plan. For the first time, she made a deliberate inspection of her face, hobbling to the washstand mirror so she could see everything Avery had done. She hardly recognized herself. It was no wonder William had been so startled. She tried braiding her hair, but it quickly became too much of an effort. She hunted until she found the frayed calico work dress she'd arrived in and her underclothes, and she put them on. Then she tilted the mirror on the washstand downward and turned sideways to look at herself. Avery had been right. She was beginning to show.

Poor baby—

"Caroline," Leah Steigermann said behind her, making her jump. She smoothed the front of her dress and turned to face her.

"You are better today, yes?" Leah asked kindly, but her eyes went to Caroline's belly.

"Yes," Caroline answered. "Better." She could feel her eyes welling with tears again, and she looked abruptly away.

"I've brought you something to eat—some of my mother's egg custard. You'll like it, I think. Come sit here." She pulled a chair closer to the fireplace with her free hand, handing Caroline the custard cup, a starched napkin and a spoon when she sat down. "Go on," she coaxed. "It's what you need now."

Caroline looked at the custard, then began to eat. It was quite delicious.

"You must eat all of it," Leah said. She knelt in front of the fireplace to add another cedar log to the fire. The smell of burning cedar filled the room and a shower of sparks flew out onto the hearth and up the chimney. "I have promised my father."

"Promised him what?" Caroline asked. She kept glancing at Leah's profile as she deftly managed the log with the heavy iron poker. Leah was very beautiful, and spoiled, and pampered, and Caroline would never have guessed that she would attempt such a mundane task as stoking a fire.

"I promised him that I'd get you to eat something so you will have strength," she said, still poking at the log. She looked at Caroline. "He's coming to talk to you."

About what? Caroline nearly asked, but the question was ridiculous. There would be but one topic of conversation for John Steigermann or anyone else—her illicit pregnancy. She closed her eyes for a moment, trying not to think about how stupid she had been.

Oh, Kader.

She had loved Kader Gerhardt for a long time. She had loved him enough to tell him so—afterward. And she had seen the veiled look that came into his eyes. She realized immediately that her love was of no importance to him. He had wanted her body, not her devotion. She kept telling herself that she hadn't meant for anything to happen between them that day. She hadn't gone looking for him. She'd only meant to return a book he'd loaned her—*Dying Testimonies of the Saved and Unsaved*. She was going to leave it on his desk, but he was working in the schoolroom. She had stood by the door for a moment watching him, surrounded by the smell of leather-bound books and India ink and wood smoke from the back draft in the small fireplace. And she had loved finding him so completely unaware.

He looked up sharply when he realized he wasn't alone. "You shouldn't be here, Caroline," he said immediately. "What if someone saw you? How would it look?"

"I—I only meant to return this," she said, flustered because he *was* here and because he was as cross with her as if she'd been one of his recalcitrant pupils.

He stood up from the desk and came closer. She waited, waited for his nearness so that she could savor his clean masculine smell. Kader Gerhardt didn't stink of sweat and horses and manure. Kader Gerhardt was a gentleman.

"You cause me a great deal of difficulty," he said, taking the book out of her hand.

"I'm very sorry to disturb you," she said, still distressed that her unannounced presence had offended him so.

"Does . . . Avery know you're here?"

"Avery? No. Avery's in town buying seed."

He had smiled then, and he'd been so kind. And how she had craved his kindness. She had been so grateful for it that she took the full responsibility for his passion. The thing that had happened between them was *her* fault. She had come upstairs to the schoolroom alone. She had let him kiss her. She had let him take her. She had let herself be completely overcome by her need for him, and she had lost herself in the touches and kisses and the rush to free her from the layers of wool and muslin that kept them apart.

And then it was abruptly over, and he'd left her lying alone, oblivious to the fact that she was shaken and still *needing* him so badly. She had tried to cover herself. She could hear children running and playing in the churchyard below.

"It's nothing," Kader said, intent now on righting his own clothes. "Just the boys playing war. They won't come up here."

And then he explained to her how this had all come about.

"You made it impossible for me, Caroline," he said sadly, as if she had deliberately set out to ruin him. "I couldn't help myself."

"I...love you, Kader," she said, and it was a long time before he answered.

"We will have to be strong, Caroline," he said finally, not looking at her. "We must behave properly—for your sake."

His idea of propriety had been to rush her from the schoolroom as quickly as possible before someone saw her there. And to make certain that she had no notion of mentioning anything to Avery. She had been devastated by his coldness. She had given him everything, and he'd only wanted her to get out.

And someone *had* seen her there. Eli Graeber, Frederich's nephew, who thankfully didn't speak enough English to understand. Since that day Kader had all but forgotten she existed. There had been no more offers to loan her books, or newspapers with the latest war news. No requests for her help with the younger children in his class. No attempts to engage her in conversation behind Avery's back at Sunday church services. No wishes for her good health sent via William. She wondered if he knew how dire her need for good health was now.

She realized suddenly that Leah had said something that required her comment. "I'm sorry, what?"

"I said I could loan you something of mine to wear."

"The dress I have is fine, Leah. I...don't much care how I look."

"Then I will go to your house and get some of your own things," Leah decided.

"No. Please—"

"I will go, Caroline," she insisted. "Avery won't say no to me."

No, Caroline thought unkindly. *And vice versa.*

"Eat," Leah chided. "Please eat some more."

Caroline shook her head. She was feeling light-headed and queasy again. "I've had enough, I think. Please tell your mother it's— How much I—"

"There," Leah said brightly, as if Caroline hadn't been about to cry again. "The fire's going. I'll go tell my father to come up. Are you all right, Caroline? You are so pale."

Caroline managed a painful smile, but she didn't reply.

Why are you doing this? she wanted to ask. *Avery certainly isn't going to love you for it.*

But she said nothing. She stared into the fire instead, feeling the heat on her battered face, and she braced herself for yet another ordeal. Leah left the door ajar, and after a moment Caroline could hear her downstairs, then John Steigermann's heavy treading up the steps to the second floor.

"Please, come in," she said when he was about to knock on the door. She saw immediately that his wife stood behind him. Mrs. Steigermann was such a frail-looking woman, her fragility exaggerated by her husband's great size.

John Steigermann motioned for his wife to precede him, and he gave her the only other chair in the room. He remained standing, towering over them both. He stared openly at the bruises on Caroline's face. It was all she could do not to turn away.

She forced herself to say what needed to be said. "I want to thank you—" she began, but he held up his hand.

"What I have done, anyone would do," he said, but they both knew that was far from the truth. Anyone might have intervened if a man were beating his horse, but not his unwed and pregnant sister.

"There is something you need to know. Frederich is going to withdraw his pledge of marriage to you," Steigermann said bluntly.

Caroline looked at him, not knowing what her response should be.

"There is no marriage pledge," she said after a moment.

"Avery gave his word on your behalf," he said. "The agreement will be set aside in the church Sunday, Caroline. *You* will have to be there."

"I?" she said in alarm. "I had nothing to do with Avery's agreement."

"Frederich is the injured party, Caroline. And he . . . says he doesn't want you. He says the baby you carry isn't his. I know you have never said that is so," Steigermann said when she would have interrupted. "But if the baby *is* his, you can say so before God in the church. You can hold him to the pledge."

"No. I don't want to marry Frederich. I *never* wanted to marry Frederich." Her face hurt to talk. She bit down on her lower lip to stop her mouth from trembling.

"You have to be there, Caroline."

"Why? I didn't have anything to do with this. I didn't even know there was a marriage planned until—until Avery—" She broke off to keep from sobbing out loud.

"There are people who believe that you and Avery were going to fool Frederich—"

"The marriage was Frederich's idea," Caroline said, incredulous that she had been reduced to repeating anything Avery said as the truth. "I didn't know about it—"

"You must go to the church. It is the only thing you can do for the reputation of your family. Not for Avery, but for Ann's daughters and for your little brother, William. You must say that the withdrawal of the marriage pledge is acceptable to you, that Frederich has done nothing dishonorable."

"I can't," she said.

"You can," he answered. "God judges us, Caroline. No one else has the right. I believe this. My wife believes this," he said, gesturing in her direction. "But there are the others, you see. Those are the people you must face in the church. You must show them that you will stand with your head up, and you will let only God decide if you have sinned. You must do this for the sake of the baby and the rest of your family. And you must not leave Frederich to take the blame for what has happened to you.''

She realized that he was looking at her bruised face again, and this time she turned her head away.

''I believe that Avery Holt has more to answer for than you, Caroline,'' he said gently. ''But you are the one who must go to the church. Frederich is a proud man and he must save his honor. You must give it back to him. *You* must say before God that you release him from the pledge.''

''I never made any pledge!''

''Avery did. It is the same.''

''It isn't!''

''There is the baby, Caroline,'' he reminded her. ''For the rest of your life you and the child will suffer the talk. It will be worse for you both if you—''

''I don't want to do this,'' she said, crying openly now.

''It's what Frederich wants, Caroline. It's his right to have everyone know he has done nothing wrong. What will you do? Will you run from here? Will you leave William and Lise and the little one—Mary Louise—to face what you have done?''

Mrs. Steigermann said something to her husband in German. He hesitated, then translated the question.

''My wife asks...if the father of the child is...away from here. If he is a soldier, perhaps I can send word for you—''

''No,'' she interrupted. ''I have nothing to say to him. Nothing.''

She hadn't gone to Kader about her pregnancy—and wouldn't. When she first knew that there would be a baby, she had comforted herself with fantasies of telling him. Sometimes she'd find him in the schoolroom again, only he'd be glad to see her and he'd stay glad even after she'd told him she carried his child. He'd sweep her into his arms and beg her forgiveness. He'd want them to marry immediately—

But she had no hopes of a happy ending. She had seen her parents' loveless marriage. And Ann's. And she knew the truth of her own situation. Kader Gerhardt didn't care about her, and to his credit, he had never claimed that he loved her. In a moment of boredom, she had been nothing but a temporary diversion. What would he give her now if she asked? Money perhaps, but never marriage. He would deny everything, and if people did think that she and Avery had tried to trick Frederich into marrying her, who would believe *her* version of the truth? Her child would still be a bastard and her begging for Kader's help would only compound her stupidity and her shame.

She forced herself to look into John Steigermann's eyes. She saw nothing but concern there. He was a good man, a kind man—but how could he expect that she face the entire congregation?

"You know I have spoken the truth, Caroline. You know what you have to do. You will not be alone. My wife and I will stand with you."

She abruptly bowed her head. She didn't care about Frederich Graeber's honor, but she did care about William and her nieces. And she cared about the child she carried. Perhaps she even cared about the German schoolmaster who had given it to her.

"You need time alone now, Caroline. We will leave you. You know what needs to be done," he said when he reached the door. "My advice is that you ask God to help you and give you strength."

She sat there, her mind in turmoil, hardly aware that the Steigermanns had gone.

Would Kader be there? she thought. *Would he sit and watch her humiliation in silence?*

Yes, she thought sadly. He would. Because they must behave properly—for *her* sake.

Chapter Three

Caroline had to wear her same worn-out yellow-flowered dress on Sunday morning after all. Avery might have obliged Leah by giving her one of Caroline's better dresses, but there was a limit to John Steigermann's free hand. He would not allow Leah to go see Avery Holt, not even for the sake of Caroline's pitiful wardrobe. He had seen firsthand Avery's loss of control, and he refused to permit his beloved only daughter to have anything further to do with such a violent man.

The upstairs smelled of the morning breakfast—fried ham and potatoes and cabbage and freshly baked black German bread. The smell of the food and the *Schmalz,* a greasy, apple- and herb-flavored pork fat the Steigermanns spread on the bread, had been more than Caroline could manage. She had abruptly retreated to her small room, and she sat down to wait by the fire until John Steigermann came upstairs to tell her it was time to go to the church. If he was surprised that she would do as he asked and let Frederich officially withdraw his marriage pledge, it didn't show. But then there was no reason for him to be surprised. His fine expectations and her obligation to him made it impossible for her not to go. It was his suggestion that they arrive ahead of the rest of the congregation. She saw the wisdom of the plan immediately. The last thing she wanted was to have to enter the church after everyone else was already seated.

The day was cold and windy. Her face looked a little better, perhaps not so swollen, but she was grateful for the loan of one of Leah's bonnets so that she could hide from the wind and from the curious stares she was bound to encounter.

She let John Steigermann take her by the arm to escort her to the wagon waiting by the back door. She felt dead inside, not afraid so much as empty. Leah was waiting for her in the downstairs hallway, resplendent in her fine brown and coral merino wool dress and her fur-trimmed cape. Caroline kept glancing at her, acutely feeling her own shabbiness both inside and out. She wondered if Avery would have abandoned Leah if their liaison in the barn had led to a baby.

No, she thought. Leah would have brought much more to a marriage than an illegitimate child. She would have brought money and prestige and land. And the rest of the men would have given Avery a pat on the back for being clever enough to get around John Steigermann.

It was a long, cold ride down the river ferry road to the German church. The church was a square, two-story edifice of natural stone built by the German settlers who had come here from Pennsylvania in the last century. It was a fitting monument to their faith and their perseverance. She tried hard not to let it remind her of the German schoolmaster.

In spite of their clever plan, Caroline and the Steigermanns were not the first to arrive. Avery stood in the sun on the front steps. He was dressed in what passed for his Sunday finery, a severe black broadcloth coat that always needed a vigorous brushing. Caroline didn't see William anywhere, and she guessed that Avery would have made him stay at home. She prayed that he had. The Holts had been shamed enough without William having to witness the proceedings today.

Avery was obviously waiting for her, and there was no way for her to get inside the church without going past him. She got down out of the wagon with difficulty and walked a few steps away from the Steigermanns. The graveyard that surrounded the church was quiet except for the wind in the trees and the rattle of leaves blown against the low stone wall. Her mother and father were buried here. And Ann and her lost babies. For a brief moment, she thought about crossing the wall to stand at their graves, but she knew already that she would find no comfort among their cold headstones. There was no comfort anywhere.

The Reverend Johann Rial's house was within sight of the church. She could see the glint of the sun on the tin roof and smell the wood smoke from the chimneys. And Avery was coming toward her. She had to force herself not to turn and run. She was afraid of him, but whatever he had to say now, she preferred to hear it alone. The Steigermanns had been privy to enough of the Holt scandal.

More buggies and wagons were arriving, and Leah came to take her arm. Caroline had to force herself not to look for Kader Gerhardt among the men who were beginning to congregate on the front steps where Avery had been. Would she think less of Kader if he came—or if he didn't?

Avery was close now.

"My father won't let him hurt you," Leah said quietly, and Caroline drew a long breath.

"Please, Leah. Step away so I can talk to my brother alone."

"Caroline, he is angry still—"

"Please," she whispered, and Leah reluctantly went to stand with her father.

Whatever Avery does, don't let me cry, Caroline prayed.

"You deserved what you got," Avery said when he was close enough, not caring if the Steigermanns heard him.

"Yes," she answered quietly. "The way Leah will if you aren't careful."

His cheeks flushed and he reached out to grab her by the arm. She drew back instinctively, expecting to be hurt again.

"What did you tell old man Steigermann about me?" Avery said.

"I didn't have to tell him anything. He *saw* what kind of man you are."

"Damn you, Caroline! You've ruined everything—"

"Come, Caroline," John Steigermann said behind her. "We go inside now. Your brother will not want to keep you out here in the cold." He offered her his arm, and she took it gratefully. She gave Avery one last look as she walked past him. The question was still in his eyes.

Who, Caroline? Who?

"I have seen by the fine attendance this morning that you are all aware of what is about to take place today," Johann Rial said from the high pulpit. He spoke in English now— for Caroline's benefit, no doubt—and his eyes swept over the congregation, coming to rest on her. She felt physically ill, and she took a wavering breath. Leah reached for her hand.

Johann waited for a moment for someone's fit of coughing to subside and for his words to be translated to the older members who spoke only German. "Those of you who are feeling relieved that my sermon has concluded," he continued, "will be pained to hear that I have more to say. To you all. I now charge each of you to remember the Scriptures.

"Behold I was shapen in iniquity and in sin did my mother conceive me. Against Thee—and Thee only—have I sinned.

"I charge each of you to remember Our Lord's admonishment— Let him who is without sin among you cast the first stone.

"It is also written that a bastard shall not enter into the congregation of the Lord even unto his tenth generation shall he not enter.

"I further charge you that this *child* in Christ be not left without salvation. Brother Graeber must follow his own conscience. But I steadfastly hope that someone among you will see fit to make an honorable and Christian offer of Holy—"

Johann Rial abruptly stopped, and Caroline could hear whispering behind her and the shuffling of feet. The commotion intensified, a collective murmuring and a creaking of pews as people turned in their seats.

"What is it?" she whispered to Leah, not wanting to look around.

"It's Eli Graeber," Leah whispered back. "He's standing."

Caroline could already hear him addressing Johann Rial in German, and there was more commotion among the congregation. Leah gave a sharp intake of breath.

"What is he saying, Leah?" she whispered, squeezing Leah's hand hard. Did Eli know about her and Kader Gerhardt after all? Surely, surely he wouldn't stand up in church and say that she had been with the German schoolmaster.

"Eli says he is willing to offer you marriage if Frederich withdraws his pledge," Leah said.

"He what?" Caroline cried, turning around now. Eli was indeed standing—and Frederich had him by the arm.

"*Sitzt sich!*" Frederich bellowed, trying to make him sit down.

Eli pulled free and began to speak over the clamor around him.

"Eli says he owns half the land, half the farm," Leah translated rapidly. "He says he has the right to take whoever he pleases—and his uncle is—"

Her translation was interrupted by another outburst from Frederich.

Sit down! Sit down! Caroline prayed, as if her litany could stop whatever Eli was doing by sheer force of will. *Oh, dear God,* she thought. *Everyone will think Eli is the one.*

Eli Graeber suddenly looked in her direction, but he was speaking to Johann Rial. Then he was making his way to where she sat, waiting at the end of the pew for Johann to join him.

"Eli wants to know what you say," Leah said.

"I don't say anything!" She sat with her head bowed, as if she could hide somehow. Everyone was staring at her—she tried desperately not to cry. She hadn't expected this. In her worst nightmare she hadn't expected this.

"Come, Caroline," Leah said, trying to get her to stand up.

"No—please. No!"

"Caroline, Eli and Johann want to talk to you!" Leah whispered urgently.

"Leah, I can't—I have to get out of here!"

She would have tried to run, but both John Steigermann and his wife had gotten up so that Eli could come into the pew and Leah was blocking the other way out. She was hopelessly trapped. Eli was actually going to address her here and now, in front of all these people.

"Caroline Holt," he said.

She forced herself to look up at him, and she was immediately struck by two things. How determined he looked. And how unhappy.

"Eli, what are you trying to do?" she whispered, knowing he wouldn't understand. Then she abruptly covered her face with her hands. *I can't bear this! I can't!*

"Caroline Holt," he said again. *"Sehen Sie mich an."*

"Eli says to look at him," Leah translated.

"Bitte," Eli said. "Don't be...afraid," he managed in English.

Caroline turned away from him. Afraid? She wasn't afraid. She was humiliated.

He held his hand out to her, much the way he had that day he found her on the schoolroom stairs.

"Come. We talk now," he said. "You come away from all these—" He gestured toward the people around them. "Their business is—*not* to know—"

He stopped struggling to find the English words and simply waited, his hand still outstretched.

A farmer's hand, Caroline thought. *A hand like Avery's. Like Frederich's and her father's.*

"*Kommen Sie,*" Eli said. "I . . . help you."

Help? she thought incredulously. He had made a spectacle of her. How could he *help?*

He abruptly reached for her hand and she let him pull her upward, not because she intended to talk to him, but because he was the only way out of this place. When had she ever talked to Eli Graeber about anything? There was only that one time, that day in the church when he'd kept Mary Louise and Lise from seeing her. How much had he understood then? How much did he understand now?

She glanced at Johann Rial. He wanted to say something very badly. Then she took a deep breath and let Eli lead her out of the pew. They followed Johann, and she meant to keep her eyes straight ahead, to look at no one in their all too public trek to the vestry. But like a moth lured into the candle flame, at the last moment, she looked at the congregation. Her eyes immediately locked with Frederich Graeber's, and she couldn't keep from faltering. The raw emotion, the anger she saw there, led her to but one conclusion. Frederich Graeber wasn't made of stone after all.

The vestry smelled of hymnals and dust and candle wax. Caroline waited for Johann to stop talking. Her breath came out in a white cloud in the frigid room, and her hands felt stiff and cold. She wanted to move to the far corner away from the door, because she truly felt that if Johann hadn't been standing in the way, she would have bolted.

"Do you understand what's happened?" Johann finally asked her.

"Do you?" she countered. She had no idea how she'd come to be in this predicament.

"Caroline, Frederich wants to talk to you."

"It's a little late for that, isn't it?"

The door abruptly opened, and Frederich Graeber stepped into the room. Caroline caught a glimpse of the people on the nearest pews, all of them trying to get a better look. She stood with her head up, the way John Steigermann had counseled. She was not going to cry. She was *not*.

Frederich glanced in Caroline Holt's direction, but he said nothing to her, closing the door firmly behind him. "I want to know what you—and Eli—are doing?" he said to Johann in German, lowering his voice so that Leah wouldn't hear him.

"What *I* am doing?" Johann said incredulously. Johann's German was corrupted by years of speaking English and sounded wrong to Frederich's ears. "This uproar is no doing of *mine,* Frederich. If anyone is to blame it is you and Avery Holt. The girl didn't even know there *was* a marriage pledge until the day John Steigermann took her to his house. My only concern is for this bastard child—"

"You know what people will think!" Frederich interrupted.

"Do *you* think the baby is Eli's?"

"If I thought that, Johann, he'd be dead now," Frederich answered, knowing full well that the only reason he *didn't* believe it was the horrified look on Caroline Holt's face when Eli made his bold offer. Clearly, Frederich wasn't the only German she held in disdain.

"Yes, and the day isn't over yet, is it, Frederich?" Johann said pointedly. "What is it you want done—or do you even know? She is *your* family member with or without the marriage pledge. Are you going to withdraw your pledge? Do you care if her baby is born a bastard or not? If you don't, then leave. I will find whatever way I can to save this innocent child—even if it is a marriage to Eli.''

Frederich made an impatient gesture. "I will not be indebted to Eli!"

"How much has *he* to do with your making this marriage pledge in the first place?" Johann asked bluntly.

"Everything," he said, meeting Johann's gaze head on.

"You would put Caroline in the middle of the trouble between you and Eli and poor Ann—"

"Poor Ann? I am the one cuckolded!"

"Ann made a wrong choice, and she is the one who died for it. I think it would be better if you did withdraw the marriage pledge to Caroline. Let Eli take her. You carry too much pain and resentment still—"

"She won't be any better off with Eli, Johann, and you know that. Eli has lived his whole life according to his whim. Ann was one of his whims. What if he changes his mind *after* he's married Caroline? Who will be looking after her and her baby then?"

"I will ask if someone else will make the offer—"

"No! I don't want any more scandal! And I told you. I can't—won't—be beholden to Eli. There will be less talk if I keep my pledge—at least they won't dare say anything to my face. Caroline Holt is my children's aunt. She has always been kind to them, and as much as I might dislike it, both of the girls need her."

"And you, Frederich. What is it *you* need?"

"I need a mother for Lise and Mary Louise."

"Can you be kind to Caroline? Can you keep from punishing her for Ann's sin?"

"Look at her, Johann," Frederich said. "We are alike, she and I. Neither of us cares what happens to us from here on. Perhaps we can do something good for an innocent child, and we can make everybody else happy in the process. I will keep the pledge. I am making the Christian and honorable offer you wanted someone to make."

"Yes, but are you sure?"

"I'm sure, Johann."

"I don't think she'll marry you, Frederich."

"What choice does she have? Now go away so I can talk to her."

"Go away? I can't leave you in here alone with—"

"Leah is here. I don't want you listening to what I say to Caroline—for her sake. There are some things that are none of your business. I want her to speak to me without you standing over her with the wrath of God."

"I don't do that," Johann protested. "I never do that."

"Go away, Johann!"

Caroline watched as the conversation between Frederich and Johann Rial abruptly ended. Johann was disturbed—she could tell that much—and one of his questions had made Frederich angry.

"What were they saying?" she asked Leah, trying hard to stand calmly and not wring her hands.

"I couldn't hear," Leah said.

Surprisingly and more than a little reluctantly, Johann left the room. Caroline needed to sit down. With Johann gone, there was no one to stand between her and Frederich Graeber's anger. She was so tired suddenly, and in spite of everything she could do, she swayed on her feet. She moved blindly to one of the straight chairs in the room, and resisting Leah's help, she sat down heavily.

Frederich immediately pulled up another chair and sat directly in front of her. He needed to be able to see her face when he talked to her, and he watched her closely. She was more afraid than she was willing to let on, and she was very pale. But she was not an older version of Ann. She looked nothing like his dead wife, and if anything in this situation pleased him, it was that.

"I know what you think of Germans—" he said.

"You know what *Avery* thinks of Germans," Caroline replied. "You don't know what *I* think about anything."

"I also know what you think of marriage," he went on as if she hadn't interrupted. Ann had told him once that Caroline was determined never to be trapped in a loveless and hurtful union like their parents'.

Caroline didn't respond to that remark, and Frederich waited. After a moment, she reached up and took off her bonnet, as if she wanted him to see her face better. She was not beautiful. He had always thought she had a kind of wasted prettiness, the kind that would have been fine enough for any man—if only she would have smiled more. She was not pretty today. Her face was bruised and swollen, and her dark hair was roached back so that it hid nothing of the damage Avery had done.

"Do you want to marry Eli?" he asked.

"No," she said, meeting his gaze. "I don't know why Eli is doing this. And I don't want to marry you. I never wanted to marry you. I didn't even know what you and Avery had planned—" She abruptly broke off and looked away. She was not going to explain this *again*.

"Why doesn't the father of this baby marry you?"

Caroline glanced at him, but she said nothing. Then she intently smoothed down her skirt as if that were much more important than his questions.

"Do I . . . know the man?"

Again, Caroline refused to answer.

"Are you that ashamed of him then?" Frederich asked next, and Caroline's head came up sharply. She looked him directly in the eyes.

"Take your marriage proposal and be damned," she said.

"Caroline!" Leah chided her. "We are in the church!"

It surprised him that he was not in the least offended. He was far happier knowing that she was still the strong person Ann had described to him. He intended only to provide her child with legitimacy, nothing more. He wanted no whipped puppy or helpless clinging vine to have to look after.

"I have decided to keep the marriage pledge," he said, holding up his hand when she would have interrupted. "Before you are so quick to say no, I remind you that *you* are the one who needs a marriage ceremony. I also remind you that my children—Anna's children—need a woman who cares about them. Beata is no mother to them. It has been hard to see them so lonely since Anna died. Perhaps you will think of a marriage to me as a way to help your sister's children as well as yourself. If you agree to it, I give you my word that I will take care of you as best I can. But I will expect you to be a good wife. I will expect you to be civil to me. I do not take Avery's place as someone you must do battle with at every turn—"

"How can you speak of marriage? You think I'm not fit to have anything to do with your children," she said.

"Yes," he answered. "I do. But you are innocent in my children's eyes and you are important to them. I have never had cause to think you unfit until now."

Caroline looked abruptly away.

"You...don't say anything about the baby," she said, realizing even as she said it that she sounded as if she were actually considering the possibility of marrying him. She looked up at him. "Can you be kind to another man's child?"

She saw a flicker of emotion cross his face. He took a moment to answer.

"The child cannot help how it got here. If you marry me, then it will be mine. There is nothing left to say about this and we are wasting time. Do we marry or not, Caroline Holt? *Antworten Sie entweder ja oder nein.* Answer yes or no."

Her eyes met his briefly, but she then quickly looked away. She said nothing, her hands clutching the folds of her skirt.

"Your right to pick and choose husbands *you* have forfeited, Caroline Holt. You can sit and cry and live on John Steigermann's charity or you can marry me," he said impatiently. "If the answer is yes, we will have the ceremony right now. Everyone who is still here will be invited to stay to witness it. There will be no hiding. People already know the reason for our marrying—or not marrying. There will be no more shame about what has happened."

"I don't even know you," Caroline said abruptly. "You're a stranger to me."

"Every person who marries marries a stranger," Frederich said. "No one knows that better than I. But I am less a stranger than most. We are part of the same family." He stared at the bruises on her face. "I give you my word now that I will not beat you. I will not let Avery or anyone else beat you. What else do you want?"

What indeed? Caroline thought.

The door abruptly opened.

"I can't wait out here any longer, Frederich," Johann said in German. "I've been talking to Eli and he—"

"This matter is between Caroline Holt and me. Eli has no part in it."

"I know that, Frederich. It's Beata I'm worried about. She's becoming a ... problem."

"Beata is *always* a problem."

"She is threatening to swoon," Johann said in English.

"Swoon?" Frederich asked, not familiar with the word.

He smiled at Johann's explanation of this terrible thing Beata would inflict upon him to have her way. He had no doubt that their sire would have capitulated immediately at such a dire threat from his spoiled daughter. The old man was long gone—and Beata still believed that the mere possibility of her keeling over in public would turn the world according to her wishes.

"Caroline Holt," he said, getting up from the chair. "We have wasted enough time. Tell me now. Do we go make Beata *swoon* or not?"

Chapter Four

Nearly everyone stayed for the wedding.

Forgive me, Ann, she kept thinking. She was a coward and she had no other choice. She clung to Frederich's arm like a person in danger of drowning, far more ashamed of having to accept his offer of marriage than of her out-of-wedlock pregnancy. She stood before God and she answered the questions Johann Rial asked her until suddenly the ordeal was over. The church emptied, and a feeble celebration began. Johann brought out three kegs of hard cider from his own cellar for the impromptu wedding guests. The men swarmed the kegs, dragging Frederich off with them as they queued up to pass around a common dipper. Their congratulations were loud and boisterous, and some of them began cracking their whips in a kind of belated *Polterabend,* the noisemaking necessary to scare away the German evil spirits the evening before a wedding. She remembered the raucous demonstration surrounding Ann's marriage to Frederich—Ann standing on the Holt front porch and laughing up at her dour soon-to-be-husband.

It occurred to Caroline, too, that everyone here accepted the obvious reason for her agreeing to marry Frederich Graeber. She was pregnant; the real father of the baby was unwilling. And while Eli had come to her rescue like some *Sturm und Drang* hero who intended to make an honest woman of her no matter what, it was Frederich's arm she held on to. She held on to his arm, and she knew the truth. She had married Frederich because on the worst day of her life, this seemingly humorless man had dared to make light of her predicament. Neither his prenuptial promises nor her great need had swayed her the way his almost mischievous remark about Beata had. She had nearly laughed in spite of her misery, and it was as if he had given her a brief and shining glimpse of the person she used to be.

What happened to that girl? she wondered, watching as Frederich accepted another dipperful of cider. *What happened to the Caroline Holt who used to dance and sing and laugh so easily?* She could remember quite distinctly a time when she had been happy. Being sent to school in town when she was fifteen had been one of the greatest joys of her life. Her mother had insisted that she be educated, paying for Caroline's three years at the Female Academy out of her own small inheritance, regardless of her husband's wishes. But today was the first time Caroline had realized that her father had been right in wanting to keep his daughter in her place. Her mother had done her no favor in giving her a taste of the kind of life *she* had come from. An education was supposed to make one better, not forever dissatisfied and longing for the things one couldn't have. Her mother had been born to live in town and go to teas and lectures and poetry readings, not she. She had been born to be a farmer's wife, to work herself into mindless exhaustion, to bear children until she died like Ann. Her fine education had done nothing to change that. She took a quiet breath. If she was thankful for anything, it was that neither of her parents had lived to see this day. Her downfall would have done nothing but fuel the contempt they had for each other.

She jumped as John Steigermann fired a shotgun in the air. He gave her a sheepish grin and she smiled. Given the circumstances of this marriage, she needed to have the evil spirits as far away as possible. It was a shame that the *Pol-*

terabend didn't work on Beata. Her new sister-in-law hadn't swooned after all, and every time Caroline looked up, Beata was whispering to a different group of women. Caroline had misjudged Beata in the early days of Ann's marriage, thinking her flighty and insecure and living in Frederich's household on sufferance much as she herself lived in Avery's. Beata always talked nervously with her hands, her pale eyes darting away, as hard to pin down as a little boy caught with the telltale remains of a pie left cooling on the windowsill. Her torso was too thick for her arms and legs, the heaviness accentuated by a dowager's hump. There were heavy lines in her face from nose to mouth and between her eyebrows. She was crude and vulgar and vindictive, and she had made Ann's life a nightmare.

Caroline huddled with Leah and tried to pretend that she didn't notice how few of the women came near after Beata spoke to them. She knew perfectly well what Beata was about. She was making sure that a hasty marriage didn't change Caroline Holt's status as an outcast.

She sighed and looked away from Beata's animated discourse with yet another group of women to find Leah watching her.

"No one will believe her, Caroline," Leah said quietly.

"Won't they? What is she saying?"

"Beata tells lies, Caroline—"

"Tell me."

"Caroline, it's better to just ignore her."

"Please, Leah. I can't defend myself if I don't know."

Leah hesitated, then gave a small sigh. "She...says you've been going to town and lying with the soldiers who are always around the depot. She says you don't know who your baby's father is."

Caroline nearly laughed at the irony. She hadn't been into town in more than a year, and Avery had refused to take her along with him the day she'd gone to the schoolroom. But she couldn't deny Beata's tales. To do so, to say she hadn't been to town in so long would only focus the speculation about who had fathered her child on the men here.

She watched Avery at the cider kegs. He had said nothing to her or Frederich since they'd come out of the church, and he was drinking heavily, pushing his way in to refill the dipper again and again. And Kader was there—apparently had been in attendance all the time, and he was clearly enjoying the celebration. She gave a sharp intake of breath as he suddenly snatched the dipper out of Avery's grasp. He lifted it high and toasted Frederich with it, slapping him on the back and shaking his hand. Then he made some remark that caused the men to roar with laughter.

"Are you all right?" Leah asked.

"Quite all right," she answered, and she realized that Kader Gerhardt was probably the only person here who was truly happy about her marriage.

She turned and looked the other way, determined not to let Kader see how forlorn she felt. She was so cold. Her entire body ached with it, and her hands trembled from the strain of the morning and the long time since she'd eaten. She wanted to speak to Lise and Mary Louise, but Beata keep them close by her side. How many times today would Lise have to hear about her Aunt Caroline and the soldiers at the depot?

"Leah, could you ask your father to tell William what's happened?" Caroline said abruptly. "I promised him I'd let him know whatever I...decided to do. I want him to hear more than just Avery's version."

She was certain that otherwise William would never believe she'd done this thing. She didn't believe it herself, any more than she believed that she could have actually asked Leah Steigermann for a favor.

"I'm...sorry for the trouble I've caused you with Avery," Caroline said. "I know you care about him, and I thank you for your help today. I don't think I could have made it otherwise. Avery is bound to have hard feelings, and I just want you to know that I'm . . . sorry."

"Ah, well," Leah said, immediately dismissing the apology. "What can anyone do about Avery?"

Nothing, Caroline thought. *Absolutely nothing.*

"I will go find my father now," Leah said. "He will see that William is told." She put her hand on Caroline's arm. "You *are* lucky, Caroline. Your baby will have a name now. And Frederich has money and land. He's quite handsome—you must try not to mind how the marriage happened."

Handsome? Caroline hadn't thought of him as ugly, but neither had she recognized his handsomeness. She looked for him in the crowd around the cider kegs to verify Leah's opinion. He wasn't there anymore. She finally saw him standing alone with a dipper in his hand at the stone wall near Ann's grave.

She couldn't keep from shivering. The wind was far too sharp for an outside celebration, particularly one as half-hearted as this one. The women were anxious to leave, and the men began seeking out Frederich again to shake his hand. Only a few people said goodbye to Caroline.

She looked around as Lise and Mary Louise came running to her, both of them clinging to her with as much desperation as she herself was beginning to feel. She forced herself to smile at their upturned faces. Blond and freckled Lise, who was so quiet and serious and old beyond her years. And Mary Louise, who was as mischievous as she was merry. Caroline wondered how much it bothered Frederich that his youngest child was dark-haired and brown-eyed like the Holts.

"Is it true what Papa says?" Lise asked earnestly. "Are you coming to our house?"

"Yes," Caroline said. "It's true." She looked across the churchyard to where Frederich stood.

Why did you do this? she thought. She had no beauty, no reputation, no virtue. She had only her availability for the wedding night and any other night he felt so inclined.

Kader!

She hugged both the nieces tightly, and she couldn't keep from shivering again. Frederich had moved to the Graeber wagon now. Beata hovered at his elbow, still talking. Both of them stared in her direction.

"Look, Aunt Caroline!" Lise said. "My tooth is loose!"

She looked down and smiled at the front tooth Lise wiggled with her tongue, then laughed as Mary Louise tried to wiggle hers as well.

"I can't do it!" Mary Louise said, grabbing Caroline around the knees, nearly toppling her. "You do it, Aunt Caroline!"

"Silly Willy," Lise said. "You're just a baby. You have to be seven like— Papa wants me," she said abruptly as Frederich gestured for her to come to him. There was no doubt in either of their minds that he meant *now*.

Caroline stood awkwardly, watching Lise scurry to see what Frederich wanted. Should she make Mary Louise follow? Was she to ride back with Beata and the children or had he made some other arrangement?

Mary Louise kept pulling at Caroline's skirts, and she bent to lift her. But Frederich walked up. He said nothing, taking the child out of her grasp. His eyes met hers over the top of Mary Louise's head. The anger was still there, she thought in dismay. She could never make peace with this man, even if she wanted to. His bitterness came solely from injured pride at his having trusted Avery Holt, and not from the fact that he'd actually ever wanted her. She was astute enough to recognize a man's interest when she encountered it, the subtle and not so subtle looks that came when one's brother or father wasn't looking. She'd never gotten any such looks from Frederich. Frederich Graeber had barely acknowledged her existence. The memory of the day Ann died surfaced in her mind again. He was a powerful man, strong from his work in the fields, and she realized at that moment that, in spite of his promise, she was as physically afraid of him as she had ever been of Avery.

Mary Louise started to cry, and Frederich seemed about to say something. But then he turned abruptly and walked back toward the wagon, with Mary Louise still crying and reaching for her over his shoulder.

Caroline stood for a moment longer, then made her decision. She wasn't going to try to second-guess Frederich. If he didn't want her at the Graeber wagon, he was going to have to say so. She gave an ironic smile. She could see herself left standing, the Graebers riding away home, freed of the burden of her presence—but it wouldn't be because she had let Frederich intimidate her. She had done nothing wrong—at least where Frederich Graeber was concerned.

Frederich turned to her the moment she walked up. "Where is Eli? We are going."

"I don't know," she said evenly.

"Get on the wagon. I don't expect to have to tell you everything."

She bit down on her reply, surprised by the surge of anger she felt.

"Aunt Caroline," Lise said, leaning over the wagon edge and holding out her hand.

Caroline took it, intending to step up on the hub of the wagon wheel. But it hurt too much to lift her leg that high. She tried with the other leg, Lise pulling hard on her hand while Mary Louise still cried for Caroline to hold her. Beata climbed in on the other side, settling herself on the front wagon seat and giving off a loud tirade in German Caroline couldn't begin to understand. People were beginning to turn and stare, and Johann was walking rapidly toward them.

"Mein Gott," Frederich said under his breath. He lifted Caroline roughly upward and deposited her beside his daughters, his broad hand resting directly over a bruise on her back. She couldn't keep from crying out. Her eyes smarted, and she bit down on her lower lip. The pain stayed.

Thankfully, Eli appeared, intercepting Johann before he reached the wagon. She couldn't bear any more heavy-handed concern from either of them today. The two men talked while Beata muttered under her breath and Frederich fidgeted impatiently.

"Eli!" he yelled suddenly, making Caroline jump.

After a moment, Eli came and took a seat beside Caroline. He said nothing to anyone but Lise, some remark in German that made her smile. Frederich looked over his shoulder once, then cracked his whip to get the horses moving. Beata's muttering immediately became loud, guttural German again, the brunt of it directed at Frederich as far as Caroline could tell.

How am I going to stand this? she thought. She closed her eyes and tried to endure. She was in agony having to sit on the hard wagon seat. Her head ached and her nose ran from the cold—and she had no handkerchief. It was all she could do not to burst into tears and wail right along with Mary Louise.

Frederich said something to Beata in German as the wagon turned into the narrow road leading up to the Graeber house.

"And what does a whore like *her* need with clothes?" Beata answered in English, looking directly at Caroline.

Eli was out of his seat and would have put his hands on Beata if Frederich hadn't grabbed him by his coat front to intervene. The horses pranced and reared nervously, and Mary Louise began to cry again.

"Enough!" Frederich bellowed. "By God, I have had enough!"

Beata clutched at Frederich's arm. "You let him raise his hand to me! You let him—!"

"Be quiet, Beata! I will hear no more!" He was still holding on to Eli, and he pulled hard on the reins with one hand to keep the team from bolting, finally stopping them in the yard. He said something to Eli in angry German, silencing Beata again when she made some remark.

Please, Caroline prayed as Frederich lifted her down. *Please let me get away from these people.*

But she had married Frederich *and* the Graebers, and she was having a baby. She tried not to think about who would help her when her time came. Beata?

Oh, dear God.

Eli and Frederich began to unharness the team, both of them still arguing. She stood for a moment, staring toward the house, a brick house two stories high. Ann had been so proud to live here. She had been too young to know that a fine house meant nothing if there was no love in it. Given Beata's present mood, Caroline wondered if she would even let her come inside without some kind of altercation.

"Aunt Caroline?" Lise said, ignoring Beata's admonishments to take care of Mary Louise. Lise was so pale, and Caroline realized suddenly how difficult this day must have been for her.

Lise and Mary Louise were the only good things to come out of this arrangement, she thought. She looked up at the sky. The sun was low on the horizon. They had completely missed the noon meal. Both children must be starved. She took her nieces by the hand and walked along with them toward the back porch as if she expected nothing from Beata but exemplary behavior. Beata hurried past them, muttering to herself. She went into the house first, but at least she didn't lock Caroline and the children out.

The Graeber kitchen was huge and smelled of smoldering ashes and Beata's before-church baking. One side of the room faced the east and had two double windows to catch the morning sun. There was a trestle table in front of one of the windows and a paneled chest-settle near the huge diagonal fireplace. The fire had been banked, but it still gave off some warmth. Caroline walked with the children to the settle, needing desperately to sit down again. She began to help them take off their coats. She felt so ill at ease here. Everywhere she looked reminded her of Ann. Ann's punched tin sewing box, the one decorated with sunbursts, sat on a small table by the settle. Their own mother's English Stafford-shire china filled the corner cupboard. The numerous bright blue and white dishes had been Ann's only wedding gift of any value from the Holt side of the family. And how Caroline hated seeing them in Beata's kitchen. Ann's heavy oak rocking chair still sat in the same corner. The back of the chair was decorated with carved roses. It had been a wedding present from Frederich, and Ann had always sat in it to feed her babies. It surprised Caroline that Beata had kept it.

There was no pig iron stove in the kitchen, only an iron box oven that sat directly on the hearth. Ann had wanted a real stove so badly. She had never really learned how to cook in the fireplace where everything had to be done over open flames or buried in hot coals. Once, she'd even set her skirts on fire.

Eli came in and began to light the oil lamps that hung on S hooks from the exposed overhead beams. She could see the room better now. The rest of the walls were lined with dressers for dishes and pots she didn't quite remember. And there were several churns sitting about, and some small three-legged stools in the corners. One bare brick wall had been sponge painted with white lead. She had to grudgingly admit that Beata, for all her ill-tempered ways, kept a spotless house.

Eli moved from lamp to lamp, glancing at her from time to time as if he expected her to cry or run or both. He seemed to have taken over the task of acting as her champion, but she wished that he wouldn't stare at her so. She was dangerously close to tears again.

I can't live here with Frederich, she thought, but it wasn't living with him that troubled her. The Graeber farm was twice the size she was used to. There would be more than enough chores for her and Beata to do. She could easily stay out of his way during the day, but what would she do at night?

Tonight?

She tried to find the numbness she'd felt earlier this morning, but it had been replaced by a kind of mindless panic. She was trapped, and the sun was going down. She had no night things. No dressing gown. No way to hide from her new bridegroom. She had only the clothes she'd arrived in. She glanced at Eli as he lit the last lamp. Perhaps he could help her. Perhaps she could just *say* it.

Eli, I'm afraid!

He left the kitchen for a moment and came back with a brimming pitcher of milk. Then he motioned for her and the children to come to the table. She got up reluctantly, while he found three large tin cups and filled them with milk. Then he disappeared into the pantry and returned with several pieces of cold corn bread.

"Beata doesn't cook when she's angry," Lise said as if she thought Caroline needed some kind of explanation.

Caroline gave a resigned sigh. In that case, it might be months before Beata prepared another meal for this household.

"Sit," Eli said, pulling out a chair.

Caroline hesitated, then sat down in the heavy Carver chair he wanted her to take, hoping that he wasn't giving her Beata's seat. All she needed was for Beata to come downstairs and find Caroline Holt sitting in *her* place.

Caroline Holt Graeber.

"*Trink,* Caroline," Eli said, holding a cup of milk out to her.

She didn't want to drink. She didn't want anything. Except to run. Or to take back the marriage vows.

"Eli, I—"

She stopped because both children were watching intently, and when she didn't take the cup, he walked to the worktable and lifted the lid on the honey pot, ladling a huge dollop of honey into the milk. He rotated the cup for a moment, sloshing milk over the sides, then brought it back to her.

"*Trink,*" he said again.

She sighed, and she accepted the cup and the piece of corn bread he pushed at her. Then she drank the milk. All of it. Apparently, he'd heard somewhere of her weakness for milk and honey.

"Papa!" Mary Louise said, grinning broadly when Frederich came in the back door. He pointedly ignored Eli, but he stopped long enough to almost smile and to affectionately pat both children on the cheek. The gesture caught Caroline completely off guard. She had never once thought of Frederich Graeber as man who could be gentle with his children. He glanced at Caroline briefly on his way upstairs, and she was struck by the peculiar notion that he was feeling as trapped by the turn of events as she.

Beata must have been waiting for him on the top step, because Caroline could hear both their voices almost immediately.

And Eli stood watching her.

"Eli, don't stare at me. Please," she said finally, hoping he had enough command of English to understand.

Whatever he answered had something to do with Lise.

"I can tell her," Lise said to him. "I like to talk for Eli," she said to Caroline.

"Mary Louise needs to be put to bed," Caroline said. "She's falling asleep in her corn bread...." No one was listening to her. She didn't want to have to endure any secondhand conversations with Eli. She didn't want...anything. He spoke to Lise for a moment in German.

"Eli says to tell you this, Aunt Caroline. We...welcome you and we are glad you are here. Don't be—" She stopped to ask Eli for clarification. "Don't be afraid of us," she continued. "No one can hurt you anymore."

Caroline abruptly looked down at her hands, completely overwhelmed by how desperately she wanted to believe that. She had to fight hard not to cry.

"Eli says I'm to take you upstairs now. He says for you to rest—and try to sleep."

She looked at him, but now he avoided her eyes.

Lise asked Eli another question.

"Come with me," she said to Caroline after he'd answered.

Caroline nodded, then stood up. She let Lise take her by the hand, looking over her shoulder once at Eli before she climbed the stairs. He was wiping the milk mustache off Mary Louise's mouth.

The room upstairs was Spartan and small and not the one Frederich had shared with Ann. Was this where Frederich slept now? Caroline wondered. There weren't enough personal things in it to be sure, and she couldn't ask Lise. She managed a smile when the child dutifully kissed her goodnight, but she kept looking at the door, expecting Beata or Frederich or both and yet another unpleasant encounter.

She sat down heavily on the side of the bed after Lise had gone and took off her bonnet, hanging it by its ribbons on the one chair. She had no water to drink or to bathe in. She had no brushes or combs.

She sat there, numb again after all and staring at nothing. Then she lay down on top of the quilts and curled herself into a tight ball. All day long, she had been fighting the tears, but now that she had the privacy to shed them, none came. She lay there, huddled in her shawl, listening to the sounds of the house. Distant voices still raised in anger. Footsteps and slamming doors. The wind moaning against the eaves. And she listened to her own wavering sigh.

In spite of the cold and the strangeness, she fell asleep, and she woke a long time later when the door burst open.

Chapter Five

"**W**here is he?" Frederich demanded, realizing as he said it that in spite of his earlier certainty, Eli was not in the room.

"What?" Caroline Holt asked. The dazed question only fueled his anger.

"The sun is up! There is work to do! Where is Eli?"

Her hair was coming down, and it suddenly penetrated that his new wife was fully dressed and still wearing her shawl and that the bed had been slept on, not in. She sat up slowly and stared at him. Her eyes were big and afraid like a child's, like Mary Louise's when Beata scared her with witch stories about the cruel Eisenbertha.

But she took her own time about answering. "I don't know."

"You don't know where he is?"

"I've said I don't know! I haven't seen him since—" She broke off, and looked away, as if she had to shore up her courage. "Since yesterday," she said, looking him directly in the eyes again. "He didn't spend the night here, if that's what you think."

Taken aback by her bluntness, Frederich stood for a moment, then abruptly left the room, slamming the door behind him.

Now what? he thought as he clambered down the stairs.

Where could Eli be? He wasn't in the barn—none of the animals had been tended. The cows hadn't been milked. The kitchen fire hadn't been lit. Between Eli's disappearance and Beata's sulking, nothing had been done this morning. The north field had to be plowed and his children hadn't been fed—and wouldn't be at this rate.

He crossed the cold kitchen and opened the back door.

"Eli!" he yelled into the backyard, as if he hadn't already looked. He listened for a reply, but he could only hear the crows in the pine tops at the edge of the field and the lowing of miserable, unmilked cows.

He turned and went back into the kitchen, and was startled to find Caroline Holt standing there.

"Are the children still asleep?" she asked.

He didn't answer her.

"Why, yes, Caroline," she answered for him. "The children *are* still asleep. Why don't you build a fire so the kitchen will be warm when they come down? Perhaps you could even cook them a little *Frühstück* since they've only had milk and corn bread since yesterday.

"What a fine idea, Frederich," she continued, her sarcasm the kind born of years of practice. "I understand it may be some time before Beata decides to participate in the household again. But you see, I don't quite know what to do with such a huge fireplace. Perhaps if you would *deign* to instruct me—for the sake of *your* children—I could accomplish—"

"You find this amusing?" Frederich cut in. By God, she was a sharp-tongued woman, whether she was afraid of him or not. No wonder her brother had beaten her—except he was certain Avery Holt hadn't beaten her for her sarcasm. He'd beaten her for the child she carried. For ruining his dream of finally owning the acre of land with a spring he'd begged the use of these past eight years.

"Oh, no, Frederich," she said. "I don't find this amusing. I find this a living *hell.*"

Frederich turned abruptly and went outside before he laid hands on her in spite of his promise. He was angry enough to do it, to grab her and shake her until all that superiority and arrogance dropped away. She was not *his* better, regardless of her fine education and her airs. He knew that she had never considered him a fit husband for Ann—but Caroline Holt had been tumbled by a man she was clearly too ashamed to name. She was like any other briar patch whore in the county, and she'd do well to remember that.

The horses rumbled a greeting when he flung open the barn door, blowing heavily and leaning out over their stalls to nudge him as he passed by. But he left them standing. He had to put the cows out of their misery first.

The milking rapidly grew into yet another aggravation, because his barely controlled anger made the cows as testy and uncooperative as he felt. The wind the past few days would have dried the ground, making it just right for plowing—and here he was doing Beata's job. Caroline Holt had been right about one thing. This was going to be a kind of hell—living in the same house with her *and* Beata. He ignored the fact that just such an arrangement had been his original plan and that he had once looked at Caroline Holt with a certain longing. He couldn't deny that he found her attractive enough for his taste and that her aloofness both annoyed and intrigued him. He had never wanted a docile wife. He had wanted this marriage to make his children happy, and, in time, he had wanted to be vindicated as a man worthy of her regard and not some ignorant foreigner.

It was only when he remembered the way Ann had died that he knew the true reason for his seeking to wed her sister. He still felt the sting of Ann's betrayal as sharply as if it had been yesterday. He cursed the day his older brother had sent Eli here to America. Eli, who had taken half the land *and* Frederich's young wife. Frederich tried not to remember the look in Ann's eyes every time she spoke Eli's name. The question had never been *whether* Ann had loved Eli

Graeber. The question had been how much. He knew the answer to that now, but Ann was no longer here to atone for the wrong she'd done, and it hadn't been enough for him that she had died giving birth to Eli's child. He still needed reparation, and Caroline was the person Ann loved best. After her children. After Eli. If he, Frederich, married her, he could make her suffer for Ann's transgression without remorse. He could insist that she be a good German wife. He could keep her pregnant—there would be no time for books and poetry and fine airs. How Caroline would hate that, and how Ann would have hated it for her.

But the actual marriage yesterday had somehow changed everything. Caroline was in his household as a wife and therefore legally and morally subject to his will, but she was also a helpless outcast in need of his charity, beloved by his children no matter how disdainful she was of him. He didn't like the turn his emotions had taken. Perhaps it would have been better to let Eli—

Where is Eli, damn him?

Off somewhere feeling sorry for himself—again, he thought.

Frederich's abrupt fit of agitation startled the cow, and she bellowed loudly, kicking over the nearly full milk pail before he could catch it. He swore and watched helplessly as the barn cats rushed forward to make the best of his misfortune before the milk seeped into the ground.

He could hear Lise and Mary Louise calling him. He left the bucket sitting and he stepped outside. They descended upon him immediately, grabbing him by the hand and pulling him along, chattering as they went. He entered the house fully expecting to find the kitchen on fire.

A meal had been laid out on the table instead—bread and cheese, jam and butter. Bacon and boiled eggs.

"Look what we made, Papa!" Lise said, pulling out his chair. "We only had two things to burn."

"Three," Caroline said, lifting Mary Louise into a chair. "The bacon caught fire twice. I couldn't find the coffee," she said, turning back to the hearth.

He hesitated, looking at her warily, as if there was some devious purpose behind all this. She glanced at him over her shoulder, and after a moment, he sat down.

"I cooked the bread, Papa," Mary Louise said, grinning around the two fingers she had in her mouth. He reached to pull them out before she ruined her fine teeth.

"She means she *found* the bread. Beata hid it in the pantry," Lise said. "We thought the water for the eggs would never boil, didn't we, Aunt Caroline?"

"Never," Caroline agreed without looking up from the hearth. She'd shed her shawl, and her face was flushed from working so close to the fire. She struggled with an iron pot, and Frederich tried not to look at the way her breasts moved under the bodice of her ugly yellow-flowered dress.

There were only three places set. Apparently, Caroline had not intended to join them, nor did he invite her. He lost himself in conversation with his daughters, listening to their convoluted story of how such a fine *Frühstück* had come about.

"Beata's going to be upset," Lise said.

"Beata is always upset," he said, spreading more jam on a huge slice of bread.

"But she's going to say we took bread she was keeping for something else."

"For what?" Frederich asked with his mouth full.

"She never says that part," Lisa answered, and he laughed.

"Don't worry, little one. If Beata wants to hoard her bread, then she must come down here and guard her kitchen herself. The biggest trouble with sulking, you see, is while you're off hiding with your long face, life will go on without you. If she stays away, there's no telling what we might do with the rest of the food in the pantry—we might even find where she hides the coffee,'' he added in a whisper.

He was smiling—until he glanced at Caroline. Then he was immediately reminded of what a disaster this morning had been.

He abruptly got up from the table. ''I have too much to do,'' he said, the reproach in his voice apparent even to him. He took another hunk of the ill-gotten bread and a slice of bacon with him. He had stayed in the company of his children and Caroline Holt too long. He had nearly let his anger dissipate, and he needed it if he was going to plow the north field *and* locate his good-for-nothing nephew.

He went back to the barn. He tossed the last bit of bacon and bread to the barn cats, and he climbed the ladder to the hayloft, fighting off a fit of sneezing that came from the dust and the pungent scent of the hay. He stood for a moment peering into the dark corners for Eli's sleeping form. If Eli hadn't gone to Caroline, then he had to have slept somewhere.

The loft was empty, and Frederich began pitching the hay into the stalls below. The cats mewed loudly for another handout, and Beata was awake. He could hear her complaining all the way out here.

He moved to the other side and looked over the edge. The door to the stall directly below him stood ajar, and the bay gelding that should have been there was gone.

Frederich stayed away from the house until shortly after noon. The kitchen was quiet when he came in, and he was surprised that there was no meal on the table. Even if Beata was still sulking, he expected Caroline to have at least managed something for the children. He didn't see the girls anywhere, but *she* was sitting on the bottom step of the stairs.

''We observe the *Mittagessen* in this house,'' he said.

She looked at him blankly.

"The noon meal," he said as if to a backward child.

"Lise and Mary Louise have eaten."

"Is there anything left?" he asked pointedly.

"I don't know. Beata took it."

"Took it where?"

"I don't know," she said again.

He swore under his breath and went looking for whatever Beata might have put aside for him—or missed hiding. There was nothing. He looked up from his search to see Caroline standing nearby.

"Have you... found Eli?" she asked, not quite meeting his eyes.

"One of the horses and a saddle is missing. Eli had some money put by. I expect he is long gone."

"Oh," she said, as if she hadn't considered that possibility.

When he looked up again, she was putting on her shawl and opening the back door. "Where are you going?"

He saw the rise and fall of her breasts as she took a deep breath before she answered him.

"This—marriage—isn't going to work. I'm going to ask Avery to let me come home."

The remark took him completely by surprise, and his temper flared. He had given her the only chance she would ever have for any kind of respectability and she was about to throw it away?

"Avery will not let you come home," he said bluntly.

"You don't know that—"

"He made too much of a show among the men of disowning you."

He walked into the pantry looking again for something Beata might have forgotten to hide. He supposed that the loss of her secret hoard of bread must have convinced her as nothing else could that the rest of them hadn't suffered enough from her self-imposed absence. Certainly it would be much more difficult to cook and eat without her if no one could find any food. He wondered what terrible thing he had done in his life to deserve Beata. And Eli. And Caroline Holt.

When he came out of the pantry, Caroline was no longer in the room. He leaned over the table to look out the window. She was walking across the field he should have had plowed by now, her gait strong for a few steps then hesitant, as if she were being forced to give in to the pain she still had from Avery's beating.

Good riddance, he thought. Let her grovel in front of Avery. And when he sent her back again, perhaps she would understand her situation better.

He looked around at a small noise. Both his daughters stood at the bottom of the stairs.

"Papa?" Lise said tentatively. "Did you let Aunt Caroline go?"

He sighed. "She went, Lise. There was no letting or not letting."

"Aren't you…worried? Uncle Avery—he might hurt her again, Papa. And we promised."

"Lise, I can't tie your Aunt Caroline to the kitchen table so she'll stay here," he said, trying not to be influenced by how hard she was trying not to cry. Lise was a gentle soul; she was concerned about all living creatures—whether they deserved it or not.

"Eli said we wouldn't let anyone hurt her again. He promised, Papa."

"Lise, there is nothing I can do," he said, in spite of the fact that he'd made the same promise himself.

"Couldn't you just—?"

"This is not your business."

Mary Louise was tugging on his trouser leg. "What is it, Mary Louise?" he said more sharply than he intended.

"I think we might cry, Papa," she advised him.

"Then you'll just have to cry. Life is full of crying. I can't fix everything." He was very careful not to look into her upturned face, into those begging Holt-brown eyes.

"Can't you please just fix this, Papa?" Lise asked. "Don't let Uncle Avery hurt her again. Please, Papa! All you have to do is just stand there while she talks to him—he wouldn't hurt her if you stood by. I know he wouldn't!"

Her mouth trembled, but she worked hard not to give in to it. Clearly, Lise expected him to stand guard indefinitely.

"Your Aunt Caroline left by her own choice—"

"No, she didn't, Papa! She left because Beata is going to be mean to everybody if she stays. Papa—"

He held up his hand to stop her.

"You don't worry about your Aunt Caroline. You don't worry about any of those people over there."

Caroline heard the back door slam, and Frederich caught up with her before she reached the edge of the Graeber land.

"I have something to say to you, Caroline Holt. This is—"

"What do you want, Frederich?" she interrupted. She stopped walking, and she forced herself to look him in the eye.

"What do *I* want? I want to keep you from making the scandal any bigger than it already is."

They stared at each other. She abruptly looked away.

"What is wrong with you?" he said angrily. "You behave as if you have some choice about what you will do! You don't. You are pregnant. Avery doesn't want you or your brat. It falls to me to keep *my* family from becoming any more of a laughingstock than it already is. I am going to keep the family's honor—the honor *you* drag through the mud as if there is nobody to suffer the consequences but you. There is only one thing to be done. You don't start everybody talking all over again about the marriage. Do you understand?"

"No," she said. "I don't!"

"My daughters are crying—Beata is starving us to death hiding everything she can get her hands on—Eli has disappeared! All this is *your* fault. Do you understand that? Going to Avery—begging Avery—will only make our trouble worse. Worse for you—worse for—"

She looked away from his penetrating gaze. She did understand after all. She understood perfectly. How terrible for Frederich to have to keep her when he wanted so desperately to be rid of her.

"Frederich, I—" she began, looking back at him. But he was staring at her clothes. "Come," he interrupted. "We go see Avery now."

"Go see—Frederich, you just said you didn't—"

"You are beginning to stink. You need your clothes. We'll go and get them, and you don't say anything to your brother about this notion you have of coming home. You can manage that, surely."

He took her by the arm to start her walking, letting go almost immediately as if he found touching her distasteful. And he kept giving her wary glances as they crossed the field.

"Say nothing!" he admonished her as they neared the house, and she had to bite her lip to suppress an angry reply. She wasn't stupid about everything. Just her choices of lovers and husbands.

She could see John Steigermann standing in the yard—perhaps advising William of her marriage as she'd asked. Under better circumstances and with a different companion, the walk here would have been pleasant enough. It was cold still, but without the biting wind of yesterday. Spring always came quickly in this part of the country; winter one week and budding leaves the next. She noted with some surprise that she was looking forward to the dogwoods and jonquils just as she always did. And she noted, too, that she was actually going to try to have a civil conversation with Avery after what he had done.

Better to ask for her clothes than for sanctuary, she thought.

John Steigermann and William and Avery were all staring at her as she and Frederich approached. They would, of course, be surprised to see her out today. She was newly married and should be attending to her wifely duties.

"Ah!" John Steigermann said immediately, waving her closer. "Frederich! Caroline! Come hear this. You will want to know the news."

"What news?" she asked, glancing at Avery as he swallowed whatever unpleasant thing he would have said to her if both John Steigermann and Frederich hadn't been there.

"The army has gone through again foraging supplies," Steigermann said. "Penn Palmer says they took every decent horse he had. Steal is what they do. Paying with pieces of paper no one wants to honor. I say we go to the garrison in town—we see what they will do about paying real money for what they take. And look at this, Caroline," he said taking a folded newspaper from his coat pocket. "You will read what this says, yes? I can't read the English so good."

She took the paper he handed her. "New call for troops," she read aloud. "The following is under proclamation of the President, extending the call under the Conscript Act, to embrace all residents of the Confederacy between the ages of eighteen and forty-five years, not legally exempt—"

John Steigermann frowned and motioned for Caroline to keep reading.

"Foreigners," she went on, "who are actual residents, will be called upon to do military service in defense of the country in which they reside."

"Let me see that," Avery said, snatching the newspaper out of her hand and reading it himself. "That's what it says. I've got my farmer's exemption—but this is going to get a lot of you Germans if you aren't careful."

"And how can we Germans be careful, Avery?" Frederich asked. "Do we go hide in the woods and leave the women and children to work the farms?"

"You can go into town and see about a farmer's exemption the same as I did," Avery said.

"That is not so easy when the man who takes the bribe changes every week."

"It isn't a bribe, Frederich. It's a *fee.*"

"Call it what name you will, Avery Holt. It is what it is."

Caroline stepped away as the discussion became more heated. She closed her eyes for a moment and took a deep breath. She was tired from the walk. And from arguing with Frederich, and before him, Beata.

Isn't there someplace where I can just live in peace?

"Caroline," William said.

She looked around at him. He was standing awkwardly, clearly embarrassed by her new status and not knowing what to say.

"Hello, William," she said, forcing a smile she didn't begin to feel.

"I got something for you," he said, motioning her toward the house.

Avery glanced at him but didn't intervene.

"What is it?" Caroline asked, letting William take her by the hand.

"I got your clothes all together," he said. "I reckon you're going to need them until Frederich can buy you some more."

"William—"

"I got your dresses bundled and everything else in Mama's old straw valise—I reckon the handle will stay on. I was going to sneak them over to you first chance I got. But since you're here, I can give them to you now. And I reckon you'll be wanting your books and all—me and Avery sure ain't going to be reading them."

"William—"

"It's all right now, ain't it, Caroline? You'll be all right with Frederich, won't you? You know I never in a million years thought *he'd* be the one you'd end up marrying. See, I never thought you'd marry at all—" He broke off, apparently realizing that his comment was less than tactful. "It's good Frederich could come over to help you carry this stuff," he decided, and he was looking at her so earnestly.

I have to come home, William.

She pursed her lips and tried to say the words, but she couldn't manage it. William was so happy for her. He thought she was safe now.

"I'll get your clothes," William said, turning and bounding up the steps into the house.

She stood there still wanting to ask Avery—to beg him to let her come home. Surely, *surely,* he'd let her. He wouldn't lose face. She could tell him that people would think the better of him—John Steigermann would think the better of him if he did this for her.

Frederich came and stood next to her as if he could feel her wavering, and William bounded out of the house with her dresses and the valise.

"Here you are, Caroline," he said, grinning from ear to ear. "Hey, Frederich, you're not mad at Caroline anymore, are you?"

Frederich took the valise out of William's hand without answering.

"There is more to bring or not?" he asked Caroline.

"I can get your books, Caroline," William suddenly offered. "Since Frederich's going to be carrying your things for you. I can put them in a pillow slip, all right? I'll be right back—"

He was off running again.

Caroline abruptly bowed her head. How could she let Frederich haul her back? And how could she ask Avery for anything?

"Stay here," Frederich said, slinging the valise at her because the ground was too muddy for him to set it down. "I will speak to your brother."

She stood there, meekly holding everything she owned in her arms, feeling like the fallen woman she was as she watched Frederich approach Avery. Her brother was wary at first. And he kept glancing at her, his righteous indignation all too apparent.

"Ja! Gut!" John Steigermann said, listening intently to whatever Frederich said.

She couldn't hear anything else.

What now, Frederich? she thought.

She kept making the same stupid mistake. She kept putting her trust in men who didn't care. Avery. Kader. And now Frederich, who seemed to actually think he could stand a marriage to a woman pregnant by another man.

After a moment, Frederich and Avery walked into the barn and closed the door, leaving John Steigermann standing. Frederich came out again, leading one of Avery's saddle horses.

"Caroline, we'll go now," he called to her.

She walked to where he stood, hating the meekness of every step she took.

"Your brother is going to lend you a horse so you don't have to walk back," he said.

She looked at him doubtfully, then handed him the valise and let him lift her and it onto the horse's back. She said nothing, trying not feel his broad hands on her waist or the pain he caused on her bruises when he hoisted her upward.

William came running with the pillow slip full of books.

"Say hello to the girls from Uncle William," he said, handing it up to her. His farm boy hands had left smudge marks on the crisp, starched whiteness of the pillow slip.

She forced a smile, her eyes meeting Frederich's over the top of William's head.

Frederich took the horse by the bridle, watching Caroline closely to see if she was going to return with him quietly after all. His right hand hurt. His knuckles were bleeding.

"Do me a favor," he said to John Steigermann in German. "See about Caroline's brother. See if I've killed him."

Chapter Six

Caroline slept fitfully and woke early. She had taken the precaution of bolting the door, but she was still surprised that Frederich hadn't bothered coming to her bed. She was surprised, too, to find Beata already in the kitchen when she came downstairs. She had resolved sometime during the night not to concern herself about Beata Graeber. She would think of nothing but the children—Ann's and her own unborn child. And she wouldn't think about Kader or Frederich. She would fix her attention firmly on the girls and on her baby to come, and in doing so, she might tolerate—at least tolerate—living here.

But the sight of Beata's smug expression when she came into the kitchen immediately put an end to her determination to endure. She had no defense against this woman, and she braced herself for whatever Beata wanted to say. She didn't have long to wait.

"So! Caroline!" Beata said with a slight smile. "Who did you find to sleep with last night? Ha!"

Beata's chopped-off laugh set her teeth on edge. She closed her eyes and bit down on her bottom lip to keep from making some retort she'd surely regret later. Both children sat at the trestle table, looking from her to Beata and back again.

"It doesn't matter what you say to me, Beata," she said

quietly. "But it matters a great deal *where* you say it."

"They will know sooner or later the kind of woman you are. It might as well be—"

Beata broke off because Frederich was coming in from the barn. He greeted Lise and Mary Louise, patting both of them on the cheek as Caroline had seen him do once before. This fatherly side of Frederich still amazed her, but thankfully he had nothing to say to her. Indeed, he studiously avoided looking in her direction at all. He looked at the table instead and said something to Beata in German. Beata immediately took offense. Frederich spoke louder. After a moment, Beata whirled away from him and went to the dish cupboard to get another plate.

Her plate, Caroline realized.

Beata set it on the table in a huff, all but throwing the knife and fork that went with it.

"Beata has no manners," Frederich said in English to Lise and Mary Louise as he sat down. "I do not expect to ever see either of you behave in this way."

"I won't wait on that—!" Beata shouted, biting off the epithet she didn't quite have the nerve to use.

"Nor anyone else, either, it seems," Frederich said. "I have twice the work to be done with Eli gone. I can't do yours as well. I intend to have peace in this house. You will see to the kitchen—and I don't mean to hide everything like a silly vindictive child. Caroline will stay out of your way. She won't bother anything that is yours. Do you understand that, Caroline?"

He looked in Caroline's direction. Her back was rigid and her chin up. And she was looking at him as if he'd just done something to remove all doubt from her mind that he was as uncivilized and crude as she'd always suspected.

He forced himself to hold her gaze, forced himself to not to let his eyes stray to the soft swell of her breasts. She was almost pretty this morning, in spite of the bruises on her face. Her hair was brushed and braided. She looked clean, freshly scrubbed. He could just smell the soap she'd used to wash in. And the dress was different—pink-checked instead of the faded yellow calico.

But he would not allow himself to be affected by any improvements in her personal appearance. Caroline Holt carried another man's child, a child he still thought of as a bastard regardless of their sham of a marriage. She still insisted on behaving as if she'd done nothing wrong. She made no excuses. She clearly disdained any kind of forgiveness. She had no remorse for the shame she'd caused the family—*his* family. "I have asked you a question," he said evenly. "Do you intend to answer me or are you as ill-mannered as my sister?"

Caroline and Beata both protested.

"Sit down!" he bellowed.

They sat.

"Good," he said, looking from one to the other. "Caroline, you will take care of the children. Do you understand *that?*" He glanced at Beata, who was about to flutter her hands and make another protest.

"Yes," Caroline said, hating the meek sound of her voice. *It's only for the children,* she thought, trying to find her resolve again. *I don't want them upset by all this animosity.*

"Are you learned enough to teach Lise here at home so that she doesn't have to be sent to the school?" Frederich asked.

"Yes," she said again.

"Good. Then I want her taught here. We will say grace now—"

But Beata had stood it as long as she could. She burst forth in angry German.

"Kader Gerhardt will not go hungry because I take my one child out of his school!" Frederich snapped in English. "You always tell me my children make too much work for you. Caroline will take care of them now *and* the schooling."

Caroline sat in silence, making some attempt to follow Frederich's German table grace and taking the bowls of fried ham and fried potatoes and fried cabbage and fried apples Lise handed to her when it was over. But, for once, her stomach didn't rebel at the sight and smell of heavy German food. She was hungry, regardless of the ill will at the breakfast table, and she ate more than she had in days. There was practically no conversation except when Frederich wanted this or that handed to him and when Beata chastised Mary Louise for giving up eating to wiggle.

Caroline looked up several times to find Frederich watching her, and she stared back at him. She would give in on matters concerning the children in order to keep peace in the household, but he wouldn't intimidate her about anything else. Yes, her presence was nothing if not disruptive and yes, she was *perhaps* indirectly responsible for Eli's glaring absence—but there was nothing she could do about it.

For heaven's sake, what? she thought when she caught Frederich staring at her yet another time. She longed for a decent bath, but she had made a point of effecting one of sorts in the freezing upstairs room. She'd changed her clothes. She didn't stink any longer, as he'd so rudely pointed out yesterday. She was trying to keep her manners at least on the same level as Beata's. She'd agreed to everything he wanted.

Beata said something to Frederich in German and he scowled. But, for once, Caroline thought that whatever Beata had said had nothing to do with her. She tried William's trick of trying to understand without having any command of the language. It didn't work.

"I've lost a day getting the plowing done," Frederich said in English.

He was looking at her again, but this time as if he expected some response. She took it for the complaint it was.

"What do you want me to say, Frederich? I'm sorry? Very well. I am *sorry*." She abruptly stood up and began clearing her place the way she would have if she'd been at home, but then she stopped. "Forgive me, Beata," she said. "If I understand the rules, this is *your* job."

She left Frederich and Beata sitting and went upstairs. Better to pace the confines of the room she'd been given than provoke another altercation. She was surprised that Frederich would remove Lise from the German school and still more surprised that he would ask—*tell*—her to teach the child, regardless of William's theory that Frederich's need for someone to school his children was at the heart of his marriage proposal in the first place. If Frederich already thought that Kader was unfit to teach German children, he could hardly think her a suitable alternative.

She walked to the window and looked down on the yard below. Frederich was harnessing the great Belgians he used for plowing. She watched as he kissed his daughters good-bye. Had he always been this kind and affectionate to them? she wondered. Or only since Ann died?

She stepped abruptly back from the window because he looked upward in her direction.

The weather had turned much warmer, and she took the girls outside to their own small garden to work. The three of them spent the morning turning the soil and weeding. Ann had helped the girls do this last year. She had been full of life then, full of hope and anticipation about the arrival of her new baby. It was only when Caroline pulled the covering of leaves away from a row of jonquils that she came close to crying. Their mother had brought the jonquil bulbs from her parents' fine garden in town after she'd married their father, and Caroline in turn had given an apronful to Ann when she'd gone to Frederich.

I miss you so, she thought, gently uncovering the tender green shoots. *I miss you and Mama both.* She looked up to find Lise and Mary Louise gone quiet and obviously worrying about her state of mind.

"Don't cry," Mary Louise said, her eyes big. She reached out to give Caroline little sympathetic hit-and-miss pats on the arm. "Papa can bring you candy next he goes to town—peppermint candy, Aunt Caroline. Then you'll feel better. Don't *cry*."

"I won't," she said. "But I think I need a hug and a kiss until the peppermint gets here."

She was immediately swamped with affection. She was so glad to be with the girls. She was glad, too, that Frederich didn't seem interested in her except as a children's nurse. Perhaps she *could* stand it here—if she didn't have to worry about whether or not Frederich would spend the night in her bed.

She abruptly looked up at the sky. The sun was lowering. "I think we've missed the *Mittagessen*," she said, getting up from her knees.

"No, we didn't," Lise said. "Beata didn't call us."

Exactly, Caroline thought but didn't say.

They walked hand in hand back to the house. Apparently Frederich had eaten and gone, because Beata had already cleared the table. She glanced up when they came in, but she didn't interrupt her dishwashing.

"I don't wait a meal forever," she said. "You heard me calling you."

Caroline took a deep breath. "No," she said evenly. "Apparently Lise and Mary Louise—"

"If you chose to ignore me then you go—"

"—and I have all gone deaf!"

"—hungry!"

Beata turned her back.

"The children need to eat, Beata," Caroline said, trying hard not to lose her temper.

"Of course they do," Beata said, but she made no move in that direction.

Caroline waited. Finally, Beata looked around at her.

"If *I* understand the rules," she said, "*that* is *your* job."

"Fine," Caroline said. She didn't mind putting together a meal for the children; she just didn't want to have to fight Beata tooth and nail to do it. She managed to melt cheese on bread she toasted in the heavy iron skillet with legs—without dragging her skirts through the hot coals or burning the bread.

The meal was pleasant enough, the rest of the day was pleasant enough, at least until Frederich returned. The sun was nearly down when he came in. He was ill-tempered and clearly exhausted. Caroline took the children upstairs almost immediately after they'd eaten to keep them out of his way. He was the old Frederich she remembered, and she didn't want Lise and Mary Louise any more distressed by the day's events than they already were.

She waited until they were both asleep and the house quiet before she unbolted the door and came downstairs again. She felt assured now that, for the moment at least, Frederich had no intention of demanding his conjugal rights, but she was still far too restless to retire. She intended to flagrantly take some wood from the back porch so that she could have a fire in her room upstairs. She wanted to create a warm, quiet place to read for a time before she went to bed. She had always been able to take pleasure in little things, a talent she would sorely need in this house.

She made her way to the worktable in the kitchen without lighting a lamp, then felt along it toward the back door. The moon was shining when she stepped outside, the night quiet and frosty. She could make out the wood box in the dark, and she loaded her arms with one log and several smaller cut pieces, hoping she hadn't included a spider. She stood for a moment looking out across the field toward the Holt farm. Avery was still awake. She could see a light from the house shining through the trees. She wondered idly why he hadn't come today to fetch the horse he'd loaned to

Frederich. That he'd loan it in the first place was amazing enough. That he hadn't come after it today was incredible.

She gave a quiet sigh. She didn't miss Avery, but she did miss William. She carried the wood high, careful of her belly.

My poor baby, she thought as she stepped inside. *Who will love it but me?* Lise and Mary Louise perhaps—if Frederich and Beata would let them.

She kicked the back door closed and crossed the kitchen carefully, not sure where in the darkness Beata might have left a stool or a churn. She stopped for a moment midway, sticking her foot out to make sure there was nothing in front of her.

"You are looking for your...husband?"

She jumped violently, dropping the wood heavily on the floor. Frederich lay sprawled on the settle in the dark. She could hear him fumbling about, and, after a moment, a single candle glowed in the darkness. She realized immediately that he must have been drinking—still was drinking. She could smell the plum brandy and just make out the bottle he held in his hand. Ann had never told her that Frederich sat up alone drinking at night.

"No," she said shortly, bending down to pick up the wood.

"No," he repeated, his sarcasm readily apparent. "Your bastard has a name, so you have no need for your *husband,* is that so?"

"Yes," she answered, and he gave a short laugh.

"A Holt who tells the truth," he said, lifting the bottle high in the air. "What a surprise. I drink to you."

She continued to pick up the wood, saying nothing.

"I asked you to look after my children today, Caroline Holt, not starve them," he rambled on. "You are nothing but trouble. What do you say to that?"

"Told," she said without looking in his direction. "You didn't *ask* anything."

"Ah. So I did. Maybe . . . I will ask you something now."

But he didn't. Caroline stood up with the wood in her arms, growing more and more uncomfortable in the ensuing silence. She could imagine what Beata must have told him about her letting the children miss the noon meal, and she could sense how much he wanted her to make some kind of excuse. She wasn't about to give him the satisfaction, not when he would believe every word Beata said just as he always had when Ann was alive.

"I want to know," he said finally. "I want to know what Anna told you about me. She always talked to you. I want to know what she said."

She looked in his direction now. The candle he'd lit flickered in the draft from the fireplace. She could just make out his face in the dimness.

"Nothing, Frederich."

"Nothing? I am wrong then," he said, taking a long drink from the bottle. "You are a lying Holt after all."

"Frederich, Ann never said anything to me about you—nothing like what you mean—"

"And what do I *mean?*"

"You want to know if she complained—criticized—"

He sat up suddenly. "You were her sister. You were her *friend.* She told me that once. I wanted her to visit with the women here—I thought she needed their help—someone to talk to—to explain. But she said she had *you.* And she told *you* nothing. Not in eight years. Not in all that time?"

"She . . . told me she was happy," Caroline offered, because it was the truth. "Just before she died. I was worried about her—but she said I shouldn't worry about her having another baby because she was so happy."

He was standing now, moving closer. She was afraid suddenly, and she began to edge away. As she turned to get out of the room, he reached and grabbed her by the arm and pulled her around to face him. The top piece of wood fell heavily onto the floor. She was off-balance and nearly leaning into him. She could smell his man-smell, leather and wood smoke, sweat and tobacco and plum brandy. She could feel the heat and the power of his body, the grip of his callused hand on her arm. It was all she could do to keep from shivering.

"Johann was right, Caroline Holt," he said, his fingers hurting. "I cannot be kind to you."

He abruptly let her go, and she staggered away from him. She backed out of his reach, still carrying the wood, all but running by the time she reached the stairs.

"What is this stick of wood doing here?" Beata asked, her shrill voice making his head pound worse. "Did you do this?" she demanded, turning on the children.

"I dropped it, Beata!" he said sharply. "Either leave it or throw it on the fire—but do *not* talk about it anymore!"

"And you don't take your brandy headache out on me!" she said.

He made a gesture of impatience, but he didn't say anything else. It hurt too much to talk. It hurt to breathe. He looked around as Caroline came downstairs.

"Good morning," she said to the girls, making a concerted effort not to notice him. He didn't blame her. He was ashamed of his behavior last night—not of what he had said to her—he barely remembered that—but of the way she'd cowered from him when he grabbed her by the arm. She had fully expected him to hurt her, and that expectation had insulted him in a way he would have been hard put to explain. He was not used to drinking and he'd taken too much plum brandy—but drunk or sober, he was *not* like her brother. He thought surely Caroline Holt should know that, but he didn't tax his aching head with the specifics of *how*.

"What will you and the children do today?" he asked, surprising himself and her.

She gave him a furtive glance before she answered, but she spoke to the plate in front of her. "I think it's going to rain," she said. "We'll work on mending their clothes. I see Beata has put out the basket for me—"

"Mary Louise is too young," he interrupted.

"She can pick out buttons and find matching thread—and learn her colors. Lise can practice her multiplication tables while we sew. Then I thought we would read—and perhaps a music lesson if you don't object."

"Why would I object?" he asked, his pounding head notwithstanding.

She didn't answer him, and Lise cast a worried look at Beata, who was tending something on the hearth.

Beata must have extended her dominion to include the piano, he decided. "I have no objection to music lessons for the girls. In time, perhaps they will play what they learn for me. You can teach Beata, too, while you're at it."

He had meant only to annoy her, but her horrified expression struck him as funny, and he laughed in spite of the pain in his head. "Is that not a good idea?" he asked Lise, smiling still.

"*No,* Papa," she assured him, making him laugh again. It felt wonderful to laugh with his children at the breakfast table.

"*No,* Papa," Mary Louise echoed.

"What are you saying?" Beata demanded from the hearth.

"I was saying Caroline could teach you to play the piano—what do *you* say, Caroline?" he asked over Beata's sputtering.

"I would be simply...honored," she said gravely, the corners of her mouth working hard not to smile, her eyes filled with mischief.

He waited until the end of Beata's long tirade in German, then stood up to go outside. "Beata thanks you for your kindness," he whispered to Caroline as he reached for his hat. "But she feels she really must decline."

* * *

Caroline realized she was smiling to herself again. She made a concentrated effort to force the smile aside.

I don't understand, she thought yet another time. Last night, Frederich had made her afraid, and this morning he had actually been trying to tease her and Beata. A Frederich who teased was as disconcerting as the one who played the kindly father—except, in all fairness, she didn't think he was playing at that.

Apparently, Beata had been disconcerted as well. She had immediately immersed herself in a frenzy of cooking, and she had been vexed all morning, taking it out on anything and everything that strayed into her path. Caroline had put Mary Louise to bed for her afternoon nap early to keep her out of Beata's way.

Perhaps Frederich had intended for her and Beata to squabble, Caroline suddenly thought. Perhaps it amused him to have them at each other, regardless of his fine speech about domestic tranquillity.

She shook her head and went back to the mending. "Three times five?" she said to Lise, only half listening to the reply. Her hands were busy. Her mind was busy. And still this morning's episode with Frederich forced its way into her thoughts.

I don't understand.

She looked up at the sound of a wagon.

"Leah Steigermann," Lise said, looking out the window. "Does that mean I can stop now?"

"For the time being," Caroline said, careful to keep her empathy for the tediousness of multiplication tables masked. "Go and let Leah in, please."

Caroline put the mending back into the basket and set Ann's sewing tin on the small table where it belonged, running her fingertips lightly over the sunburst pattern. She stood up and smoothed her dress over her rounding belly, feeling acutely self-conscious and sinful again.

"I'm bringing the rain," Leah called as she swept through the door. "And I've come early especially to see how you are." She gave Lise a small hug before descending on Caroline.

"I'm quite well," Caroline said, suffering her embrace. The gray poplin dress with the cream satin trim Leah wore was heavily spotted with raindrops and likely ruined, a fact that appeared to cause her no concern at all.

"Scoot now," Leah said to Lise. "Run tell Beata I'm here—something smells wonderful. What *is* Beata cooking?"

"I don't know," Caroline said. "I'm not allowed to lift the lids."

"No doubt," Leah said, smiling. "She's going to be very annoyed that I've come already. And where is the bridegroom?" she asked, making herself comfortable on the settle.

"I don't know," Caroline said truthfully.

"Ah, well, it's you I've come to see. I *know* I'm early," she said again, "but..." she added, leaning forward and trailing off dramatically. "I wanted to make sure you'd heard the news."

"What news?" Caroline asked, a bit relieved to know that there might be some other news in the community, a tidbit of gossip that had nothing to do with her.

But her relief was short-lived.

"The news about Avery, of course. Has anyone told you?"

"Leah, what are you talking about?"

"*Avery.* I usually avoid these tedious hospitality gatherings, but I had to come when I heard. I was sure Frederich wouldn't say anything. You know how closemouthed he is. And Beata wouldn't tell you—where is Beata, by the way?"

"Upstairs," Caroline said, holding up her hands in bewilderment. "Leah, I don't understand. I don't know why you're early—I don't even know what you're early *for.* And

I haven't heard anything about Avery—is William all right?" it suddenly occurred to her to ask.

"William is fine. This has nothing to do with William. This is about Avery and Frederich—"

"For heaven's sake, will you tell me?"

"Gladly," Leah said. "Frederich has given Avery the original marriage settlement...." She gave another dramatic pause. "Frederich gave Avery the acre of land with the spring for you, Caroline."

"He—"

"And then, *then,*" Leah interrupted, "he knocked Avery down—several times, Papa said. For hurting you the way he did—and for some remark he made about you when you came to get your clothes. Now, I ask you. When has anyone ever bested Avery in a fight? You should see your brother, Caroline. His face looks worse than *yours.* And he's going around telling people he ran into a door," she added with a chirping laugh. "I love Avery dearly, but it's so funny, Caroline!"

"Leah, you must be mistaken. Why would Frederich—?"

"Because you're a Graeber now, of course. He has to uphold the honor of the Graeber family, no matter how much he might...well, you know what I mean."

Yes, Caroline thought. She knew exactly what Leah meant. It was perfectly obvious that Frederich found it nearly impossible to tolerate her presence here. He'd made no secret about that.

She abruptly sat down on the settle beside Leah. Frederich should never have given Avery the acre with the spring, not for her, not when she'd—

She looked around because Beata was coming down the stairs, Lise and Mary Louise both in tow. Beata had changed her dress and her hair had been parted in the middle and swept back in wings that might have been attractive on someone less sour.

"These children are not ready!" she said, thrusting the girls forward. "You sit and gossip and leave your work for *me*."

"Beata—"

"You see what I have to endure," she said to Leah. "Laziness!"

"Do you suppose, Beata," Caroline said with as much dignity as she could muster, "you could advise me as to *why* the children need to be ready?"

"Lazy and good for nothing!" Beata hissed at her.

Caroline stood up, her hands clenched at her sides. She had had enough of Beata's riddles and always being in the wrong.

"It's our turn, Caroline Holt," Beata snapped. "And you know that! You deliberately try to embarrass us—with dirty children for everyone to see!"

"Well, we can fix that quickly enough," Leah said, standing up as well. "I'll help. I'll do your hair," she said to Lise, taking her by the hand. "Would you like that? Let's go upstairs—no, you take Mary Louise and go on and I'll bring some hot water. Beata will let us have a big kettleful, won't you, Beata?"

Beata made a gesture of disgust and turned away.

"Something smells wonderful, Beata," Leah continued, giving Caroline a wink behind Beata's back. "I'm *so* glad I came. Mother and Father will be along soon. They asked that I give you their regards and say how much they are looking forward to your fine cooking...."

The back door opened, and Frederich came in. He looked around the room, his eyes falling immediately upon the girls, who still stood at the bottom of the stairs.

"Why aren't they ready?" he asked Caroline.

His query provoked a sound of frustration and anger from her that he might have protested if he hadn't been so taken aback. She pushed past him and ran up the stairs, leaving everyone in the room staring after her.

"Well, well," Leah said to him, carefully holding a hot copper kettle away from her skirts. "Hello, *door*."

It fell to Frederich to fetch Caroline. He had waited patiently for her to ready the children—which she did with Leah's help—and now he was waiting for her to bring herself to the supper table. The guests were ready to be seated. Exasperated by Caroline Holt's rudeness, he abruptly went upstairs.

He found her sitting in her room in front of the small fireplace and clearly startled that he would open her door without her leave.

"How far will you go to embarrass this family?" he asked without prelude.

She looked at him, but she didn't respond.

"We are waiting the meal for you!"

"Why?" she asked, the icy control in her voice pushing him to the edge.

"Why! You ask *me* why? Why are *you* behaving this way? I expect this kind of tantrum from Beata. I would have hoped to see better from you. They taught you nothing at that fine school in town? You do everything you can to upset the evening? You knew it was our turn to extend the hospitality and you keep everybody waiting—"

"I didn't know anything of the kind!"

"We talked about this at breakfast yesterday morning, Caroline Holt."

"*We* didn't—"

"Beata said plainly that tonight was the night for the hospitality supper!"

"In what language?" she cried, throwing up her hands.

He stared at her, then frowned. *What language?*

"German," he admitted finally.

"It...wasn't my intention to embarrass you any more than I already have," she said quietly. "I didn't understand what was expected of me. I...still don't."

"You are to join the family for the hospitality supper," he said. "You are to behave well and do nothing to cause more talk."

She looked into his eyes. He had apparently taken it upon himself to thrash her brother senseless, but *she* wasn't to cause any more talk.

"I haven't changed my dress. I'm not fit—"

"It doesn't matter," he cut in.

No, she thought, still looking into his eyes. What did it matter if *she* had made herself presentable? The more unkempt she was the more credence she would give Beata's complaints.

"Anything...else?" she asked,

"You will take care of my children—see that they don't get too tired and that they don't become a nuisance to the guests," he said, looking away from her steady gaze.

She stood up. "And what lie do we tell the guests about Eli's absence?"

"No lie. We will tell them—I have already said all they need to know—that he isn't here."

She clearly had some retort to that and he waited for her to say it. She didn't.

"Whatever remark you want to make, do so. I want no reproachful looks all evening."

"I don't give reproachful...!" Caroline began, but she bit down on it. "I have no remarks," she said instead.

Incredibly, he laughed. "You Holts can never tell the truth, can you?"

"All right! If you want a remark, this is my remark. If you gave Avery that acre of land with the spring, then you are a *fool!*"

"Without a doubt," he agreed. He turned and left the room, clearly expecting her to be following along behind. And she did follow, hurrying so that she might get in another gibe. But she realized as soon as she reached the bottom step that, instead of making barbed remarks, she should have been asking Frederich who was on the guest list.

It was raining still, a cold, bone-chilling rain, and the daylight had nearly gone. All the lamps had been lit. And Kader Gerhardt stood warming his hands in front of the sitting room fireplace.

She faltered at the sight of him, perhaps would have run if it hadn't been for Mr. Steigermann's greeting.

"Ah!" John Steigermann said, stepping forward to vigorously shake her hand. "Marriage is agreeing with you, Caroline. Is that not so, Frau Steigermann—see, there are roses in her cheeks!"

Mrs. Steigermann gently scolded her husband, then smiled in Caroline's direction. Caroline could feel herself blushing. Given the condition of her face, it would have been most difficult to tell the rose from the bruise. But she took her time greeting Steigermann and his wife and then Johann Rial. She had herself in hand by the time decorum required that she say something to Kader. He was so certain she would protect him still, as certain as she had been of his love *before* she'd lain in his arms. There was no reason he shouldn't be sure of her. She had stood before an entire congregation—with him there in the sanctuary—and said nothing. He would have no misgivings about coming here now.

"Frau Graeber," he said to her, giving a little bow. He was freshly barbered, immaculate as always. He wore his usual schoolmaster's garb, the severe black wool suit and white shirt she had always found so becoming to his pale hair and eyes.

"Mr. Gerhardt," she responded, keeping her hands in the folds of her skirts so that he—no one—would see them trembling.

She made no pretty apology for having kept everyone waiting. She made no offer to help Beata put the food on the table. She was fully aware that she would be condemned whether she did or didn't. She stood back as the others adjourned to the table, half expecting Beata not to have set a place for her again. When everyone was about to be seated, she went to stand between Lise and Mary Louise. Kader immediately came to assist her, pulling back her chair with his usual European flair.

"I have missed you," he whispered in her ear as she was about to be seated and he slid her chair forward.

She could feel her cheeks flush, and she kept her head down, fussing with her skirts and helping the children get situated.

Kader took the seat directly across from her.

"How do you like this rain, Frau Graeber?" he asked her immediately. His voice was politely neutral, in spite of his whispered remark, but his eyes burned with a kind of intensity she might not have recognized if she hadn't seen it so apparent that day in the schoolroom.

This is your baby I'm having, Kader.

The thought rose in her mind in spite of all she could do. But she immediately let herself remember. His coldness. Her humiliation.

No, she thought sadly. *This is* my *baby.* And she would not let *her* child suffer for its mother's poor choice of a sire.

"I don't mind the rain," she said without looking at him.

"Neither do I," he agreed, smiling now. "It reminds me of the springtime in Germany—"

"You are fortunate enough not to have to venture into the wet and cold unless you choose to do so, Mr. Gerhardt. Johann and Frederich—and Mr. Steigermann—likely don't find such a downpour nearly as fascinating."

Frederich had been speaking to Frau Steigermann. He looked up at the mention of his name, but he made no comment.

"Tell me, Caroline, did you hear that all of Aaron Goodman's sons have enlisted in the Confederate army?" Kader persisted, blatantly using her given name.

"Is that so?" John Steigermann leaned forward to ask. "The oldest boy asks to marry my Leah at least twice a month. Who shall we have suffering on our front porch now, Leah?"

"Oh, Papa," Leah said, clearly basking in her father's teasing.

Caroline looked down at her hands, because the Goodman brothers were all friends of William's, and he had followed their lead in more things than she cared to remember.

"You must not worry that William will catch the war fever, Caroline," Frederich said from the head of the table. "He will do his duty to his family first."

She didn't reply, surprised that he recognized her concern. But she didn't miss his far from subtle reminder. William would do his duty to his family—unlike certain others of the Holts. But perhaps he wouldn't have a choice. The newspaper she had read for John Steigermann had indicated that he wouldn't, nor would any man seated at this table.

"William is just a boy," she said abruptly, causing everyone to look in her direction. "He is too young to go to war."

"What a fine table the Graebers have set for us! Shall I deliver the grace now, Frederich?" Johann said heartily, his pulpit voice already in place.

The thanksgiving prayer began, and Caroline jumped in her chair because she suddenly felt Kader's foot firmly pressed against hers under the table. She kept her eyes down, and she squirmed to move away from him. A woman's good reputation was the only protection she had against unwanted attention. When hers had been spotless, it had been no deterrent to Kader Gerhardt. Clearly, he now considered her as immune to insult as any other woman of ill repute. She fought hard against the welling of tears. If she had had any doubt as to his lack of regard for her before, she had none now. As soon as Johann finished, she slid her chair noisily back from the table a few inches, ignoring Frederich's less than approving glance.

"Caroline, can you hand nothing?" Beata said sharply when Caroline didn't immediately accept the bowl she offered.

"I'm very sorry, Beata," she said quietly, because she had been trying to avoid Kader's overt gaze rather than anticipate Beata's bowls. She took the dish of sweet potatoes and tried to ignore the derogatory comment Beata made under her breath, fully aware that both Johann Rial and Kader must have heard it.

Thankfully the children were behaving—if she couldn't. The table conversation continued in German, and Kader turned his attention to John Steigermann and Frederich, pausing between courses to flatter Beata—at least Caroline assumed it was flattery because of Beata's simpering response. After a time, Lise fell into quietly translating some of the discussion. She hesitated once when her father looked at her, but Frederich nodded his permission for her to continue.

"Mr. Gerhardt says he thinks perhaps Napoleon III will help the South in the war," she whispered. "Papa says we should pray not. The French will want far more in return than they give. Mr. Steigermann says the army came to his farm yesterday—to buy grain with worthless paper."

Caroline ate little, keeping her attention on the children as Frederich had ordered her to do. She surmised as the meal progressed that this "hospitality supper" was some kind of regular event, whereby the various German families took turns inviting the schoolmaster and the clergy to dine. She surmised, too, from Kader's heated glances, that he expected far more from the new Frau Graeber than sitting down with him to a hearty meal. What did he think she would do? Sneak out of the house at night and meet him in the schoolroom?

Lise stopped translating, and Caroline poured Mary Louise more milk, trying to guess what Beata was saying to the group and still keep Mary Louise from snatching her cup away mid-pour.

"Ha!" Beata concluded, and everything at the table stopped.

Caroline looked up, immediately recognizing the vulgar, chopped-off laugh. Leah, for once, was completely at a loss for words, and John Steigermann reached out to pat his wife on the hand. Beata wore her smug grin and she kept looking to Kader for some indication of his approval. Even Johann Rial seemed speechless.

"Caroline," Frederich said, and she glanced in his direction. He had spoken quietly, but he was clearly angry. "Will you take Lise from the table now?"

"Why?" she asked pointedly, because she had no intention of letting Beata's vulgarity drive her from the room.

"Take her," Frederich said.

She looked at Lise then. The child sat with her head bowed, her mouth trembling.

"Lise is crying," Mary Louise said, trying to reach her sister's arm to pat it much the way she had patted Caroline's in the garden. "Am I going to cry, Sister?" she asked Lise.

"Go with your Aunt Caroline, Lise," Frederich said. "You and Mary Louise both."

"Perhaps Beata is the one you want to send from the table, Frederich," Johann Rial said, and Leah laughed.

"Ich—?" Beata said, waxing indignant.

"Caroline, take Lise upstairs," Frederich said again.

The child was crying openly, and Caroline put her arm around her.

"Come, Lise," she said gently. "We'll go now."

"It's my—fault—" Lise said, crying harder. "I didn't *tell* you, Aunt Caroline. Beata talked about the hospitality supper—being tonight—but she said it in German. I didn't say it in English for you. Beata and Papa are mad at you again—and it's my fault—''

"No, dear heart, it is *not* your fault I'm ignorant of the language. Come along." She stood up and took Lise by the hand. "Good evening," she said to the guests in general. "I have very much enjoyed—" She broke off. She hadn't enjoyed anything, and she couldn't make herself say it, regardless of what a good upbringing required.

"Good evening," Lise murmured, trying hard not to sob out loud.

"Am I going to cry?" Mary Louise asked again as Caroline led both girls out.

"No, Mary Louise, you're not," Caroline assured her. "This is nothing for you to cry about."

"Then Papa better bring us a *lot* of peppermint candy," she decided as they climbed the stairs.

Caroline left the room without glancing back.

I am never going to stand this, she thought. *Never.*

She helped the girls get ready for bed. Lise stopped crying after a time, lapsing into a worrisome kind of silence broken only by the barest of responses to Caroline's conversation.

"This isn't your fault," Caroline said as she kissed Lise good-night.

"Is it *my* fault?" Mary Louise wanted to know.

"No, it is not," Caroline assured her. "Here is your kiss, too. Now go to sleep."

"Are you going to tell us a story?" Mary Louise persisted.

"Once upon a time there was a little girl named Mary Louise and she was such a good little girl, she stopped talking and went right to sleep. *The End.*"

"No," Mary Louise said, giggling. "That's not it! Tell about—about—the—"

She couldn't remember and had to hop out of bed to confer with Lise.

"King Midas," Lise said, her voice scratchy-sounding still from crying.

Caroline managed to get Mary Louise back where she belonged, and she began the story of the king who loved gold above all else. Mary Louise, for all her energy, dropped off to sleep almost immediately. Caroline gamely told the rest of story for Lise's benefit, but she could hear lively conversation—Kader's voice—from downstairs. Clearly, Beata's remark—whatever it had been—hadn't dampened the evening. After a time, she sighed heavily and sat in silence, her mind irrevocably going to the baby she carried.

"It's still raining," Lise murmured, just on the edge of sleep.

"Yes," Caroline said.

"Aunt Caroline? Don't leave until I go all the way to sleep, all right?"

"All right," Caroline said.

"Mama used to do that. Sit here until I went to sleep. I wish Papa..."

Lise didn't say anything else, and Caroline waited to see if she'd dropped off.

"Aunt Caroline?" Lise said when Caroline was about to stand.

"What is it, Lise?" Caroline asked kindly, reaching out to pull the quilt higher on Lise's shoulder.

"Is there any music?"

"Music?"

"From downstairs."

"No. No music."

"I thought I heard it—but I...didn't, did I? I...wish Papa would play his fiddle again. He used to when people came to supper. Mama and I would waltz and waltz all round the table. He hasn't played in such a...long time. That's how I know...he's still...sad...."

Caroline sat there listening to the rain and to Lise's quiet breathing. After a moment, she got up from her chair and quietly left the room. And she sat by her bed for a long time in the dark, trying with all her might to imagine Frederich Graeber fiddling a waltz.

Frederich heard the squeaking of the third step from the top of the stairs. He lay quietly, just on the edge of sleep and thinking that it must be Mary Louise, prowling the house again, looking for Ann as she had done so often since her mother's death. Her nighttime searches were always likely when she had gotten overtired or upset, and seeing Lise so distressed this evening would have been more than enough to disturb her sleep.

He forced himself to sit up on the side of the bed in spite of his exhaustion. Mary Louise never cried when he found her wandering about, never expected to be scolded. She always seemed glad to have located him at least. Sometimes he drew the milk jug up from the cold bottom of the well, and they'd share a cupful before he put her back to bed. Sometimes they just sat in the big rocking chair in front of the fire until she grew sleepy again.

But Mary Louise was in her bed when he stopped outside the room she and Lise shared. They were both sleeping soundly. He listened for a moment, then moved quietly down the stairs, avoiding the telltale third step he was certain he'd heard. Beata hiding things again, he thought. Or Eli come sneaking home.

He had made a point of not seeking Caroline out when the guests had finally gone and he came upstairs. Beyond simple charity, he refused to be concerned about her. His only concern was Lise. His older daughter was far too sensitive for her own good, and Caroline was once again the cause of Lise's tears. He was aware that Caroline would have asked him about Beata's crude remark. She would have asked in that proud, blunt way she had, and he would have told her. Then she would have looked at him with those eyes of hers, and he would have felt sorry for her. He did *not* want to feel sorry for Caroline Holt.

He could see partway into the kitchen when he reached the bottom step. The fire had been built up. He could smell the burning wood. The room danced in shadows. After a moment, he heard a wavering sigh.

He stepped closer. Caroline was kneeling on the hearth beside a porcelain pitcher and basin, one shoulder and one breast bare. She worked to get her other arm out of the sleeve of her dress and the chemise she wore underneath it, letting both garments hang downward from her waist.

The fire popped and hissed. One of the smaller logs shifted. Caroline waited for the sparks to subside, then she carefully began to wash, her movements tentative, as if the water was still too hot or the procedure too painful. Her back was to him, and he imagined that he could smell the pungent scent of the lye soap as the steam rose upward. He could almost but not quite see the dark mottling of the bruises on her forearms and back, and he could hear her soft cry of pain when she touched a place on her shoulder too heavily with the wet cloth. Until this moment, regardless of her battered face, he hadn't realized how much Avery had hurt her.

She moved closer to the fire and turned slightly. He could see one breast lined in firelight. She was completely unaware of him.

He stood transfixed.

Watching.

When she began to gently soap her breasts, his lips parted and he drew a shaky breath, feeling himself grow hot and heavy with desire. She was so...beautiful. He hadn't known she would be so beautiful. In his fantasies of revenge he had simply taken her, his will over hers, his right as her husband. He hadn't cluttered his mind with any of the details.

He couldn't tear his eyes away. His hands ached to touch her in the same way she was touching. He wanted to step into the room. He wanted to grab her and push her down right there on the hearth and—

No! I will not think of her in this way!

Not when he knew now who was likely the father of her baby. He had seen her stricken look when she realized Kader Gerhardt was in the room. If any other woman in the community had been in Caroline's situation, he would have immediately suspected the schoolmaster, but he had honestly thought *she* would have had better sense. He had more or less convinced himself that she had been tumbled by some man from the town, some old classmate's brother or cousin, some rich, fast-talking dandy she had no experience in knowing how to resist.

He realized immediately that he was describing Kader Gerhardt.

He abruptly turned away. Tomorrow, spring planting or not, he would go looking for Eli.

Chapter Seven

Caroline got the girls ready for church well ahead of Beata's complaints. Both nieces were fed, clean and dressed in the proper attire. They had nothing to do but wait for the arrival of John Steigermann's wagon—an arrangement Frederich made before he left. Mary Louise was still full of questions about when her father would return, but there was nothing Caroline could say to satisfy her. She had not been made privy to Frederich's itinerary, and neither, she suspected, had Beata.

Frederich had been gone three days, and she couldn't account for the feeling of vulnerability his absence precipitated. Frederich was in no way her champion, in spite of the fact that he had kept the marriage pledge after all and had allegedly knocked Avery down. That had been the result of his and Avery's long-standing animosity; she had only been the excuse, and she was not to be flattered that Frederich had done violence supposedly on her behalf. It annoyed her greatly to keep finding herself looking and listening for his return—when they could hardly be civil to each other and when she locked her door against him every night.

Even so, she was flooded with relief when Frederich walked abruptly through the back door. Both his daughters ran to him. He said something to Beata over the clamor of their greeting. John Steigermann was taking them to church,

Caroline thought Beata replied. Then, Frederich asked for something to eat—a request that Beata clearly did not receive kindly.

"I'll get it," Caroline said, realizing that there was something, after all, to William's claim of being able to guess what was being said without actually speaking the language. She ignored both the Graebers surprised expressions and turned to get the leftover biscuits and ham from the niche in the hearth wall that served as a warming oven. She got down a plate and a tin cup from the cupboard as well, but Beata stood firmly planted between her and the table.

"I thought you didn't understand German," Beata said, her hands on her hips.

"I don't—"

"You understand when it suits you to understand!"

"I know the word for breakfast!"

"You are trying to make *me* look bad!"

"You don't need me for that!" Caroline broke off and gave a sigh. She did *not* want to start the day with yet another altercation. "I thought you wanted to finish dressing," she said in a normal voice. "You've said at least ten times that Mr. Steigermann would be here soon."

Beata still hesitated, but apparently the possibility of missing a ride to church outweighed her need to quarrel. She would want to be in church this Sunday, the first Sunday after the so-called wedding. Everyone would want to talk to her today. Everyone would want to hear all about Caroline Holt and Frederich Graeber.

Frederich sat down to eat with Mary Louise on his lap.

"You aren't ready for church," he said when Caroline put the plate and cup down in front of him.

"Aunt Caroline's not going to church," Lise said helpfully.

"Aunt Caroline *is* going to church," he answered, filling his plate with biscuits and ham. "There is no declining or accepting, as *she* pleases. She will go."

Caroline stood for a moment with the coffeepot in her hand, ignoring the cup Frederich deigned to hold out to her. "No," she said, the quietness of her voice in no way indicative of the anger she felt. She set the coffeepot down carefully just out of his reach, and she untied her apron. "Caroline is *not* going."

She turned away then and walked purposefully toward the stairs, because she wanted him to understand that she was not having a tantrum like Beata. She was simply... leaving, and she didn't realize that Frederich had followed her until she had gone into her room and tried to close the door.

"I am not going!" she said, trying to keep him out, but he was much too strong for her, and he pushed his way in past her.

"How many times do I have to tell you these things?" Frederich said. "Do you listen to anything I say to you?" He crossed the room and jerked open the clothes cupboard, searching through it and bringing out the unbecoming wren-brown frock he'd seen her wear to church. "You will go!"

She stood rigidly in the center of the room, and she looked from him to the dress and back again. He expected some kind of angry retort, but she said nothing, and suddenly tears began to spill down her cheeks. She made no attempt to wipe them away. Her mouth trembled, but she made no sound. She simply stood there with her head up, the way she had stood in front of the congregation when they'd gone through with their farce of marriage.

"You are not going to give these people more to talk about, Caroline Holt!" he said.

"It's Graeber," she said. "Not Holt. Graeber!"

She covered her face with her hands then and abruptly sat down on the side of the bed.

"I can't stand anymore," he thought she said. After a moment she took her hands down and looked at him. "I can't—face the—stares and the whispers—" she said, struggling for control.

It's Kader Gerhardt you don't want to face, he thought, knowing how much worse he would think of her if she were clamoring to get to church to see the man. But even he would admit that she had given Gerhardt no encouragement at the hospitality supper. He had heard her remark to the schoolmaster when he'd professed to loving the rain. If anything, she had insulted him.

"You are no better to face the stares and whispers than the rest of us, Caroline *Graeber,*" he said. "And there is nothing that can happen in the church today that will be any worse than you—than *we*—have already been through. We will not hide. Who doesn't know everything by now, tell me that?"

They don't know you sleep alone, she thought. And she had no doubt whatsoever that Beata would tell them. What distressed her, though, was how much she minded. Of course she didn't want Frederich to consummate the marriage, and yet she didn't want people to know how disinclined he was to do it.

Frederich thrust the dress at her. When she didn't take it, he threw it over the back of the chair.

"Did you find anything about Eli in town?" Caroline suddenly asked, her voice barely a whisper.

"No. I didn't. No one has seen him. Now get ready for church—or you can go the way you are. It makes no difference to me."

"I'm sure it doesn't," she said, incredulous that she could have been waiting expectantly for this man's return. He was right, however. She was not the only one affected by this scandal, and John Steigermann had already explained what needed to be done. She would let no one sit in judgment of her. She would have to wait until people forgot—

No. People would never forget. She would have to bear this, now, until some other scandal came along to take their collective attention. And she would enjoy the respite until they remembered again.

"If you are worried about Avery—"

"I'm not worried about Avery," she said. "Fighting is all my brother understands. If you've bested him at that *and* given him the marriage settlement, you've made a friend for life. He won't bother me as long as I'm living under your roof."

She took a deep breath, then stood up and reached for the dress. "Do you at least give me the privacy to put this on?" she asked.

Frederich could feel himself blush, as if she had somehow become privy to the thoughts he'd had about her these past few days, thoughts that easily could have driven him into the arms of some whore in one of the houses down by the railroad depot in town if he'd given in to them even for a second. He forced himself not to look at her. He would not let himself be caught in those great, sad eyes that pleaded for help even while she tried to drive him away.

"I'm going to feed the livestock," he said abruptly.

"They've been fed," she said, taking a certain satisfaction from his surprised look. "I'm not entirely the burden you think, Frederich. I was born and raised on a farm. I know what needs to be done when the lord and master is gone, and I know how to do it."

"I spoke to John Steigermann—"

"And I spoke to him afterward," she said. "I saw no point in being any more indebted to him than I already am. There was no reason for him to have to come here every day to do something I can do. I fed the livestock and—"

"And ruined them, too, likely!"

"I did nothing of the kind. I followed the instructions you gave Mr. Steigermann—"

He left her standing and went straight to the barn to make a painstaking inspection of his property. Everything seemed perfectly in order—to his great relief and to his annoyance. None of the animals had been starved or overfed. The stalls had all been cleaned out. The cows had been milked.

He began to tend the horse he'd ridden to and from town, more than a little perplexed by this new facet to Caroline Holt. He *had* considered her useless in anything that mattered, and it did not please him to discover that he'd been wrong.

He looked around to find Caroline and his daughters standing in the barn doorway. Caroline was not wearing the dress he'd all but thrown at her. She had changed to a dark blue one instead, one with black trim and a red ribbon at the neck.

"Any dead bodies?" she asked mildly.

"Who did the milking?" he asked without answering, still looking for a cause for complaint.

"Me, Papa," Mary Louise said. "I can milk good."

"You let Mary Louise—" Frederich began, turning on Caroline.

"Of course not, Papa!" Lise interrupted, rolling her eyes. "It's too dangerous. We did the singing part—"

"Singing? What singing is this?"

"Papa, we sat in the hay pile and sang some songs. Did you know if you sing to the cows, they give more milk? Hurry, Papa," Lise said, grabbing him by the hand as if she didn't see the all-too apparent signs that he was far from mollified. "You're the only one not ready for church."

He gave a heavy sigh. He was trying hard to hang on to his anger, but he couldn't when he looked into Lise's upturned face. "Go," he said, shooing his children ahead of him. "Go quick and find me a clean shirt."

He followed along after them, taking long strides so as not to have to walk alongside Caroline.

"A 'thank you, Caroline' would be in order," she said behind him.

"If not for you, I would not have been gone in the first place," he answered unkindly.

She stopped walking, and he looked back, half expecting to see her in tears again. But she wasn't crying. She was staring at him, the fleeting, little quirk of a smile he'd seen now and then firmly in place.

"Touché," was all she said.

Caroline hardly heard the sermon, so intently was she concentrating on hearing everything else. She tried to focus her attention on the hymnal instead of the overt whispering, on standing when she was supposed to stand, and sitting when everyone else did. But she was not participating in the service at all, and she felt everyone's attention so acutely that she actually thought any noise from her, even interspersed among countless others, would make her even more conspicuous than she already was. It wasn't only her bruised face that turned heads. She was conspicuous by her very presence here.

Neither Avery nor William had come to the service this morning, a disappointment in William's case. She had maintained the small hope that seeing her younger brother would make whatever else she had to endure worthwhile. She hadn't really expected Avery to put in an appearance—if he truly was wearing the evidence of Frederich's fists.

But Kader was there, smiling and gallant and seeming intensely affected by her arrival. He would have actually made a point of speaking to her if Frederich hadn't circumvented it.

How peculiar, she thought. It was as if her show of disinterest and her obvious unavailability had made her desirable again in Kader's eyes, pregnant or not.

Learn from all this, Caroline, she admonished herself as she stood yet another time. Two rows ahead of her she could see the back of Beata's bonnet. Beata had made a great show of avoiding her since their arrival, and Caroline was thankful for small favors. At least Frederich hadn't insisted that they sit together to further the hypocritical show of Graeber family unity.

She tried harder to concentrate on what Johann Rial was saying, but she began to feel more and more queasy. She should have eaten breakfast—would have eaten if she'd known Frederich would force her to come to church.

Johann finally ended his sermon, and she meant to get to the outside quickly, hurrying Lise and Mary Louise along ahead of her the second he concluded the benediction. But the aisle was crowded and progress slow. As she reached the main doors, she faltered. She could see the group of men congregating just outside, men who turned and looked in her direction as she approached.

"What's wrong?" Lise said at her elbow.

"What's wrong?" Mary Louise repeated.

"Mary Louise, don't say everything *I* say," Lisa said, and Caroline gave both of them a hard look. Frederich stood waiting on the front steps.

"Something's wrong," Lise immediately advised him.

Frederich looked at Caroline sharply, but he made no comment. There were too many people around. He noted immediately how pale she looked and just as he noted that, she had seen the group of men who stood on the flagstone path between her and John Steigermann's wagon. There was nothing subtle about the way they looked at her or about the sudden burst of laughter that erupted after someone's remark.

"Take my arm, Caroline," Frederich said to her quietly. She looked at him but she didn't do as he asked. "Take my arm," he said again. "You don't have to do this alone."

Her lips parted, trembling slightly as she gave a small, wavering sigh. But she reached to put her hand on his arm, her touch tentative and hesitant at first. He was beginning to understand her, to realize that she'd rather die than ask for help, particularly from him, and that she hated her vulnerability in this situation because it gave her no choice. She let Lise carry her Bible, and she took Mary Louise by the hand and walked with him, her grip on his arm tightening when she realized he had no intention of circumventing these leering men. He headed directly toward them, causing them to have to step aside to let him pass.

When they were nearly through the grinning crowd, Frederich suddenly turned to the closest man.

"You wanted to say something to me, Karl?" he asked, and the man flushed bright red.

"Ah, no, Frederich—"

"I thought you did, Karl," Frederich persisted. "I thought you wanted to say something to my face instead of behind my back."

"Frederich, please don't," Caroline whispered, completely incredulous that he would initiate such a confrontation with her on his arm.

He ignored her.

"Please!" she pleaded, still whispering.

Frederich looked at her then. She was near tears or fainting. Or both.

"Come," he said abruptly, as if confronting the man Karl had been her idea. He walked on with her, leaving the men staring after them.

Regardless of the light-headedness she felt, she let go of Frederich's arm. "Why?" she said, her voice trembling. "Why did you do that?"

"So they will know."

"Know what! That you can hold me up to their ridicule any time you like?"

He looked at her, surprised that she didn't understand. "You must leave these things to me," he said.

"To you? So that you can embarrass me? Humiliate me—?"

"Is your embarrassment—your humiliation—any worse than mine?" he asked quietly. "I did not send you to face them alone, did I?"

She looked away and didn't answer. She stepped away from him and walked toward the Steigermann wagon.

"Papa?" Lise said at his elbow, her face filled with concern.

"Go with your Aunt Caroline," Frederich said.

"Are you mad at her?" The word *again* hung in the air as if it had been said.

"Lise, don't ask me about things you're too young to understand!"

"I'm sorry, Papa," she said, her voice barely a whisper. She gave him one last look before she scampered away.

He gave a heavy sigh. *How long?* he thought, Job-fashion. How long would his family be in turmoil because of this one woman? And he still wasn't done with it. He had one other thing—one other person—he needed to confront today.

He began to look through the crowd for Kader Gerhardt. He saw him on the church steps talking to—trying to escape from—Beata, who clung to his arm as she related some obvious tale of woe. And whatever she was saying seemed to catch Gerhardt's attention after a moment, so that he wasn't trying to get away from her anymore.

Frederich walked in their direction, again feeling his disappointment in Caroline Holt. He expected Beata's kind of silliness where Gerhardt was concerned. Beata was far too impressed by the man's claim of a high-placed German family. But how could Caroline Holt have let herself become infatuated with such a man? She was more than a simple farm girl, regardless of her claim this morning. She had gone to the female academy and lived in town for a number of years. She should have been able to see Kader Gerhardt for the arrogant womanizer he was.

"Beata tells me you are withdrawing Lise from my school," Gerhardt said before Frederich could speak his mind. "It won't do—"

"I have no intention of justifying my decision to you," Frederich said.

"Frederich!" Beata protested. "Such disrespect! Herr Gerhardt is the schoolmaster. He is—"

"John Steigermann is waiting, Beata," Frederich interrupted rudely. "And this is not your business."

She stood looking at him, clearly weighing whether or not she wanted Kader Gerhardt to see her petulant side. After a moment, she smiled at the schoolmaster. "Herr Gerhardt," she said elaborately. "I look forward to your joining us for supper again soon. I trust you will forgive us the bad impression we must have—"

"The only one who needs forgiveness for a bad impression is you, Beata," Frederich cut in. "And *he* is not the one you should ask for it. John Steigermann is waiting."

She gave him a withering look but managed to smile at Gerhardt one last time before she turned to go.

"My daughter will be taught at home," Frederich said.

"I was guaranteed a certain income to come to this God-forsaken place, Graeber. With the older boys joining the army, the school can't afford to loose even one pupil—"

"You came here to get away from a cuckolded husband who would have killed you, schoolmaster," Frederich said bluntly. "And you were lucky to find so forgiving a man as Johann Rial to accept your services. Don't look to me to maintain your salary."

They stared at each other, Frederich again wondering what Caroline could have ever seen in this man.

But he knew what she had seen. A fine education and clean hands. Not some dirt-stained, ignorant farmer like her brother. And like Frederich Graeber.

"Surely you are not going to let the Holt woman teach her," Gerhardt made the mistake of saying, and Frederich grabbed him by his shirtfront.

"She is Frau Graeber to you and I suggest you remember that."

Gerhardt smiled and pulled Frederich's hand away. "The nights are long, are they not, Frederich? And there is no comfort from the grave—"

Frederich would have grabbed him again, but Johann Rial was there suddenly and stepped in front of him.

"Frederich, I don't know what this is about, but I do know this is *not* the place for it," Johann said, a hand resting firmly on Frederich's chest. "Kader, there are people waiting in the foyer to pay you their monthly school fees. I suggest you go and take the money they have managed to scrape together to give you." He stood with his hand on Frederich until Kader had gone. "What is this with Kader?" he asked, his voice quiet so the passersby couldn't hear. "Something wrong is happening here, Frederich. I think I should know what it is, and I ask you now, as your very longtime friend."

"It is nothing, Johann. I . . . have a short temper."

"Now *that* is the truth," Johann answered. "But it doesn't answer my question."

"There is no reason for you to be concerned, Johann."

"Indeed. If a brawl between the most prominent farmer in the county and the schoolmaster on my church steps is nothing for *me* to worry about, then let me ask this. What is happening now between you and Eli? Where is *he* this morning?"

"I don't know."

"You don't know?"

"I don't know, Johann! Does that make you happy? He ran off the night of the wedding. I've been to town—to ask if anyone had seen him. No one had."

"Why would he run off now? He stayed when you found out about him and Ann," Johann said, Ann's name abruptly a whisper because of a group of passersby.

"How should I know!"

"None of this should have happened, Frederich."

"*You* are the one who stood in the pulpit and asked for a volunteer husband."

Johann ignored his sarcasm. "What will you do?"

"Do? What is there to do? He owns half the Graeber land."

"Then how are things with you and Caroline? You have consummated the marriage?"

Frederich didn't answer him.

"I tell you this now, Frederich. If you don't, that child she carries will never be yours. Caroline is very strong willed. I will speak to her—"

"No!" Frederich said. "She has been shamed enough. She doesn't need any lectures on her marital duties from you."

Johann stared at him for a moment, then nodded. "You are a good man, Frederich," he said, and Frederich laughed.

"You confuse 'good' with 'trapped,' Johann. I must go. John Steigermann is waiting."

"I will pray about this, Frederich," Johann assured him, but Frederich held up his hand. He had had enough outside intervention in his life to last him a long while yet.

It was clear to him when he climbed into the back of the Steigermann wagon that both Caroline and Beata were still angry with him. He could tell by their rigid backs. But he couldn't help that, and he sat down on the wagon floor with his legs stretched out in front of him. His only regret was that Lise was upset. Only Mary Louise seemed to be her usual cheerful self, and for that he was grateful. She climbed over the back of the seat as the wagon jerked forward, barely missing tumbling headfirst onto him. But she didn't want to sit on his lap. She wanted to sit where she could stare unabashedly into his face.

He closed his eyes, dozing in the warm sunlight as they rode toward home, John Steigermann still humming the last hymn, and his wife and daughter quietly chatting. He wondered idly what it would be like to have a peaceful family like John Steigermann's. Even with Leah in it, Steigermann couldn't have the aggravation *he* had.

After a time, he opened his eyes. Mary Louise was still watching him.

"Mary Louise, what is it?"

"I think I might cry," she advised him, her face puckering just enough to show him the possibility.

"Indeed? Is there any particular reason for this crying?" he asked.

"Nobody brought any candy from town," she said gravely.

"Nobody brought candy? Who says this about the candy?"

"*Me,* Papa. Didn't you *hear* me?"

He laughed out loud, his eyes meeting Caroline's when she looked around to smile over her shoulder. But both their amusement immediately faded.

The ride home seemed to take forever, and Frederich realized his aggravation was far from over the moment they rode into the Graeber yard. William waited on the porch steps, his face clearly worried. He stood up immediately and bounded forward, before the wagon stopped.

"The army's at our place, Frederich," he said, without taking the time for amenities. "And they're taking a lot more grain sacks than Avery wants them to have, I can tell you. If you got anything you want to keep, you better start hiding—"

"Too late," Frederich said, looking past William toward the open field. A number of gray-uniformed horsemen were coming along the edge of the woods. He reached to lift

Beata and then Caroline over the side of the wagon. "Take Lise and Mary Louise inside," he said to Caroline as he helped the children down to the ground.

"They are *our* soldiers, Frederich," Caroline said.

"Yours perhaps, not mine. Soldiers are always the same. They are here to steal whatever they can. Take my children inside."

She gathered the girls to her, but she lingered to speak to William. He hadn't combed his hair today. It stood up in cowlicks all over his head. She forced herself to resist the impulse to mother him and make some remark about his lack of grooming. "You've grown a foot," she said instead, and he grinned from ear to ear.

"I don't know why—I ain't had a thing decent to eat since you left. Avery ain't no cook, that's for sure."

"William," Frederich called to him. "You stay to eat with us."

Caroline glanced at Beata, who wanted to object but for some reason didn't, and William's grin widened.

"Much obliged, Frederich. I sure was hoping to get fed. And I was kind of hoping to get that horse of Avery's, too, while I was at it."

"Is that the reason Avery sends you?" Frederich asked, his eyes still on the line of horsemen coming along the edge of the plowed field.

"Lord Almighty, no!" William said. "Avery's too scared to send me to do that."

"Why would Avery be afraid for you to get his horse?" Caroline asked.

"Aw, you know. If he sent me, Frederich might say for him to act like a man and come get it himself—boy, he's been as mad as an old wet hen since him and Frederich had their little discussion. So I thought I'd see if I couldn't get it for him as long as I was over here." He eyed Caroline closely. "You know, your face looks a damn sight better than Avery's does."

"William, don't swear," Caroline chided him, annoyed both by his tactlessness and by his language.

"Beg your pardon," he said, his response run together and automatic from all the years Caroline had clearly wasted trying to teach him how to behave. He did, however, manage to look a bit sheepish.

"You're a good brother to Avery," Frederich said, patting the boy on the back. "You take the horse—but you stay to eat with us first—if *our* soldiers don't take Beata's Sunday chicken right out of the pot."

Caroline ignored his sarcasm and walked with the girls and William a few steps toward the porch.

"William," John Steigermann called. "Do they pay money to Avery for the grain?"

"Same piece of paper you got, Mr. Steigermann. The one you have to take to the garrison in town," William said, and John Steigermann shook his head.

"You'd better go, John," Frederich said. "If they come to your place again, you'll want to be there."

Mr. Steigermann added a final comment to Frederich in German, then cracked his whip sharply, and the wagon lurched forward.

"Go inside, Caroline," Frederich said again, because the first of the soldiers was about to ride into the field near the far corner of the yard.

"Frederich—"

"When these men are gone, we will talk."

She allowed herself to look into his eyes; it was the only way she could halfway tell what he was actually feeling. This time, however, his eyes told her nothing.

"Where's Eli?" William asked, looking from one of them to the other.

"None of your business!" Caroline said. "Come inside—all of you."

"This is exciting!" Lise said as Caroline hurried along. Beata was already at work in the kitchen, but they all congregated to watch Frederich and the Confederate officer from the window. The officer seemed to be doing all the talking. Frederich stood silent and grim. After a moment they walked off to the barn.

"Reckon that soldier's going to come out looking like Avery?" William wondered, taking a few boxing jabs at the air.

"William, for heaven's sake!" Caroline said.

"You ain't *seen* our brother, Caroline. I'd worry for anybody going off with Frederich when he's looking the way he's looking right now."

But the officer came out of the barn looking fine. He stood talking to Frederich for a time, then handed him a piece of paper.

"Is he the same one who came to the house?" Caroline asked William.

"That's him. Kept asking me why *I* wasn't in the army. Said he had boys younger than me in his company—I'm going outside," he said abruptly.

"William, don't," she said, but to no avail. She had to catch Lise by the dress tail to keep her from following after him.

William went to stand beside Frederich, his thumbs hooked in his trouser pockets. And he kept looking at the boy soldiers who waited for their commanding officer to complete his transaction. They did indeed look younger than William. After a moment, the officer mounted his horse and left, and Frederich and William came back inside.

"That was good, Frederich," William said. "Caroline, you should have heard. Boy, that officer didn't like what Frederich told him a little bit. Tell her what you said, Frederich."

But Frederich clearly didn't feel like enlightening her. "Go wash your hands, boy," he said, "if you want to sit at this table."

The meal went peacefully enough, Beata softening somewhat in the wake of William's earnest praise. She even sent a sweet potato pie with him when he was ready to leave. The prospect of such a wonderful delicacy later had him grinning from ear to ear.

He gave Caroline an awkward hug.

She held the pie while he mounted Avery's horse. "Goodbye, William," she said, handing the pie up to him and fighting down an absurd inclination to cry. She missed her little brother so.

He took the pie, looking back at her once to give her a big grin as he rode off toward the Holt fields.

Frederich stood at her elbow. "We will talk now, Caroline," he said without prelude. "Wait," he said when she turned to go into the house. "We will walk down the road a bit—unless you want Beata to hear."

She looked at him doubtfully.

"You don't feel like walking?" he asked.

"No, I feel fine," she said immediately. "I can walk."

She was still afraid of him. He could see the wariness in her eyes. Of what was she so afraid? he thought. He had given her his word not to beat her. She must know by the very fact that he had married her that he kept the promises he made.

But she was not afraid of a beating, nor was she afraid of walking out with him. She was afraid that very soon he would want her in his bed. He knew that she had taken to locking her door at night, and how that insulted him. He had done what he could to save her reputation. He had the right to take her—and she locked him out, when he'd had no intention of forcing himself on her. It galled him that, regardless of his willingness to marry her and make a home for her, she still found him so unacceptable. A stupid, ignorant foreigner. A farmer with hands too dirty to lay upon Caroline Holt. He was all those things, and there was nothing he could do about it. Perhaps he should tell her how little *she* appealed to him with her sharp-tongued sarcasm and her superior air.

And her unborn child.

Except that it wouldn't be true. He did think of her in that way. He thought of her all the time, remembering the way she looked that night before the fire. He had ached to touch her then. He ached to touch her now. It was all he could do not to reach up and catch the strand of dark hair that had blown across her cheek.

"Lise! Mary Louise! *Kommet!*" he abruptly called, and the girls came running, dancing around them in a burst of youthful energy.

"How much grain did the army take?" Caroline asked as they began walking down the winding road that led from the house. The sun was bright, warm until the wind blew. The trees in the woods beyond Frederich's newly plowed fields were just beginning to green. The day reminded her of the time when she and Ann had taken the children on that last picnic, the time when Ann had told her she was pregnant yet again.

"Too much," Frederich said grimly. "Fifty sacks—ten percent, the officer says. Everything was done very politely this time, but they will be back as long as there is anything left to take, and politeness will fall by the way."

She made no comment, walking slowly, savoring the feel of the sun on her face. One good thing about having no reputation to speak of—she didn't have to worry about whether she got freckles anymore. She stopped long enough to admire a bunch of violets Lise and Mary Louise picked, smiling to herself as they ran off again.

The smile faded. "Please," she said. "What is it you want to say?"

She didn't know what she expected—nothing really. Something about the children perhaps. Some instructions he wanted to give without Beata's interruption. She glanced at him. He was staring at her intently.

There is no guile in this woman, Frederich suddenly
thought. She was nothing like Ann, nothing at all, and what
she wouldn't bluntly say, her face gave away—like her fear
of his church-sanctioned, carnal intent. Like the identity of
the father of her child.

"*I* am the head of this family," he said after a moment.

She gave a short laugh. "Yes, and what a trying job *that's*
become."

She glanced at him, surprised to find him actually smiling.

"Yes," he agreed. "Trying."

"*That* is what you wanted to say to me? I assure you I
know the chain of command here, Frederich."

"No," he answered. "Lise! Mary Louise!" he abruptly
called to his children. They both came immediately.

"What, Papa?" Lise asked, breathless from the joy of
running back and forth like a colt let out to pasture.

"What, Papa?" his smaller daughter, the echo, asked.

"I have found something in my pockets," he said. "I
think these things must be for you." He began searching,
bringing out two small paper packets from inside his coat.
He handed one to each of the children.

"Thank you, Papa," Lise said in her quiet way.

Mary Louise sniffed the packet. "Peppermint! Peppermint! *Peppermint!*" she cried, bouncing up and down.
"Thank you, Papa—did you bring Aunt Caroline some,
too? She needs it—didn't you get her some, Papa? I said she
would cry without it. Did you forget?"

"No," Frederich assured her. "I didn't forget."

He brought out yet another packet and held it out to
Caroline. The gesture caught her completely off guard. She
couldn't remember the last time anyone had given her any
kind of gift, and she stood looking at it, suddenly awash in
an impulse to cry—precisely what the peppermint was de-
signed to prevent.

"It is important that you have this, Caroline," Frederich said pointedly, still holding out the candy. She looked at him. His eyes shifted ever so slightly to the children, both of whom were waiting expectantly to witness her pleasure at receiving such a treat from their father.

"Thank you," she managed, finally taking it. "Thank you very much indeed."

She looked away across the plowed field to keep from crying.

"I think you better eat one," Mary Louise advised her. "I think you better eat one *now*."

"Yes, you're right," she said, forcing a smile. She opened the paper as the girls went running off again, realizing that she really was going to cry after all. She swallowed hard and turned away from Frederich.

"Thank you," she said again, incredulous that such a simple gesture could reduce her to tears.

"It is nothing."

"It is to them." She wiped at the corner of her eye with her fingertip. "And . . . to me."

She looked at him then, acutely aware of the two thoughts that suddenly filled her mind. That Frederich Graeber's eyes were intensely blue, and that regardless of what he'd said to her that night she'd found him drinking in the dark, he perhaps had some capacity for kindness where she was concerned after all.

"Caroline," he said when she turned to walk back to the house. "The thing I wanted to say to you."

She stopped and waited, clutching the peppermint sack tightly in her hand.

He hesitated, and she thought for a moment that he had changed his mind. But then he took a deep breath. "You don't have to worry about Kader Gerhardt."

Chapter Eight

Frederich knows.

The thought stayed in her mind all the time. But how he could have possibly found out about Kader she couldn't imagine. Had he simply guessed? Had she somehow given herself away? Kader would never have said anything. She was certain of that. And now, when she looked into Frederich's eyes, the overt animosity that had been there earlier was gone. It had been replaced by something very akin to disappointment—as if he had gone against his better judgment and allowed himself to hope for the best where her strength of character was concerned—and he had been gravely disappointed. It both angered and saddened her.

Her nerves stayed on edge in anticipation of a further discussion. She stayed out of Frederich's way as much as possible, so much so that Beata even remarked on it. She couldn't believe Frederich would suddenly announce that she didn't have to worry about Kader Gerhardt and then just let it drop. And if he did ask her about him, what would she say? As her husband, she supposed he had the right to know, but how could she make anyone understand that she had thought that she loved Kader Gerhardt, that she had thought him honorable and worthy and that she, who had always prided herself on her independence, simply hadn't known how to say no?

"Was haben Sie?"

Caroline looked up sharply from the button she'd been sewing on Mary Louise's pinafore, startled because she hadn't realized Frederich was anywhere around. She stopped and waited, as common courtesy required—courtesy and her indebtedness to him for the legitimacy of her child and for her daily bread. Even so, she refused to be put at a disadvantage because she didn't understand the German language.

She allowed her eyes to just meet his before she went back to sewing.

"What's wrong with you?" he said in English.

She nearly laughed. Wrong? He was seemingly privy to a secret she'd intended to take to her grave, for one thing.

"Nothing," she said, trying to sound at ease in spite of the fact she was desperately worried now that he really would ask about Kader.

"You are feeling well?" Frederich asked instead.

"I am fine," she answered, blindly jabbing the needle at the hole in the button.

"I think you don't eat enough," he said.

I don't understand, she thought. His speaking to her in English was no more helpful than his speaking in German. Frederich Graeber did *not* concern himself with whether or not she ate.

"You cannot make a baby out of nothing, Caroline. You must eat more."

"Frederich—"

"I need to know if you are well because I need your help," he said, clearly not interested in whatever remark she'd intended to make. "Are you?"

"Yes," she said without hesitation.

"I thought I heard you last night. Walking about."

"You didn't," she said evenly, again looking him in the eye. When she locked her door, it stayed locked, she almost said. She half expected him to call her "a lying Holt" again, but he didn't. Once again, she bent her head over the loose pinafore button to discourage further conversation. He was waiting when she glanced up.

"Put that away. I have another job I want done."

"Indeed," she said, not quite under her breath.

"Indeed," he assured her.

She dutifully followed him out of the kitchen and onto the back porch, waiting where he said to wait until he'd brought a bucket and a sack of potatoes that were ready to sprout.

"These come from the relatives in Pennsylvania," he said as he slung the sack onto the porch. "They are very fine. I want them cut for planting on Good Friday and I want none of the eyes wasted."

"You can't get *all* the eyes, Frederich," she said, watching him open the sack wider.

"Even so," he said. "Hold out your hand."

"*Why?*" she asked pointedly.

"So I can see what size knife is best for you to use," he replied, just as pointedly.

"Forgive me," she said, thrusting out her hand and trying to ignore his rough fingers on hers. Did he seem to want to touch her more often these days or was it her imagination? She abruptly dismissed the notion as ridiculous. "I am unaccustomed to such attention to detail," she added to annoy him.

He glanced at her, but he made no reply. He went into the house and came back with a small knife from the kitchen. "Don't let Beata see you with this."

"Oh, of course. Let's have as much drama surrounding the potato cutting as we possibly can," she said, taking the apparently purloined knife. He held on to it a little too long, forcing her to pull it out of his hand. She glanced up at him. The mouth wasn't smiling, but there was something almost mischievous in his eyes.

What are you doing? she thought. *Are you teasing me? Are you being cruel?*

"I think you like drama, Caroline Holt," he said.

"What I like is Beata occasionally in something less than an apoplectic fit."

She reached into the sack and picked a potato, looked at it, then cut it into what she deemed the appropriate number of chunks to separate the maximum number of eyes.

She was aware of Frederich's scrutiny, but he made no comment. After the third potato, she looked at him. "Well?"

"Too slow," he observed. "But the cutting good enough."

"Oh, thank you. I was truly worried."

She sat down on the porch steps while she worked, surprised to find that her belly was beginning to take over her lap. She knew she was pregnant certainly, and yet she didn't somehow. The mounting number of changes in her body were always catching her unaware. Sometimes she went for hours without thinking of the baby at all, and sometimes, when she did remember it, did notice some overt change in her body, she was completely overwhelmed. Like now. This latest discovery—that she was losing her lap—left her with the ridiculous urge to cry. She had to concentrate intently on the potatoes, swallowing hard and taking great care not to look in Frederich's direction. She desperately wanted him to go away and attend to whatever pressing matters he surely must have if he'd allowed himself to ask her for a favor. She never wanted to give him the satisfaction of seeing her so overcome by her situation that she would weep.

But he was mending a piece of harness, as engrossed in it as she was the potatoes.

"Do you know about the *Geburtstagstisch*?" he asked after a time.

"No," she answered. "Yes," she immediately amended, because she felt more in control now and because she didn't want him to think she was totally ignorant. "It's a German birthday custom, isn't it? A little table with gifts on it—Ann told me about it.''

"Yes. The birthday table. It's Lise's birthday soon. I want to ask if you know of something she wants. There is little money to spare until the army pays for the grain—if they pay. But I want to find something for her table. Something that will make her..."

She looked up when he didn't go on.

"Happy," he concluded.

Their eyes met; he was the one who looked abruptly away. She frowned, marveling again at this side of Frederich's nature. If he was such a good father, why hadn't she ever seen it when she visited Ann here? Perhaps he had been a good husband as well. She had told him the truth the other night; Ann had never complained about him.

"I've only heard Lise mention one thing that she wanted—and it doesn't cost any money," she said.

"What is it?"

"She wants you to play your fiddle again."

Frederich said nothing. His face registered nothing. For a moment, Caroline thought he hadn't understood her.

"I have no use for fiddling," he said finally—and in a tone of voice she was hard-pressed to define. Angry? Annoyed? Yes, annoyed. As if she'd deliberately set out to insult him.

"Oh, I'm sure," she said, her own annoyance rising. She would never understand these people.

He immediately accepted the gauntlet she'd thrown down. "What does that mean?" he asked, moving closer. "*'I'm sure.'*"

She stopped cutting and looked at him. "It means that so simple a request from a little girl who loves you with all her heart would be lost on a man like you."

"Ah! A man like me. A man too rough and unlearned for such a fine lady as *you* are?"

"Don't!" she said, her eyes locked with his. "We both know what *I* am. I accept that you think the worst of me. There is no need for your sarcasm."

Frederich gave a short laugh. "My sarcasm. Yes. We have a lot of trouble here if we don't keep in hand *my* sarcasm."

She abruptly went back to cutting. Frederich could see how agitated she was. He expected her to vent her aggravation with him on the seed potatoes, but she didn't. She was still as exact with the knife, as careful of the precious eyes, as she had been before—a marked difference between her and Beata, he realized. Beata would have ruined every potato that came to her hand—even if they all starved this winter—just to get even.

The image of Caroline bathing before the fire rose in his mind, regardless of his resolve not to think of her in that way. He didn't want to be thinking of her in *any* way—except as the disgrace she was.

But she was sitting in a patch of sunlight, her dark hair as shiny as a raven's wing. He fought down the intense urge to reach out and loosen it from its pins. He wanted to see it tumble down her back. He wanted to bury his face in it. He wanted to pick her up and carry her upstairs to his bed in broad daylight—

Damn Eli for this! Damn him to hell!

If Eli hadn't stood in church and offered to marry her, *he* would never have been forced to keep the marriage pledge. Caroline Holt would be out of his life. He wouldn't be looking for her a hundred times a day and he wouldn't be tormented by these perpetual thoughts of ending his celibacy. Kader Gerhardt had been right. The nights were long and there was no comfort from the grave.

"Your brother is coming," he said abruptly, grateful for the diversion even if it were another Holt.

Caroline looked up, expecting to see William, but Avery was coming across the field. She immediately got up to go into the house.

"There is no need for you to run from Avery," Frederich said.

"I'm not running. He's only here because he wants something. Since it isn't in *my* power to give him anything, I have no desire to watch him ingratiate himself. I have things to do inside."

"You have things to do out here."

"When he's gone," Caroline said, going inside in spite of Frederich's objections. And she nearly bumped into Beata as she closed the back door. To her immense surprise, Beata had been standing before the washstand mirror. Primping?

Yes, Caroline decided. And it wasn't the now-where-does-this-strand-of-hair belong? kind. It was the kind a woman resorted to when a particular man had unexpectedly arrived. The dour Beata Graeber had actually been primping for Avery Holt.

Obviously startled by Caroline's sudden entrance, Beata went immediately back into the kitchen.

Caroline looked in the direction Beata had gone, and then through the window at Avery. As far as she was concerned, Beata Graeber was the perfect comeuppance for Avery Holt. She felt mischievous suddenly, and she threw open the back door.

"Avery!" she called brightly. "Do come inside!"

He and Frederich both looked at her as if she'd lost her mind.

"Come on," she coaxed, holding the door wider.

Avery stood doubtfully, then peered past her as if he expected to find some devious trap had been laid for him. He was not far from wrong, only Caroline hadn't done it. She glanced over her shoulder. Beata, the Spider, was waiting in her parlor—and positively beaming.

"Come in," Caroline coaxed further. "How is William?"

"Fine," Avery said warily, coming onto the porch. "What are you up to, Caroline?"

She glanced at Frederich, who had the look of a man who might be wondering the same thing.

"What could I be up to, Brother?" she said. "We both know *I* am no match for you. My," she said, looking closely at his face. He did indeed look worse than she did—but then he had the land and the spring he'd coveted for years to console him. She, on the other hand, had nothing.

"Beata, may I ask you this one favor?" she asked, turning in Beata's direction. "Could we make my brother welcome? Give him some coffee? Or cake, perhaps? I know Avery loves your cooking. He's said so so many times."

Avery gave her a dark look, but she felt no fear—because of Frederich, she suddenly realized. Frederich had told her she didn't have to run and she believed him.

"*Avery* is always welcome," Beata said.

Caroline stood back to let Beata drag him the rest of the way into the house. She smiled slightly to herself, surprised that Frederich stood with her. She went out onto the porch, looking across the field toward the woods beyond. She loved this time of year, the abrupt change to springtime and greening trees. A few more warm days and redbud and dogwoods would bloom.

"What *are* you up to?" Frederich asked.

She looked at him, but she didn't reply. She sat down on the steps and returned to the task of potato cutting instead.

"I want no more Holts in my family," he said.

Caroline took no offense. She wanted no more Graebers in hers. "Don't worry, Frederich. Avery might seduce dear Beata if he got half the chance, but marry her? Never."

"You are a blunt-speaking woman, Caroline Holt," he said.

"I can *be* blunt," she said, reaching for another potato. "I have no reputation to preserve and nothing to lose by speaking the truth. Men don't allow women to speak the truth very often, did you know that? Our lot in life is to keep all of you flattered and cajoled and thinking everything is just fine no matter what terrible thing is going on."

"Beata isn't good enough for your brother then."

"Beata isn't landed enough. Avery isn't about to marry a woman who isn't going to inherit good farmland. Leah Steigermann is more what he has in mind."

"Well, he won't manage that except over John Steigermann's dead body."

Caroline glanced at him. Frederich had no idea how much Avery had already managed. If John Steigermann ever learned what had happened between Leah and Avery at the corn shucking, there would indeed be a dead body. The question was whose?

"We all have our troubles," she said.

"And Leah is *your* friend."

"No, she isn't. But she's been kind to me—for whatever reason. Her infatuation with Avery, I suppose. I'd hardly even spoken to her before...before John Steigermann took me to stay in their house. It's hard accepting kindness from someone you think is...?"

She didn't go on, and Frederich made no comment. He sat down on the top step near her and looked out across the field as she had done. It struck her suddenly Leah had been right, that he really was not...unhandsome. He was in his late thirties, but he had a boyish look about him, when she looked past the beard. And he was tired. She felt a stab of guilt. Eli had run off the moment *she* came into the household, regardless of his fine welcome speech, and Frederich had suffered the consequences. If there was an innocent party in all this, she supposed it must be he. He had kept his marriage pledge—the sacred German *Verlobung*—and being cold and humorless was no sin to anyone but her. Actually, she had come to the realization that he really wasn't cold *or* humorless—except toward Holts.

"Tell me what Lise said—about the fiddling," Frederich said abruptly.

Caroline told him everything she remembered in spite of his imperious tone.

"Strange," he said. "The things that make children feel better—safe. When I played the fiddle for her and Anna, I was still..."

He suddenly stood up, incredulous that he had been about to reveal even a small part of his private pain. He had to be on his guard with this woman. He had to remember who and what she was.

"I can be blunt as well, Caroline Holt," he said, looking down at her. He moved slightly so that he could see her face. "Tell me. Why do you bolt your door at night? Tell me," he said again, because she looked so startled and because she abruptly turned away from him. "Are you thinking that you can have a marriage that is not consummated annulled?"

She took a deep breath before she answered; he could feel her struggling for control.

"If the marriage was annulled," she said, finally looking at him, "then my baby would be a bastard. I don't want that. The reason I agreed to marry you in the first place is to keep that from happening."

"But *you* have decided that we will have a marriage in name only—and you still expect me to take care of both of you—you and this other man's leavings."

"The child is innocent. Those were your words, were they not?" she said quietly, and she forced herself to hold his steady gaze. "The truth is I expect nothing from you. Nothing. I can't even guess why you kept the marriage pledge."

"I've told you the reason."

"Christian charity?" she suggested.

Frederich ignored her sarcasm. "You are important to my children. You make them happy. But I don't want them to be hurt ever again by your bad behavior—especially Lise. I expect you to remember that if—*when*..."

She thought he was going to say Kader's name.

"...the *man*—comes around you again." He stepped off the porch. "And as for locking your door, Caroline Holt, *if* I wanted you, I tell you now a locked door wouldn't keep me out."

Caroline stared at him, speechless, and she took his last remark for the insult it was. She didn't have to lock her door, because, married or not, she wasn't fit for Frederich Graeber.

Her throat ached. She could feel her eyes welling.

"I'm going to the fields," he said, clearly indifferent to the fact that he had wounded her to the point of tears. "Finish the potatoes. I leave entertaining your brother to Beata."

He walked away, and she sat trembling, struggling not to cry. She was still wiping furtively at her eyes when Avery reappeared.

"Where's Herr Graeber?" he said as he walked out onto the porch. "You know, Caroline, I have to thank you for putting me in Beata's pocket like that. The cake and the coffee were fine. And the conversation was really...what's the word? Enlightening."

"How nice."

"Beata's given me all her best theories."

"Beata wouldn't know a theory if she fell over it," she said, careful not to look at him.

"Ah, now, there's where you're wrong, Caroline. She's got some remarkable ideas about who tumbled you. I must say some of them I hadn't even considered. She does have a logical mind, that Beata. And, of course, she doesn't hold anything against *me*."

"Lucky you. It's too bad Leah doesn't feel the same way."

He suddenly grabbed her by the arm, his grip hurting "If you say anything about me to Leah—*anything*—you'll regret the day you were born—"

"I already regret the day I was born, Avery. You're wasting your time and your threats. You and Beata are just alike. I don't *have* to say anything to make people think ill of you. Both of you manage that very nicely all by yourselves."

He abruptly let go of her and smiled, and it was only when she saw Frederich coming in their direction that she realized why. Avery was indeed on his best behavior with Frederich about.

"Don't get too far above yourself, Caroline," he said, and he walked off to ask Frederich for whatever favor he had come about.

She stared after him, mindful of her resolution to do the best she could for Ann's children—even without Frederich's admonishments. And she had the presence of mind to know that flinging the whole sack of Pennsylvania potatoes at Avery's head would be contrary to that goal.

She took up her task again with great care and deliberation. But then she suddenly stopped and let the potato fall. She put her hands gently over her belly, waiting and still. After a moment, the soft fluttering in her womb came again. There would be no forgetting now that a baby was coming; she had felt her daughter or her son irrevocably announce its presence. And the question that had been in her mind for so long surfaced yet another time.

What am I going to do?

Chapter Nine

Everything inside her, everything around her was changing. The days passed relentlessly, one after another, propelling her toward the event she couldn't escape. The war that should have been over by Christmas raged on. More and more of the men—and boys—were leaving, and she worried all the time about William enlisting. Did a soldier facing his first battle suffer the same fear for his life as she did for hers? What would happen to her baby if she died in childbirth and wasn't here to take care of it?

She gave a sharp sigh and tilted the mirror on the washstand downward to stare at herself. No matter how many petticoats she wore or how high she tied her apron, there was no way to hide her pregnancy now. Her back hurt all the time, and her feet swelled in the summer heat. She had to be careful not to take off her shoes until bedtime, because she couldn't get them back on again.

How much longer? she thought. Two months? Three?

She had quietly begun trying to get things ready for her confinement after everyone had gone to sleep, sewing together some of Beata's hoarded newspapers and some pieces of rags to make a kind of pad to protect the bed. The rags had been easy to come by; she'd shredded one of her own shabby dresses. But she had had to slip secretly into the Graeber attic to look for the newspapers and for the herb book Ann had brought with her when she married Frederich. The book had been useless in Ann's last labor, but still Caroline wanted to have it at hand. It had been compiled by the first Holts who came to this country from England more than a century ago. The pages were filled with pressed specimens of native herbs and numerous spidery notations about the ailments they were supposed to treat. It had taken her a long time to find the book—it had been stuck away in the trunk that held Ann's clothes and the rest of the remnants of her short life. Caroline had removed the book and carefully hidden it in her room. Beata would react in the extreme if she learned that Caroline Holt had been snooping through ''her'' attic, and while she should be used to Beata's rantings by now, she was too tired of late to want to endure yet another tirade.

And she still had no plan as to what to do when her time finally came. She hadn't been able to bring herself to ask Leah and Mrs. Steigermann for their help. Could she deliver the baby herself? She didn't know, and she woke night after night dreaming of herself cold and dead like Ann and being carried out of the house with a lemon under her chin.

She abruptly moved the mirror so she could see her face. She barely recognized her own reflection these days. She was nothing but a pair of frightened eyes.

She realized suddenly that Lise was talking to her, and she forced herself to smile. ''Woolgathering,'' she said. ''What did you ask me?''

''If we can take Papa a picnic basket—Mama and Mary Louise and I used to—when he and Eli were out working in the fields. He needs a picnic, Aunt Caroline.''

''He needs a picnic, Aunt Caroline,'' Mary Louise said.

She looked down into their earnest faces, ashamed of how badly she wanted to say no. Of course Frederich's children missed him. He was gone to the fields before they woke up and he returned long after they'd gone to bed. And they didn't want to avoid him at all costs as she did.

"He's very busy these days," she said anyway. "He might not want to be bothered."

"We wouldn't bother him, Aunt Caroline. We could just bring him the basket and leave it in the shade—and he could eat when he rests the horses. He needs a surprise—please, Aunt Caroline."

"Please," Mary Louise said. "He needs jelly bread."

"Jelly bread," Caroline said, trying not to smile.

Both children nodded.

She sighed, outnumbered. Ann's children asked for so little, and there was no reason why they couldn't take Frederich his *Mittagessen*—except that she could see no easy way to extract a basket full of food from the Holy Pantry without precipitating an attack from Beata. She decided to confront the problem head on, to grab the first basket she could find, fill it up and run—hopefully without having to wrestle Beata to the floor to get out of the house.

But Beata wasn't standing guard over the pantry for once, and Caroline managed to put enough into the basket for all four of them—she and the children could picnic, even if Frederich chose not to join them.

The walk was pleasantly cool and unobstructed on the wide, shady path that led to the field where Frederich was working. And, if one kept going, one would eventually reach the Steigermann house. The path was part of an intricate off-road network that enabled the men and their horses or oxen to get to each other's farms more quickly during the harvest season—and the army to shamelessly forage.

But she didn't see the army out and about today. She thought she could hear the faint jangling of tack and harness and Frederich's low commands to the team off through the trees. She hadn't talked to him or even seen him for days, and she slowed her pace in dread of having to encounter him now, walking along and trying to listen to Lise and Mary Louise singing about the chicken who wouldn't lay an egg instead of listening to the pain in her lower back.

Did all pregnant women suffer this constant ache? she wondered. She couldn't remember Ann having complained of it, and today it seemed to have crept around to the front as well. She felt vaguely ill, not sick enough to lie down and not well enough for this outing.

"I hear Papa," Lise said abruptly, but it wasn't Frederich she heard. It was a horse and rider coming along the path behind them.

Caroline took Mary Louise by the hand to keep her out of the way, but she didn't turn to see who approached until the rider was nearly abreast of them. She looked upward and directly into Kader Gerhardt's eyes.

"*Guten Tag*, Frau Graeber," he said cheerfully, reining the horse in.

Caroline kept walking, and she didn't answer. She would not exchange pleasantries with Kader Gerhardt as long as she had a choice.

"Frederich allows you out here alone with the army around?" he persisted, letting the horse—a fine sorrel gelding the congregation had provided for him—keep pace with her. The saddle and bridle looked new—and expensive. Caroline wondered idly who would have bought them for him.

"We're taking Papa a surprise," Lise said proudly, holding up the basket of food.

"Ah! I just saw him through there," he said, gesturing toward the trees and the field beyond. "You and your sister will run along quickly now and take the basket to him, yes?"

"Wait," Caroline said, trying to intervene, but the girls were only to happy to scamper ahead. She stopped walking.

"Why did you do that?" she asked, forcing herself to look up at him. He was a fine figure on a horse, and the handsomeness she had once admired so was still apparent.

But how insignificant it had become now that she knew the ugliness within. He was so much like Avery, and why hadn't she seen it?

"Because I want to speak you, Caroline—"

She abruptly started walking again, causing the horse to shy and toss its head.

"You and I have nothing to speak about," she said.

"I want Lise to come back to the school," he said, sending the horse along after her. "People are talking."

She stopped to give him an incredulous look. "Are they?" she said.

"It doesn't look good, Caroline."

"I'm afraid you will have to see Frederich about that," she answered. She gestured toward the field. "I believe you know where he is."

"But you must explain to him."

"Explain what, Kader?"

"That his taking Lise out of the school the way he did is a slur upon my reputation."

"I have done all I will ever do for *your* reputation."

He stared at her for a moment. "Forgive me," he said stiffly. "I had thought that you maintained a certain regard—"

She couldn't keep from laughing at his injured tone. "Oh, Herr Gerhardt, please," she said, walking again. "You credit me with much too much Christian charity—or stupidity."

"What is it you want, Caroline? I thought you understood my situation!"

"What do *I* want? I want to attend your funeral, Herr Gerhardt—wearing a red taffeta dress. Good day, now. Do enjoy your ride."

She walked away from him, stepping off the path to cut through the trees. The ground was too uneven for her no longer light-footed tread, and she was out of breath almost immediately. But she pushed herself to walk faster, startling Frederich in the field when she burst forth from among the pine trees. She was certain that his frown deepened the closer she came. He looked over his shoulder toward the children, who were standing in the shade at the edge of the field waiting for him to come around again and toward the path where Kader must surely have just come past.

She stopped for a moment to catch her breath, then approached Frederich across the hot field, squinting in the sunlight and trying to fight down the light-headedness that threatened to overtake her. It occurred to her suddenly that perhaps she was glad to see him.

"Now what's wrong?" he asked as soon as she was close enough, immediately taking away any notion she had that she might welcome being in his company.

"Nothing is wrong. The children only wanted to bring you a picnic."

He was watching her closely, for what she had no idea— a guilty countenance because she'd run across Kader Gerhardt in the woods? She was completely innocent, but still it was all she could do not to avoid his eyes. "I have no time for picnics, and you know that," he said.

"Very well. They're *your* children. I'll send them out here and you can look into their little upturned faces and tell them that. Heaven knows, it won't bother *me* if you choose to go hungry."

"Choose? You think I choose—"

"No," she interrupted, immediately regretting the remark. He was sweating profusely in the heat, and she could see, almost feel, his weariness. "I don't think anything of the kind. Lise and Mary Louise miss seeing you, that's all. I...just couldn't say no to them. We'll leave the basket for you."

"Wait," he said when she turned to go. "You are here now. I might as well eat. You can help me with the horse."

She looked back at him. Help with the horse?

He called to the children, motioning for them to come to the wagon he had left under the big hickory tree in the middle of the field.

One of the Belgians was limping badly.

"Caroline," he said, unhitching it from the harrow and leading it into the shade. "Come and stand by his head."

"Why?" she asked. Surely he didn't think that she could control such a huge animal.

"Because he likes women better than he likes men. You talk to him while I see to his hoof."

She hesitated, wary of any creature so large as this one. It easily dwarfed any horse she'd ever ridden.

"Koenig—Caroline. Caroline—Koenig," Frederich said impatiently, as if it were the lack of introductions that stood in the way.

She tried not to smile. Frederich stepped forward and took her by the arm, leading her to where he wanted her to stand, much in the same way he'd led Koenig.

"How do you do?" she said gravely to the horse. It gave a soft rumble and began pushing at her pockets with its nose.

"Hold his head," Frederich said.

"Frederich, I can't keep this horse from doing whatever he wants to do."

"I know that—but he doesn't. Talk to him."

She frowned, then abruptly talked as Frederich lifted the ailing hoof, her words of praise halfhearted at best, and less so when she realized how amusing Frederich was finding this.

"Keep talking," he said.

She sighed and talked on, her conversation punctuated by the scraping noises Frederich was making against the hoof.

"How bad is it?" she asked.

"Bad enough. He will have to stay out of the fields a few days. I didn't know you were afraid of horses."

"I'm not. I'm *not*," she repeated in response to the look he gave her. "This isn't a horse. This is a giant."

"Did you know this about horses—that some like a man's voice and some like a woman's?"

"No."

"When you buy a horse, you find out which one he is before you part with your money."

"As you did, I suppose?"

"I didn't buy Koenig. I bred him. I had to take what I got."

"You could have sold him."

"Not with two little girls treating him like an overgrown dog—"

Koenig suddenly shied, and she hung on to his bridle, talking to him again as if he were a puppy or a kitten.

"Does Avery come to the house again?" Frederich asked.

"It's not my doing," she said defensively. "I gave him no invitation."

"Have I said anything about anyone's *doing*?" He finished with the hoof and tied up the horse. "Come," he said to the girls, lifting them into the back of the wagon so that they wouldn't have to sit on the ground. He lifted Caroline as well, without prelude, taking her by surprise. She lowered herself carefully to the sack of feed he had brought for the horses, letting the children sit next to her. And, pressed for time or not, she would have had to say Frederich was making an effort to be cordial. He let Mary Louise and Lise empty the basket, and he ate heartily, more than properly appreciative of the purloined bread and cold boiled potatoes and cheese and blackberry jam they had brought him.

"I must remember to say thank you to Beata," he said.

"I...wouldn't do that," Caroline said, wiping the remains of Frederich's jelly bread off Mary Louise's face. When she looked up, he was actually smiling.

"No? Why not?" he asked with great innocence.

"You know why not," Caroline assured him, and he surprised her by laughing out loud. She wasn't comfortable with a Frederich who laughed, and she still wasn't at all certain whether he had seen her talking to Kader.

The shade was cool and dappled in sunlight. The birds sang, and the bees buzzed around them. A noisy flock of crows roosted in the tall pines at the edge of the field, and the pungent smell of newly turned ground filled the air. And, well-fed and happy in the wake of the success of their surprise, both Lise and Mary Louise fell promptly asleep in the back of the wagon, their heads resting on the feed sack.

Even more uncomfortable in the ensuing silence, Caroline began gathering up the remnants of the picnic and putting them into the basket. She could feel Frederich staring at her, and she abruptly moved to rouse the girls to take them home.

"Leave them for now," he said. "It is better to let Beata get over having her pantry raided before you go back."

She had no argument with that. She had no desire to encounter an incensed Beata. But Frederich seemed to be in no hurry to return to the field, regardless of his earlier remark. She sat awkwardly, feeling his eyes on her again and not quite knowing what to do with her hands. She stopped just short of resting them on her belly.

She glanced at him. She had always thought herself unattractive, and she felt her ugliness even more acutely under his gaze. He'd had no hesitation about bluntly *saying* that he didn't want her. She supposed that Beata must have told everyone by now that Frederich and his new bride slept apart—hence Kader's certainty that she would still be under his influence.

"Your shirt is too thin," she said abruptly. "You are going to get sunburned out here."

"I have no better shirt," he said. "My wife doesn't sew."

For the briefest of moments she thought he meant Ann, and she nearly challenged the remark. Ann is a fine seamstress, she almost said.

But Ann was dead, and *she* was his wife now. She'd had no idea he needed shirts, and how could she possibly defend herself without precipitating a major listing of all her *other* wifely shortcomings?

She forced herself to look at him, finding his eyes waiting.

"Mary Louise doesn't wander around in the dark anymore," she offered quietly. "And Lise—"

"Lise has remembered how to laugh," he finished for her.

He continued to stare at her, leaving her flustered and even more unsure. She had intended to counter his criticism by pointing out at least two positive results his marriage to her had brought; she certainly hadn't expected him to agree with her.

But his agreement was short-lived. "Why aren't you doing your part?" he asked.

Her chin came up slightly. "My part? I don't know what you mean," she said.

"Johann says the church women have committed themselves to knitting a supply of socks for the soldiers from the German community. I want to know why you aren't helping."

"How could I help? I didn't know anything about it."

"Where do you think Beata goes every Thursday afternoon?"

"I haven't cared where she goes—I've been far too busy rejoicing at her absence."

"I can't put you in the wrong, can I, Caroline Holt?" he said.

"I didn't think I was ever out of it."

"If you aren't, it is your own fault."

"My fault—!" She abruptly broke off, forcing herself to stay calm. The children were sleeping. She was not going to get into an argument with Frederich over socks. "Are you telling me you expect me to go knit?" she asked with a calmness she didn't feel.

"I'm telling you that Johann remarked on your absence."

"And my absence reflects on you," she suggested, "regardless of whether or not I'm welcome."

He didn't answer, a maddening habit he had, she realized. The silence lengthened, and she shifted her position on the feed sack, and shooed a fly away from Mary Louise's face.

"You're going to have to tell me precisely what it is you require of me," she said finally, forcing herself to make some effort to maintain the Graeber standards, obscure though they may be.

"I thought I had already done that. I thought I said plainly enough that I wanted you to stay away from Kader Gerhardt. I have just seen how much attention you paid to that...."

She got up from the feed sack, and he with her, but she couldn't get out of the wagon without his help. He jumped down first, holding out his hands to her. She didn't step forward. She had done nothing wrong and she absolutely was not going to be put in the position of having to explain!

He said something to her quietly in German, still holding out his hands. She looked into his eyes, trying to decipher his meaning.

But she couldn't. Whatever he'd said had sounded almost... kind, and she'd learned too well that any kindness from Frederich was always followed by some cruel remark. "I don't understand," she said. "But it doesn't matter. I never understand you, regardless of what language you use."

She let him lift her down, trying to ignore the feel of his warm hands through her dress, trying to ignore a sudden and ridiculous neediness that washed over her.

If I could just—oh God!

She wanted to lean against him. She wanted to explain to him about Kader. She wanted to tell him how afraid she was to have a baby, and she wanted him to put his arms around her and tell her everything would be all right, the way she'd seen him do a hundred times with Lise and Mary Louise. She wanted to feel his strength and his protection just for a moment so she wouldn't be so alone. Who did she have in this world to rely on but him—and who despised her more?

She bit down on her lower lip to keep it from trembling, forcing herself to step away from him the moment her feet touched the ground.

"Is he waiting?" Frederich asked, and she whirled around. She would have struck him with her fist if he hadn't caught her hand.

He restrained her easily, but she still struggled in spite of the fact that she was appalled by her own behavior. In a fit of blind anger she would have actually bit him. She was no better than Avery.

She abruptly stopped trying to get loose. "Please," she said, her voice barely a whisper.

Frederich let go of her then. He stared at her for a moment, as if he had something he wanted to say, the look of disappointment she had come to expect all too apparent. Then he picked up the leather strips he wore to protect the palms of his hands when he worked in the fields and he walked away, leaving her standing.

I'm not going to cry, she thought, watching him go. *I am not going to let you or Avery or Kader Gerhardt make me cry!*

But she was going to cry, and if she didn't get out of here, Frederich would hear her wailing like a child. She managed to get Lise awake, and together they half led, half carried

Mary Louise back to the house, wishing all the way that she could just disappear from this place the way Eli had.

What is going to become of us?

He hadn't had the nerve to say the words to her in English, because there was no *us,* and he knew it. They were not friends and they most certainly were not man and wife. They were simply strangers who tolerated each other for the sake of propriety. It had startled him that Caroline was still afraid of him, afraid enough to physically try to fight off his accusations if she had to. He had no idea how to go about trying to make things better. He was a proud man. He had been held up to public ridicule because of her. If she would just—

Just what? She was civil enough, he supposed, helpful enough, dependable enough when it came to his children. But what an exasperating woman she was! She wouldn't be ashamed of her pregnancy. She never seemed to care if he was disgruntled. She said whatever she had to say—or made light of him, which was worse. She looked nothing like Ann. She behaved nothing like Ann. Ann had cowered under Beata's tyranny, and he was fully aware that he, perhaps wrongly, had aggravated the situation by refusing to involve himself in their arguments. He could have been a better husband. He could have been kinder, given Ann more allegiance, so that Eli wouldn't have been able—

He didn't know what to do, and he hated the not knowing. In spite of Caroline's sad eyes, there was music and laughter in his house these days. Many an evening he had been able to continue working because he could hear her playing the piano and Mary Louise and Lise singing, hear them laughing together in a way that made him smile and not mind so much the overwhelming fatigue that had beset him since Eli had gone.

He gave a sharp sigh. Why had she been talking to the schoolmaster? As far as he knew, no one but he had realized that Kader Gerhardt had fathered her child. But he didn't know why Caroline had kept him from suffering any of the consequences. Did she love him that much? If she did, then Gerhardt's indifference must have been nearly more than a proud woman like her could bear. God, how he detested the man! He had always disliked him, even before he knew about Caroline. Gerhardt was the epitome of everything he'd come to this country to escape, that terrible system of a man being judged by his father's social status instead of by his own worth. And if that was the crux of what this new war was about—a man having freedom to accomplish whatever he could, then perhaps it was just—if one could only tell which side had the truer cause.

But he was not going to concern himself about the war, and he was not going to feel sorry for Caroline Holt. He had enough to do to keep his family fed. And, he had enough sense to know that breaching her locked door was not the solution to the problem, regardless of Johann's unsolicited advice. He simply must not allow her to become a necessary part of his life. He must not spend the day hoping to catch a glimpse of her. He must not remember the way she looked by firelight. He would keep his mind on other things. Like where to hide the grain and the livestock before the army came foraging again. Like how to do the work of three men alone.

Easy enough, except that whenever Caroline came near, he forgot all those things, forgot his need for revenge on an unfaithful wife, forgot everything except the fact that he wanted to touch her. Her soft woman smell overwhelmed him, the essence of it so subtle as to be missed if one were not careful.

And he would have been far better off if he had missed it. Whether real or imagined, it filled his mind, tortured his body.

He wanted to lie with her.

He wanted her to come willingly to his bed. He wanted to make her forget the schoolmaster. He wanted to take the contempt she had for Frederich Graeber and turn it into desire. He wanted her to roll in his arms and whisper his name.

My wife, he thought bitterly.

He moved too abruptly, causing the Belgian to shy.

"Easy, old man," he said to the gelding, catching him by the bridle. "You be glad you don't have to worry about such things."

Chapter Ten

He could hear Mary Louise crying long before he reached the house. The back door stood ajar, and she sat on the porch near the edge, her legs straight out in front of her and her head bowed, wailing loudly.

"Mary Louise!" he called, trying to manage the horses and see about her as well.

She got up immediately, bounding out into the rain and wrapping her arms around his knees.

"No—Mary Louise, you'll get wet," he said, reaching down with one hand to try to lift her.

But she was already wet, soaked to the skin. "What is it? What is wrong with you?" he asked.

She wouldn't let go of his legs, and the unlame Belgian began to prance nervously. "Caroline!" he yelled toward the house. "Come get this child!"

No one answered him.

"Caroline! Beata!" He tried to bend down. "Come here, Mary Louise. Tell Papa what—"

She immediately grabbed him around the neck, still crying.

"What is it? Are you hurt?" he asked, standing up with her. He tied the Belgians to the porch post with one hand and stepped under the shelter of the eaves out of the rain. He stood for a moment, letting Mary Louise cling to him before he made her look at him.

"What is the matter?"

"I'm—lost—Papa," she managed to say between sobs, hiding her face in his shoulder again.

"Lost? No, you're not lost, Mary Louise. Stop crying now. Stop."

She lifted her head and looked at him doubtfully, her face threatening to crumple again.

"Where is your Aunt Caroline?" he asked, his annoyance at finding Mary Louise unattended rising—and his anxiety. The mental picture of Caroline and Kader Gerhardt talking today rose unbidden in his mind.

"Asleep," Mary Louise said, sticking her fingers into her mouth.

He pulled them out again. "Asleep where?" he asked more sharply than he intended.

Mary Louise began to cry again. "I'm lost, Papa!"

"Mary Louise—"

He swung himself and her onto the porch and carried her inside the house. Caroline's apron hung on the peg by the washstand. No one was in the kitchen. The kitchen clock ticked quietly on the mantel—twenty minutes until five. "Caroline!" he called. "Lise!"

There was no answer.

"Mary Louise, where is everyone?"

Still carrying her, he started up the stairs.

"Making—socks," she said.

"Making socks?"

He reached the landing and walked down the hallway to Caroline's door. It wasn't locked—for a change—but the room was empty, the bed neatly made. He tried to set Mary Louise down, but she clung to him harder.

"Caroline?" someone called from downstairs.

He went back toward the landing, still trying to soothe his fretting, rain-soaked daughter. Leah Steigermann stood at the bottom of the stairs.

"Oh, Frederich," she called. "I came to see if Caroline is all right."

"I don't know where she is," he said bluntly, because it was the truth.

Leah stared up at him, a slightly perplexed frown on her brow. The frown deepened.

"I don't understand," she said as he came down the stairs. "She came to help with the knitting—I saw her walking across the yard with the children, but she never came inside. Lise did—she's still there with Beata. But Caroline and Mary Louise—well, Mary Louise is here so Caroline must be here. I just wanted to make sure she was all right. I thought she might not be feeling well if she came all that way and didn't stay." She kept looking at him as if she expected him to explain it.

"Mary Louise," he said firmly, making the child look at him. "Where is your Aunt Caroline?"

"Asleep," she said again, only one finger in her mouth this time.

"Asleep where?"

"I think I might cry, Papa—"

"I think we have had enough crying. You must tell me—now—where is your Aunt Caroline?"

"All lost, too," she said. "All lost, too, Papa."

"Take her, Leah," Frederich said, handing Mary Louise over. He took a deep breath. More discord, more disharmony in his house and in his family. He hated it. "You said Caroline came to Johann's for the knitting?"

"Yes—but she never came inside. Johann had me cutting one of those awful 'war' cakes—a pitiful thing it was, too—not nearly enough sugar at all. It was a while before I went in with the rest of the women. Caroline wasn't there—no one had seen her."

"The schoolmaster was there?" he forced himself to ask.

"Kader? No, of course not."

"Well, where would she go?" he asked sharply.

"I don't know, Frederich."

He walked to the back door and looked outside, torn between his anxiety at her absence and his need to think that nothing was wrong. Perhaps she'd gone into the church to be alone, or she'd seen something that needed tending in the barn or—

Or she'd simply abandoned Mary Louise and gone to Gerhardt.

The Belgians still stood in the rain—and Leah Steigermann's horse and buggy.

"I'm going to look around out here," he said, stepping off the porch into the mud. He untethered old Koenig and led him into the barn, leaving the other Belgian standing and calling Caroline's name once as he went. He put the lame horse into his stall.

"I tend to you later, old man," he said to him, then walked to the back barn door, his eyes scanning the yard, the orchard, the privy beyond. The rain was coming harder, wind-driven against his face. The door to the privy had blown open. There was no sign of Caroline there or any place else.

He walked back through the barn.

"Leah!" he called as he made his way to the other Belgian. "I'm going to ride back to Johann's."

"But I just came that way," Leah said from the doorway. She had Mary Louise by the hand.

"Did you look for her along the path?"

"Well—no. It was raining so hard. I thought she'd be here— "

"I'm going. Stay with Mary Louise—find her some dry clothes. If you would be so kind," he added when he remembered he should not be giving her orders.

"Yes, of course. Frederich!" she called as he swung up on the Belgian's back. "What do you think has—"

"I don't know," he interrupted. But he had his suspicions. Gerhardt had had a change of heart, a sudden recognition of his obligation to his unborn child and to the woman who must love him, and today, in plain view of Caroline's so-called husband, he had convinced her to come away with him.

He turned the big-hoofed Belgian sharply and prodded him around Leah's carriage, heading toward the path and the church. And he pressed the lumbering beast hard, slowing down from time to time to let his eyes scan the line of trees or the field beyond.

He abruptly decided to take a short cut across Avery's acreage of clover, unmindful of the damage the Belgian's great hooves would do. He saw Caroline near the middle of the field and only seconds before the horse would have stepped on her. She was lying facedown, one hand outstretched as if she'd been reaching for something. He reined the horse in hard and slid to the ground.

"No," he heard himself say as he rushed forward. "No!"

The rain pelted down on her. Her hair, her clothes were soaking wet. He grasped her shoulders and turned her over. The ground under her was still somewhat dry—she must have been lying here when the rain first started. He tried lifting her upward. Her head dropped backward, her bonnet slid off and dangled over his arm.

"Caroline—Caroline!"

She was so still. He stroked her face, pressed his cheek against hers.

"Caroline—" he whispered. "*Mein Gott.* Caroline, can you hear me!"

He ran his hands over her, searching for some injury, some wound. Perhaps she'd been shot by a hunter or by the foragers, those bored, careless young soldiers who had nothing better to do than to steal livestock and grain and fire off their guns as a lark.

"*Bitte,*" he said, the only prayer he could manage. He found nothing to account for her present state.

"Caroline!" he said again, desperate now and giving her a shake. This time her eyes fluttered and she attempted to lift her hand. He caught it and held it against his chest as her eyes closed again.

The rain came harder; he had to get her home. He managed to lift her off the ground, but when he approached the Belgian with his burden, the animal shied violently, whirling away and galloping off across the field.

He swore out loud. He should have brought Leah's buggy, and even as the thought came to him, he knew why he hadn't. He hadn't expected to find Caroline—except with Kader Gerhardt.

He shifted her in his arms so he could carry her more easily. Her head lolled against his shoulder. He began walking back the way he'd come, as fast as he could walk, his body hunched to try to protect her from the pouring rain. By the time he reached the trees and the path, she was beginning to rouse again. She gave a soft moan, then made a sharp mewing sound, and she stiffened so that he nearly dropped her.

"Caroline," he said, kneeling down with her.

"Hurts—so—" he thought she said. She suddenly clutched the front of his shirt. "Mary Louise—where—"

"It's all right," Frederich said, trying to see her face. "Leah has her."

"Leah?" she murmured, dazed. She made the mewing sound again and doubled up, her head nearly touching her knees. "Frederich—" she managed. "I'm—it's the baby—"

"Caroline, we have to get you home. I'm going to lift you up. See if you can put your arms around my neck. Try, Caroline. That's it—we get you home quick now—so your baby can be born."

"No. No!" she protested as he stood up with her. "It's too soon—Frederich—oh!"

Too soon?

He had no idea if that was truly the case or not. He'd never bothered to find out how far along she was in her pregnancy. He had simply resigned himself to watching her grow bigger every day with another man's child.

Too soon.

Too soon.

He carried her along, overwhelmed suddenly by the realization that this had happened before.

Not like Ann. Please, God, not like Ann.

He called out loudly as he approached the house, and Leah met him on the porch. He was completely winded and had to let her help get Caroline inside.

"Where's—Mary Louise?" he said, looking frantically around the kitchen.

"She's asleep—what's happened?" Leah asked as they made their way up the stairs. "Is Caroline all right? Frederich, what's wrong with her!"

"The baby comes now," he said, and Leah immediately faltered. If he hadn't been in her way, she would have bolted.

"Leah, you have to help me," he said.

"No, I can't—I don't know what to do! I'll go get somebody—"

"And who do you think will come here—for her? Would your mother come?"

"Yes—no, she can't. She's sick again. She's been in bed all week—Frederich!" she said in exasperation because he wouldn't step aside.

"I need you to help me!"

She stopped trying to get by him.

"I need you to help me," he said more quietly. "The second door there."

But she still hesitated, and Caroline gave a ragged moan.

"*Bitte!*" he said for the second time that afternoon, he, who never said "please" to anyone.

Leah nodded and hurried ahead of him to open the door and to turn down the bed. She began to help him get Caroline out of her wet clothes.

"Where are her night things?" she asked, moving away and leaving the removal of garments to him.

He said nothing, his pride keeping him from stating the obvious. He had no intimacy with his wife whatsoever. He knew nothing of this room or her. Leah began to search without his direction, finding them in a lower bureau drawer. She brought a nightgown quickly and helped him bring it over Caroline's head, neither of them looking at her nakedness.

Caroline began to shiver, the shivering abruptly overtaken by another hard contraction. Frederich covered her with the quilt, then hurriedly left the room long enough to bring another one from his own bed.

Caroline moaned loudly as the contraction intensified.

"She's so cold—shall I heat some bricks?" Leah said anxiously.

"Yes," Frederich said. "Do that. And heat some water—make her something hot to drink. There may be some coffee—if you can find it. I don't know. Something—anything—"

"I'll see about Mary Louise on the way down," she said, and he nodded. When he looked back at Caroline, she was trying to get out of bed.

"I need them—" she said, reaching toward the small armoire.

"What?" he asked, making her lie back. "What do you need?" He searched her face, trying to decide if she was lucid.

"I put—the things—in there."

He moved to open the armoire door. "What things?"

"Behind—the dresses—oh!" she said as another contraction overtook her. She was pale and shivering again when the pain eased. "Please," she told him. "I need them—"

He looked inside the armoire, seeing nothing but a bundle lying in the bottom. "This?" he asked her.

She was watching him intently, and she held out her hand for it.

"Yes," she said, clutching the bundle to her. "Frederich, you have to—go. You can't be—here—please!"

He understood that he was the last person she would want now, but he also knew that he had no intention of leaving.

"You can't do this alone, Caroline. No one else is here but Leah. The other women—I don't think there is time for any of them to get here." He had to force himself to look in her eyes. The reason he gave was the truth—but not the first truth. The first truth was that she was still an outcast, regardless of her marriage to him.

She closed her eyes. The tears squeezed out of the corners and ran down the side of her face into her hair.

I am your husband, he almost said. But he had been Ann's husband as well, and in his anger and humiliation he'd stayed away when she was dying.

He took the bundle out of her hands and untied it, recognizing the purpose of the sewn-together newspapers and rags immediately. The herb book he had not seen in a long while, and he didn't want to remember when it had last been in his hands.

But the memory surfaced anyway, the driving need he'd had to pack away every reminder of the faithless Ann Holt. Lise had had to plead with him not to take away the rocking chair and the sewing basket with the sunburst design, or every trace of her would have been gone from his sight.

He put the book aside, and he had to literally force Caroline to let him arrange her and the bed for her labor. She kept trying to push him away, then clung to him as another contraction began, her fingers digging painfully into his arms.

She abruptly let go, her body limp; the next pain came almost immediately. This time he gave her his hands to grip. The rain fell outside the slightly open window; the wind drove it into the room from time to time. He made no move to close the window because the room felt oppressively hot and humid to him. But Caroline still shivered, her teeth chattering in her need to get warm and in her fear.

Of course she would be afraid, he thought. She had been with Ann at the last, and in this very house.

Leah returned with a kettle of hot water and towels, ones Beata would shriek over when she knew how they had been used. He took them and the kettle out of Leah's hands and poured some hot water into the washbowl, wetting one of the towels so that he could wipe Caroline's face. She let him without protest until another pain came. She was in agony, and he knew of nothing to do to help her. There was no doctor to send for. The German community had always relied on its own people for these things, its own women for the birth of a child. He could only let Caroline writhe and drag on his hands, watch her bite down on her bottom lip until it bled.

"The horse came back—I put it in the barn. And I found some tea," Leah whispered, her face as worried as he felt. "I think Beata hid it for a rainy day." She gave a slight smile, because both the weather and the events certainly qualified. The smile faded. "I'll go get it."

"Mary Louise?" he asked when she reached the door.

"Still asleep. I think she must be worn out. Who knows how much wandering around she did before she found her way home."

But there was no time to get the tea.

"No, please! *Please*—!" Caroline suddenly cried, her body curling upward, her hands clutching her knees.

Frederich and Leah both turned to her, but she no longer needed their help. Her body sagged back against the bed; her eyes closed. She said nothing, asked nothing. Her eyes opened again and held his, the question she couldn't bear to voice there for him to see.

This time she didn't fight him when he moved the quilts. The child had come—too soon, as she had feared. But there was no baby's cry, no sound in the room at all but her ragged breathing and the rain.

Chapter Eleven

Why am I still here?

The question came to her every time she opened her eyes. She hadn't meant to survive, certainly hadn't wanted to. She had been ill enough to die. She knew that. She remembered very well the fever and the pain in her chest that had followed the baby's birth. The hushed voices. There had been some kind of committee meeting to decide what exactly ailed her. Johann had been in the room. And Mr. Steigermann. And Beata. A fever, from lying too long in the rain before Frederich found her, they decided, not knowing how badly she wanted to leave this world.

But, regardless of her desires, she was unquestionably... alive.

She turned her head at a small noise. Frederich sat in the only chair in the room, sound asleep. He was close enough for her to reach out and touch him if she wanted.

She didn't want to. Instead, she watched him sleeping, surprised at how young and vulnerable he looked. He had hurt the back of his left hand on something since she had last noticed—a while past, she decided, because she could see that the cuts were healing. And he was missing a button on his shirt—another fault of hers, of course. No new shirts. No buttons on the old ones. Her illness must have been grave indeed for him to keep a bedside vigil for such a worthless wife. He had kept no such vigil for Ann.

But Ann had died so quickly.

So quickly.

The worthless and shameful Caroline was still here. There must be little rejoicing in the German community at that. She couldn't fathom why God, who surely must want to punish her, could have let this golden opportunity slip by.

Ah, but he was punishing her, she suddenly thought. He had duly noted her sins, found her guilty and sentenced her to remain *here.*

She gave a wavering sigh and let the sorrow she had been trying to keep at bay wash over her.

My baby!

Frederich was awake immediately. He leaned forward and rested his big calloused hand on her forehead without her leave, his familiarity much more disconcerting than his newfound concern.

"Gut," he said, more to himself than to her.

She closed her eyes. When she opened them, he was waiting.

"The fever is leaving, Caroline. The fever is leaving—and you are not, no matter how much you want it. I am going to bring Lise and Mary Louise in to see you now."

"No," she protested, surprised at how weak her voice sounded.

"Yes," he answered. "They have worried enough. They will see you are awake with their own eyes."

He left then and returned almost immediately with the girls. But he didn't let them come into the room. He stood in the doorway and lifted Mary Louise up so that she could see.

"Blow your Aunt Caroline a kiss," he said to her. He took Lise by the hand, because both girls had grown suddenly bashful. They hesitated, hiding their faces against Frederich for a moment before they did as he asked.

Caroline forced herself to look at them, trying hard not to cry.

"We're glad you're better, Aunt Caroline," Lise offered after a moment. She glanced at her father to see if she'd spoken out of turn. "I've got another loose tooth—want to see it?" she added, apparently deciding that she had not. She opened her mouth wide and wiggled a remaining front tooth with her tongue.

"Can you come out and play?" Mary Louise asked.

Caroline managed a smile. "Soon," she whispered without meaning it. With considerable effort, she returned their blown kisses.

Frederich's eyes held hers for a moment, and if he wanted to say something, he didn't. He set Mary Louise down instead.

"Go let Beata give you your supper," he told them, sending the girls on their way.

He stood for a moment, making sure they had gone, then came into the room and sat down on the side of the bed—yet another familiarity Caroline found disconcerting. And he didn't *say* anything. He simply waited, as if his being here was something she required of him.

Sit here and wait until I can think of something you can do for me.

But there was nothing he could do for her, nothing anyone could do for her. She didn't want to be here, and if she must, then she just wanted to be left alone.

"You are hungry?" he asked.

She shook her head and looked away.

"Sleep then," he said. "Tomorrow you will get up for a little while."

She had no intention of sleeping or of getting up, but she did both, not at Frederich's insistence but at Leah's. Leah wanted Caroline to get out of bed, to bathe and to dress, to eat—and she wouldn't be put off by anything Caroline said or did. She simply offered the one threat that couldn't be ignored.

"If you don't, I will go get Frederich."

Caroline found the entire process of returning to the living exhausting, but less so than fighting Leah Steigermann's iron will. At Leah's insistence, she even visited briefly with Lise and Mary Louise, dutifully drinking the beef tea and toasted bread they so precariously brought her.

But she couldn't keep from crying. They were so dear and loving and she should be grateful to still be with them. She wasn't grateful, and in spite of all she could do, the tears coursed down her cheeks. Lise took her cue from Leah, ignoring the silent weeping, feeding Caroline bits of bread she had to force down and holding her cup. It only made the crying worse.

"We'll go now," Lise said, when Mary Louise was about to make some observation.

"But she needs peppermint," Mary Louise whispered.

"Then we have to find Papa and tell him," Lise whispered back. "We've got to hurry," she said to Caroline, all but carrying Mary Louise out the door.

"They love you very much," Leah said after they'd gone. "You're very lucky—"

"I don't feel lucky," Caroline said, sniffing heavily. She was so tired of being Leah Steigermann's charity case. If her brother disowned her, if her child died, Leah came to the rescue—and she didn't want to be rescued.

"Caroline, you would be dead if it weren't for Frederich—"

"I don't thank him for it."

"Well, you should. He fed you when no one else could— or would for that matter. I don't know how many nights he stayed up with you—trying to keep you from hurting yourself when the fever was so high you didn't know where you were—trying to get your fever down. You almost *died,* don't you know that?"

Caroline said nothing. She wiped at her eyes with the back of her hand.

"And people think *I* am spoiled and selfish," Leah said. "I'm going now—but I'll be back. And, yes, I know you want to be left alone. But I'll be back *anyway,* because Frederich wants it. You know what the saddest thing is, Caroline? I know you don't thank Frederich for saving your life, but the saddest thing—the *saddest* thing—is that he knows it, too."

"He should have let me go. It would have solved all his problems."

"No. It would have solved all of *yours.* His children— your nieces—love you. Did you think he would just sit and do nothing and let their hearts be broken again? You have a reason to be here, Caroline."

Caroline gave a sharp sigh and turned away. Her hands were trembling. She wanted to lie down; she wanted to run as far and as fast as she could. When she looked back again, Leah had gone. She abruptly put her face into her hands.

For the nieces.

She did love them. She loved them with all her heart. She had been willing to endure her marriage to Frederich for their sakes. Why couldn't she find any of that determination now?

She lifted her head after a moment to listen—Frederich's heavy tread coming up the stairs.

Give her time.

Johann's sage advice. Johann, who had never lived his life around a woman.

Frederich forced himself not to stop at Caroline's door, nor did he seek her out the next day or the next. He let more than a week pass because he had thought—hoped—that if he left her alone for a time, she would want to rejoin the family again. But she still kept herself apart from them, hiding in her room, speaking to no one. If she came downstairs at all, it was in the night after all of them had gone to bed. She was eating; his children reported that news to him. She must be getting physically stronger. He could hear her walking back and forth overhead sometimes.

But he missed her, as his children missed her.

No. He missed her as a man missed the woman who was important to him. How was it that he had gotten so used to talking to her—when it seemed as if they had never talked at all? And how many times a day did he have to stop himself from going and asking her what she thought about this or that? The price of corn. The war news. The livestock. Things he should have talked about with other men—with Steigermann, or heaven forbid, Avery.

He made a decision while he was grooming old Koenig. Lise was sitting on the porch nearby, earnestly trying to sew a tear in one of Mary Louise's dresses and finding the task hard going because Mary Louise still had the dress on.

"Lise, where is your Aunt Caroline?" he asked.

She looked at him in surprise. He knew where Caroline was. Everyone knew where Caroline was. But she was a tactful child. "Upstairs, Papa," she said.

"Upstairs, Papa," Mary Louise repeated.

"Stay here," he said when Mary Louise would have followed him inside, even if it meant dragging Lise and the needle and thread along behind her.

"But, Papa!"

"No 'buts.' You stay out here with Lise."

He went up the stairs quickly, ignoring Beata's sniff when he passed her in the kitchen. How eloquent were Beata's disgruntled noises. With one mere sound she could fully communicate how much she disproved of the attention he was paying to his ailing wife.

Caroline's door was closed as usual. He didn't knock. He was not worried about whatever state of dress or undress he might find her in. He was her husband. He had delivered her child. She had no secrets from him.

She was sitting in the chair by the window, perhaps reading, perhaps not. He approached her immediately and took the book out of her hand.

"Stand up," he said.

"What?" she said, not certain yet whether or not she should be worried.

"Stand up," he repeated, taking her by both forearms and bringing her to her feet.

"Frederich, what—"

He didn't take the time to explain. He simply lifted her up and carried her toward the door.

"Frederich, put me down," she said as he stepped into the hall, struggling to get out of his grasp.

"You have been in this room too long," he said.

"Frederich! Put me down!"

"No," he said simply, and he kept walking toward the stairs.

"Frederich—Frederich, what are you doing!"

"Trying to keep from falling down the stairs and breaking both our necks," he said. "Excuse me, Beata," he said when he reached the bottom. "You are in the way." He swung Caroline around so that Beata had to duck to keep from getting hit by Caroline's feet.

Both his children looked sharply around when he stepped out on the porch.

"Papa!" Mary Louise said. "Can't Aunt Caroline *walk?*"

"Can but won't, Mary Louise," he said, going down the porch steps.

"Damn you, Frederich!" Caroline hissed at him. "Put me down!"

He ignored her, setting her on old Koenig's back instead. It occurred to him that perhaps she had never sat on a bareback horse, but he was not deterred. "You and I are going for a ride," he said, swinging up behind her. He kept a firm hand on her to keep her from jumping off.

"I don't want to go for a ride!"

"I don't remember asking," he said.

"Can *we* go?" Lise asked, shading her eyes from the sun with her hand.

"Not this time," he said. "You stay here with Beata."

He turned the horse sharply and headed him away from the house. Caroline was sliding off, but this time it was not on purpose. She had no way to keep her seat but to hang on to the horse's mane, or to lean against him—which was clearly out of the question. She was not wearing stays. He could feel the warmth of her skin through her dress when he set her in a less precarious position.

"Why are you doing this?" she asked as he turned Koenig down the wooded path toward the church. Her voice sounded as if she might be crying, but her back was rigid with anger.

"There are things I want to say to you."

"What kind of things?" she cried, startling a blue jay out of a low pine tree.

He didn't answer her, and she gave a sharp sigh.

They rode for a time in silence. It was cooler in the shade, and even in the wake of her anger, it was not entirely unpleasant, riding with her like this on a slow-moving horse, dappled in sunlight. The air was ripe with the smell of decaying leaves and pungent with smell of injured, living trees where someone had been chopping. And there was her scent—lye soap and clean, sun-dried clothes, and woman. He watched as the patches of sunlight glanced off her hair. Dark hair that wasn't all dark after all, he noted. It was rich with highlights of red and brown and gold. She had beautiful hair, and once again he fought down the impulse to put his hand on it.

He waited until they had reached the edge of the churchyard before he spoke.

"You don't ask me anything about the baby," he said quietly, and she stiffened as if he had physically hurt her.

After a moment, she gave a quiet sigh and bowed her head. "Why don't you ask me, Caroline?"

She shook her head and said nothing.

"It was what you feared," he went on. "She came too soon, this little girl. She didn't cry—you know that. You remember that. She didn't breathe, Caroline. There was no chance for her. I am very sorry for that because I think she would have been very...beautiful. Steigermann—"

He stopped. He could feel her trembling.

"Go on," she said without looking at him, her voice barely a whisper.

"Steigermann made the coffin for her. He wanted to do that—for you. Avery gave the wood—"

"Avery?"

"He gave the wood—a very fine piece for the making."

He reined in the horse by the low stone wall and slid off. She kept her face averted when he lifted her down.

"Your little girl is here, Caroline. With Anna. I thought you would want that—"

She looked at him then, disbelieving, her incredulous look wounding him deeply.

"What did you think I would do with your daughter, Caroline?" he asked, gripping her arms. "Do you think I understand nothing? You were too ill to ask. I did what I thought you would want." He abruptly let her go and moved away from her. "I will wait here," he said.

She hesitated, then stepped through a broken place in the low stone wall. He watched her walk toward Ann's grave, tentatively at first, and then with a firmer step. She stood by the graves for a long time, until finally, she reached down to touch the small headstone.

He stopped watching then, moving farther away to leave her to grieve alone. She was so sad. He wanted to do something for her, anything that would make her feel better, but he knew only too well that she wanted nothing from Frederich Graeber. He adjusted old Koenig's bridle, checked his formerly ailing hoof to see how it fared, speaking to him softly, not realizing that Caroline had returned and was standing close by.

When he looked over his shoulder, she gave a small shrug and crossed her arms over her breasts.

"It's green," she said.

"Yes," he answered, understanding her remark. "William did it—cut the sod to cover the grave. He took it from a meadow on the Holt land—a place you liked to go when you were a little girl, he said."

"There were . . . flowers on the grave."

"Mary Louise and Lise bring those from time to time," he said. "It's been more than a month, Caroline." He watched her steadily. She took a deep quiet breath.

She said something he couldn't hear, more to herself than to him.

"Are you ready to go now?" he asked, and she nodded. She went to stand by the horse so that he could lift her up again, but she still had that vacant, detached look about her, as if she hadn't quite agreed that she would be staying in *this* world and not going to the other.

"There is one other thing," he said. "If you need to speak to him—to Gerhardt—I won't keep you from it—"

"No," she said immediately, finally meeting his eyes. "I don't need to speak to him. *She* meant nothing to him. I have understood that for a long while." She reached out to wind her fingers absently in the horse's mane. "Was there a . . . service for her?" she asked, her eyes sliding away from his.

"Yes. Johann said the words. The Steigermanns were there. And your brothers."

"And you?"

"Yes. Me."

He didn't have to say that Beata didn't come. He moved to her side and lifted her onto the horse. Then he stood on the low wall to climb up behind her. As they rode away, she turned to watch the place where the baby lay as long as she could.

But she didn't say anything more. The ride back was quiet and undisturbed, and he savored the time with her, letting the old horse find his own way in his own good time.

Caroline.

He wanted to find some words that might help. He wanted to touch her. He did nothing.

"Frederich?" she said as they were about to ride into the yard. She turned around as far as she could to face him. He put his hand on her waist to keep her from falling.

Her eyes searched his. "Thank you," she whispered.

He didn't know what to say. He was completely unprepared for her gratitude. He was unprepared even for her acknowledgment of his presence. He said nothing, and she abruptly put her arms around him and pressed her face against his shoulder. "Thank you, Frederich. I won't ever forget—"

He held her tightly, awash in emotion, afraid that she would suddenly remember who he was and pull away. He touched her cheek with his rough hand, stroked the dark hair he'd been so longing to touch.

"I would do anything for you," he whispered—in German—because he was a coward where she was concerned and because he needed to voice the thought to himself as much as to her.

He held her, feeling her sorrow and his own, determined to keep her close like this for as long as she would allow it. But the horse pranced nervously, and she abruptly let go of him and slid from his grasp to the ground, hurrying into the house without once looking back.

He sat there, completely overwhelmed by the realization that he couldn't deny the truth any longer. He cared far more for this exasperating woman than he ever intended, and he wanted her—as a friend, a lover, as a wife.

And now she was grateful to him—her unrelenting grief over the death of her child had made her vulnerable enough to let him see it. Somehow it only compounded his loneliness.

What now? he thought. But he knew. He didn't want her gratitude any more than he wanted her incredulity that he was capable of behaving as if he were a decent, civilized man.

I should have let Eli take her.

If he had, then perhaps they both would have been out of his life now and he could live in peace.

He gave a sharp sigh and looked toward the house. He saw Caroline moving back and forth in the glow of the lamp in that solitary upstairs room, the place where he was not welcome. And Beata stood watching him from the kitchen window below.

Chapter Twelve

When the dream began, the baby was crying. Frederich had been wrong when she said she didn't cry—Caroline could hear her so plainly. Her baby daughter was in her cradle there on the other side of the room, and all in the world Caroline had to do was go to her.

But the room changed—doors where there had been none. And people—Johann preparing to read in his book of rituals, and Leah Steigermann dressed in black.

Wrong, some part of her thought. *Wrong for Johann to come here with his book. Wrong for Leah to wear mourning. Don't you hear her crying, Leah?*

I'll get her, she thought. *I'll bring her so you both can see—*

She couldn't move her legs, couldn't tell where the cradle sat anymore. And the baby cried and cried—

I'm coming! she wanted to say, but she had no voice. *Please, little one, I'm coming—*

She could still hear her, but now Beata stood in her way and wouldn't move aside no matter how hard Caroline tried to get past.

Get away, Beata!

Oh, I'm sorry, Beata said quite distinctly. *I thought you knew!*

And then she smiled—that terrible smile she had—Beata, victorious.

No! I don't know! I don't! Caroline tried to say, but Lise came bursting into the room, her hands clasped over her heart, her eyes bright with excitement.

"Aunt Caroline! Papa is going to play again!" she cried, jarring Caroline awake.

"What?" Caroline said, disoriented and still in the clutches of the dream. She tried to sit up, looking wildly around the room, her heart pounding.

Where is my baby?

But she knew instantly. The sun was shining and the birds were singing. And her baby lay at Ann's side in the German cemetery.

"He's playing the fiddle again, Aunt Caroline! It's my birthday present. Any song I want! 'Old Blue,' 'Aura Lee'— anything!"

"What?" Caroline said again, but Lise didn't hear her. She whirled away, dancing out the door and into the up-stairs hallway.

Caroline lay back and closed her eyes.

Lise's birthday.

She took a deep breath and willed the dream to fade, letting the harshness of reality take its place.

There is no baby. There is nothing.

She had to force herself to get out of bed. She had to force herself to do everything these days. She stood for a long time staring at her face in the mirror. She had to try harder. She was not going to spoil Lise's special day, and she took un-usual pains with her toilette before she put on the stark mourning dress. Three months. One wore black for three months after an infant died. Who decided such things? she wondered, and how could that be enough time when more than a month had already passed and she didn't even re-member it?

Beata was already at work in the kitchen when Caroline came downstairs. She immediately sniffed and turned away. Certainly Beata had cause for complaint. Caroline hadn't been doing "her job" these past few weeks, and it was clear that—Lise's birthday or not—Beata was not in a forgiving mood.

She dismissed Beata with a sigh and tried to concentrate on more pleasant things—how proud Ann would be of her wonderful older daughter. The *Geburtstagstisch,* the birthday table, stood ready near Lise's chair, stacked with presents from all of them, even the Steigermanns and William and Avery. Caroline added her gift to the pile, a small silver brooch that had belonged to her mother. She had had no money with which to buy a gift and no time, because of her illness, to get anything made. She thought that Lise would like the brooch. It would make her feel grown-up and ladylike.

But it was Frederich's music that would give Lise the greatest joy. Caroline hadn't known that he had changed his mind about playing the fiddle for her birthday. He hadn't said anything about it. Since that day at the cemetery, he hadn't said much about anything.

The first bawling notes of "Old Blue" came drifting in from the porch, but Caroline made no attempt to go out and join the others. Frederich had become stern and cold and German again—at least where she was concerned. She would never understand the contradictions in the man. He had shown her great kindness when she needed it, and if she could believe Leah Steigermann, it was because of his determination that she was even alive. The only thing she really understood was that there had been no change in their arrangement. He intended that she look after his children, but he didn't want her as a wife.

She looked out the window. Lise sat as close to Frederich as she could without interfering with his playing. He stopped long enough to take a request, then began another song, a waltz that Caroline didn't recognize. She listened to the haunting, three-quarter-time melody, seeing in her mind's eye the occasion Lise had talked about, when Ann was still alive and she and Lise had danced around the room to the lilting music of Frederich's fiddle.

She heard Mary Louise coming two-feet-on-each-step down the stairs. Someone had taken over yet another of Caroline's duties and dressed her for church—Frederich or Lise, she supposed. When Mary Louise reached the bottom step, she immediately ran into Caroline's embrace.

"Good morning," Caroline whispered in her ear, because she loved whispering. Or perhaps Mary Louise had had to tiptoe around so much while Caroline was ill that she hadn't realized it was all right to make a little noise now.

Mary Louise giggled and leaned back, taking a moment to stare into Caroline's eyes. Caroline understood the process, the need Mary Louise had to determine whether her aunt would be more herself today or whether she would be crying again.

"Is it my birthday, too?" Mary Louise asked, also in a whisper.

"No, not today. Yours will be here at Christmas time."

"Is that tomorrow?"

"No, love. About four months from tomorrow. Don't you want to go listen to your papa play?"

Mary Louise nodded, and Caroline let her go, abruptly turning around, because she felt Beata's eyes on her. She *always* felt Beata's eyes on her.

"What is it, Beata?" she asked pointedly, in spite of the fact that she'd slept too late and she'd let someone else dress Mary Louise for church. It was senseless to expect any kind of truce with this woman.

"You won't get above yourself in this house, Caroline Holt," Beata said.

"What are you talking about?"

"I see how you watch Frederich," Beata said knowingly. "I see what you are planning. I know the lies you tell him—"

"Beata, I don't know what you're talking about."

"The things you are saying about me! He doesn't believe anything you tell—"

"I haven't told him anything!"

"You think he wants the likes of you in his bed? Ha! He will keep you in your place—you are no better than that sister of yours—!"

"If you have something specific you want to say about me or my sister, for the love of God, say it!" Caroline cried.

The music from the porch abruptly stopped. Frederich came into the kitchen with both children in tow; it was clear that he—that all three of them—had heard the exchange.

"Go upstairs now," he said to Lise. "Help Mary Louise finish getting ready. We leave for the church soon."

Lise stood for a moment, looking from one adult to another, her face worried and upset. Caroline would have reached out to her, but Frederich said something in German to Beata, a remark that precipitated yet another of her harangues.

I can't stand this! Caroline thought. She gathered up her skirts and walked rapidly out onto the porch, all but running down the steps and away from the house. She didn't realize that Frederich had followed her until she was well inside the barn.

"Caroline!"

She abruptly stopped and turned around, expecting him to criticize her again for yet another disruption of his household. But he remained silent, watching her closely— for signs of hysteria, she supposed, not understanding that she would cry only for her lost child. She refused to shed tears over anything Beata Graeber said, whether she understood the words or not.

She gave a wavering sigh. She had lost her temper and she shouldn't have. It was Lise's birthday. She should have made a better effort to keep the peace—for Lise's sake. She wanted to tell Frederich that, but she didn't. "What do you want?" she said instead.

"What do *you* want, Caroline Holt?" he countered.

The inside of the barn was dark and quiet. She could smell hay and dust, horse and weathered wood. The Belgians gave a low rumble and went back to munching their morning corn. Narrow shafts of daylight came through the cracks in the wall.

"I want to be left alone," she said, feeling close to tears after all.

"Few of us will ever have that luxury, Caroline Holt. I want to tell you this. You are well enough now. I want you to come to church this morning."

So, she thought. Everything was back to normal again. Her baby was gone forever and Frederich was making his proclamations, to which she would dutifully comply. She stared at him. He held her gaze, until she was the one who looked away. He was a big man, and his presence and his piercing gaze crowded her so much that she wanted to turn and run.

She made a concerted effort to stay calm and not to back away. "I don't think—"

"People are saying that your shame and your guilt have driven you to madness," he said bluntly. "There is nothing I can do to stop the talk. They need to see you at church so they will know it isn't true."

"Isn't it?" she asked sadly. In those first days after the baby's death she had certainly felt mad. Perhaps she still did. And no wonder Beata watched her so closely. Everything Caroline Holt said and did must be duly noted and reported. If she didn't eat, didn't sleep, if she walked all the way to the churchyard in the dark of the night—well, the more bizarre the better.

"No," he said, coming closer. "You are grieving for your baby. You are not mad—"

"Don't!" she cried. "Don't give me your consummate understanding! How can you know? You don't *feel* anything!"

She regretted the remark instantly, but it was too late to take it back. He looked at her a long moment, then turned and walked away.

"Frederich, wait," she said, following after him. "I didn't mean—"

"I *feel,* Caroline," he said without looking back at her.

She caught his arm. He jerked free of her grasp, but he stopped walking.

"I'm—sorry," she said. "I didn't mean to...hurt you."

He answered her in German. She didn't understand.

"How can you hurt a man who doesn't feel anything?" he asked in English. "I will tell you what it is *I* feel. I feel *your* sorrow. And I feel your contempt. All the time. Do you think I am too stupid to know these things?" He took a step closer. "I don't want you to be *sorry* and I don't want your pity any more than you want mine."

"Please..." she said, because he was crowding her again. She could feel the heat and the power of his body. She tried to move away. He wouldn't let her get by.

"*Mein Gott.* You're still afraid of me. Even after—"

She looked up at him when he didn't go on. "Yes," she whispered.

He reached for her then. She saw his intent, and she stood there, rigid and unyielding. She would feel nothing, give nothing. She would be as unemotional as she'd accused him of being.

But his arms were warm and strong, and the sadness was going to overwhelm her again. She pressed her face into his shoulder. He smelled of soap and cedar-scented Sunday clothes. His calloused hand stroked her cheek. After a moment he made her look at him, his eyes searching hers—not for permission but to understand—it was almost as if he were the one who was afraid.

He said nothing. Instead, his mouth touched hers, tentatively at first and then harder and so insistent that her lips immediately parted. He tasted her, again and again, as if he was starving and she the morsel that would save him. The ensuing rush of feeling took her breath away.

She wanted more.

More...

There was no tenderness in him, and she needed none. She had been alone for so long, empty for so long. And driven by the intensity of her desire, she strained against him to give him access to her mouth, to let him touch her wherever and however he wanted.

She gave a small whimper when his hand slid to her breast. Her body arched in pleasure. Her breasts grew heavy and her belly warm. She clutched the back of his shirt to keep from falling. The sudden weakness in her knees made her sag against him.

He pressed her closer. She could feel his hardness, feel him trembling. She could feel herself trembling.

"Papa!" Mary Louise called suddenly from somewhere outside.

It was he who stopped, tearing his mouth away from hers, his body rigid, his breath coming in ragged gasps. She could only cling to him, impatient and needy.

"Papa, it's church time!"

The barn door creaked loudly behind them, and Frederich pulled her deeper into the shadows.

"Papa, Beata's getting *mad* now!" Mary Louise insisted, her voice nearer still. "Papa—!"

He turned Caroline abruptly around, but he didn't let go of her. "I don't want your pity," he said roughly against her ear before he sent her reeling into the sunlight. "Stay away from me—for both our sakes—"

He doesn't want the likes of you in his bed.

Stay away from me—

Yes, she thought. *I won't make that mistake again.*

She tried to keep her mind on Johann's sermon. She should be thinking of the pitfalls of human wickedness he so eloquently put forth and not Frederich Graeber. She could see him across the aisle and two rows up. She could see the way his hair lay on the back of his neck. She could see and know how it felt in her hands, know how his mouth tasted—

She closed her eyes against the rush of feeling. The desire was still there, in spite of his rejection, in spite of the fact that he hadn't looked at her even once since they'd left the house. She might have been someone he'd never even met.

Or perhaps she was. She didn't recognize herself anymore. She didn't know where those feelings had come from. How could she have behaved so wantonly, when he had made it painfully clear from the very first that he had no interest in her beyond her caring for his daughters?

"—the wicked!" Johann said loudly, and she tried again to listen to whatever he was saying. But her eyes and her attention went immediately to Frederich. He had been right about her coming to church, regardless of the fact that he now obviously wished that she hadn't. When she came downstairs to leave for church with the rest of the family, she'd thought for a brief moment he was going to tell her that she couldn't go.

But she wouldn't have missed Beata's dismay for the world. What a liar Caroline Holt's appearance in church must have made of Beata Graeber. Caroline was behaving so well, too—on the surface at least. It was only in the barn with Frederich that her craziness unloosed itself and she lost all sense of propriety and decorum. She had learned nothing from her experience with Kader Gerhardt. She still mistook complete indifference for high regard.

Mary Louise was tugging at her sleeve. "Pee-pee," she whispered loudly enough to draw smiles from Leah Steigermann and the rest of the people around them.

Caroline took Mary Louise by the hand, putting her finger to her lips to show her that no further discussion regarding nature's call was necessary, and she guided her as unobtrusively as she could down the aisle to the side door, opening it just wide enough for them both to slip through. An armed soldier—an officer—stood outside on the steps.

"Morning, ma'am" he said, touching the brim of his hat. "Captain Elijah Brady, at your service. Church over?"

"No," Caroline said, looking down as he took her firmly by the arm. "What—?"

"I need you to come over here now, ma'am," he said, pulling her along.

"Sir, what are—you don't understand—I have to take this child to the privy."

"She'll have to wait."

"She can't *wait*—she's just a little girl." She looked around at the group of soldiers that seemed to have encircled the front of the church. "Are you foraging again? There's nothing to forage *here*—"

"As a matter of fact, ma'am, there is—Sergeant Alexander!" he snapped, making a red-bearded man off to his left jump.

"Are you ready, Alexander?" he asked as the man rapidly approached.

"Yes, sir, Cap."

"Keep this woman out of the way—you got all the doors covered?"

"Ah, yes, sir. Come on, ma'am," the sergeant said to Caroline, pushing her along. "You best get on over that way."

Mary Louise was clinging to her skirts and she nearly stumbled.

"I don't—wait—what is happening!"

"Conscription detail, ma'am. Sometimes a gun or two will go off, so you're going to want to keep yourself and your little girl out of the way."

Caroline tried to look over her shoulder. The captain and three other men were about to enter the church. They flung both doors wide, letting them bang against the opposite walls as they strode inside; she could hear the congregation abruptly stop singing.

She tried to sidestep the sergeant, who still wouldn't let her by.

"I'm telling you, ma'am, I got a captain here who loves his work. You ain't wanting to get in his way—"

"I have to hear what he's saying!" she cried. She jerked free of the man's grasp, meaning to fight him off if she had to. "My brothers are in there!"

And my husband.

He shrugged and let her go. Mary Louise was wailing now, but Caroline managed to half carry her close enough to see down the center church aisle. The captain was standing in front of the pulpit, talking loudly. He hadn't bothered to remove his hat.

"—you people to know I have government authority and I don't want any trouble—because you will sure as hell get more than you can give if you try to interfere with me. Now, here it is! All men of good health between the ages of eighteen and forty-six are hereby conscripted into the army of

the Confederate States of America!'' He paused, waiting for
the clamor of voices to subside. "There are no exceptions!
Do you all hear that? *None.* So I don't want anybody crying to me about planting or harvesting or pregnant wives.

"Reverend, I'm sure you have some birth records around
here. Go get the book so we can start weeding them out. All
you new soldiers will be leaving for camp as soon as that's
done, and *no,* none of you are going to run on home to get
something first. Whatever you think you have to have can
be sent to you at Garysburg.

"Let's get at it, Reverend! I don't have all day! All of you
women go outside and wait—*now,* ladies! You can farewell
these new soldiers when we're done here."

The women began coming out, hurried along by a young
soldier who tipped his hat courteously to each one but who
kept them moving. Caroline could hear Avery's raised voice
announcing his farmer's exemption and the answer he got.

"You are exempt if you pay the government to let somebody else get shot in your place—*for which,* I can assure
you, it is too late now! You are in the army, son!"

Lise came out. An obviously frightened Beata fluttered
along after her, trying to hang on to her hand. A woman
behind them suddenly swooned when she reached the bottom step and Caroline dragged Mary Louise out of the rush
to loosen the woman's stays and find someone refined
enough to be carrying smelling salts.

When had it come to this? she thought in a panic. When
had it become all right to *steal* soldiers for an army? No. She
knew when. She had read the notice in the newspaper for
John Steigermann. And she'd been too involved in her own
troubles to note its import. She looked around her at the
women who cried openly and the dry-eyed women who refused to believe they were about to lose their husbands and
brothers and sons. *How naive we all were,* she thought, *to*

think that the most that would be required of us was knit-ting socks.

The old men were filing out—and several underage boys. Leah Steigermann ran to her father. Caroline tried to see inside the church again, but the gathering of people trying to revive the woman on the steps blocked her view.

She reached down and picked up Mary Louise, because the child still had to heed the call of nature. She staggered a bit under Mary Louise's weight because she was not yet strong.

"Where are you going?" Beata cried, grabbing at her arm. "You have to be the one! You have to tell them they cannot take Frederich! He is *your* husband!"

Caroline pulled her arm free. "You forget, Beata, even if I could do something, he wants nothing from the likes of me." She tried to walk on, but Mary Louise was too heavy for her. She faltered and finally had to set her down, caus-ing her to protest loudly and renew her crying.

Leah immediately stepped forward. "Let me take her," she said. "Let me take you, pumpkin," she said to Mary Louise, easing her grasp free of Caroline's skirts. "Come with me, Lise," she said around Beata. "Come walk with me and tell me about your birthday. Have you opened your presents yet?"

"Aunt Caroline?" Lise said, close to tears herself. "What's going to happen to Papa?"

"I don't know, Lise. Go with Leah now," Caroline said. "So Mary Louise won't cry so hard."

Leah's eyes met Caroline's over the top of Lise's head. "Sit down someplace," she said quietly. "You look terri-ble."

For once, Caroline felt no resentment at needing Leah Steigermann's help, but there was no place to sit down, re-gardless of how terrible she might look. She could only stand and wait—and hope that she didn't keel over and add another fainting woman to the pile. She couldn't tell what was happening inside the church now. The big two-over-two windows were open, but she couldn't get near to them because of the ring of soldiers. The front doors had been closed. She could hear only a raised voice she thought was Avery's from time to time.

Leah returned almost immediately with the girls. Mary Louise was no longer crying, but she was no less upset. And Lise. Her birthdays would never be the same again. They would always be the anniversary of *this*. Caroline gave her a small smile, one which Lise managed to return. But her smile abruptly faded and Caroline put her arms around her. She could feel the child trembling.

There was some kind of commotion from inside the church. Caroline kept looking at the double doors, but they remained closed. She realized suddenly that the men were coming out the door on the other side, the one she and Mary Louise had exited during the church service. She realized, too, that perhaps Captain Elijah Brady had lied about letting the women "farewell" their men. In a maneuver that must have come of practice, the new conscripts were immediately surrounded and ready to be marched away down the dirt road that eventually led into town.

"Hurry," Caroline said, taking both children by the hand, her eyes searching the line of men for Frederich. "Do you see him?" she said to Lise.

Avery was coming out of the church, a soldier at each elbow.

"You keep an eye on that one," Sergeant Alexander said to one of the men.

"I'm not doing anything!" Avery said.

"Not yet you ain't," Alexander said. "You boys watch that farmer and I mean it!"

"Papa!" Lise suddenly cried, and Caroline saw Frederich at the same moment. He was trying to get closer but a soldier immediately blocked his way, prodding him back into the group.

"You keep this up, Fritz, and you and me is going to tangle," the soldier warned him.

Caroline tried to get abreast of him, pulling Lise and Mary Louise along with her.

"Caroline, will you take care of my children?" he said around the soldier. "Caroline—will you!"

"Yes, Frederich," she said, distressed because he was.

"You give me your word?"

"Yes!" Of course she would take care of Mary Louise and Lise. What other plans did he think she had?

"Where is Johann?" he said, sidestepping the soldier again. "Find him, Caroline!"

But Johann Rial was coming out of the church.

"Johann!" Frederich called to him. "Bring Beata here!" Johann immediately took a protesting Beata by the arm and escorted her in Frederich's direction.

"Beata, you listen to this," Frederich said when they were close enough to hear. "Caroline is to take care of my children. I don't want any misunderstanding about her authority. I don't want you trying to take over while I'm gone. Johann, do you hear?" he said around the soldier, who was determined to keep him in the ranks. "Caroline is to take care of my children!"

"Yes—of course—" Johann said.

"Are you listening, Beata?" Frederich said. "I don't want you telling people I left you to say what is best for my daughters—or anything else. Caroline will do as she sees fit."

Beata clamped her mouth into a tight line, her eyes bitter, but she said nothing. Johann glanced at her nervously.

"Frederich—" Caroline began but he wasn't listening. He had no time to listen.

"Caroline, take this..." he said, trying to give her the money from his pockets. "If you need advice, you ask Johann. Beata has—no say. None—do you understand?"

She didn't answer him, because part of the money he'd handed her slipped through her fingers. The other women were swarming around her, trying to get closer to their men.

"Do you understand!" he cried.

"Yes!" she answered, holding on to Mary Louise to keep her from getting stepped on while Lise tried to gather up the coins.

"Caroline!" Avery interrupted from Frederich's other side. "You get my livestock fed, you hear! Get John Steigermann to help you!"

But she had no interest in taking orders from Avery. "Where is William, Avery? Are they taking him?"

"He's up at the front of the line—grinning like a damn fool," Avery said. "He's going for a soldier, Caroline—and that suits him just fine. You're going to have to send us what we need—put the things in a box or something and let Johann bring it. You go see Aaron Goodman's boy—the one that came home with his leg missing—he'll tell you what we need. And you tell Leah to write to me—Caroline! Did you hear me?"

"You!" Sergeant Alexander suddenly bellowed.

"I'm not doing anything!" Avery bellowed in return.

"Not you, farmer—him!" he said, pointing at Frederich. "When were you in the army? How long ago?"

Frederich didn't answer him. There was absolutely nothing showing on his face.

"Don't you start off on the wrong foot with me, Fritz! These boys are going to need all the help they can get and you got the look about you. Now you answer me. Were you in the army—yes or no?"

"Yes," Frederich said finally, taking Caroline completely by surprise.

"What are you grinning at, cabbage head?" the sergeant yelled at Avery after all.

"Who me? Not a damn thing," Avery assured the sergeant, but he didn't stop grinning. "Frederich, you are just chock-full of startling declarations, you know that? I didn't think you could top the one where you said you were going to marry Caroline anyway, but I'll be *damned* if you ain't—"

"Quiet in the ranks! Where the hell do you think you're going?" the sergeant yelled, because Frederich stepped forward to embrace his children. He picked up Mary Louise and stroked her hair, and he managed to kiss them both before he was forced back into line. Caroline walked a few steps closer to get the girls, and his eyes locked with hers for a brief moment.

"Don't let—" he said, but he didn't go on.

She pursed her lips to tell him that she didn't understand, but he was looking past her, and she turned around to see. Kader Gerhardt stood a few feet behind her.

"I want you to go now," Frederich said. "Now, Caroline. Take my children. *Bitte!*" he said when she hesitated. "I don't want them to watch this—"

"You get these boys ready to march, Fritz!" the sergeant yelled.

Frederich ignored him, reaching out as if he was going to try to touch her.

But then he abruptly turned and walked away without a backward glance.

Chapter Thirteen

It took Caroline weeks to realize that she would have to take charge of more than the children if they were all going to survive. At first, she found herself paralyzed by indecision—something she had suffered not at all when Frederich and Avery were still here. How easy it had been to give unsolicited advice on crops and sales and purchases when one didn't have to take responsibility for the consequences. More and more problems arose—sick animals and debris-filled wells, unpaid debts and *Beata*—until she awakened one morning with the certain knowledge that the time for behaving as if Frederich would return any minute had ended. He wasn't here and she had no realistic expectation when he might come home—if he ever came home at all.

Her first proprietary act had been to move as many of Avery's cows as she could find into the Graeber herd, because it was suddenly obvious to her that her most sensible course was to consolidate everything. Her second proprietary act had been to delegate the care of Mary Louise and Lise to Beata. Beata's already hostile nature had hardly been improved by Frederich's publicly assigning Caroline Holt his authority—legal wife or not—and the new arrangement did nothing to lessen her ire. Beata didn't seem to understand that everything had changed, and the truth was that Caroline simply couldn't manage all the outside chores and the girls' schooling and meals alone—a shortcoming that Beata never ceased belaboring.

They had no word from Frederich, no letters and no messages sent via the German neighbors as they returned from their hurried visits to the army camp near the Virginia line. Caroline decided after a time that it was better this way, better that she should make her own decisions and her own mistakes, better that she not think of him at all.

Except that the memory of that last Sunday returned again and again, regardless of her resolve. She couldn't keep from remembering. Frederich. The warmth of his body. The touch of his mouth and hands. The sound he had made when her arms slid around him—

And the humiliation.

His words still hurt. *Stay away from me—for both our sakes*—as if she had deliberately enticed him into the barn. As if she were a woman with some low and unscrupulous design. She certainly had no difficulty staying away from him now—except that it should have been out of sight, out of mind, and it wasn't. She had been up since before dawn, dragging buckets of water to fill the huge wash pot and getting the fire started under it so she could set about boiling and scrubbing the clothes that should have been done a week ago. The sun was hardly above the trees and already she was exhausted. She was cold in spite of the physical effort it took to get the clothes clean, in spite of the fire that still smoldered under the iron pot, and she was still remembering.

She looked across the field toward the Holt farm. The cornstalks were cut and the stubble ready to be plowed under. A mist rose from the bottom land as the sun pierced the long shadows, and a flock of crows roosted noisily in the tall pines. Frederich should have been out walking the furrows behind the Belgians. She should have been hearing the sound of jangling tack and harness. She should have been hearing blowing horses and Frederich's chirping whistles and low commands. Sometimes he sang in a rich baritone voice as he worked—some unidentifiable German song she had been too superior to ask him about.

Frederich Graeber played the fiddle for his daughter and he sang in the fields. It was as if this Frederich and the stern man who had been Ann's husband were two different people.

Frederich—

She looked sharply at the sound of an approaching horse, afraid that the army had come foraging again, but it was Johann Rial making his rounds already this morning. He waved to her briefly as he dismounted and stepped up on the porch to speak to Beata. She let herself relax. Nothing bad then. If something had happened to William or Avery or Frederich, he wouldn't tell Beata first.

Poor Johann, she thought. He was much too tender-hearted to have to be a messenger of death. How many times had he brought the news that another soldier had died of mishap or disease since that Sunday the men were taken? Three? Four? And they hadn't even faced the real enemy yet.

Johann stood on the porch talking to Beata for a moment, then he came in her direction. In spite of her logic, her sense of dread immediately returned.

"Caroline," he said cheerfully. "Hard at work, I see."

She made no reply, her hands clutching the wet dress she was about to hang.

"I have had a letter from your husband," he went on. "Frederich wants you to come to Garysburg."

She stood there, amazed at the sudden rise of anger, amazed that Frederich, even so far away, had been able to do this to her again. She closed her eyes for a moment. She would never understand him. Never.

Kiss me, Caroline. Stay away from me, Caroline. No, drop everything and come to Garysburg, Caroline.

She flopped the dress over the top rail of the fence to dry, and she kept hanging wet clothes, sidestepping Johann Rial because he was in the way.

"He wants me to bring the children?" she asked finally. For their sake and their sake only would she comply.

"No. He said to leave them with Beata or the Steigermanns."

"Then no," she answered.

"Caroline," Johann said with his minister's patience, as if she'd somehow misunderstood and it fell to him to explain. "You are his wife. He wants you to come to Garysburg. He has made arrangements for me to take you there before the company is sent into Virginia—you *are* his wife?" he asked pointedly.

"You yourself performed the lovely ceremony, Johann."

"That is *not* what I meant. I want to know if this marriage has been—"

"Johann, I can't go to Garysburg," she interrupted, ignoring his heavy-handed prying. "I don't *want* to go to Garysburg, and even if I did, I'm trying to keep two farms going—how can I go to Garysburg? And how do you know he's even there still?"

"Because I've had no word otherwise. Caroline, he expected you to come with me when I took the men their supplies—"

"Why in heaven's name would he expect that?"

"I can't say—you would know better than I. I can only say that he was most disappointed."

She gave him a doubtful look, but she said nothing.

"Are you writing to him at least?" Johann persisted.

"Yes, Johann, I am writing to him. Lise copies down all the receipts and expenditures I've had since he left, and I add a note at the end if there is anything else important enough to report. I suspect he knows far more about his assets and liabilities than he did when he was still here. Do you want to read the next one? I see no use for you to take me to task over letter writing. I can assure you that Beata is keeping him apprised of my every move." She snapped one of Lise's pinafores sharply and draped it over the top rail.

"I wish you would reconsider—"

"Johann, I can't go!"

"He's in grave peril, Caroline—you know that. All of them are. If you won't consider your husband, perhaps you might consider that your brothers—"

"Oh, certainly Avery is pining for me to come for a visit," she interrupted.

Johann ignored her sarcasm. "I am going to be blunt. I think something must have happened between you and Frederich to make him so anxious to see you, and I think you might regret it sorely if you leave anything... unfinished."

She stopped fussing with the wet clothes and looked at him. It wasn't what had happened between her and Frederich. It was what hadn't happened. There was nothing "unfinished" between them. Their marriage had never begun.

"Winter is coming," she said. "There is too much to be done here."

He sighed heavily. "And that's another thing. Beata says you are staying every night at your brother's place."

"I am," she said, throwing clothes over the rail again.

"Do you think that... wise?"

"Wise or not, it's the only way I can manage. I work here with Beata until sundown. Then I put the girls to bed, and I go to Avery's so I can feed the stock that is still there. I stay the night because I'm too tired to do anything else and because I'm on hand in the morning when the animals need to be fed again. Then I come back here and work all day. It's the only thing I can do until Mr. Steigermann can help me move the rest of the livestock to pasture here. Or would you have me running back and forth and never getting any sleep—so it will be more acceptable to Beata?''

He made no reply to that, but he hadn't given up. ''I don't know what Frederich will think about it.''

''He will think the worst, Johann—just as Beata does. And you. All the men are gone, Johann. What mischief can a wanton like myself possibly get into?''

''I have made no accusations, Caroline, and that is not what I meant. It's dangerous for you to stay there alone— there are soldiers about nearly all the time now. There are men escaping from the prison in town—''

''I don't think they come this way.''

''These are desperate men on the run—how do they know which way is safe for them to go? You need to let me take you to Garysburg. You need to speak to Frederich about this situation. It will worry him, Caroline—''

''Johann, please!''

''I haven't done wrong, have I? In allowing your marriage to Frederich to take place? I did have my misgivings. I did think that perhaps he shouldn't have honored the marriage pledge, feeling the way he did—but you understand that it was for the child's sake.''

''It's too late to worry about any of that now, isn't it?'' she said quietly, forcing herself to meet his earnest gaze.

''All right,'' he said after a moment. ''You must forgive my tenaciousness. It is a pastor's duty to be so.''

''You are like an old mud tortoise,'' she said, not unkindly. ''Latch on and never turn loose until it thunders— that's you, Herr Rial.''

He smiled broadly. ''Think about what I've said. Whenever you decide, I will take you to see your husband—but it will have to be soon. From what I could tell, the company is nearly ready to be sent off.''

She stood for a moment after Johann had gone. How simple it would be if she didn't *want* to go to Frederich, she thought. How simple it would be if she didn't miss him, if she didn't worry about him night and day. She had no idea why Frederich wanted her to come to Garysburg, except that there was no baby now, no reason for the Graeber-Holt alliance to continue and no reason why he shouldn't be free of her if he wanted. Perhaps he even had a lawyer waiting. Her locked door would give him ample grounds for an annulment—Beata would surely support his claim.

And she couldn't very well say that to Johann Rial.

"Stop it," she said out loud, hanging the clothes with renewed vigor.

She had no time for any of this. She had to make plans for harder times. The army was still foraging. She had to find places to hide enough food to get them through the winter. She had to find a way to get Avery's remaining livestock here and alive, and God only knew what she and the girls would do in the spring.

She reached for the last article of wet clothing—a homespun blue-plaid shirt she'd managed to find the time to make for Frederich, bartering for the cloth with some dried cherries Beata didn't know she had and getting up early to sew it before she fed Avery's stock. She had wanted the shirt clean and soft and ready when Johann took the next box of supplies to Garysburg. It had seemed the least she could do.

You see? she thought as she draped it over the rail. *Your wife* does *sew.*

But she doesn't go to Garysburg.

What do you want from me, Frederich? she thought, feeling close to tears when she hadn't let herself cry in weeks now.

"Aunt Caroline?" Lise said behind her. "Mr. Rial says he forgot to give you the letter from Uncle William."

Caroline took a deep breath and reached out to take the envelope Lise presented, immediately recognizing William's undisciplined scrawl. Her beloved younger brother was no scholar, but he was a faithful correspondent. She couldn't keep from smiling in anticipation, because William was nothing if not candid. No one would give her a better indication of how he and the others fared.

I take pen in hand to say I hope you are well, Caroline. Your little brother is behaving—no whiskey and nothing else that wuld make you worry for him. I think he is turning into a good soljer. Frederich says so and I have drilled enough to be a general. Avery will be a good soljer, too, if he can learn to keep his mouth shut. Dont nobody here know nothing about soljering but your husband, Frederich. Did you know he was in the army in Germany? He says he werent no older than me when his daddy sent him in. He says he had to go because he wasnt the oldest son and he kept getting into trouble—that don't sound like our Frederich, does it? I am staying close to him when the shooting comes. He says just don't step on his feet.

She smiled again.

We all think you shud tell Mr. Rial or John S. if you need anything. Avery says dont go selling any of his animals without he says so. Did Lise like the birthday present from me? She dont say in her letter, and I didnt like to ask. Everybody is thinking we will get into the fight soon. The regement missed the shooting at Malvern Hill. They got put watching prisoners before they even got to where the fighting was. But there werent no shame in it to my way of thinking. A soljer has to do as he is told. Frederich says dont worry about being skared. He says a man what says he aint afraid of a battle is a liar or a fool, and anyway it goes away when the shooting starts.

Avery wants to know did you tell Leeah S. to write to him. He aint got a letter yet and he thinks maybe she's writting to Mr. Gerheart instead of him. He goes on all the time about how maybe Mr. Gerheart is trying to take his place with Leeah and he's come close to pounding Mr. Gerheart a couple of times. Frederich had to make them quit. We are all tired of hearing about it so if you could get Leeah to write to him maybe Frederich and me cud get some rest. Its time to go eat so tell everybody hello from William or Uncle William if its Mary Louise and Lise. Tell Beata I surely do miss her pies.

Respectfully, from your brother at Camp Long in Garysburg, William T. Holt.

P.S. Frederich says he means for you to come up here.

Caroline reread the last line, stopping short of frowning because Lise waited expectantly.

"Is it a good letter?" she asked.

"Yes. Uncle William says hello," Caroline said, making a mental note to tell William that Lise hadn't mentioned his birthday gift because she had never opened it. She had put Frederich's fiddle and all of her gifts away until her father came home again.

"I thought so. You *smiled,*" Lise said wistfully, and Caroline felt a pang of remorse about her recent, humorless state.

"I hope Uncle William doesn't die," Lise went on matter-of-factly. "What would we do if he got shot and died, Aunt Caroline? What would we do if Papa got shot and died?"

"Let's don't borrow trouble, all right? We just have to try to take care of everything here—and you keep remembering your father and Uncle William in your prayers—"

"But I'm afraid it won't help, Aunt Caroline. It didn't help Mama."

Caroline put her arms around her. "We'll still pray, though. No matter how it comes out, we'll still pray as hard as we can." She leaned back to look at Lise's face and move a tendril of hair out of her eyes. "Did Mr. Rial forget anything else?" she asked, hoping to change the subject.

"No. He just left—I guess to find out about the money."

"What money?" Caroline asked. She picked up a bucket and dipped it into the iron pot to fill it with soapy water to take to the pigs.

"Papa's money," Lise said, following along with her and taking hold of the rope handle to help without being asked. "Beata says she knows Papa left plenty of money for us— she just doesn't know what you did with it—"

Caroline stopped walking, sloshing soapy water on them both. "What *I* did with it?"

"That's what she said. She wants to send some of it to Mr. Gerhardt. He's not used to rough army life. He needs to buy things to keep him in the comfort he's accustomed to."

"Over my dead body," Caroline said under her breath.

"What, Aunt Caroline?"

"Nothing—go help Beata keep up with Mary Louise, all right? I'll see you at the *Mittagessen.*"

Caroline propped open the gate to the empty hog pen and dumped the water into the trough, causing the pigs to run forth from their hiding places, squealing with anticipation. She stood back out of the way, rather proud of her self-control. She had emptied the soapy water onto the pigs instead of onto Beata's head. Beata Graeber was worse than *all* the Seven Plagues of Egypt, she thought, but it wouldn't help having Lise any more upset than she already was.

She kept carrying soapy water, intending to finish the task and not worry anymore about Frederich or his overly generous sister. She found Leah Steigermann waiting for her at the iron pot when she returned from her fourth trip to the hog pen.

"Caroline," Leah called, tripping out to meet her with great attention to where she stepped. "I came to tell you Johann brought me a letter from Avery today."

"Why?" Caroline asked bluntly, because Leah Steigermann, of all people, would know that she wouldn't have much interest in anything Avery had to say.

Leah smiled. "Because Frederich wrote something in it for you."

"Oh," she said with little enthusiasm. Her pride had been sorely damaged of late, but it was still viable. It was incredible how much she didn't want Leah to know what transpired between her and Frederich.

"He wrote to me," Leah said, taking the letter out of her pocket and opening it, "because he writes better in German—which you wouldn't be able to read—and he says he doesn't trust Beata to translate for you. Very sensible, I think." She moved the back page to the front. "Here it is— Frederich writes that the company is going to join Lee's army in Virginia before the week is out. He thinks they will go into battle soon and he wants you to know that he will take care of William the best he can. That's all he says. This is dated the last of August—nearly a month ago. They are long gone by now, don't you think—are you all right?"

"Yes, I—it just surprised me, that's all. I thought—"

She didn't say what she had thought. Of course she knew that Frederich and William would be going into harm's way. She just hadn't expected the news to affect her so strongly. Her relief at no longer being ordered to come to an army camp was completely overwhelmed by her concern for William. How long did it take to turn a farm boy into a soldier? she wondered. Surely more time than this, regardless of William's thinking he'd "drilled enough to be a general."

She looked around to find Leah watching her.

"You should have gone to Garysburg," she said.

"Is there nothing about my personal business people here don't know?" Caroline said in exasperation.

"Not much. You should have gone to Garysburg," Leah said again. "You treat your husband very badly, Caroline."

"I do not, and you don't know anything about it."

"I know you owe him everything and you give him nothing."

"I am taking care of Lise and Mary Louise. I am taking care of his property—"

"Yes. His property. Not him. Do you think Beata doesn't tell how things were between you and Frederich?"

"There was nothing for her to tell."

Leah sighed. "Exactly. But you already know what I think, Caroline. I told you on your wedding day you were lucky to marry him. *I* would have married him gladly if you hadn't—" She stopped, apparently because of Caroline's incredulous look. She gave a small shrug. "My father wanted him for me. We would have done very well together, Frederich and I."

"But you *love* Avery," Caroline said, still incredulous and coping now with a new emotion she would have sworn was jealousy.

"Yes, of course, I love Avery—but he is a man for pleasure—*not* a man for marrying. Ah! How shocked you are! How is it you are so shocked, Caroline? You should understand."

I don't know anything about pleasure, Caroline almost said. She could feel her face flush and she looked away.

"I'm sorry," Leah said kindly. "It wasn't that way with the other man then."

"No," Caroline said, reaching down to pick up the bucket. "It wasn't that way."

"Then that is another reason why you are lucky to have Frederich. I think he would be an accomplished lover—"

"Leah!"

"What?" she said, laughing.

"You shouldn't say these things!"

"No?"

"No!"

"Don't you want to know what I—what other people—think about your husband?"

"I know all I need to know."

"I hear my father and Johann talk. You don't want me to tell you what they say?"

"Certainly not—" She broke off and gave a resigned sigh. "Tell me," she amended. She was ashamed of her ignorance in matters concerning the man she'd married, but not ashamed enough to let an opportunity like this pass her by. She hardly knew anything about Frederich Graeber—and what little she did know kept changing. She glanced at Leah, expecting her to be laughing still. She wasn't.

"Tell me," Caroline said again with an in-for-a-pound bravado.

"They talk about why his father sent him to America," Leah said. And about his first wife."

"Why would they talk about Ann? She was a good wife to—"

"No, not Ann—his *first* wife. His German wife. Are you done carrying the bucket?" Leah asked. "I don't want to keep you from your work."

"Never mind the bucket—what German wife?"

"Well, I *think* she was his wife. It was all very tragic. It happened when he was a soldier in Germany. Frederich wanted to marry the daughter of a very prominent man, but her family had already arranged a marriage to someone else, someone with a lot of money—a banker, I think. Anyway, Frederich deserted from his company and ran off with her. They were caught, of course, and his father had to pay a fortune to get him out of the trouble it caused—the girl's reputation was ruined. Then Frederich's father sent him to America to keep him from bringing any more scandal down on the family—but Frederich stole her from her parents' house and took her with him.''

"But what happened to her? I don't remember that Frederich had a wife when he came here."

"She caught the fever and died on the voyage over. She had to be buried at sea. I think she is the reason Frederich wouldn't take another German wife. He would marry because it was required of him, but he didn't want to be reminded of her. He told Father once that he would never go home to Germany again. The sea was too terrible a place to him, because it was *her* grave. Father says she is the reason Frederich wanted your baby to have a place beside Ann—so that the baby wouldn't have to lie all alone—Caroline, I'm sorry. It makes you sad still. I shouldn't talk about the little one.''

Caroline didn't reply. She was thinking of the day Frederich had taken her against her will to see the baby's grave. She was thinking of how much comfort it had given her to know that the baby rested beside Ann. She was thinking of the accusation she had made in the barn. She had been angered by Frederich's presuming to understand her grief, and now she had discovered that, in all probability, he had.

And she was thinking of Ann. Poor Ann, who hadn't known there was no way she could matter to him.

"I was right then," she said, more to herself than to Leah.

"About what?"

Caroline looked at her for a moment, as she decided whether or not to answer. "About Frederich—and Ann. He didn't care what happened to her. All he wanted from her was a male heir—"

"No, Caroline—"

"She *died* trying to give him his son when she wasn't supposed to have any more children—what?" she said, because of Leah's troubled look.

"I think you misjudge him, Caroline."

"I was there, Leah."

"Don't you care for Frederich at all?"

"I think he is very kind to his children—and very hard on his wives."

"But he is kind to you."

"To me? No, Leah. He isn't kind to me."

"But of course he is, Caroline. How can you say that? He would never hurt you—the way Avery did—and I've told you. You are alive because of him."

"You don't understand."

"Then explain it to me."

Caroline sighed again. "I suppose he *is* kind—some-times—"

"He is kind enough to write and try to keep you from worrying so about William."

"Yes," Caroline agreed. "*Sometimes* he is kind—but then he isn't. I never know what to expect from him. It's as if he suddenly remembers who I am and how I came to be here—and he can't abide it."

"I don't think that is what he is remembering," Leah said.

"What then?" Caroline asked.

Leah stared at her for a long moment, then shrugged. "I think he remembers what happened with *her*. I think maybe he's afraid of you."

"Leah, why would Frederich be afraid of *me*?"

"Because once he let himself care for a woman so much that it cost him everything. I think he is afraid to let anyone else have that kind power over him again. You are strong, Caroline. You would never just settle for whatever he thinks he wants to give."

Caroline gave a short laugh. "Strong? You are the one person who knows better than that."

"Oh, yes. I have seen you at your worst. But you don't stay at your worst, do you? Look at you now—after all the bad things that happened to you, after nearly dying. You keep Frederich *and* Avery's farms going. Everyone is talking about it—that prissy Holt woman with her town airs, knowing what to do. Everybody is hiding their cabbages and potatoes and hams in more than one place—because Frederich's wife is doing so. Everyone is letting the pigs run in the woods—harder for us to catch, yes, but much harder for the army, too, if they want to take them—because Frederich's wife is doing so. Everyone is keeping the ten percent of grain and corn set by and ready to give the army when it comes, so they don't go looking for more—because you do it. Father and Johann both tell people it is better that the army takes the ten, like Caroline says, than the fifty. You see?"

"I see that people are worrying that I might be right, not expecting that I am."

Leah smiled. "How is it you understand other people so well and not your husband?"

"No one can understand Frederich Graeber, Leah. He keeps changing the rules—stay and eat with us, all right? Maybe you can put our Beata into a better mood."

"I will happily stay to eat," Leah said. "But, my dear Caroline, I cannot do miracles."

Caroline smiled. "And will you write to Avery and set his poor neglected heart at ease?"

"No," Leah said, returning the smile. "I am engaged now, you see."

"Engaged! Leah, when? To whom?"

"Oh, two weeks now," she said airily. "Like Avery, he is a dashing soldier. I have known him a long while. He wrote to my father, and my father gives his blessing if I want it."

"And *do* you want it?"

"Of course—it's time I was married. You took the best man. I must take the only suitable one left. Tell me, shall I make a good schoolmaster's wife?"

Chapter Fourteen

Oct 20

Dear Caroline,
I don't have to worry no more about what hell is like, for I have seen it with my own two eyes on that sunk down road to Sharpsburg. I am proud to say no body can give me the White feather. All the officers in this regement got killed. Frederich is the one that took us through. One of the generals didn't like us letting a sarjent and a German tell us which way to go, but Frederich got us dug in where we could shoot Yankees and do some good. Me an Avery both would be dead if it werent for him. I for one am glad he is in the family and in this company. You know I found out I could run shoot and eat all at the same time?

        Respectfully, your brother Pvt. William T. Holt

P.S. Avery wants to know if its true Leeah S. is marrying Mr. Gerheart. I told him if he wanted to know so bad he could ask Mr. Gerheart, for he is right here. But he says ask you. Can you send me some drawers? Mine is all full of holes. We are all pretty Holy if you want to know the truth.

William's effort did nothing to alleviate the anxiety Caroline had endured since the word came of the September battle. But she set about answering him immediately, not because she wanted to announce Leah's impending marriage, but because Johann was going to Virginia to try to find out about the men who had been wounded at Sharpsburg, and sending a letter with him was the best opportunity she had for William to get his answers. She spared no detail about the preparations for the nuptials—the gathering of women who met as often as they could to sew the wedding dress and the trousseaux—usually in Beata's kitchen because the Graeber farm was centrally located and more sewers could attend. She even advised William who would stand at Leah's side and hold the bouquet when the time came for exchanging the vows. She did *not* tell him that Caroline Holt as matron of honor in Kader Gerhardt's wedding had to be one of life's most ironically cruel jokes.

But, there was no way she could tactfully get out of it, unless she feigned illness on the big day—whenever that might be. She had tried pointing out the obvious—that Leah couldn't possibly want The Scarlet Woman of the County standing by her at the altar. Leah was not discouraged, however. Caroline Holt was her friend, scarlet or not.

In time, Caroline began to appreciate the situation. Somewhat. It was bound to annoy Kader far more than it upset her, and in lieu of wearing a red dress to his funeral, she decided that this must be the next best thing. She rather relished the idea of being conspicuously on hand for the "or forever hold your peace" part of the ceremony. She knew that she should be ashamed of the pleasure her lack of charity gave her, but there it was, and it was no use pretending otherwise. If her presence at Kader's wedding caused him undue anxiety, so be it. Turnabout was fair play; he had certainly been a sore point at hers. She would never forgive him for his indifference to his unborn child, just as she would never tell Leah or her family that he had been the father of her baby. Her doing so would serve no purpose but to cause the Steigermanns embarrassment and pain. She owed them too much to do such a thing, but that part, Kader didn't have to know.

She hardly remembered the month of November, there was so much work to be done. The severely cold weather had lessened the army's foraging, but it was nearly all Caroline could do to keep enough wood cut. Sawing oak logs with a two-handled saw and Beata on the other end was inconceivable torture. Beata absolutely refused to learn that one never pushed, one always pulled, and it was only when Caroline threatened to hoard the wood and burn it in the fireplace upstairs for herself and the children *only* that Beata finally began to get the gist of the procedure.

Occasionally.

By the latter part of December, Caroline had been driven to stealing Avery's already-cut wood, taking the wagon to the Holt farm every day or so for another load, rather than trying to maintain a woodpile with no help save Beata's.

The sky was heavily overcast and the afternoon freezing cold when she returned home from yet another forage. The coldness had the damp and wet kind of feeling to it that preceded a snow. Had there been any rings around the moon last night? She didn't know. She had been too exhausted to look.

She could hear laughter from the house as she drove the wagon into the yard—Leah's sewing circle hard at work. It still surprised her that Beata allowed the women to meet in her kitchen. Leah had worked a miracle after all. Her announced engagement to Kader Gerhardt had certainly eliminated Beata's nagging for money to send him for his "comfort."

She unhitched the horses quickly—with a skill she had never aspired to possess—and put them into the barn, leaving them with more feed than she should have as a token of her undying gratitude for another successful trip. Frederich had told her once that old Koenig had no idea that she couldn't keep him from doing whatever he wanted to do, and she earnestly hoped to maintain the deception.

She hurried across the barnyard and began unloading the wood, stacking it in the woodbox by the back door. At one point, she thought she heard whispering from inside the house, and she dismissed it as a sign of how little progress she'd made. She was a fallen women to be talked about behind her back, and clearly she would remain so. The last armload of wood she carried into the kitchen, fumbling with the door until Lise came to open it. She glanced at her niece, then back again. Lise was positively beaming.

"Hurry, Aunt Caroline!" she said, shooing her along with her hands but not touching her so as not to interfere with the load of wood.

"Aunt Caroline! Aunt Caroline!" Mary Louise cried behind her. "Guess—"

But Lise snatched her up midsentence and walked quickly toward the pantry.

The kitchen was warm and full of women in the process of sewing as Caroline expected—except that no one seemed to be working at the moment and Johann Rial stood in their midst.

"Are you sewing trousseau now, Johann?" she asked, walking in his direction because he was standing on the hearthstones in the approximate location where she needed to put the wood. Leah and Mrs. Steigermann stood shoulder to shoulder on either side of him.

"Oh, yes!" he said brightly. "No—I mean no, Caroline."

Caroline looked at him—at all three of them—noting that they all wore the same expression. But she made no comment, stepping closer with the wood. Neither of them moved aside.

"I need to set the wood down, please," she said finally. Surely Johann wouldn't be smiling like this if he'd brought bad news.

"Shall we let Caroline do that?" Johann asked Leah and Mrs. Steigermann. "Shall we let her put down the wood?"

They grinned at one another and immediately parted, giving Caroline full view of the rocking chair behind them. Frederich sat in it, a thin and exhausted, chilled-to-the-bone Frederich.

The wood spilled out of her arms. "Oh—oh!" she heard herself saying. She rushed forward, in spite of the onlookers, kneeling by the chair, both her hands gripping his arm. "Frederich—what are you doing here? It's not William, is it—?"

"Your brother is well, Caroline. Both your brothers are well. They are with the regiment in the winter quarters in Virginia."

"When did you get here? How? Johann said there were no furloughs," she said, her eyes searching his.

"We cleaned him up for you, Caroline," Leah said behind her. "You should have seen him when he got here. You should have *smelled* him."

Frederich gave a tired half smile. "You are glad to see me, Caroline?"

"Glad?" she repeated as if she'd never heard the word before, and she suddenly remembered herself. She stood up immediately. "Look who's here!" she said to Lise, who had returned with Mary Louise from the pantry.

"We surprised you!" Lise cried. "Mary Louise was going to tell *everything!*"

"We surprised you!" Mary Louise said, ignoring the accusation and immediately climbing onto Frederich's lap.

"Yes," Caroline said, rattled still. "You surprised me." She began to pick up the spilled wood and stack it on the hearth, feeling Frederich's eyes on her every move and dropping several logs again in her haste. "I have to see to the horses," she said abruptly, because the room was too small suddenly and she had the overwhelming urge to cry. Frederich was here—when she *never* would have expected it. She hadn't been given any time at all to see how she might feel about the possibility. He was just *here* and she didn't know what to say or do, not with everyone watching.

She managed a smile of sorts as she escaped to the outside, and she stood on the porch for a moment trying to decide in which direction she wanted to flee.

"The horses are that way," Frederich said behind her. "Or have you moved them, too?"

She immediately turned on him, fists clenched. "Don't!" she said. "I don't want to hear it!"

"Hear what? I have only asked a question. *One* question, Caroline. Have you moved the horses?"

"No," she said, her chin still up.

"So do we go see about them or not?"

"Not," she answered, stepping off the porch. To her dismay, he came right along with her. "The horses are fine," she added, because he looked so tired.

But she didn't stop walking.

"Don't you have something to do?" she said pointedly over her shoulder, because he continued to follow.

"I'm doing it," he advised her.

"You look terrible," she said, hoping he would take the hint and go sit by the fire again.

"So do you," he countered.

She stopped walking, trying to find some indignation to fling at him. And she might have—if he hadn't been so right. She did look terrible. She needed clean clothes and a bath and her hair washed. She needed a good night's sleep. She needed—

She looked up at him. "We heard about the battle at Fredericksburg."

"Not too bad for the regiment this time," he said. "Mostly we were held in reserve and never needed."

"I see," she said, fully aware that she didn't see at all.

"You didn't answer my question. Are you glad to see me?"

She made herself look at him. It wasn't gladness she was feeling. Gladness wasn't weak knees and wanting to cry at the mere sight of him. "No," she answered.

"I'm thinking that I am going to kiss you anyway," he said.

"Kiss—Frederich, everybody is watching—at the windows—you can't—"

He chuckled softly. "I didn't say *now,* Caroline."

"What you *said* was for me to stay away from you."

"I was feeling sorry for myself that day. I no longer have the time for such things."

"Indeed," she said, still not sure whether to be angry or flattered, or to run or stay.

"Indeed," he assured her. "Come. Show me what you've done to my farm—come," he coaxed, because she made no attempt to do as he asked.

They walked together over the barnyard. Whether he approved or disapproved of her numerous burial pits for cabbages and turnips and potatoes, she couldn't tell. He had questions, of course.

"They are trenched?" and "How much straw?"

"How did you get the cornstalks plowed under?" he asked when he saw the north field.

"John Steigermann and Aaron Goodman's boy—"

"Jacob—the one who lost his leg? He can manage a plow, then?"

"Yes. He walks with the wooden peg they gave him, and he falls a lot—but he won't put up with anybody trying to help him. He and Mr. Steigermann went around to all the farms to get the plowing done. I let them use the Belgians—because they're a good team," she said. "Easier to manage."

She waited for his disapproval, but he merely nodded.

"I saw Jacob Goodman as I came in—talked to him. Old Aaron tells the boy all the time that God has punished him for running off to the army with his brothers and leaving his father all alone."

"Yes," she said, because he was looking at her as if he expected her to do so.

"He would be happier out of his father's house. His sister cries over him all the time—it makes him ashamed that he is not a man anymore. What do you think about him staying at the Holt place—keeping it up, paying a rent with part of whatever he can grow until Avery gets back?"

"What do *I* think?" she asked incredulously.

Frederich sighed. "Yes, Caroline. You are the only other person here."

"Very well. I think Avery would have a fit if you let Jacob Goodman live in his house."

"I had in mind that *you* would let him live there."

"Oh, of course. How silly of me not to realize who gets to face the wrath of Avery Holt here."

She glanced at Frederich. He was smiling.

"I like you when you're like this," he said, walking off in another direction.

This time, *she* followed. "What do you mean 'like this'?" she asked, ready to be insulted.

"Sharp-tongued," he said over his shoulder. "Sort of...like Beata," he added.

"I am *not* like Beata!" she said, and he laughed out loud.

"Which well did you have the trouble with?" he asked.

"How did you know about the well? Never mind, I know. Beata told you."

"Beata," he agreed. "And half the county. John Steigermann says you put on William's old clothes and he lowered you down on a rope."

"There was no other way—I couldn't very well dangle *him* on the rope."

"Were you afraid?"

"Of course, I was afraid. I'm not a complete idiot."

"John says you were very brave. But Beata says you are going to hell for wearing men's britches." He paused, apparently to hear her sharp tongue again. She didn't oblige him.

"You got the well cleaned out?" he asked.

"Yes, for now."

"Good. I hate going down in wells. It's good I have somebody to send in my place when it needs doing again."

He was teasing her, blatantly, and she simply didn't understand.

"Did you see the stars?" he asked.

"Stars?"

"When you went down in the well. If you look up at the sky, even if it's daylight, you can see the stars."

"Yes, I saw them—Frederich, what are you doing here?" she asked bluntly.

"My children are here. *You* are here. You don't write to me—" He held up his hand when she was about to protest. "You don't write to me," he said again. "You tell me how many sacks of corn I have, not how my family is. You don't come when I send for you. What else could I do—?"

He abruptly stopped talking as the geese on the far edge of the field became noisy and unsettled. Caroline immediately saw the reason—a group of gray-coated men on horseback coming along the edge of the woods, their hats pulled down, their bodies hunched against the cold. Frederich stepped nearer to the shed, out of their line of view.

"Into the house," he said, taking her by the arm and pulling her along the side of the barn to stay out of sight. "You—and the others—haven't seen me. Do you understand? One of you must take Mary Louise upstairs so she won't say I'm here—"

"Frederich, wait!" she cried, holding on to him. "What have you done? Have you deserted the army?" she asked—*again* she almost said.

"There was no other way."

"Frederich, they'll hang you if they catch you! It was in the paper. They are hanging deserters in Richmond—"

"Yes."

"What are you going to do?" she cried, trying to keep up as he walked her rapidly toward the house. "Maybe they're just foraging again—"

"They aren't foraging."

She looked past him to the approaching line of soldiers. Their progress was slow. Nothing about the Graeber farm had alarmed them—yet.

"Come into the house," he said. "Hurry before they see us—when they're nearly here, I'm going to try to make it to Avery's. They've come from that direction, so it may be that they've already been there. Johann!" he cried as he flung open the back door. "Take my hat and coat! Hurry!"

Johann stood for a moment, completely bewildered as Frederich tore off his coat and flung it at him.

"Put them on, Johann," Frederich said. "The army is coming. I want you to take Caroline back outside."

"Frederich—" Leah said, stepping forward.

"No questions," Frederich said. "Where are the girls?"

"Upstairs," Leah said. "Lise is looking for your fiddle and her birthday presents. What—?"

"No questions, Leah," he said again. "Keep them up there out of the way—Caroline, *I* am glad. Do you understand?"

"No," she said, trying to get Johann into the coat.

"To see you," he added. He reached out and touched her face, much the way he might have done if she had been Lise or Mary Louise. Then he moved around her and grabbed up his rifle and blanket roll and hurried out. She stood for a moment, watching him go.

"I don't understand," Johann was saying, but she hardly looked at him. She took him by the arm instead and dragged him and Frederich's hat out the back door. She understood the plan now. If the army had seen her with Frederich in the yard, then "Frederich" needed to still be here when they arrived.

"Caroline," Johann whispered urgently. "Would you kindly tell me the purpose of this subterfuge I'm perpetuating?"

"We don't want Frederich hanged," she said simply.

He blinked. "Oh."

She stuck the hat on his head. "Now walk with me and ask me some farm questions."

Caroline's hair was still wet when she braided it. She had long since run out of things to wash, including herself, and she could still hear the soldiers down in the kitchen, still hear the muffled laughter from time to time at some remark Leah made. Clearly, these men were not going to leave until they were turned out.

She left the room and crossed the hall, stepping quietly so as not to wake the children. She pushed open their door slightly. Both of them appeared to be sleeping.

She pulled the door to again and walked quickly to the room that had been Frederich's. She never came in here, and she didn't stop to inspect it now. With trembling hands, she lit a candle and opened the huge armoire in the far corner, riffling through it until she found Frederich's heavy work coat. She held it to her face for a moment, but it only smelled of cedar and not him.

There was little else in the armoire she thought he'd need. All his shirts and socks and drawers had long since been sent to him—the last of drawers after William's complaint that they were all "Holy."

She snuffed the candle and put it and some apples she'd been hiding from Beata into the pockets. Then she carried the coat into the hall, leaving it on the floor by the back staircase. She'd pick it up on her way out.

If she ever got the chance to be on her way out.

There was a roar of laughter from downstairs. She took a deep breath to steady her nerves before she made her way down the steps to the kitchen. All the soldiers were still seated around the table, still eating and drinking whatever Beata kept finding to give them.

"Mrs. Graeber, ma'am," they all said more or less in unison when she reappeared, scraping their chairs back to stand up as she entered. She realized immediately that she had been gone from their company long enough to make their officer suspicious, so she smiled graciously—she hoped—and tried to subdue the resentment she felt for these men who stayed safe on the home front instead of having been on the sunken road to Sharpsburg with Frederich and William.

She glanced around the room. Mrs. Steigermann and the other women had long since gone. Only Johann and Leah remained, and both of them were beginning to show the strain. Johann kept pulling at his collar, fearful, no doubt, that he would be put in the position of having to lie. Dressing like Frederich was one thing. Saying outright that he hadn't seen him was something else again. As far as she knew, none of the soldiers had specifically said they were looking for deserters, but she was certain that Frederich had been right. These men were not foraging.

But the person Caroline was really worried about was Beata. Beata could be mindlessly spiteful with no regard whatsoever for the consequences. She glanced in Beata's direction and tried to remember her mood before the soldiers arrived, but, unfortunately, she had become so used to ignoring her ire that it hardly registered anymore. Caroline's only comfort was that as long as these men were here, they weren't out looking for Frederich.

"I was just about to ask for you, ma'am," the officer said. "The weather, I expect, will turn most foul. I would consider it a kindness if you give us and our mounts shelter for the night."

Caroline stood for a long moment. She was taken completely off guard. She certainly hadn't expected that they might want to stay here. If their horses were all shut up in the barn and Frederich thought the soldiers had gone and returned to the house, he could walk right into them.

"Ma'am?" the officer said again.

"I leave it to our clergyman, Mr. Rial, to say, sir," Caroline answered. "We are only women and children here. I simply don't know if it would be... seemly."

She smiled slightly. The officer didn't.

"Well," Johann said too heartily. "We can hardly let our gentlemen suffer in the cold when it is in our power to do otherwise. I believe that if they stay in the—"

"Please, stay here by the fire, sir," Caroline interrupted, glancing at Beata. It was immediately clear to her that Beata had come to believe all her own lies about how Caroline Holt had become illicitly pregnant. Her obvious indignation that Caroline would openly solicit the presence of soldiers in the house was something to behold. "I think that it would be proper," Caroline went on pointedly, "if Mr. Rial also remained." She gave Johann a pleading look. Regardless of what Beata thought, the last thing she wanted was a bunch of soldiers milling around outside. "If you will excuse us, we ladies will retire now. Mr. Rial can see to whatever you might require—"

She abruptly stopped because Mary Louise was standing barefoot at the bottom of the stairs.

"Papa?" she said, wandering into the room and peering into the soldiers' faces. "Papa!"

"He's not here, darling," Leah said. "Of course he isn't."

"He *said* we can surprise Aunt Caroline again," Mary Louise insisted. "She's *easy* to surprise. Papa! Where did you go? I can't find you!"

"Where is your papa, little girl?" the officer asked.

"Here," Mary Louise said, looking up at him. "He's not lost. I got lost and Aunt Caroline got lost and—but Papa didn't—"

Caroline and Beata both stepped forward, Beata reaching the child first and snatching her up off the floor.

"You see!" she said, immediately turning on Caroline. "She is sleepwalking again!"

"Give her to me, Beata," Caroline said, reaching out for Mary Louise, because her eyes were big and afraid.

But Beata turned away and kept going. "I don't give her to *you! You* are no more her aunt than I am! Who are you to take her? You let soldiers stay in this house—my brother should have never married you!"

"I want to talk to that child!" the officer said loudly, but Beata ignored him, holding Mary Louise closer and railing in German as she mounted the stairs.

"The little girl *is* sleepwalking again," Johann said, stepping into the man's way when he would have followed. "She did so after her mother died—and it appears that it has come back now that her father's been away. I'm sure that Frau Graeber would rather that you had not been made aware of the animosity that exists between her and her sister-in-law, but, please, do not cause the lady of this house or the little one any more distress tonight. Perhaps in the morning—"

"We have been put on the alert for deserters, Reverend," the officer said, clearly unmollified. "The biggest group of conscripts came from this vicinity. That child's father, I think, is one of them—and *she* believes that he is here."

"I can assure you he is not," Johann said truthfully. "Do you want to search the house? Frau Graeber will not object—if the word of a man of God isn't good enough."

"Mrs. Graeber," the officer said, suddenly turning to Caroline. "Where is your husband?"

She looked at him evenly and told the truth as far as it went. "We had word that he and both my brothers and Miss Steigermann's fiancé were in the line at Fredericksburg three weeks ago. The fighting was very fierce there, I'm told—but I'm sure you've heard all about it." There was just the slightest pause before the word "heard," just enough to convey the reproach Caroline intended. "Search the house if you like. You will find nothing but our continued hospitality."

He stared at her across the room. "I can assure you, ma'am, your hospitality is both recognized and appreciated. I will not search your house, but I will see the child in the morning. I bid you good-night."

Caroline gave him a slight nod and took Leah by the arm.

"Good night, Mr. Rial," she said to Johann.

She walked slowly up the stairs with Leah, putting her finger to her lips when Leah would have spoken while they were still in earshot.

"I'm going," Caroline whispered when they were in the upstairs hallway. "Please, Leah, take care of the girls for me."

"Going where?"

"I have to look for Frederich," Caroline said, still whispering. She grabbed up the coat she'd left by the back stairs. "I have to warn him."

"Caroline, shouldn't you wait until the soldiers are asleep?" Leah asked, wringing her hands.

"No, I'm going now—before one of them decides to sleep on the bottom step and I can't get out."

"But what do we tell them if they miss you?"

"Tell them I went to the privy. Tell them Beata and I quarreled again and you don't know where I went." She buttoned Frederich's coat and pulled her shawl up over her head.

"Caroline, it's so cold out—"

But Caroline didn't hesitate, giving Leah a quick hug before she slipped down the stairs. She could hear the soldiers talking when she reached the bottom, and she waited long enough to determine that all of them were accounted for before she opened the pantry door and crept inside. She was in total darkness. She didn't dare light a candle; the soldiers might smell the burning wax or see the light under the door. It had been someone's idea to put a small outside entrance in this thick-walled room as a way to bring in potatoes and turnips without having to drag them through the house, and she had to feel along the wall for it, realizing finally that Beata had baskets and wooden boxes stacked directly in the way. She set about trying to move them, carefully, one at a time, her heart nearly stopping when several of the baskets toppled over.

But the noise apparently hadn't penetrated into the kitchen, and she went about finding the door again.

It was locked. Caroline lifted the handle and pulled it as hard as she dared, but she couldn't open it. She tried again and again, finally resting her forehead against the cold wood.

Now what?

She looked over her shoulder. The sounds from the kitchen were much quieter now, and she would have to be quieter as well.

Maybe it isn't locked. Maybe it's just stuck.

But she couldn't budge it. She began running her hands along the door frame, searching for a latch of some kind. She found nothing. She tried to reach higher, thinking that Frederich might have put it out of a climbing child's reach.

Nothing.

Her eyes were growing more accustomed to the darkness. She could see some light coming through the cracks in the door that opened into the kitchen. She would have to wait until the men were all asleep and slip across the kitchen and outside that way.

She leaned against the wall and slid downward to sit on the floor and wait. Her hand immediately touched a piece of wood at the bottom of the door—a wedge, she realized. The door wasn't latched. It had a piece of wood jammed under it to keep it closed.

With some difficulty, she pulled the wood out. The door immediately swung open. She scrambled upward and hurled herself through it to the outside, moving as fast as she could go in the dark toward the Holt farm. It was only when she reached the shelter of the woods that she dared to stop and look behind her. There was no activity from the house. No one had heard her and sounded the alarm.

She gathered up her skirts and began to run.

Chapter Fifteen

Frederich heard her long before she saw her coming through the trees. The night was so cold and the sound of her footsteps echoed across the frozen ground. He recognized her immediately, but he stayed in the shadows and watched her go into the house.

He waited—for her to come back out again—for whoever might be following her to catch up. He looked upward at the night sky. There was no moon visible, no stars. He marveled that she had been able to find her way, except that she, unlike him, had been born here. She had been a child here, played in these woods and along these paths. Of course, she would know the way, even in the dark. All the time he'd been hiding around Avery's abandoned house, he had expected her to come to him—with no real reason for him to do so, except that he wanted it. She'd been greatly taken aback by his arrival, but civil to him, if barely. And just when he'd given up the idea of seeing her one last time, here she was, and he was all undecided again.

But then, he had always been undecided when it came to Caroline Holt. He didn't want to risk capture. He fully intended to return to his company as soon as he was satisfied that his family—that *she*—was all right, but he had no delusions. He knew that if he was caught, he would indeed be hanged. He was a foreigner, a German. And conscripts as a whole were considered cowardly and undependable in battle by the military and the civilians alike. Even so, he waited, knowing that he should be well on his way into town before daylight.

But then he suddenly moved out of the place where he'd been hiding. He was wasting time, when he knew better than anyone that he had no time to spare.

Caroline could find no sign that Frederich had been in the house. The place was deathly quiet. She didn't call out to him. She moved carefully in the dark and touched the pig iron stove. It was cold. She couldn't keep from shivering. Her teeth chattered as she tried to find the candle she'd brought in her pocket. She fumbled along the shelf near the stove for the tin matchbox, her fingers finally locating it, but not where she expected it to be. Perhaps Frederich had been here after all, she thought.

She lit the candle at the moment the back door opened, startling her so much that she dropped it and the match tin on the floor, scattering matches everywhere, the lit candle flaming brighter in its downward fall.

"Put that out!" Frederich said, and she immediately fumbled along the floor to reach it only to have the flame die of its own accord. It rolled away from her fingers and she left it lying.

"I thought you'd gone," she whispered, her voice shaking with the cold. He didn't come any closer. She couldn't see his face. "I came to tell you the soldiers are still at the house. I was afraid you'd come back while they were—"

"Are you sure you didn't bring them with you?" he interrupted, and her heart sank. What if she had?

"I don't think so. These aren't men who would want to be out on such a cold night. The officer asked me where you were—because Mary Louise woke up and came looking for you. He may suspect but he isn't sure—"

She looked up sharply at the sudden burst of rain—no, sleet—against the house. The bad weather she'd expected all afternoon had finally arrived.

"Have you had anything to eat?" she asked, looking back at him. She could just make out his form in the darkness. "I've got some apples in my pockets. Your pockets," she amended. "It's your coat I'm wearing. I thought you would need it—"

"I've stolen one of your brother's coats," he said, his voice strained.

"If you don't want apples, I can look for whatever else might be here to eat," she went on in a rush. "But I'll have to light the candle—if I can find the candle."

She thought that it had gone the way of the scattered matches, and she got down on her hands and knees to feel for it in the dark. She found a number of the matches and the tin box they were in, but no candle.

"I don't want anything to eat," he said, coming close to her. He reached down and took her by the arm to bring her to her feet again. "I haven't been waiting for you here so that you could bring me apples."

"You've been waiting?" she asked, trying to see his face in the darkness.

His fingers tightened on her arm. "Yes! Did you think I deserted the army to get apples? I came home to see you, Caroline, so that I could talk to you. So that I could tell you how it is with me. I'm afraid I'll die and never get it said—" He abruptly released her and moved away again. She followed after him, coming as close as she dared.

"I am so *tired* of this," he said after a time. "We are never going to understand each other."

"I understand," she said.

"No, Caroline Holt, you do *not*. I was wrong to come home. I was wrong to stay here trying to see you. I'm leaving now. With the weather this bad, I'll have a better chance to get to town without being caught. Kiss my daughters for me...."

He flung the door open and she shivered in the blast of cold wind. It reminded her suddenly of that cold March day when Avery had come home to tell her of her impending marriage.

He slammed the door closed behind him, and she stood for a moment before following him.

"Frederich," she whispered. "Frederich!" she said louder as she opened the door.

The sleet pelted down; she could hear it clicking against the porch boards all around her. The steps were already icy. She had to hold on to the railing to keep from falling.

"Frederich," she called, trying to catch up to him as he walked rapidly away from the house toward the path in the woods. "Frederich!"

He didn't slow down. She had to run hard to try to close the distance between them.

"Frederich," she said when she was close enough for him to hear her. "Whatever—you came—to say, I want you to—say it. My baby is—gone. The reason for this so-called—marriage is gone. If you want it, you can be—free of me now. I know—I owe you my life. I owe you—your—free-dom—"

"I can never be free of you," he said over his shoulder, still moving away from her in the dark.

"The marriage can be—ended legally—you've done your duty—even Johann would agree. I have no reputation—to lose. I won't hold you to the vows—"

"I don't want to end marriage!"

He stopped walking so suddenly she nearly ran into him. "I don't want . . . to end marriage," he said again, his voice gone quiet, his back still toward her.

"Then what do you want?" she said in exasperation.

He turned around, but she still couldn't see his face in the dark. The sleet beat against them both. She couldn't stop shaking in the cold.

"I want us to be together," he said. "I'm tired of being your enemy, Caroline. What little is left of this night, I want to spend with you. I want to lie in your arms and I want to forget everything else. I want you to make me forget where I've been and what I've done—"

He abruptly started walking again, and she grabbed his arm, all but falling against him. "Frederich—"

"Let me go now, Caroline," he said gruffly. "Before we hurt each other any more—"

"No—wait—the question you asked me today, Frederich—I *am* glad to see you. I am! I've been so afraid for you. I couldn't bear it if anything happened to you. I couldn't bear it!" She held on harder when he would have put her aside, nearly falling again.

But then he abruptly stopped trying to get away from her. He simply stood there, suffering her undignified attempt to detain him.

"I want you to come back with me," she said, trying to see his face in the darkness.

"Did you not understand what I want from you? I can be more blunt if you didn't—"

"Come back with me!"

He whirled around and gripped her by both shoulders; she thought he was going to shake her—he was surely angry enough to do that and worse. But he swore instead, German words she didn't precisely understand. He took her by the hand and began walking toward the house again, pulling her along after him.

He all but carried her inside, flinging his gear to the floor and reaching for her as soon as he had kicked the door closed. His hands pulled at the front of her coat, freeing enough buttons so that he could touch her. She closed her eyes and arched against him when his hand found her breast.

But this was not what she wanted. This was far too much like that shameful time with Kader, rushed and furtive and illicit, with no love and no respect.

"Wait," she said, pushing against his chest to keep his hands out of her bodice. "Frederich, wait—Frederich!"

He abruptly stopped, his breath coming in heavy gasps.

"Please," she said, trying to slip from his grasp.

"What—?" He lurched after her, catching her easily and pulling her to him.

"No—not here. I want to make a place for us," she said, trying to hold him at arm's length. "I don't want my wedding night on the kitchen floor. Give me—just a few minutes. Then come to me—find the candle I dropped and come upstairs—please—"

"Caroline—"

"Please!" she whispered urgently.

He gave a heavy sigh.

"Frederich, I need to do this!"

"All right," he said after a moment, because he knew her well enough to know that there was no way short of brute force to do otherwise. But he held on to her as long as he could, letting her fingers slip through his, trying to see which way she went in the dark. He heard her going noisily up the stairs, bumping into something that caused her to cry out along the way.

"Caroline?"

"It's all right. You're going to need that candle," she assured him, and he smiled in the darkness. After a moment, he could hear her overhead, then not at all.

He took a deep, ragged breath and tried to find the lost candle. His hands still trembled, more with desire than from the cold. He knew perfectly well that he should go now, before the army came looking for him, before he had the time to think about this amazing turn of events. The risk he was taking was great, and he prayed to God that Caroline was right, that these home guard soldiers were not the sort of men who would relish being out in the cold if they could help it.

He found the candle finally, when he stepped on it and cracked one end. It took him a moment to fix it, and he moved away from the window before he lit it. Then he used it to look around the room, wondering how long "a few minutes" might be. He'd been here in the kitchen a number of times in the past, but he'd never been upstairs. He and Avery had had a kind of grudging, mutual agreement to help each other when the need arose, and he'd come inside with his brothers-in-law to drink lemonade or coffee, depending on the weather. Caroline had almost always been there, aloof and unapproachable.

Come back with me.

That she should have said such a thing to him was incredible. He still half expected to wake up and find himself among a dozen snoring men in a makeshift log-and-mud hut in Virginia.

He had no idea of the time. Before midnight? After? How long did he have with her? A few hours? Or no time at all? *Caroline.*

He picked up his gear and walked toward the stairs. She was waiting for him on the first landing, another wavering candle in her hands. She said nothing, and neither did he. He simply followed her—wherever she wanted to take him, he didn't care.

She had uncovered her hair. If he had had a free hand, he would have reached out to touch the thick braid that hung down her back. She led the way to the second story, then up another flight of stairs to the attic space.

"Do you think we can have a fire?" she asked along the way, her voice so matter-of-fact that it unsettled him. *He* was nervous about this sudden change in their relationship. Why wasn't she?

"The windows are very small," she went on. "I don't think anyone who passed by would see the glow in this weather."

"They'll smell the smoke, Caroline," he said.

"Oh. Yes. I didn't think—"

"It won't matter," he said quickly. "If the soldiers come here, it will be because they believe they have a reason. A smokeless chimney isn't going to keep them away."

She had to make him move down a step or two so that she could open the door at the top of the narrow attic stairway. Her hand rested on his shoulder. He felt her touch much deeper than that.

"This is where you stayed? When you lived here?" he asked as he followed her into the room.

But it was more than a room. As far as he could tell, the space took up the entire top floor of the house. He stood awkwardly, looking around him.

"Yes," she said. "It was too hot in the summer and too cold in the winter—but I needed a place away from..."

She didn't go on, but he understood. It would have been hell for a quiet, bookish person like her to live in the same house with Avery Holt. She would have needed some kind of sanctuary. It occurred to him that it must have been hell for her to live with him as well.

Everything looked swept and tidy. The bed—her bed— had a high headboard with oak leaf carvings and a thick feather mattress. The pile of quilts covering it had been turned down. He found the gesture both endearing and erotic.

She had other small candles lit, most of them on the hearth where a fire had been laid. He could see a stack of books in the shadowy recesses of the room, perhaps the same books she'd brought to his own house that day William had given her her belongings in a pillow slip. But she hadn't been up here long enough to arrange all this—she must still stay here sometimes, he thought. Beata had writ-

ten to him, complaining bitterly about Caroline's sleeping
in her brother's house every night after all the men had gone
for soldiers—and her implication had been anything but
that Caroline was sleeping *alone.* But Johann Rial had taken
it upon himself to explain the situation to him in a lengthy
letter, answering all the questions that he, Frederich, would
have had too much pride to ask. He had believed Johann,
and he knew Caroline well enough to know that she still
grieved for her child and that she would want some kind of
respite from living with Beata.

His eyes strayed to the bed again, and this time Caroline
caught him at it. She glanced quickly away.

So, he thought. He wasn't nervous by himself after all.

He set his rifle and blanket roll on the floor near the
hearth and knelt down to light the fire. The wood had been
well laid and it caught immediately. When he stood up
again, Caroline was still standing where he'd left her.

Come here, he almost said, but he immediately changed
his mind. He was taking no chance of offending her—or
scaring her, from the look on her face now.

He walked to her, but he said nothing. He allowed himself the luxury of simply looking at her, at her pretty face
and her hair, at the swell of her breasts his coat didn't hide.

His eyes returned to her face in time to see her lips purse
with the question she didn't ask.

What are you doing?

"I am looking," he said as if she'd asked it. *Looking as
long and as much as I like.*

There was a sudden cessation in the rattle of sleet against
the windows and the roof, but he didn't let it interrupt his
intent. She stood very still, suffering his inspection, glancing at him from time to time and clearly trying to decide
what he might be about next.

He took her by the hand and led her to the bed.

"Sit down," he said.

It surprised him that she did so. He knelt in front of her and began to untie her shoes. Startled, she tried to move away.

"I can do it," she said. He could see her breath in the freezing cold.

"I need you to let me do this for you," he said, looking into her eyes. "I need these things to remember. Do you understand?"

She didn't answer him, but she didn't pull away again.

He removed her shoes and left the stockings, then stretched up to unbutton her—his—coat. He didn't take it off her, though she obviously expected him to. The room was so cold still; she was having to hold herself rigid to keep from shivering.

He abruptly stood up and pulled back the quilts, lifting her into the bed still fully clothed and covering her carefully. Then he walked back to the fire to add another cedar log. The room smelled of burning cedar now, and the noise of the sleet beating against the windows and roof had given way to the soft, powdery whisper of snow.

He looked out the small high window near the chimney. There was nothing but blackness, no lights from the Graeber house visible through the bare trees.

When he turned and walked back to the bed, he saw that her eyes were closed, and they stayed closed even when he sat on the edge beside her.

"Caroline?"

She looked at him. "I'm doing what you were doing," she said. "Finding things to remember."

"What things?"

"The smell of the cedar burning," she said. "And the candles. I can hear the snow against the roof and the wood pop and hiss as it burns—and you walking across the floor. When I was a girl, I used to think about—about—"

She abruptly stopped and looked away.

"About what?"

She gave a quiet sigh.

"Tell me," he said.

"I don't want you to think any worse of me than you already do."

"Tell me," he said again. "I want to know what you thought about when you were a girl."

"All right," she said, looking at him again. "I thought about a night like this. With my husband—here."

The log he'd just added fell out onto the hearth, causing a shower of sparks to shoot into the room. He got up and walked to the fireplace, pushing the log back onto the andirons again.

Not Kader, he thought as he worked. *She wouldn't have known him then.*

He forced the thought aside. He wanted to believe that she no longer thought about the schoolmaster—just as he no longer thought about his own past. But that was by choice on his part. The past was too painful to be remembered.

He stood up, realizing that he was wasting time worrying about Kader Gerhardt, and he took off her brother's coat. He was acutely aware that she watched him. He took off his tattered CSA uniform jacket and pulled out his shirttail before he sat down on the bed again to remove his shoes. He was so weary suddenly. Not just physically, but weary of spirit as well. He had told Caroline the truth. He just wanted to be with her. He wanted to forget everything—all the ghosts that wandered through his life to haunt him. He wanted only the pleasure she could give him.

She made room for him when he climbed into bed.

"This reminds me of when I first came to this country," he said.

"This?"

He smiled. "Being in bed with all the clothes on. I stayed with the Pennsylvania relatives that first winter—the oldest daughter was being courted by a young man from the next farm. He would come to visit—it was so cold there—and they would go to bed with all their clothes on to stay warm while he convinced her to marry him.''

"Bundling,'' she said. "I think it's called bundling, but I didn't think anyone did that anymore.''

"Well, it was a shock to me—just off the boat. Nothing should have shocked me then but that surely—'' He broke off and didn't continue.

"Did she marry him?'' Caroline asked after a time.

"I don't remember,'' he said, looking in her direction. He had been careful not to touch her yet, and he marveled that he was actually talking to her—as if they were an old married couple. Talking—when that was the last thing he wanted to do.

She had turned a bit toward him, and he reached up to touch her braided hair, letting his fingers work into the end of the long braid to undo the plaiting. He wanted very much to see her with her hair unbound. She suffered this without comment.

"You have beautiful hair,'' he said, because it was true and because he felt he should say something.

"Thank you,'' she said with a primness she must have learned in her town school. "Frederich—''

He stopped trying to undo the braid and waited for her to speak her mind. He had no doubt that there was something she wanted to tell him. He knew the look. In the months they'd lived in the same house, he'd learned that about her, too.

"Say whatever it is you want to say, Caroline,'' he said when she didn't go on.

But she shook her head and sat up and took her arms out of the coat, pulling it out from under her and spreading it on top of the quilts.

"I don't want to say anything,'' she said, looking anywhere but at him.

She lifted her mostly unbraided hair out of the way and began to undo the buttons on the bodice of her dress. He took over the task after the second one, and if that alarmed her, it didn't show. He helped her get the dress over her head and the petticoats down. He brought a corner of the quilts up around her shoulders, noting that her chemise was very plain except for the ribbon ties. No lace. No embroidery. He could see the thrust of her breasts against the muslin.

He caught her hand and placed it on the top button of his shirt. She hesitated, then began to undo each one as he had for her. He watched her face as she worked, wondering if he should tell her how long he'd thought about this—about her willing participation in the first time they would make love.

She felt his scrutiny, and she suddenly stopped.

"Frederich, don't," she said. "Regardless of what you think, I'm not—I don't know what's expected of me. I don't know how to behave. Don't give me something improper to do just so you can be offended—"

"I'm not offended, Caroline," he said, reaching up to touch her face with his fingertips. "I'm living something I've thought about for a long time—come here. Come here," he said again, pulling her to him and wrapping his arms around her. She was stiff and unyielding for a moment, then she relaxed against him. "Why do you think I took your shoes away from you the first thing?" he asked, teasing her now and giving her an abrupt squeeze. "So you can't run off. So I can get you to bed and keep you there." He kissed her on the cheek and then on the ear, making her give a nervous laugh.

But then he was serious suddenly. He cupped her face with his hand so that he could look into her eyes.

"I don't want you to be afraid of me," he said. "I *hate* it that you're always so afraid. I'm not Kader Gerhardt. I won't hurt you. I want you, Caroline. I want to look at you and touch you. I want to be inside you—" He kissed her eyes and her mouth and her eyes again. "We have so little time. Don't hide from me," he said, because her eyes had remained closed after the last kiss. "Caroline."

She opened her eyes. He thought that she might cry.

"Is there nothing about me that pleases you?" he asked.

She looked at him a long time before she answered. "Your body," she said finally. She took him completely by surprise, and he showed it.

"You're very strong," she went on quickly. "You work so hard and your strength never fails you. The girls and Beata—and I—we all know we're safer in this world because of you—I'm sorry," she suddenly whispered. "I've said the wrong thing. I told you I don't know how to behave."

He lay there with his arms around her, staring into her eyes, regardless of how much she didn't want that now, and trying to decide if she was telling him the truth. The fire popped loudly, and one of the candles began to flicker and smoke. He dared to kiss the corner of her mouth.

"What else?" he asked shamelessly.

She gave a small sigh. "Your...eyes," she went on, surprising him further. "Because they're so blue."

"Yes, blue," he agreed.

"And...so sad," she said, bringing up a hand to touch his face. "So...sad, Frederich."

She kissed him then, gently on the mouth, lingering until he felt it deep in his belly.

His arms tightened around her. His hand slid to cup her breast. "Caroline..."

"We have so little time," she reminded him, and she kissed him again—*she* kissed him, releasing all the hunger and the need he'd had all these months.

He tried to show some restraint, but the ribbons on her chemise had come undone, giving him access. The scent and the feel and the taste of her smooth white skin left him trembling. And she was clearly surprised that he would touch her breasts in such an intimate way. He was certain suddenly that Gerhardt had never done that, and the thought pleased him immensely. He suckled her gently, then harder, making her body arch in pleasure.

He had on too many clothes. They both had on too many clothes. He abruptly sat up and pulled his shirt off over his head, then removed his trousers underneath the covers with no thought as to where they went when he kicked free of them. Then he sought the drawstring on her drawers—he no longer had drawers of his own to worry about regardless of her diligence in sending him several pairs. She didn't protest his attempt to untie the string, but neither did she help him. When they were both naked, he gathered her to him again, stopping long enough to look into her eyes. She looked back at him, and if she was afraid now, he couldn't tell.

"My beautiful Caroline," he whispered to her in German as his mouth covered hers—because he was afraid to say it in English.

He kissed her long and hard. His hands stroked the length of her, until her body rose to his touch, until she sighed, until he found the hunger in her that matched his own and her knees parted. He moved her under him and kissed her again.

"Caroline," he whispered, because he wanted her to look at him. He wanted her to *know* that it was he, Frederich, who would take her now, and he would do it with a love and a respect he could never voice. He had no words for the intensity of his feelings for her, none in English or in German.

"Caroline," he said again, and she reached up to place her hands on his shoulders, her eyes locked with his when he entered her. The pleasure was so intense that he nearly cried out with it.

"Love me," he said in German, and then again, *"Love me."*

And whether she understood him or not, she wrapped herself around him and gave him the oblivion he so desperately needed.

Chapter Sixteen

Caroline reached down to draw the covers over them both. She thought that he was awake, but she wasn't certain, and she lay there, listening to his quiet breathing. His arm was still thrown over her, but he had turned his face away. If she moved her head slightly, she could press a kiss against his shoulder. She wanted to very badly, but she didn't do it. She wanted to touch him, to run her hands over him and feel the lean muscled hardness of his body.

After a time, he turned his head to look at her and to kiss her mouth gently, so gently that once again she had the sudden inclination to cry.

"Are you all right?" he asked.

"Yes," she said, avoiding his eyes.

"You are overcome with regret now that it's done?"

"No," she said truthfully. She regretted nothing and she felt no embarrassment at what had passed between them. She turned slightly so that she could see his face. "I didn't know it would be like this with us."

"It wouldn't have—if we had married the way I intended—without all the... trouble."

He was much closer to the truth than he realized, she thought. If there hadn't been the "trouble," she would never have married him at all. She gave a quiet sigh. She hardly recognized herself anymore. He had said once that

she felt only contempt for him—and it had been true—then.
But somehow, living in the same house with him, watching
him with his children, having him take care of her when the
baby died, had changed everything. *She* had changed. She
had become an entirely different person almost without her
notice. She'd come from the "prissy Holt," who feared
marriage and who held the Germans in more disdain than
she would have cared to admit, to the woman who shamelessly lay abed with Frederich Graeber and who was more
than a little happy to be there.

"Will you tell me something?" she suddenly asked, realizing that perhaps she was not so changed after all. "Will
you tell me about your German wife?"

He stiffened against her, as if that was the last thing in the
world he expected. He moved away from her and turned
over onto his back to lie staring up at the great wooden
beams that supported the roof of the house.

Caroline waited.

"There is nothing to tell," he said after what seemed to
her a long time.

"Her name at least?"

He turned his head to look at her. "Her name was Sybilla."

"Did Ann know about her?"

"Ann? No. Not unless it came from the same person who
told you."

She ignored the remark. "You loved her—Sybilla?"

"Caroline, this is not something I want to talk about. I
don't ask you about Kader Gerhardt."

"But I can tell you about him—now."

"Can you? You...you don't care that he will marry
Leah?"

"I—it hurts my pride that he cared so little for me and my
child. But I won't let him and his indifference rule my life.
I didn't know what he was about. God knows, with a
brother like Avery, I should have, but I didn't. I thought

only beautiful women like Leah Steigermann had to worry about being seduced. I didn't realize that there were men like Kader—men who knowingly lie to achieve the conquest and then excuse themselves by reasoning that the woman must have known all the attention and the flattery meant nothing. I was so starved for kindness then—perhaps I wouldn't let myself think a man so thoughtful and so refined could have only seduction in mind. But I have suffered the consequences for my stupidity—''

"Your marriage to me, you mean?"

"No, that is not what I mean—"

"'A living hell' is what you said."

She abruptly sat up. "And *you* said for me to stay away from you—why do you always do this? Why do you make me think that there's a chance for us to have some kind of truce and then spoil it?"

"I don't know," he said truthfully. "Something in us both, I think—"

She attempted to move away from him, and he caught her arm to keep her from getting out of bed, pulling her to him and making her lie down again.

"Sybilla has nothing to do with you," he said. "Nothing."

"I'm only trying to understand—"

"Why?"

"Because I need to."

"All right. If you want to know about Sybilla, then I'll tell you. It's not a very pretty story—but then you know that already, don't you? You want to hear my side of it? I will tell you. I thought nothing could keep us apart—not our families, not the army and not her marriage to a rich man. I thought I could just steal her out of her father's house and go to America and live happily ever after—and why not? If I was banished to this place, there was no reason why I couldn't take her with me. The boy I was then loved her beyond reason—and she is dead because of my foolishness.

She died of a fever on the boat. They sewed her body into a canvas sack and threw it over the side—there had been a lot of bodies thrown overboard by then—old people, children, babies. The fish had already learned to follow the ship for the next feed—"

She made a small sound of protest, and he abruptly stopped. "You *asked,* Caroline."

"Frederich, I told you. It's only because I'm trying to understand,"

"What can knowing about Sybilla help you understand?"

"It helps me understand *you*. I see now why you were so worried about what I might do to the family name. You had redeemed yourself. You stayed in this foreign place for your father's sake. You made a success of the land. There was no Graeber family scandal here. I see how hard it must have been for you to marry me—if I didn't behave well—or perhaps even if I did, then everything—Sybilla's dying—would have been for nothing—"

"I don't want to talk about any of this," he interrupted. He rose on his elbow so he could see her face. "I don't want to *talk,* do you understand that?" His hand reached upward to deliberately caress her breast. She realized immediately that he expected her to be offended—perhaps wanted her to be. It was something he'd done time and time again—made some attempt to insult her—whenever she came too close to him.

She held his gaze, and she made no move to shrink from his bold touch. His thumb began to stroke her nipple, a direct challenge to her willingness to accept him and his uncouth intent—except that she didn't find him or his intent uncouth at all. She wanted to be with him again, in that intimate way, however shameless such a desire might be.

She could feel her eyes welling, but she didn't look away. "If we are enemies," she whispered, "it's because you keep us so."

He abruptly laid his head against her breasts, and she put her arms around him.

"Can't we start from here and now?" she whispered. "Frederich, can't we?"

"Caroline—"

"You are right that Sybilla has nothing to do with me. Neither does Ann. And Kader Gerhardt has nothing to do with you. All that is past. If you don't want the marriage ended, then can't we just make the best of what we have? Can't we help each other and..." She stopped because she was crying openly now. It occurred to her that he might not want anything from her but *this*, her willingness to lie with him and let him take his pleasure.

But there had been pleasure for her as well, intense pleasure, the kind she had never imagined could exist between a man and a woman.

She gave a wavering sigh and tried to stop crying, but he gathered her to him and began stroking her hair, comforting her with soft German words she didn't understand. It only made her cry more.

"I don't know—what's *wrong*—with me," she said finally, struggling hard for control.

"It's what happens sometimes," he told her, still stroking her hair.

"What happens?" she repeated, not understanding.

He leaned back so that he could see her face. "There is a sadness afterward." He reached up to move a strand of hair out of her eyes. "When the pleasure is strong, so is the sadness after."

She looked at him doubtfully, and he smiled.

"No, don't laugh at me," she said, hiding her face in his neck. "Please—"

"I don't laugh at you," he said. "Never. Kiss me now. Kiss me, Caroline—" His mouth sought hers, hungry and urgent and she responded in kind.

At one point she broke away so that she could see his face. He was in such peril now, whether he stayed here or returned to his company.

"I don't know what's going to happen to us," she whispered, pressing herself against him, but she knew as well as he did that this might be the only time they would ever have.

They came together quickly, lovers now and no longer strangers, their intense need of each other quickly brought to a fever pitch and quickly met.

Afterward, they lay tangled in each other's arms, and Caroline realized that she must have slept, because faint daylight showed in the high windows when she opened her eyes. She stirred in Frederich's heavy embrace, afraid for him again. He couldn't hide here indefinitely. What would she do if anything happened to him?

They both heard the noise downstairs at the same instant. Someone had come into the house, someone trying to be quiet. Frederich thrust her aside and began grabbing for his clothes.

"Stay here," he whispered.

"No, Frederich. I'll go—"

"Stay here, Caroline!"

She began to hurriedly search for her own clothes. Only half-dressed, she followed him when he crossed the room to the door, helping him on with his coat, the one she'd been wearing. It still had apples in the pockets. He reached for his rifle and his blanket roll and then for her, hugging her fiercely before he stepped out onto the narrow stairway. He looked back once, and then he left her there. She could only stand and watch him go, because she had no choice. She waited for a moment longer, shivering on the landing and listening hard. After a time, she heard Frederich's voice, but not what he said or whether anyone answered.

She abruptly closed the door and hurried to find the rest of her clothes, dressing as quickly and as quietly as she could. There was no way that she would stay up here while

who knows what was about to happen downstairs. Her eyes
went to the rumpled bed.

Am I your wife now, Frederich? she thought.

She had wanted this night as much as he had, and she had
let him know it. There had been no declaration of love between them; she hadn't expected it. It was just that she
wanted that, too. She wanted him to say the words—in either language.

Caroline, I love you.

She pushed the thought aside and put on her shoes.

What a piece of irony that was, she thought. The con-
temptuous Caroline Holt hopelessly smitten with her unwanted German husband.

She gave a quiet sigh and tiptoed to the door, listening
again before she came out.

What if I have another baby? she thought. Would Frederich be glad? Yes, she decided immediately. He would. She
felt a sudden pang of loss and sorrow. Had her daughter
lived, Frederich would have been a good father to her. She
had no doubt about that.

She began to move quietly down the steps to the second
story landing. She couldn't hear anyone talking now. She
couldn't hear anything at all. There was nothing but a dead,
cold silence in the house.

She came down the rest of the way, expecting to find the
kitchen empty. Beata stood in the middle of the room, her
arms folded over her breasts. And Frederich—Frederich
stood by the window, trying to find enough light to read
whatever he had in his hand.

"What's wrong?" Caroline asked.

Neither of them answered her.

"Beata?" she said, coming closer. "Are the soldiers
gone?"

Beata turned away and said something to Frederich in
German. He abruptly crumpled the sheet of paper he had in
his hand.

"What's happened?" Caroline said. She kept looking from one of them to the other.

Frederich held up the fist that still held the paper. "This is yours."

"Mine? What is it?"

"John Steigermann carried it from town yesterday. And Beata brought it to me. She was afraid I would leave without knowing what you were about to do. She was right to bring it. This..." He stepped forward and held it out to her. "*This* I needed to see. I wouldn't believe it otherwise."

"Frederich, what are you talking about?"

"I'm talking about how you fooled me, Caroline Holt. I'm talking about how I believed you. And last night I—" He stopped.

Beata said something in German again, something about soldiers that Frederich ignored, because he never once took his eyes off Caroline's face.

Caroline took a deep breath. "I don't know what you mean," she said carefully. "What is that?"

"It's a letter from Eli," he said, his voice cold. "To you."

"Why would he send me a letter—I can't read it. I can't read German."

"You are never guilty, are you, Caroline? No one can ever make you behave as if you have done wrong."

"Frederich, what are you talking about?"

"This is the money he sent for you to come to him," Frederich said, snatching up some paper bills from the table and all but throwing them at her. They fluttered to the floor between them. "And the letter he had translated into English. English, Caroline! Eli has gone to a lot of trouble to make sure you understand him...." He began to smooth out the crumpled page, and read aloud

I gave my word to take care of you, but I have failed. I thought I could leave things as they are, but it is too painful to think of you there with Frederich when I know how you feel about him. I want you to come here. I am sending you the money. You can have a new life and I can keep my promise. I know you have no reason to put your trust in me. That afternoon in the church I would have stayed with you, helped you, but I understood how much you didn't want Mary Louise and Lise to see you—

"You and Eli were together—in the church—with my children there!"

"No, that's not true," she said, horrified that he could think such a thing of her. "It wasn't like that—I was *in* the church at the same time he was that day, but I wasn't *with* him."

"Then what does he mean about staying longer with you—about keeping the girls from seeing you?"

"I was very upset. He was...concerned. I didn't want Mary Louise and Lise to find me in such a state—"

"Why were you upset?"

Caroline glanced at Beata and remained silent.

"Why were you upset, Caroline?"

"I am not going to answer that," she said, and he grabbed her by the arm.

She stared into his eyes, refusing to cower, and he abruptly let her go.

"Why did Eli stand up in church and ask to marry you? I thought he did it as an insult to me—to show everybody that *he* had more charity for Anna's sister than I did. Why does he write this letter behind my back, Caroline? Why does he send you money?"

"I don't know!"

"You don't know?" he repeated incredulously. "I have been a fool where you are concerned—but I am *not* that besotted—no wonder you don't care if Kader Gerhardt marries Leah. What is he to you?"

"Frederich, this makes no sense—"

"I am done with the Holts! Do you understand? I don't want you! You take the money and you go to Eli! You let him keep his *promise!*"

"There was no promise!"

"Enough!" he cried. "I have had enough!"

She stood there trembling, trying not to cry. He picked up the money from the floor and slammed it on the table, adding another bill to the pile from his own pocket.

"You see?" he said, his voice cold and hard. "Never say I don't leave a woman like you her fee."

She stared at him, so wounded by the insult that it was all she could do not to turn away. She gave a wavering sigh and shook her head. He believed this thing about her, and she couldn't change his mind. She had only to look into his eyes to know that. She stood there, willing herself to be strong, trying hard to ignore Beata's presence in the room.

In one swift motion she picked up the money and flung it back at him. "Take your *fee* and be damned," she said.

Chapter Seventeen

She stood at the window and watched him go, striding away from her and their marriage and their night together without even once looking back. And Beata fluttered along behind him, assuring him, no doubt, of how much better off he would be now that he had come to his senses. Even when Caroline could no longer see either of them, she still stood there, her eyes searching along the line of woods for some sign of the army. The anger she felt was surpassed only by the fear she had for his safety. Even now.

How can I be worried about what happens to him? she thought, but she knew the answer as soon as the question had arisen.

I am being punished still.

And what better retribution could there be for her than for her to truly love Frederich Graeber? In spite of everything she had felt about Germans in general and Frederich in particular, she loved him.

She moved to another window. She could see her own reflection in the wavy glass.

I have no tears. My heart is breaking and I have no tears. Frederich!

She finally sat down at the kitchen table, and she kept trying to remember what had happened the few times she'd had any society with Eli Graeber. He had been there when

Ann died, but she had been too distraught to even speak to him. There had been that afternoon in the church, of course, and when he'd stood up in the congregation and asked to marry her. The only other time he had spoken to her had been her first night in the Graeber house—when Lise had done the translating.

What had he said then? Don't be afraid? He had made no promises to her as the letter implied. She knew nothing about a promise.

I don't understand!

But if he had sent her money those first weeks after she'd married Frederich, in all likelihood she would have used it. She would have taken herself and her ruined reputation and her pregnancy as far away as possible. Why had Eli thought she needed money *now?*

She gave a sad smile.

Actually, she did need it—thanks to his cryptic letter, though apparently it was only *she* who found what he had written a mystery. Frederich—and Beata—seemed to understand it perfectly. It fit all their preconceived notions about Caroline Holt.

"I don't understand," she said out loud. And there was nobody to explain it, except perhaps Eli, and she didn't even know where he was, regardless of the letter and the money and the invitation to make her escape.

The memory of Frederich's face rose in her mind. She had been devastated by his anger, and there was nothing she could do about it. He believed the letter. He believed every aspect of it—that at some point in time she had behaved in such a way as to make Eli think his money and his summons to his side would be welcome.

She closed her eyes at yet another humiliation. Beata had heard every word Frederich said to her. For once she wouldn't have to make up her sordid tales. And likely she was already running neighbor to neighbor with the news.

Frederich is done with Caroline Holt. He is going to send her back to where she came from.

She looked around in alarm because someone stepped up on the back porch, but she made no effort to go and see. She had heard no horses—not the army then—and not Frederich, who would have barged right in. She was hardly in a state of mind to receive visitors. Perhaps the intruder would go away, she thought. Or perhaps it had already begun—the parade of people coming by to see with their own eyes the further downfall of the notorious Caroline Holt.

Someone has to tell her to stay away from the decent folk.

Whoever it was knocked loudly. She began to pace the room.

"Leave me alone," she whispered. "Go away and leave me alone!"

The knocking grew louder then abruptly ceased. She waited a moment longer, then made up her mind. She had no choice but to show herself. She hadn't been run to the ground, and she wouldn't cower here as if she had.

I have done nothing wrong. Nothing.

She glanced at the money still lying on the kitchen table in a pile beside Eli's letter.

Never say I don't leave a woman like you her fee.

Frederich had paid for her favors. There was nothing he could have ever done that would hurt her more than that.

She stood for a moment longer, then went to the window and looked out again. Last night's snow hadn't amounted to much after all—just a light dusting over the icy ground. And she had been too happy in her husband's arms to notice.

Johann Rial stood on the porch in the feeble winter daylight, quietly smoking his pipe.

She gave a heavy sigh. She could ignore him—but it would only postpone the inevitable. Johann thought he had a soul to save, and there would no deterring him from his vocation. She walked to the back door and opened it.

"Come in, Johann," she said, her voice sounding much more distressed than she would have wanted. She cleared her throat, hoping to subdue the tears that threatened to come after all.

He looked around at her, then knocked the ashes out of his pipe, saying nothing until he entered the house.

"I've come to take you home," he said.

"I am home."

"No, you are not, and you know it—"

"You've wasted a trip, Johann," she interrupted. "I'm staying here. Did Frederich send you?"

"Caroline, what have you done?" he asked, sidestepping her question.

She closed her eyes and fought down the flood of anger at his assumption of her guilt. When she opened them, he was staring at the money and the letter.

"I want to know what has gone wrong with you and Frederich," he said, looking at her. He didn't add the word *now,* but he might as well have.

"Haven't you heard?" she asked. "I'm leaving my husband and my nieces and running away with Eli Graeber. Of course the small fact that I have no idea where he is and I haven't spoken to him since the day I married Frederich shouldn't..." The sarcasm she had always used to protect herself suddenly slid away. Her mouth began to tremble and she abruptly put her face in her hands.

"Caroline, you are overwrought. If you refuse to come with me now, then I'm going to light a fire. This room is freezing. And...we can talk. It has been a very long time since my last meal, so you will forgive me if I also invite myself to sit at your table."

"There is nothing here to eat," she said tearfully.

"I'm sure I can find something—where does Avery keep his brandy?" he added when she looked at him.

She had to struggle hard for control before she answered. "In the cellar," she said. She was so tired sud-

denly, and she hadn't eaten, either. She sat down heavily in
the nearest chair, and she put her head down on the kitchen
table, hiding her face in her arms, trying to regain her self-
control. She could hear Johann moving about—getting
wood, opening the door to the stove, lighting kindling and
then a candle so he could see to get down the cellar stairs.

After a time, he came back with a jug of plum brandy—
plum brandy that Frederich had made—and a handful of
withered potatoes. Then he went outside and drew a bucket
of water. Every rule of social decorum she had ever learned
demanded that she get up and help him, but she simply
couldn't manage it. He scrubbed the potatoes himself and
put them into a pot to boil, and only then did he pour both
of them a generous helping of the brandy.

"Drink it," he said, setting her cup down hard enough to
slosh the brandy over the sides. He pulled out another chair
and sat down across from her.

"I've never cared much for spirits—"

"Drink it," he insisted in a tone very close to his pulpit
voice. "All of it. And when you are calm enough, you explain this—this—fiasco to me."

She gave a short laugh. "Would that I could, Johann,"
she said, taking the cup.

"Make an attempt," he said.

She took a swallow of the brandy—it made her cough—
and then another, feeling it burn all the way down. She
looked at Johann and tried to force a wavering smile, but
the smile died and slid away.

"I want to know what happened, Caroline."

"Beata brought a letter," she said tonelessly, because that
seemed to be the crux of it all. "From Eli Graeber."

Johann stared at her across the table. She took another
drink from the cup, a long one this time. It burned less going down, but she still wanted to cry.

"What exactly does this letter say?" he asked.

She was dangerously close to crying now, and she picked it up and pushed it in his direction. He smoothed it out and began to read, looking up at her sharply at one part of it.

"You were with Eli in my church?" he asked, his disappointment at even the possibility of such a thing all to obvious.

"I was *in* the church at the same time he was on that particular day. But I was not *with* him," she said for the second time, fully aware that while she could deny this particular sin, she could not deny that she had been in the schoolroom with Kader.

"This is all of the letter?"

"I suppose. I didn't see any more pages."

"Was Eli the father of your child or not?" he asked bluntly.

"*Not,* Johann," she said. "I've never said more than ten words to Eli Graeber in my life—and those few he could barely understand. But Frederich thinks—"

"I know what Frederich thinks."

"Then suppose you tell me."

"He thinks that you and Eli have made a fool of him. He thinks Eli is the one who made you pregnant. He thinks that Eli, in a fit of conscience, tried to do the right thing and marry you, but he was afraid to go against the marriage pledge. So he ran off and left you here—but now he's had second thoughts. Now he wants to take care of you just as he promised. And he's sent you the money to come to him."

Yes, she thought. She could see how Frederich's logical German mind could arrive at that conclusion—anyone would for that matter. The only problem was than none of it was true, and Frederich hadn't trusted her enough to even listen.

"He thinks all of that and you want me to go back to his house?" she asked.

"There are the children. I trust you aren't going to abandon them to Beata. You did give Frederich your word to—"

"He isn't going to let me keep my word, Johann."

"Caroline, you don't know whether he will or—"

"Is the army still about?" she interrupted.

"They've left the Graeber house, but where they've gone I couldn't say."

"And where is Frederich?"

"Trying to make some sense of this. He is very angry, Caroline."

"He is not the only one who is angry! I haven't done anything wrong. It wasn't Eli. It was never Eli. Frederich has known for a long time who..." She had to stop to keep from crying. She looked at Johann sadly. "I don't know what to do."

The fire was burning hot now. The iron stove began to pop and strain with the heat. She got up to close the damper.

"You need to talk to Frederich before he goes—or is taken. If they catch him, I think they'll send him to the prison in town. It is a terrible place, Caroline. You have to talk to him now. You *have* to if you are ever going to sort this out."

"You don't know how disinclined he was to listen."

"He is not a cruel man, Caroline," he said when she sat down again. "I remember that you once thought so—after Ann died."

"Yes. It has taken me a long time to get past his treatment of her that day. She was so young when he married her."

"She was what we call the *Backfisch*—young—yes, but of age. She wanted the marriage. You know that. Frederich was her first infatuation, her *Schwärmerei*. And I must tell you that what you saw the day she died, you didn't understand—"

"What I saw was his indifference. He wanted a son—she wasn't well enough to have any more children—but he didn't care about that. He didn't care if it killed her."

"You are very wrong."

"I was *there,* Johann."

"Yes, you were there. But you still didn't know the truth."

"What truth?"

"The truth I'm going to tell you now. I had thought that it wasn't my place to speak about it, that people would be hurt unnecessarily—that *you* would be hurt, Caroline. But there is too much at stake here. Frederich's children need the both of you—"

"Johann, please! Just tell me what it is or go away!"

"All right. There is a reason why Frederich is compelled to believe that letter."

"Reason," she repeated. "And the 'reason' is also the 'truth'?"

"It is," he said, ignoring her resurrected sarcasm. "Eli never wanted to come to this country—any more than Frederich had before him—and his efforts to learn how to live here and to do his part for the family were halfhearted at best. To say that Eli Graeber was unreliable would be an understatement—perhaps you did know about that part of it. Eli made it very clear that he was no farmer and he had no intention of becoming one. It didn't matter to him that he owned half the land or that Frederich needed his help. It only mattered that his father had forced him to come to a place he didn't want to go. But whether his resentment of Frederich and his father is what caused him to do what he did, or whether it came out of loneliness or some other genuine emotion, I can't say. I only know the end result. Your sister died when she miscarried her child—but the baby that killed her was not Frederich's—"

"That's not true! I don't believe you!" she cried. "Ann would never have—"

"The baby was Eli's, Caroline."

"I don't believe you!" she said again. She stood up, but there was no place she could go to get away from Johann's revelation. *Ann and Eli? Never!*

"Yes, well, there is a great deal of disbelief floating around this day," Johann said. "But for whatever reason—revenge on his part or human weakness on hers—Eli and Ann *were* lovers, Caroline. The day she died—before you arrived—I heard her confession. And without Frederich's knowledge or permission, I arranged for her to see Eli alone. The promise Eli mentions in this letter I believe was made then. I believe his promise was to her, not to you. I think he promised to take care of the three most important people in the world to her should they ever need it—Mary Louise and Lise—and you."

"No," Caroline said, but one incident after another surfaced in her mind. Ann's suddenly learning to speak German. Ann's refusal to worry about her pregnancy—her happiness regardless of the fact that her life was in danger. And it was because she was so in love with her baby's father, Caroline realized. Eli.

Oh, Ann—

"Who else knows?" she asked abruptly. "Avery? William?"

"No. Only Beata."

Yes, Caroline thought. *Beata.* All those thinly veiled remarks she'd made about the Holt women—Beata had been trying to tell her about Ann and Eli for months, and she would feel free to say whatever she liked to whoever would listen after today.

Caroline drew a long, shaky breath and began to wander about the room. "Ignorance *is* bliss, isn't it, Johann? Or it was."

"I only wanted you to understand—"

"What I *understand* is how hopeless it is for Frederich and me. And it's always been hopeless, only I was the only one who didn't know that. Why did he ever want to marry me in the first place?"

"I don't know, Caroline. The children were a big part of it, I think."

"If it's true that Ann betrayed him," she said, because she still didn't want to believe that it could be so, "then that has overshadowed everything. I have never had a chance to find a place in Frederich's life and he must have despised me because of what my sister did. And you knew it all the time. You knew that Eli and Frederich hated each other because of poor—dead—*guilty* Ann—and you said nothing—"

"I told you. I did not feel that I was at liberty to—"

"I was alone. I was as desperate as a woman can be. How could you let me walk into a terrible situation like that so unaware?"

"It was for the child, Caroline."

"And what child is that, Johann?" she said bitterly.

"I did the best I could for you—"

"You'll have to forgive me if that brings me no comfort whatsoever. Dear God, when I think how utterly useless all this has been!"

"He has changed since he married you, Caroline. He has changed a great deal—"

"Changed? No, Johann. You said he was not a cruel man." She picked up the money Frederich had given her. "Ask me about this. Ask me what Frederich paid me for, and I'll tell you how cruel he can be."

"People say things in hurt and anger. Things they'd don't mean. Things they hardly realize they've said."

"Some people, perhaps. But not Frederich."

"You have a duty here, Caroline."

"To whom? To the man who thinks he has good reason to hate Ann and me both? To the man you deceived me into marrying?"

"To your husband."

"I don't have a husband, don't you see that? There is no marriage and never has been. And there is nowhere to go from here. Frederich can't believe me on my word alone. He can't—or won't—and nothing I say will change that."

"Caroline—" He stopped, the gravity of the situation all too apparent on his face.

"Have you told him what you suspect about Eli's promise, Johann? That it was made to Ann?"

He didn't answer her.

"I see," she said. "You have. If he won't believe you—a man of God—what chance do *I* have?"

"You have none—if you won't even try to talk to him."

"Well, I won't beg for his forgiveness when I've done nothing wrong. And I will never live in his house again, Johann. If you are going to play the go-between, you can tell him that. You tell him that I know nothing about Eli's letter, but if he believes it, then it might as well be so. I don't know what he wants from me. I have never known—except perhaps to take care of Mary Louise and Lise. I love them dearly, but I'm sure that is of no consequence to him. I'm sure he will make other arrangements for them now. The only thing I ask is that you speak to them for me, Johann. Help them understand that I just can't be with them right now."

"If you'd just come back with me, Caroline—I am pleading with you—before it's too late. It's the only way for you—"

"No! Johann, no."

"I don't know what else to say to you—except that I accept much of the blame for this. I can try to talk to Frederich again—"

"He isn't going to listen."

"Caroline I—I will remember you and Frederich in my prayers."

Yes, why not? she thought. *Prayers are all Frederich and I have left.*

But she said nothing and she didn't go with Johann to the door or try to persuade him to stay and eat their meager fare. The potatoes were beginning to boil. She sat and listened to the steam lift and then rattle the lid, and she waited until she was certain that she was alone. Then and only then did she dare to let her mind return to the earlier question.

What if I have another baby?

Frederich forced himself to let Johann make his report in his own good time. He kept to the pressing job at hand, chopping a felled tree in the woods well away from the house, his impatience rising as he tried to hang on to what little of his dignity and his pride remained.

"She won't come back here," Johann said finally.

"You asked her to do that?" Frederich said, the question out before he could stop it.

"I did."

"I have not said I wanted—"

"She won't come," Johann interrupted, "regardless of what you want."

Frederich split the next piece with much more force than was necessary. The air filled with the pungent smell of raw, injured wood.

"What do you expect?" Johann said, dodging a flying chip. "You and Beata take sides against her—"

"Is that what she said!"

"No, that is what *I* said."

"You saw the letter?"

"I did."

"And?"

"And I believe she is innocent."

Frederich rested the ax on the ground. "You saw—read— the letter and you believe she is innocent," he repeated.

"Yes."

"Then you are an even bigger fool than I have been," he said, picking up the ax again. He split two more pieces and set up a third. "Is she going to him?" he asked as he brought the ax down hard. For a moment he thought that Johann hadn't heard him.

"I told you I believe her," Johann said. "I believe that there is nothing between Eli and Caroline. But I think—" He stopped.

"What, Johann? What do you think?" Frederich said impatiently.

"I think *you* can drive her to take the only recourse she has. Without your protection, Beata will make sure she is ostracized here. I can preach tolerance from the pulpit and forgiveness and not casting the first stone—but, as sorry as I am to say it, I doubt that it will help her situation. If you abandon her now, if you accuse her unjustly—"

"I don't *accuse*, Johann! It is all there in the letter!"

"If you accuse her unjustly," Johann said again, "Eli's offer will be the only beacon in the storm. He has offered her a new life—"

"Yes, he makes her such pretty promises."

"Frederich, I am going to say again what I have said to you and to Caroline. This 'promise'—I think it was made to Ann, not—"

Frederich made a noise of disgust and attempted to walk away.

"Not to Caroline," Johann continued, following him. "She didn't know about Ann and Eli, Frederich."

"So she says."

"No. So I have seen. I have dealt in human misery all my adult life. I am not easily fooled—regardless of what you think. I know she didn't know, just as I know that you—"

He stopped walking. "What?" Frederich said when Johann didn't go on. "You know what?"

"I know you love your wife."

Frederich stood there, saying nothing. He had known Johann Rial a long time—too long to make a denial, even to save face. Yes. He loved his wife, and if there was anything at all he could be glad about, it was that he hadn't been foolish enough to tell her.

"The problem with you and Caroline is that you are too much alike—you are both too stubborn and too proud for your own—"

"I can't just forget about that damned letter!"

"You may have to, Frederich. You may have to because it's either that or tracking Eli to Pennsylvania to get his explanation. And there's the small matter of a war and your army enlistment in the way—not to mention your conspicuous absence from the ranks now. I'm telling you, if you—"

They both looked around at the sound of a wagon—John Steigermann driving his horses hard.

"They are coming!" Steigermann called before the wagon stopped rolling. "Old Aaron Goodman saw you talking to Jacob yesterday. He has told the officer that you are home—no! No!" he said when Frederich would have made a run toward the house. "You come with me. I will hide you in the wagon. If I can get you to town—if I can get you on a train headed to Virginia, they will have no cause to look for you."

Frederich stood for a moment. He didn't have his rifle or his gear. He had left them with Caroline—deliberately left them, he realized now. Even in his anger, he had had the presence of mind to arrange an excuse for seeing her again.

"Johann," he said, clasping his shoulder. "Tell my children I've had to go—tell Beata what's happened."

"And what shall I tell your wife, Frederich?" Johann asked gravely.

"Tell her—" He broke off and shook his head. "Nothing," he said. "I will tell her myself." He began walking rapidly away. "John Steigermann! You drive to the ferry road and go toward town. I will cut across from Avery's and meet you in the hickory woods—"

"Frederich, it's too dangerous!" John Steigermann called after him.

"Do it, John!" he called back.

"You be careful!"

Frederich began to run, waving his hand to show that he had heard the admonishment, and he kept running, deep into the woods toward the Holt farm. He stayed off the path, cutting through the underbrush and the brambles to keep out of sight. The briars caught his hands and face as he rushed headlong into the thickets. He had to get to her. He had to tell her—

Tell her what? he thought. He could hear his heart pounding in his ears and his chest began to burn with the exertion.

I believe you?

No. He couldn't tell her that, because he didn't believe her. He knew what Eli was capable of doing and he had seen the letter.

I don't believe you, Caroline.

I don't believe you!

And God help me, I want you anyway....

As he reached the edge of the woods, he stopped running, creeping forward, tree to tree to stay out of sight. There was no one about the Holt place that he could see. He moved farther to the right. The house had small-paned nine-over-nine windows. It was difficult to see inside. He couldn't detect any movement at any of them.

He started violently at a noise behind him, but it was only one of the pigs Caroline had set loose to graze on the hickory nuts that were plentiful on Avery's land.

He stood for a moment, impatient and desperate. He had no more time. None. With a faint curse, he stepped forward, walking quickly across the rough ground and into the yard. He felt no sense of alarm until he had nearly reached the porch. The back door was ajar and through it he could just see Caroline sitting on a kitchen chair. When he was about to call out to her, she abruptly stood up, only to sit down again—hard. Too late, he realized that she hadn't done so by choice. The first soldier stepped out from the side of the house to his left, pistol drawn. Then two more from the barn. And finally, the officer came out onto the porch, dragging Caroline with him. She was afraid, and Frederich instinctively took a step forward.

"Stay where you are!" the officer said, his revolver aimed at Frederich's head.

"Don't hurt her," he said. "She has done nothing—"

"Except perjure herself on your behalf. Such loyalty is to be admired, I suppose, even if it is wasted. Keep your hands where I can see them—Toby, you know what to do!"

The soldier, Toby, rushed forward, eager to show that he did indeed understand his duty. He emptied Frederich's pockets on the ground, then brought his hands behind his back and tied them skillfully. He left a long end and pulled Frederich over to the porch with it, making him sit down on the edge while he secured him to the porch post. Frederich's eyes met Caroline's briefly; she was visibly trembling.

"Take her inside," Frederich said. "She's cold—"

"You don't give orders here, Dutchman!" the officer said, but he thrust her aside and back into the kitchen. She didn't stay, hovering just behind the officer, coming as close as she dared.

"What's going to happen—?" she tried to ask.

"She has nothing to do with this," Frederich said again.

"Then she has no need to worry," the officer said. "You, on the other hand, have a great deal to answer for."

"What are you going to do with him?" Caroline cried.

"Go back inside!" the officer said loudly. "Now! Toby—get her out of the way!"

Toby stepped forward, but he was not nearly so certain of his ability to handle a distraught woman. And she was that, Frederich realized. But was she worried for herself or for him? His eyes met hers again. She didn't look away. He was overwhelmed suddenly by the memory of last night. He remembered the taste of her and the feel of her around him.

How could she have lain with him, loved him with such abandon if she hadn't meant it?

He abruptly looked away.

"I have the authority to hang deserters." the officer said.

"Then you'd better be sure that is what I am," Frederich answered.

They stared at each other.

"You watch him," the officer said to this men. He turned and went back inside, taking Caroline and Toby with him. Frederich could hear her say something as the door closed, but he couldn't understand the words. In frustration he abruptly pulled hard against the porch post.

"Hey!" one of the nearest soldiers yelled. "You behave yourself now, Fritz! You ain't getting loose and you ain't going nowhere—except maybe the prison in town, so you might as well situate yourself right where you are and save yourself some trouble."

Frederich "situated" himself, but it took all his self-control to do it. Every now and then he could see Caroline walk past the window, but he couldn't tell what she was doing.

Toby came back outside, standing at several different places on the porch until he found one to his liking. *He's just a boy,* Frederich thought. *Like William. Like thousands of others.* He glanced up at him several times; each time the boy was staring at him.

"That your wife in there?" Toby asked finally.

Frederich didn't answer him.

"She's ... pretty, ain't she? I think she's real pretty," he offered next. "And she sure is worried about you. How long you been married?"

"Not ... long," Frederich said after a time, because the boy was so earnest and so like William when he needed to talk.

Toby grinned. "That right? I reckoned that you was still a bridegroom—ain't nobody else would do something this crazy. I'm wanting to get married myself—soon as I can find somebody that'll have me."

Frederich smiled at this irrepressible boy in spite of himself, in spite of the predicament he was in. But his amusement died quickly, fading into a grim desperation he couldn't hide.

"You had anything to eat?" Toby asked him.

Once again, Frederich didn't answer him, but the boy was undeterred.

"Well, it won't hurt to ask if I can feed you," he said, opening the back door and stepping inside.

Toby was gone a long time. Frederich sat there, his hands numb from the cold and the too tight rope around his wrists. He kept trying to form some plan, but his mind fretted over his not having cut enough wood and not having celebrated Lise's birthday. He was caught, and he should be regretting his impulse to see Caroline one last time.

No, he decided. Whatever happened, he regretted nothing, not the marriage, not last night. Nothing.

Caroline.

The door abruptly opened, and she came out. She carried a red-checked cloth with something in it—potatoes, hot potatoes that steamed in the cold air. She came quickly down the steps and stood on the ground beside him.

"He said I can give you these—they're too hot," she said, glancing at the door.

Too hot and his hands were tied.

She opened the cloth more to let the potatoes cool faster.

"He wants me to ask him to untie you," she whispered. "I'm not going to do it." She let her eyes meet his.

He nodded his understanding. It would give this officer great pleasure to deny her such a favor.

She began to break apart one of the potatoes. The steam rose. He could smell it and his stomach rumbled with hunger. He could smell the soft woman scent that was her.

My wife, he thought. *Mine.*

"He's going through your gear," she said, feeding him a piece of potato and then another. Her fingers touched his lips and quickly withdrew. "He's read the letter of commendation—from the Sharpsburg battle. You didn't tell anyone—"

"There was nothing to tell. I was trained for the military. The training will take a soldier where he needs to go without his effort. There is nothing to commend in that."

"William said you kept him alive—and Avery."

He didn't comment. "More..." he said, nodding toward the potatoes, because he was hungrier than he realized and because he might never be this close to her again.

She fed him another portion, and another, and she kept glancing at the door and at Toby who paced around the porch, obviously trying to hear.

"What's going to happen?" she whispered.

"I don't know. Caroline, listen to me—"

She looked at him.

"If I've given you a child—"

"No," she said sharply. "I've been trapped by that once. We both have. I won't let it happen again."

"What do you mean?" he said too loudly, causing Toby to step closer. "You wouldn't try to..." He stopped because she looked so stricken—as if he had physically hurt her.

"I mean it's over," she said. "I'm giving this dying marriage its coup de grâce, and whatever comes of last night is no concern of yours."

"You would go to Eli anyway? Even if—"

"There is no going to Eli!" she whispered fiercely. "How can I make you understand? There is no going to Eli!" She bowed her head for a moment, then looked up at him and gave a heavy sigh. "It doesn't matter. I just want you to answer me one thing. Why did you marry me in the first place? Tell me that. Why?"

Her eyes searched his. He waited a long time to answer.

"I don't know," he said truthfully, because there was no one reason he could name but a thousand he couldn't. He had married her because at the time he had needed to. It was as simple as that and as complex.

"I married *you* because I thought I was supposed to suffer for my sin," she said bluntly. "And how well you have provided that."

"*Mein Gott,* you are a sharp-tongued woman!"

"If I am, it's because men like you and Avery have made me so."

"I don't know what you expect from me!"

"I expect you to believe me!"

"How can I?" he said. "How—can I?"

"Because you have enough trust in me to do it. For no other reason than that, Frederich."

He stared at her, and she shook her head.

"I thought we had come so far, you and I—from that terrible wedding ceremony to last night when we were—" She broke off and looked away. "I was wrong," she said, looking at him. "Nothing has changed. You still look at me in that way and I finally understand what it means. You don't see me. You only see Ann. If it was revenge on her you wanted, you have it—only she can't feel it. *I* feel the hurt, not her—"

He hadn't realized she was about to cry, but the tears suddenly spilled down her cheeks. She stood there, her face completely impassive in spite of the tears, and she folded the rest of the potatoes inside the red-checked cloth and stuffed it into his coat pocket. Then she stepped away from him.

"Caroline…" he said, forgetting that he was tied. The rope brought him up sharply. "You ask too much of me!" he said, still straining against his bonds.

She turned to face him. "I ask nothing. I'm worth having, Frederich. Sinful as I have been, I'm worth having! And I don't want the kind of marriage we've made."

He looked around at the sound of horses—five or six Confederate soldiers coming up the road that led to the house. A foraging wagon followed along behind them. Toby immediately summoned the officer, then came to untie Frederich from the post.

"You never should have come home!" Caroline whispered, her mouth trembling.

No, he thought. *I shouldn't have.* Then he might have lived for a time ignorant of yet another betrayal at the hands of a Holt.

He looked at her, trying to take in everything about her. If he had not come, he would have been ignorant of what it meant to finally be her husband.

Toby was dragging him off the porch and pushing him along toward the wagon. Caroline stood nearby, her arms folded over her breasts.

"Whatever happens—if they kill me or not—if the war kills me or not—you are done with us?" he managed to ask her in passing.

"Yes," she said, her eyes locked with his, her beautiful, still crying eyes. "There is no 'us' Frederich. I have no place—I *want* no place—in this thing between you and Eli and Ann."

Toby gave him no time to say anything else and shoved him on. He looked over his shoulder to see her one last time.

Yes, he thought. He was foolish enough to love her, but how fortunate he was to have never said so.

Chapter Eighteen

*P*lease...

She began and ended every day with that one-word prayer, but if she had had to say exactly what she was petitioning for, she would have been hard-pressed to do so.

Please keep Frederich safe?

Please don't let me be pregnant?

Please let me have Frederich's child?

She stayed in the Holt house, desperate for some word of what had happened to him. Johann Rial had been to the garrison in town several times and had learned nothing. If Frederich had been imprisoned there, his name was not on any roster. If he had been sent to Castle Thunder in Richmond, no one would say. Whatever the trouble between her and Frederich, she wanted no harm to come to him. She even tried to convince herself that imprisonment might be safer for him than the battlefield. But she kept remembering the small notice in the newspaper about the execution of a deserter from the 18th Virginia Battalion in Richmond. She even remembered his name—Daniel Kennedy.

She constantly looked for some task to do to keep from worrying, because the reminders of Frederich here were far more disturbing than they would have been in the Graeber house. There was no place she could turn without reliving some painful event, and sleeping in the bed they had shared offered its own exquisite torture. Sometimes she dreamed of lying in his arms again, with no anger between them and all the time in the world. Sometimes she woke in a terrible nightmare, afraid and lost and unable to find him. She dreaded the arrival of any letters from William or Avery. They would soon learn of her estrangement from Frederich—either from the other men in the company or from Beata. She didn't worry about Avery's reaction—his only concern would be whether she had jeopardized his ownership of the acre of land with the spring. It was William she worried about. William loved her and believed the best of her, regardless of whether she deserved it. She couldn't bear for him to be told this terrible thing about her and Eli. And if she was thankful for anything it was that he didn't know about Ann.

She harbored no illusions about the reality of her situation. It was no wonder that she had nightmares. She was utterly alone. Beata had cut her off completely from the children, sending her belongings to the Holt house via Johann almost immediately. And the worst of it was the certain knowledge that she, the proud, town-educated and once proper Caroline Holt, had meant even less to Frederich Graeber than she had to the indifferent, lecherous schoolmaster. The confederate officer had threatened her with arrest for aiding an army deserter, husband or no. Perhaps she would have been better off if he had done so and locked her away in a place that had no painful memories.

In spite of Johann's reassurances that he spoke to the children regularly, she missed them both terribly. One afternoon she walked in the cold air almost to the edge of Graeber land, close enough to see the house through the bare trees, hoping for some glimpse of them, however brief. But she saw no one, and as she turned to go, she heard the C scale being diligently practiced on the parlor piano, over and over, interrupted for a time by some equally diligent banging.

Mary Louise and Lise, she thought, giving a half smile. What Ann's children lacked in expertise they made up for in enthusiasm. She missed them so! But at least Beata was carrying on some kind of normal routine for them. Caroline had no idea what the girls might have been told about their father, and what they had been told about their Aunt Caroline, she didn't even want to consider. It was better that she hadn't seen them, she thought as she walked home. Better that than to provoke Beata into another one of her self-righteous fits. There was still enough of the Holt pride left, however, to let her imagine herself knocking on the Graeber back door and challenging Beata to do her worst.

But Beata had already done her worst and there was no help for it. None. Caroline kept thinking about Eli's letter as she walked along. She had read it again and again without enlightenment. She accepted that the promise Eli mentioned must have been to Ann—but why had the letter come now? That, she didn't understand.

Johann Rial was waiting for her when she finally reached the house, and once again, his surprise arrival made her expect the worse. Johann had no guile, and she had only to look into his eyes to know if the news he brought was bad, but she was walking into the afternoon sun and she could barely see him.

"Have you found him, Johann?" she asked, immediately asking the question that haunted her night and day to keep from prolonging her anxiety.

"Not Frederich, no," he said. "But I have found Eli."

She stepped up on the porch, but she made no comment.

"I have been sent word that he's with his—and Frederich's—Pennsylvania relatives."

"Word from whom?"

"From a German clergyman in the area."

"I see," she said.

"Eli wants to come back here, Caroline," Johann added quietly, and she looked at him in alarm.

"I have answered that that would be most unwise—because of the conscription—as a landowner he's bound to be taken. And because of the position he has put you in."

She gave a quiet sigh and looked out across the fields toward the Graeber place.

"You have nothing to say about this, Caroline," he said after a time.

"Beata could use his help," she said, still looking away.

"She wouldn't have his help for long—just until the next conscription detail—if indeed she'd allow him to return. He *is* a sinner in Beata's eyes."

"A sinner who owns half the land," Caroline said simply.

"Yes," Johann agreed. "There is that."

"Now that you know where he is, I want you to send his money back to him."

"You may have need of it."

"I don't want to ever have to use Eli Graeber's money. And I won't—if it's not here."

"I was thinking that you might need it for Frederich. If it turns out that he is in prison—here—or elsewhere. You may need a bribe to see him."

She looked at him. "I'm afraid he's dead, Johann. I'm afraid I'll never know what's happened to him."

"You must be strong, Caroline. I think Frederich will come through this. I think he will come back to you."

"You don't understand. Just before they took him away—I told him the marriage was over—whether he lives or dies. I meant it. I still do."

"Caroline . . ." He stopped and sighed.

"The children are all right?" she asked.

"They . . . miss their Aunt Caroline."

"I want to see them, Johann."

"It isn't wise. You know how Beata is. They are the ones who will suffer if you challenge her. You must be strong," he said again.

She gave him a sad look.

"You must be strong," he insisted. "And you must pray."

Yes, she thought. *I can do that at least.*

She prayed all through February and March as she tried to work Avery's land. She prevailed upon Johann to recover some of the Holt stock from Beata, identifying the cows by their notched ears so that Beata couldn't later accuse her of perpetrating some kind of thievery. A few of the chickens returned on their own, enticed by the scattered trail of corn she left from the woods to the chicken lot. She had eggs and milk and cream for butter at least, and enough pieces of dried cow stomach lining left to make several batches of cheese. She found two brown paper packets of seeds she'd saved and dried and put away so carefully last year, and she started early seedlings in egg shells to give herself a head start when the danger of frost had passed. She readied the beds for planting cabbages and onions. What few hams remained in the smokehouse she moved to the attic space where she could keep an intense vigil to ward off the beetles and the rats and the foragers.

It had occurred to her that she might greet the spring in the same condition as she had last year—pregnant and abandoned, but that was not the case. She was relieved when her monthly bleeding finally came, and sad, because her marriage to Frederich Graeber would indeed count for nothing.

Still there was no word of him. She didn't know what to do, where to look. For all intents and purposes, he had completely disappeared. She agonized over what kind of situation he must be in. She knew he would not write to her, but he would write to Johann or Beata—if he were able. And Johann was certainly working on Frederich's behalf, sending out letters to his commanding officers, reminding them of Frederich's Badge of Distinction at Sharpsburg. She thought Johann was likely writing to Eli as well and getting the letters north via his network of German clergy, who seemed to be undeterred by either the Confederate or the Union lines. He gave her no reports about those writings, however, and she asked for none.

In the middle of April a letter from William came:

Dear Caroline I take pen in hand to ask you a question. Everybody is saying how you wont live with Frederich any more. Nobody knows where he is got and Avery and me wont to know what is the matter with you. Both of us is worrying more than we shud—we got this war business to take care of and we aint got the time to be vexed over you leaving your husband. Avery is already upset enough on account of Leeah S. marrying Mr. Gerhart—though between you and me he dont act like a man about to get married. Him and Avery are going to get into it yet and Frederich aint here to keep them straight. It is too much for me. Cant you tell us what happened with you and Frederich so me and Avery will know how to act?

Respectfully your brother in the army, William

P.S. If you see Frederich, you tell him to come back here because this company needs him if you dont.

P.P.S. If you get a letter from Avery I wuld not read it. That is my best advice.

She didn't get a letter from Avery, and she didn't answer William's. There was nothing she wanted to say to him, no explanation she wanted to make. The first week in May, Johann brought news that the 5th North Carolina had been in a battle near Chancellorsville, Virginia. The names of the soldiers from the German community had been copied from the casualty lists and hand-delivered by Jacob Goodman—

one killed, ten wounded and captured, one missing from among the families here, and Caroline knew all of them.

Jacob also brought a letter for her; she recognized the fine script on the envelope immediately, even without a return address. Incredibly, it was from Kader Gerhardt. She had the presence of mind to thank Jacob as was expected, all the while giving thanks that it was he and not Johann Rial who had been the bearer. Regardless of what it said, she had no wish to get into a discussion about it with Johann.

The letter was very brief and to the point, beginning with the terse salutation, Frau Graeber, and ending with Kader's signing himself Herr Gerhardt. The in-between was equally as cold, and it advised her that, in view of her notoriety and her sullied reputation, she could not reasonably expect to stand in such prominent attendance at his marriage to Fräulein Steigermann—regardless of Fräulein Steigermann's generous but misguided invitation to do so. He had already advised his soon-to-be bride that decorum must be observed, he said, and he expected Frau Graeber to comply with his wishes and not inflict any more embarrassment upon him and his intended on this their most special day.

Caroline read the letter two more times, then she walked out onto the porch and stood staring at nothing. She crumpled the letter slowly in her fist, just seconds away from an observation only one so allegedly notorious and sullied as she could make—when she realized that she had visitors.

"What are you doing, Aunt Caroline?" Lise asked politely from the edge of the porch, as if there had been no time at all since their last meeting.

"What are you doing, Aunt Caroline?" Mary Louise echoed, full of giggles. She rushed forward and grabbed Caroline around the knees.

Caroline stuck the balled-up letter into her pocket and smiled broadly, happier suddenly than she'd been in weeks.

"Oh, nothing, my loves," she said, hugging them both hard and trying not to cry. "Just wondering where I can get myself a red dress."

Their visit was bittersweet and flagrantly clandestine, in spite of Lise's assertion that Beata had them out looking for some of her hens' nesting places and that there certainly might be some around here. To her great relief and her disappointment, neither of the girls seemed to be any the worse for their Aunt Caroline's absence. Beata was humorless and quarrelsome, but she would never deliberately neglect Frederich's children—unless she felt threatened. It was Beata's mindless need to keep Caroline Holt from getting "above herself" that caused Caroline concern. She knew how reckless a jealous and indignant Beata could be, and for Mary Louise and Lise's sake, she resolved to stay in "her place." No confrontations with Beata over the children. No arguments over property. Nothing.

She didn't let the girls tarry long, no matter how badly she wanted it. She walked with them back across the field toward the Graeber house after only a short while.

"Papa's got lost," Mary Louise told her as they neared the woods path. "I got lost and you got lost and Papa got lost. Lise's looking for baby chicks—but *I'm* looking for Papa."

"Papa's gone back to the army, silly," Lise said. "Hasn't he, Aunt Caroline?"

"Yes," Caroline said, willing herself to believe it. She hated having to lie so shamelessly, but for their sakes—and hers—she did it.

"No," Mary Louise said. "He's *lost. Everybody* gets lost—even Mama. And even Eli—you're going to get lost too, Lise."

"I am not."

"Are too, are too. Lost, lost, *lost!*"

Mary Louise ran on ahead, but she turned abruptly and came running back again when she realized that Lise hadn't followed.

"I won't come with you any farther," Caroline said to them, trying her best to sound calm. "Give me a goodbye kiss—"

"Can't you come back with us, Aunt Caroline?" Lise asked. She clung to Caroline's hand and kissed her cheek. "Can't you?"

"No, honey, I have to stay here."

"Why, Aunt Caroline?"

"It's too hard to explain. I don't exactly understand myself. It's just—better this way. For you and Mary Louise especially."

"Because Beata will get really mad and hide the food," Lise said.

"Yes, that's part of it—"

"Don't you like us anymore?" Mary Louise asked, holding on to Caroline's skirts.

Caroline looked from one of them to the other. "Of course I like you. You are my very own nieces. I love you. I love you both with all my heart."

"Then don't you like Papa?" Lise asked.

"Yes," she said carefully. "I like him—"

She stopped, because she could hear Beata calling the children in the distance and because she was on the verge, not of lying, but of telling the awful truth. Shouldn't somebody know that she loved Frederich Graeber?

"Go now," she said abruptly, giving them both another quick kiss. "Hurry, so Beata won't fuss—go!" she said when they still would have lingered.

They reluctantly began to walk away from her.

"I think you better tell Papa, Aunt Caroline," Lise called over her shoulder. "I think you better tell Papa you like him, because I don't think he knows it."

She stood staring after them for a long time. No, of course, Frederich wouldn't know. He only knew that she couldn't abide being married to him. He only knew that she had the real opportunity to leave him and his children for a life with Eli. It would never occur to him that she liked—loved—him.

But perhaps she didn't love him. Perhaps it was something else. She was perfectly aware that she would do anything for him—except live with him as a surrogate Ann. Not even for Frederich would she take on Ann's sins or her punishment for them; she had enough sins of her own.

Hopeless.

She saw the word in her mind as sharp and clear as if it had been written in black ink on a clean white page. She closed her eyes for a moment, standing quietly until she could see—feel—yet another word.

Please...

But God was in no hurry to answer such vague prayers, and heaven must be inundated by more exact ones from people who were worthy of having their petitions granted. There was nothing she could do except let the days pass, one after another in a relentless sameness until she hardly knew the day of the week anymore. The weather grew insufferably hot by the last of June and then hotter still in the first week of July. She went to bed each night with a palmetto fan in her hand, listlessly fanning herself until she fell asleep, only to wake up in the oppressive heat and have to do it all over again. The only real opportunity for rest and respite came in the early-morning coolness just before dawn—but the blackberries were at their peak now and more than plentiful, and she had to go berry picking before they were all gone. She left the house just at daylight, and she wore long sleeves and gloves buttoned tightly at the wrist in an admittedly vain effort to keep out the chiggers and ticks. Her apparel was comfortable enough now with the sun low, but she would suffer in the heat later. If she were not faced with the prospect of starvation and if she did not love blackberries so, she would have lain abed this day in a perfect example of the utterly useless and slovenly person Beata had always maintained she was.

She got through the one-for-the-bucket-and-two-for-me stage quickly enough and began to pick in earnest until the sun climbed well above the trees. She had carried two buckets with her—the small berry bucket she could maneuver better in among the briars and a larger one to empty the berries into. Only when the larger bucket was nearly full did she stop. She was so hot! The air weighed heavily around her. It was as if she had to push her way through it to move. She could feel the rivulets of sweat rolling down her sides under her clothes and down her face and in her hair. Her dress stuck to her back, and she wished belatedly that she'd brought a bottle of water to drink and that well-used palmetto fan.

In the distance, the German church bell began to ring before she was halfway home, and she looked around in surprise.

It's not Sunday, she thought. *Or is it?* It wouldn't surprise her if she had missed it.

She kept walking. The bell was still ringing when she reached the house, not a Sunday kind of ringing, but a steady, ominous pealing that went on and on. She wanted to walk to the church and see, but she didn't. Some days she felt up to being notorious in the eyes of her neighbors. Today, she did not.

She carried the blackberries inside and busily began to wash them and spread them out on her mother's willow platters to dry. She had cream and no sugar. She would whip the cream and eat it on a big bowl of the berries anyway.

She was nearly done when she heard someone come up on the porch. The door was open, and she looked around as Leah Steigermann rushed inside.

"Leah, what—" *are you doing here?* she was about to ask, because she assumed from Kader's letter that any society between them was now forbidden. Leah's having made no attempt to come and see her since that letter arrived certainly indicated that that was the case.

"Caroline, Johann sent me," Leah interrupted. She was out of breath from running and her hair had come undone. "—a terrible battle in Pennsylvania—"

"William?" Caroline asked in alarm, stepping forward.

"He's on the casualty list, Caroline—"

Caroline made a sharp sound.

"And Avery," Leah went on. "And the Ehrnhardt brothers—and the Leherle boy and Tobias Kruse—and two of the Goodmans—more than thirty of them just from here—so many—so many, Caroline..." she was crying openly now. "And Caroline," she said, coming to take her by the arm. "Frederich—"

"What about Frederich?" Caroline cried. "Tell me!"

"He's on the list, Caroline."

Chapter Nineteen

Please!

What did it mean to be on the list? she thought.

Missing? Wounded? Dead?

No, not dead!

Please!

William and Avery—oh, Frederich!

It could mean anything, and she knew that. She went looking for Johann, the blackberries left lying and Leah in tow. They were halfway to the church when it occurred to her that she should have asked.

"You've had no news of Ka—your fiancé?" she said over her shoulder.

"Nothing," Leah said. "He's been ill—he may not have gone on the campaign—Caroline, what will you do? Frederich and Avery *and* William—all three of them—"

Do?

Yes, she thought. She must *do* something. But her mind refused to consider what that might be. She could only think of getting to the church and speaking to Johann and nothing else. If there were any details, he would know them, and she blessed him for sending Leah to tell her. Who knew how long it would have been before she heard; she wouldn't have come to investigate the ringing of the bell.

And the bell was still ringing. When they were in sight of

the church, it abruptly stopped, the ensuing silence as ominous as the pealing had been.

She picked up her skirts and began to run, leaving Leah to keep up or not as she would. People were already gathering at the church, old men and young boys still on horseback and straight from the fields, and women standing in silent little groups. No one spoke to her as she approached. She stood off to herself, her arms folded over her breasts in some effort to brace herself to hear whatever Johann might have to say.

After a moment, he appeared, standing under the shade of the fieldstone arches at the front door.

"The battle began on Wednesday last near Gettysburg, Pennsylvania," he told them without prelude. "The telegraphed report is that it raged for three days and that as much of the army as was able has retreated back into the comparative safety of Virginia. I will read the names of men who have been killed or wounded or who are unaccounted for. Our church is open—you may spend as much time there as you need to in communion with Our Lord...."

She waited, listening for *her* names. It seemed to take forever before he read them.

William Holt and Frederich Graeber, wounded and unaccounted for.

Avery Holt, wounded.

Unaccounted for. Unaccounted for.

Dead, then?

No, I won't believe that!

But the battle had been nearly a week ago. If they had been wounded, who knew what their status was now? She had to talk to Johann. At one point, she thought that Leah had come close to her, but when she glanced in her direction, it was not Leah at all, but Beata who had come to stand so near.

Beata turned to her, her eyes red with weeping. She looked haggard, terrible, but still Caroline expected some barbed remark, so much so that she drew back when Beata attempted to put her hand on her arm.

"Where are the children—?" Caroline tried to ask.

"Are you going to go and get him?" Beata interrupted, her hands fluttering. "Are you?"

"How can I go get him, Beata? Frederich is unaccounted for. They don't know where he—"

"Not Frederich! Avery! You have no reputation to guard. A woman like you can travel without an escort—a woman like you can go into the hospitals and look for him. Go get him! Bring him home! He must be in Richmond—or—" She broke off to wipe her eyes. "Don't you know he *hates* the hospitals? He said if he was ever wounded, he wanted to come home. He wanted to die *here* or get well *here*—he can't abide being in a hospital!"

"Beata—"

"You go and get him!"

They stared at each other, until Beata abruptly buried her face in her hands. Caroline was at a complete loss as to what to do. Never in her wildest dreams had she ever envisioned herself trying to comfort Beata Graeber. Yes, she had seen Beata primping in the washstand mirror at the prospect of seeing the handsome Avery Holt—but then she'd seen Beata fawning about Kader as well. She'd had no idea that Beata's infatuation for Avery ran this deep.

"I must speak to Johann," Caroline said, sidestepping Beata and leaving her standing. She looked back over her shoulder once. Beata was still crying.

She stood on the sidelines and waited until Johann had finished reading the list, then waited again while he spoke to each of the distraught people who approached him.

"Johann, how can we find out what's happened?" she asked finally.

"I've already done all I can for now, Caroline. I've wired a message to the German clergy in the area. I've sent them the names of all those who are missing and wounded. They will search the hospitals in and around Richmond and let me know. It will take time. We can only wait."

"Frederich..." She couldn't complete the thought. Everything—the fear and the love and the longing she felt—suddenly coalesced at the mention of his name. She stood there, trying not to let herself be overwhelmed by the rush of emotion. She was only a breath away from wailing like Beata.

"The battle was very terrible, Caroline," Johann said. "I can offer you no reassurances."

"Why didn't we know he was back in the lines? Why didn't he tell us—you?"

"I can't answer that—perhaps a letter will come still."

"He said once that he would do his best to take care of William."

"Then you can be certain that he did. Frederich is a man of his word."

Yes, she thought. How else would she have come to be married to him?

"We can only wait," Johann said again. "Will you come into the sanctuary with the others?"

She shook her head. She left the church and went to the low stone wall instead, stepping over it when she neared the baby's grave. The grassy sod William had brought from the meadow to cover it was dying in the summer heat. She sat down on the ground because her legs refused to hold her any longer.

I think you better tell Papa you like him....
Is there nothing about me that pleases you?
Whatever happens... you are done with us?
Frederich!

She didn't cry. Not that day or the next. By the third day after the news had come—and regardless of what she had said to Beata—she made up her mind, and she went looking for Johann Rial.

She found him in the church with his sleeves rolled up, diligently sweeping the stone floor that had become heavily tracked in this time of worry and sorrow.

"Will you take me into town?" she asked without prelude.

"Town? Why?"

"I'm going to Richmond—"

"You can't go to Richmond, Caroline. You can't travel alone—"

"Beata has so kindly pointed out that a woman of my ill repute needn't worry about that."

"You can*not* go to Richmond."

"Johann, I *am* going. I have Eli's money and I'm going. I have only asked you to take me into town. I have *not* asked for your permission."

"Caroline, you don't even know if Frederich—if any of them—is in Richmond—"

"I can't find out anything staying here—"

"I told you there are people checking the hospitals. Caroline, I was there after Sharpsburg. I know how difficult finding a particular soldier can be. It will take time—do you have any idea how big the Chimborazo Hospital is? There must be a hundred and fifty buildings in the hospital compound—and that's not counting all the men in the tent city on the heights. And there are other hospitals in the city besides. He may not even be in any of them. Sometimes a soldier is taken into a private home—or he may be a prisoner of war and halfway to some Northern prison, Caroline!"

"I know that. I know he may be dead. But what if he's there? What if he's so wounded that he can't say who he is? None of your 'people' know what he looks like—or what William looks like. Or Avery—I have to go myself. I may not find him any other way, Johann!" she said when he was about to interrupt. "I have to. If you won't take me to town, then I'll find somebody who will. Or I'll walk. Either way, I'm going."

"Caroline—"

"I'm going, Johann!"

He looked at her a long moment, then set the broom aside. "I suppose then—since Frederich Graeber is my friend and I have given him my word to keep his wife from harm—I will accompany you."

"No. I'm sure Eli's letter will have released you from that obligation—"

"You are mistaken, Caroline. You and Frederich both are *always* mistaken about each other, and truthfully, I am worn out with it. But—be that as it may. If you *will* go on this quest, then I will go with you—for Frederich's sake and for the rest of the people here who are waiting for some word. Day after tomorrow. It will take me that long to make arrangements. We will go to town then and try to catch a train to Richmond, and we will see what we shall see."

She waited until the next day to go to the Graeber house. After she had packed a change of clothes and what few medical supplies she could put together—a sheet to tear up for bandages and her needs, some dried plantain and catnip and camomile. She had honey—an especially important cure for wounds, according to the old Holt family book of herbs and remedies. But she was afraid the stone jar would get broken in transit, so she saturated strips of muslin with the honey and packed them in an oilcloth pouch. If worst came to worst, she supposed she could eat it. And now all she needed was the book itself. It must still be in the Graeber house in the armoire upstairs. And Beata or no Beata, there was nothing for her to do but to go and get it. She needed to tell the children, too, that she was going to look for their father.

Beata was nowhere to be seen when she arrived. Mary Louise and Lise were quietly playing with their dolls in the shade on the back porch. The day was so dusty and hot, but a breeze stirred the trees at the corner of the house from time to time.

"Beata's upstairs with another headache," Lise said when Caroline asked. "We have to be quiet." She looked up at Caroline and sighed. "I knew Papa would get shot," she said. "I knew it."

"Lise—"

The child shrugged and went back to tying a pink ribbon around her doll's waist. "Nothing you can do about it, I guess—just like Mama. Do you think he's dead?"

"I don't know," Caroline said truthfully. "That's why Reverend Rial and I are going to the hospital in Richmond to look for him. That's why I came here now—to tell you that we're going."

Lise looked up at her again, her face grave and resigned. "It won't do any good, Aunt Caroline."

"Won't do *any* good," Mary Louise echoed without taking her attention from her doll.

"We are still going to try our best," Caroline said. She sat down cross-legged on the porch beside them, and Mary Louise immediately climbed into her lap.

"Then can we go with you?" Lise asked.

"No, Lise. It's a hard trip and the war is in Virginia. Your papa would be very upset if he thought you and Mary Louise weren't safe here with Beata."

"I know a secret," Mary Louise said, squirming in her lap until she could whisper something in Caroline's ear. But Caroline couldn't understand for the giggling.

"What? Tell me again—no, tell me out loud."

"Lise's got a sweetheart!"

"I do not!" Lise cried.

"He's going to marry her in fifty-hundred years—"

"Ten years!" Lise cried, realizing immediately that she had given the "secret" away.

Caroline smiled and reached out to give Lise a hug, thinking that Ann should be here now. Here was Lise—deep in the throes of puppy love—and how Ann would have smiled.

"He's a soldier and his name is Toby, and he says he'll wait for me to grow up," Lise said shyly. "Do you think he will?"

"Well," Caroline said, trying not to let her own experience cloud her answer. "I think it's always best to judge a man by what he does—not what he says. I must go see Beata now," she said, lifting Mary Louise off her lap and getting to her feet. "Toby, did you say? Is he one of the foragers?"

Lise gave a crooked smile and nodded.

Toby, Caroline thought. *The one who took your father away.*

But she said nothing more, and when she was about to go into the house, Beata, somewhat disheveled-looking, appeared in the doorway.

"I need my mother's herb book—I'm going to Richmond," Caroline said, deciding immediately that, for once, Beata wasn't pretending to be indisposed. Her forehead was deeply creased and her eyes puffy and squinted as if they had become sensitive to daylight.

"You'll bring Avery home?" she asked immediately, her voice husky and very un-Beatalike. Once again Caroline marveled at Beata's flagrantly displaying her heart on her sleeve.

"I will if I can."

"If he's . . . dead, you will still do it?" she asked so quietly that Caroline barely heard her—neither of the children seemed to. Beata studiously avoided her eyes.

"If I can," Caroline said again. "He's my brother, for all our differences."

"Take the herb book," Beata said in a normal tone. "You may need it for . . ." She didn't say for whom. She stood aside to let Caroline pass instead, and under different circumstances Caroline might have taken exception to Beata's so graciously giving over what didn't belong to her in the first place.

But this was not the time. She had far too much to worry about to let Beata insult her.

The book wasn't in the upstairs armoire where she'd put it months ago. There was nothing in it now. She needed—wanted—the book, because she couldn't bear the thought of actually finding Frederich or any of the rest of them and not having some way to help them, however ineffective the home remedies the book contained might be. She came out into the hall and called over the banister.

"Beata, it isn't in the armoire where I left it."

Beata said something she didn't quite hear, and after a moment Lise came bounding up the stairs.

"I know where it is, Aunt Caroline—Beata had to use it when Mary Louise had the croup," Lise said, walking rapidly down the hall and into Beata's room. Caroline stood in the hallway, unwilling to have Beata come upstairs and find her trespassing. She could see the bed through the open door—Beata had been lying down from the looks of it, and there were letters scattered about on the quilt as if she had been reading them.

From Avery? she wondered. Had they come to some kind of "understanding" through an exchange of letters that would account for Beata's lack of discretion where her feelings for him were concerned?

No, she decided immediately. Avery had been too concerned about Leah's engagement to Kader to have pledged himself to Beata. And besides that, he would never pledge himself to anybody. She took a small breath and tried not to think about what condition he and the others might be in now.

In a moment, Lise brought out the herb book. Beata was busy in kitchen when they came down the steps. She eyed them closely—apparently to make certain the book was all that was taken—but she said nothing, and neither did Caroline.

"You'll come back, won't you, Aunt Caroline?" Lise said as they walked out on the porch. "Even if Papa and Uncle William and Uncle Avery don't?"

"I'll come back," she said, hugging her tightly for a moment and then Mary Louise. "Be good girls for Beata."

"We will—except sometimes I go and get Papa's fiddle," Lise said. "Beata says leave it alone, but sometimes when Mary Louise and I hold it and we try really hard, we can just about almost hear him play it. Is it all right if we just hold it, Aunt Caroline?"

"I don't think your papa would mind," she whispered to them. She stood for a moment, looking into their upturned faces, then she slipped from their grasp and hurried away, the book clutched tightly in her arms.

Chapter Twenty

She kept thinking about what William had written after Sharpsburg.

I don't have to worry no more about what hell is like, for I have seen it with my own two eyes....

She had thought that, intellectually at least, she was prepared to go into the Richmond hospitals. She had seen death before, but she had never seen it on such a scale as this. She had no point of reference, and the reality of these men's suffering was far beyond anything her uninitiated mind could ever have conceived. The sight and the smells of such mutilation was nearly unbearable, and the cries of fear and pain went on and on in every crowded barracks she entered.

She could hear them in her sleep at night.

Mama! Mama...!

But she kept looking.

I am ready for the storm. No one is going to give me the white feather, William, she promised as she waited for Johann to accompany her into yet another hospital ward. Three days of searching Chimborazo's one hundred and fifty buildings from dawn to dark had yielded nothing. She had located men from the North Carolina regiments, some of whom belonged to the Fifth, but none of them had been able to give her any information.

But she kept on looking—when she was already exhausted from the harrowing five-day train trip to get to Richmond. Johann had found her lodging of sorts with a middle-aged German clergyman and his huge family, but the house was terribly crowded and she didn't understand any of their rapid German enough to communicate. A constant object of curiosity for the children, she slept in her clothes in a curtained alcove in the wide upstairs hallway—or tried to. The street noise that never abated and the strangeness of the house and her profound worry kept her awake every night until just before time to get up again. She couldn't eat and her head ached all the time.

On the fourth morning, Johann came to the house early and was waiting for her to come downstairs.

"I want you to stay here today," he said.

"No, Johann—"

"Caroline, you are exhausted. I will continue the search. You must rest—sleep. You look terrible."

"I'll sleep later, Johann. When I know. I can't stop now. I can't . . ."

They both looked around as the clergyman came into the room. He nodded to her, but he spoke in German to Johann, giving him a folded piece of paper from his coat pocket. Johann read it quickly.

"It's from another colleague here in the city, Caroline. He says he has located an F. Graeber on the rolls at Winder."

"Winder?"

"It's another of the military hospitals—"

"Then we must go. Now."

"Caroline, don't get your hopes up," Johann warned her.

"Oh, please, Johann. Don't worry yourself about that. It's been a *long* time since I've been burdened by *hope*."

Camp Winder was not nearly as large as Chimborazo— but it was no less intimidating. They found the ward the note had indicated, but the Invalid Corps attendant, a young man with his left arm missing, stopped them from entering.

"I'm looking for Frederich Graeber," Caroline said, too upset to let Johann do the talking. "He's a North Carolina soldier—the Fifth Regiment. He's German. We got a message this morning saying he's here—in this ward."

"No," he said without looking up. "No Graeber. No Germans."

"But—"

"I'm telling you. There is no Graeber in this ward."

"*Was* he here?"

The man ignored the question.

"I want to look," she said, her voice trembling in spite of all she could do.

"It ain't no use looking—"

"Please!"

The man glanced at Johann, then shrugged his permission and stepped aside. But he was right. She and Johann peered into every face. None of the men here was Frederich.

"But he was on the roll for this ward," Caroline said to the attendant. "Could he have been moved to some other one?"

"There is only one place a man goes from here," the man answered.

She had already pursed her mouth to ask him where, but then she realized that he meant the cemetery that was clearly visible through the windows behind her. Several burials were going on even now. She stood there, struggling not to cry.

"Has he got any relatives here in the city or close by?" he asked after a moment. "Sometimes a man's family will come and take him out."

She shook her head. "I am his only relative here."

"Then I'm sorry, ma'am," he said, finally meeting her eyes. He had the same stunned look that Jacob Goodman always wore, and she wondered if all the men who had endured an amputation did as well. She tried not to think of what might have happened to Frederich and William.

"We will leave you the address of the place where Frau Graeber can be reached should you encounter her husband—Frederich Graeber," Johann said pointedly, looking at the man hard enough to quell the objection he clearly was about to make. The man reluctantly took the slip of paper Johann gave him.

"I don't think you ought to get your hopes up, ma'am."

The opinion of the hour, Caroline thought. "We will have to look in the other wards," she said.

"I'm trying to tell you as kindly as I can that it's likely a waste of time—"

"Then why was his name on the roll?"

He didn't answer her. She looked at him until his eyes slid away, and she let Johann lead her outside and make her sit down on a bench by the barracks entrance. There was no shade, and the sun bore down on her. She felt light-headed, and worse, defeated.

"We have to look in the other wards," she said again.

"You sit for a moment. I'm going to look over here."

He meant the cemetery, and for once, Caroline made no effort to participate. Her sleepless nights and her fatigue and the overwhelming July heat had suddenly caught up with her, and she sat and watched him move up and down the rows of rough-cut wooden markers, until finally he stopped. She realized immediately that he had found a name he knew.

She didn't wait for him to call her. She got up from the bench and walked rapidly to where he stood, clearly startling him with her sudden presence.

"Caroline—"

"Who is it?" she asked, trying to see around him. "Johann, who—?"

He stepped aside so she could see.

The breath left her in a soft "oh" sound.

"I'm so sorry, Caroline," he said as she dropped to her knees. He bent to help her, but she made no effort to stand.

"No," she whispered. "Oh, no, Johann—"

She reached out to the wooden marker, letting her fingers touch the name:

Pvt. William T. Holt

5th North Carolina Regiment

Company "K"

Pennsylvania Campaign

She hardly remembered the walk back to the clergyman's house. She was aware on some level that the sun was still hot and glaring and that the streets were crowded and she was jostled again and again as Johann moved her along. She didn't object when he insisted that she come with him. She didn't object to anything except William's death.

Little brother, she kept thinking. *Little brother—*

He's just a boy!

Oh, William, how can I bear to never see your face again?

She let herself be delivered into the capable hands of the clergyman's wife, oblivious to the German words that the woman and Johann exchanged. She drank the glass of amber liquid that was offered her, and she lay down on the little alcove bed as she was bidden to do. She even slept for a time, waking in the early dawn, not knowing where she was.

But then it all came rushing back to her, and she lay there, the tears quietly spilling down her cheeks until the sun came up.

Had Frederich been with William when he—when they both were wounded? Had William suffered? She needed to know these things and that was yet another reason she had to find Frederich.

The house was very quiet when she finally arose. She tried to maintain the quietness as she came downstairs to the kitchen, her sadness weighing so heavily upon her that she felt years older than she had just yesterday morning. Her hands shook. She was glad that there was no one about. She helped herself to a piece of corn bread that sat on the back of the kitchen stove and filled a tin cup with water from the bucket on the small table by the back door. She ate her meager fare because she needed it and not because she was hungry. She had to return to Winder today. There were still the other wards to search and the rest of the cemetery.

After a time she became aware of the murmur of voices—two people speaking in German somewhere. Johann? she wondered as she listened. She needed to talk to him and she got up to go find him.

The voices came from a room down the hallway and on the opposite side. She knocked quietly on the door, and there was a long moment before she was bidden to enter. When she opened the door, she saw the clergyman's plump wife—then her husband. The woman immediately stood up, and Caroline couldn't begin to follow whatever she was saying.

"Excuse me—I don't understand—"

"*Bitte,*" the woman insisted, taking Caroline into the hall. She grabbed Caroline's bonnet from the hall tree, then her own, then her husband's wide-brimmed straw "preacher's" hat.

Caroline put the bonnet on, because there seemed no way to do otherwise, and she let herself be rushed out the door, the clergyman taking one arm and his wife the other.

"*Beeilin Sie sich!*" the woman urged her as they hurried along the street.

"Oh, what's wrong?" Caroline said more to herself than to them.

They both answered her in a jumble of incomprehensible German.

Their destination was a small house on a back street several blocks away—too far away to be rushing so in this heat. She could only guess that something had gone wrong with the lodging arrangements and she was being relocated elsewhere—in which case she should have brought her valise—or something had gone wrong with Johann. What if he was ill or injured? she thought. He was so absentminded and the opportunity abounded at every turn to be run over by some kind of military wagon.

But he was not ill or injured. He stood waiting on the shaded front porch, and he came immediately down the steps to meet her.

"Caroline," he said. "I have found him, I have *found* him. He is here in this house—"

"Frederich?" she dared to ask.

"Yes, of course—didn't I say that? The family here—the mother is German and she has taken him in—arrangements were made—"

"Johann, I want to see him! Does he know I'm here?"

"I don't know—she says he isn't awake much of the time. You must prepare yourself, Caroline. I believe he is very badly hurt—"

"Johann—"

The clergyman's wife said something in German, and Johann put his hand on Caroline's shoulder.

"She says that you must forgive them for their haste in getting you here, Caroline," he said quietly, looking directly into her eyes to see if she truly understood.

She took a long, shaky breath, then nodded.

Before it was too late—as it had been with William.

He released her then, and she followed him up the steps and into the cool, dark hallway of the house. A young girl waited just inside, her hair in long braids that had been pinned on top of her head.

"My mother is done washing him," she said. "She says you can come up now."

"I will wait here," Johann said.

Caroline looked back at him once as she mounted the stairs. She meant to say thank-you, to tell him how much she appreciated his efforts, but she couldn't manage it. Her knees were trembling, her heart pounding.

He is very badly hurt....

The lady of the house waited at the top of the stairs with her arms full of bed linens.

"Your man knows you are coming," she said to Caroline in heavily accented English, and she caught the young girl's sleeve when she would have continued down the hall. "That door at the end—he is there."

"Thank you," Caroline said. "Thank you for all you've done."

"Nein," the woman said. "You don't thank me for my charity when there is none. I am a poor widow. I must make money however I can. I was paid for his care."

"Paid?"

"Go now," she said. "While he is awake. He is very tired. It is hard for him to wait for you—"

Caroline hesitated a moment, then walked quickly on. She took a deep breath before she pushed open the door the woman had indicated. The room was located on the corner and very small, but it had two windows, both of which had been opened to give cross ventilation. A maple tree shaded one of the windows, leaving a patch of mottled sunlight on the floor, the leaves rustling in a random breeze and scattering the sunlight from time to time.

There was nothing in the room but a rocking chair and a small table with an oil lamp, and a waist-high four-poster bed. She walked quietly forward, moving so she could see Frederich's face. His eyes were closed. He wore no nightshirt, and he was covered with a freshly ironed sheet, one heavily bandaged arm and leg exposed. And he had so many small wounds, scraped and nicked places on his face and hands and arms as if he had been dragged for a long distance. She could smell the wood ash scent of the strong soap he'd been bathed in, see that his hair was wet and neatly combed.

She stood by the bed, watching him closely, not knowing if she should disturb him. After a moment, she took off her bonnet and hung it by the ribbons on the back of the rocking chair. When she turned back to the bed, he was waiting.

"Frederich..." she whispered, leaning toward him, but he held up his uninjured hand.

His eyes searched hers for a moment, eyes that were fever-bright and full of pain. He licked his lips and attempted to speak. She leaned closer, intently aware of the monumental effort he was making.

He closed his eyes briefly, then tried again. "You are... not a widow... yet," he whispered.

"Don't!" she said, reaching out to touch him. He visibly winced, expecting her to cause him more pain. "I'm sorry," she said quickly, drawing her hand back. "Frederich—"

"What will you do... for me?" he asked.

She didn't understand, and she stared at him without answering.

"Tell me," he whispered. "What will... you do?"

"Anything," she said, hoping that was the answer he wanted and that she could oblige him.

"Then get me... out of here."

She hesitated. She had heard him perfectly, but in these past few days she had learned only too well how precious a decent bed for a wounded soldier could be.

"When you're able—" she qualified.

"No! Now! You take me—out of here. I won't abide his charity—"

"Frederich, I don't understand. Whose—?"

"I can't bear it! Get me out, Caroline. Get me home. I want to see my—children before I die—"

"Frederich—"

He reached out to grab her arm. She could feel his fever through her sleeve. "Will you—honor—none of your marriage—vows then?"

I don't deserve that! she almost said. But perhaps she did. She had locked her door against him. She had never obeyed him. And she had only come to him now because she feared he was dead.

"Frederich, you aren't able to travel—"

"No? You should have—seen me when I got here. I am going to die anyway, Caroline—"

"No," she said. "You aren't going to die." She stepped closer so that she could look into his eyes. "You aren't going to die—but if you are determined to get home, I will help you."

"You—swear it?"

"Yes."

"Say it—"

"I swear. I will do everything I can to get you home."

She took his hand, and he relaxed visibly, his eyes closing as he gave a long sigh. She stood there for a long while— until she was certain that he slept. Then and only then did she finally let go.

Chapter Twenty-One

Is she crying?

Frederich couldn't tell in the darkness. She was sitting by the open window. He could see her profile every time the lightning flashed. He could hear the rain falling steadily on the windowsill.

He had awakened abruptly at the storm's height, thinking he was back at Gettysburg and hearing the heavy guns.

Oh, the guns!

There had been a time in his life when he had come to love a summer storm, and by that he had known that his conversion from a disgraced German *Soldat* to a North Carolina farmer had been complete. But would he ever hear the sound of thunder again and not remember the fighting at Gettysburg?

He drew a deep breath.

Yes, she was crying.

Don't, damn it! Don't!

It made him angry that she cried. It made him angry that she hid it from him. If she would just do as he asked and get him away from here! He stirred restlessly and the movement made him moan. She was immediately by his side, ever mindful of his needs. But she asked him no questions. He hated questions; she had learned that the first day. She wiped his face with a cool wet cloth without his leave. He was burning up—it felt wonderful.

I can't remember, he thought, knowing all the while that it was more that he wouldn't. He recalled the wide, open field—the blazing hot sun—men throwing off their piecemeal jackets and rolling up their shirtsleeves—the wild artillerymen with no shirts at all. That terrible sense of urgency—trying to get the cartridge boxes distributed—trying to find water to fill the canteens. Hurry! Hurry!

William taking his shoes off.

Get those shoes back on, boy!

Aw, Frederich—the damn things hurt!

Get them on! If we have to run back across this field, there will be too many things you won't *want to step in.*

Avery and Kader Gerhardt at it again—Avery pelting the pompous schoolmaster in the back of the head with a green apple just for the fun of it.

And all the while, he, Frederich, doing his duty, forcing himself not to think about *her.* He had been certain that he would die. *What if I never see you again!*

But he hadn't died. He was here, hanging on, and William, that gentle, laughing boy, was in his grave. Did Caroline know?

I don't want to tell her. I had to tell her about the child—I can't tell her about William, too. Oh, God, I hurt so!

There was never any respite from the pain. Even his eyes hurt—no, the sun was up.

Too bright in here—what happened to the night? What happened to the storm?

"Drink this, Frederich," someone said—Caroline?

"Why are we still here?" he muttered, turning his head away. "I want to be gone from this place—"

"Drink," she said again, catching him so he couldn't turn his head away. "I know it tastes bad, but it will help the pain—"

"No—"

"Yes," she countered, always herself no matter what. She forced the liquid into his mouth, overwhelming him with it so that he had to swallow or choke.

"Again," she said.

"No—"

"Yes."

"Leave me—alone—"

"Drink it!"

He drank deeply. It was the only way to get rid of her. But when she moved away from the bed, he immediately found that he didn't want to be rid of her after all.

"Caroline—!"

"I'm here, Frederich."

"Caroline—why? Tell—me—"

"I don't know what you're asking me, Frederich."

"*Why?*"

"Shhh," she soothed him, wiping his face again with the cool cloth.

"Where are my children?" he asked abruptly. "Where are Lise and Mary Louise?"

"At home, Frederich. With Beata."

"I want to see them—"

"I know. You will see them. As soon as I can find us a way to get there."

"No doctors, you understand that? No—doctors—"

"Frederich—"

"Promise me. I will keep my arm and my leg or—I will—die. Promise me!"

"Yes, all right. I promise you—sleep now. Sleep—"

The guns!
No. No, it's thunder. A storm—I remember—
Caroline by the window—is she there?
He turned his head. There was no window.
Where am I? What is this place? The storm—it must be still the same storm—or is it another one?

"Are you here?" he asked abruptly, startling himself with the sound of his own voice.

"I'm here, Frederich," she said immediately from somewhere he couldn't see.

"What is this place?"

"It's an empty warehouse. It's where we have to wait until the train comes."

"Is it night? I can't see you."

"Yes."

"Then why aren't you—sleeping?"

"Because Trudy says the thunder makes you have nightmares and I thought you might wake and not know where you were."

"Trudy?"

"The woman who was taking care of you."

Yes, he thought. He remembered Trudy. A soft woman with big breasts. She spoke to him in his own language—the kind of woman he might have wanted if he hadn't been so besotted with Caroline Holt, the kind of woman who would take money from Eli to let him stay in her house.

"Stop crying," he said.

"I'm not crying."

"I—heard you—when the rain was coming down. You thought I couldn't hear—"

"That was before—when we were still in Trudy's house—several nights—a week ago, not now."

"Caroline, I want to know why you are crying."

"I'm not—"

"I can hear you—"

"William is dead, Frederich! He's dead—"

The memory suddenly rained down upon him—all disconnected—in bits and pieces. But he remembered.

Oh, God!

Lying on the ground—the hot July sun beating down on him, his eyes, his mouth full of dirt. Blood—everywhere. He couldn't move his arm and leg. Men—*things*—lying on

top of him. A canteen—close—close—he couldn't reach it
no matter how hard he tried. He was so thirsty! His eyes
burning and burning. His face scraped and burning. He
could hear the wind high in the trees at the edge of the field.
There was shade there—a cool breeze and shade—

It hurts—who is that moaning so?

William? Caroline, I'm sorry!

So thirsty…

The pain!

I hurt so bad!

Dead and dying. Dead and dying everywhere!

Caroline!

Someone turning him over, making him scream in pain.

*Who are you? Where is William! Don't leave the boy
here! No! Don't leave the boy here!*

Someone speaking to him in German, dragging him up
off the ground.

*He is too far gone, Frederich. We have to hurry—their
soldiers are coming—*

Then leave us both, damn you!

The jarring farm wagon. William crying and crying in the
rain.

Geben Sie ihm etwas! Give him something! But there was
nothing anyone could give him.

Don't cry, William. Please—please!

Who is there? Who—?

Hands lifting him, giving him food and drink, binding up
his wounds, covering him against the rain.

Why have you come? I want nothing from you!

*It doesn't matter what you want, Frederich. I will do my
penance for Anna—*

He lay in the dark for a long time. He realized now that
they were not alone. He could hear the stirrings of other
soldiers around him, wounded men who moaned in pain—
or was it *he* who did so?

"Caroline—"

"What?" she answered immediately.

When he didn't say anything else, she came closer to him.

He stared up at her, trying to see her face in the darkness and thanking God that she could see his. "He ... didn't suffer, Caroline. William didn't suffer."

She made a small sound and bowed her head. He reached out with his good hand to pull her forward until she had to kneel down beside him. She turned her face away from him, but he kept pulling. He could feel her trembling.

"Come here," he said.

"No. No—there are people here—"

"Come—Caroline—"

"I—am supposed to—take care of you—"

"Caroline, come here."

She abruptly capitulated and rested her head on the edge of the stretcher, careful not to touch him, her face still turned away. He couldn't get his arm around her, couldn't touch her except in an awkward, backhanded way.

"He didn't suffer, Caroline," he said again, brushing her soft hair with the backs of his fingers, praying she would just accept what he said and not ask any questions.

"I can't bear—leaving him in that—desolate—place," she said in a voice full of tears.

"He is with his comrades, Caroline," he whispered to her. "Your William will not mind being there with them. After the Sharpsburg battle—he gave me the money—for his *Leichenbier,* he said. He wanted all the men in 'K' Company to gather and drink to him if he was killed in battle. He would be there, he said—with bells on. He was a good and brave soldier—a joy to us who fought alongside him. I will miss him all the rest of my life...."

She suddenly turned to him, pressing her face against his shoulder.

How long they stayed like that, he didn't know. He woke with the sun shining and her gone. He kept turning his head, trying to look for her—listening for her voice. She had apparently left him on his own with no one around to even bring him a drink of water or a chamber pot. Other men lay on their stretchers around him, abandoned as well, only none of them seemed as concerned about it as he.

He was hot and sweaty and miserable when Caroline finally returned. She came bearing gifts—bread and soup to eat and some hot water and soap. He suffered her ministrations in a surly kind of silence—which she implicitly ignored. She bathed him as best she could. She changed the honey-soaked bandages she insisted cover the wounds on his arm and thigh. He was perfectly aware that his short temper had forced her into this dearth of conversation, but he resented her not making an attempt to talk to him all the same.

He waited until she was done before he asked.

"Why did you come back?"

"What?"

"Why did you come back?" he said again.

She turned and looked at him, and incredibly he could feel his eyes begin to well and his control slipping away from him.

"Why are you here, Caroline?" he demanded in spite of the tears he couldn't subdue. "I'm not—strong anymore. Can't you see that? I'm not—strong—*anymore!*"

"No," she said quietly. "But your eyes are still blue."

The fever came again, trapping him in some hellish place where his enemies and his dead comrades pursued him without mercy. Even so, he knew that Caroline was with him sometimes—and Johann.

No. Johann was not here. Johann had stayed in Richmond. Caroline was here with him—on the train.

When he finally woke and knew that for certain, it was raining again, a quiet steady rain that drummed against the stopped railway car and rolled down the dirty windowpanes. All the seats in the car had been ripped out to make room for the stretchers. Caroline sat on a straw valise near his head.

"Where are we?" he asked her, and her startled look gave him a clear indication of just how long it had been since he'd said anything that sensible.

"Virginia still," she said, watching him closely. "Somewhere."

"What's wrong? Did you—think I was going to—die?"

"Yes," she said.

"I didn't—so don't—stare at me."

"I'm not staring. I was only...thinking."

"About what?"

"About Lise. About something she said I should do—something I should say to you."

"What?"

"I—it's—not important."

He moved his head so that he could see her better. For the first time in a very long while, it didn't pound in protest. "Maybe you had better—say it anyway—before it's—too late."

"I don't think it—"

"Tell me, for God's sake!"

"Very well. She said I should tell you that I... like you. She said she didn't think you knew."

He frowned.

"I... like you, too," he said cautiously, because he must truly have been at death's door to bring about such a revelation.

She looked at him a long moment, and then, incredibly and in spite of their present situation, she laughed, that beautiful lilting laugh he had missed for so long.

"You'd think *one* of us would be happy about it," she said.

* * *

Eventually, the train jolted forward, and the pain that had only been relentless, now became excruciating. He tried to put his mind on something else.

"Do you know how the—courtship is done—in Germany?" he asked her abruptly. She sat close by, alternating fanning him and the nearest soldier with a palmetto fan, ever alert in case either of them wanted a piece of bread or a drink of water.

"How would I know that?" she asked somewhat cautiously.

"Perhaps—Lise told you," he suggested.

"She didn't. Neither did Avery," she added significantly.

He chose to ignore her allusion to their own marital arrangements.

"First, there is the—consent," he said, struggling to keep his mind firmly on the topic and not the fiery pain.

"Her consent?"

"No, the parents. Her father. A *Degensmann* comes— asking the father—if his daughter will agree to a marriage."

"To the...*Degensmann?*"

"No—no. *Degensmann* means swordsman—because such a person once carried a sword on this kind of—mission. He doesn't ask for himself. He asks for the—man he represents—and if *that* man is very brave, he will go along with the *Degensmann* and he will stand at his side with a bouquet of flowers—for his bride-to-be. And always he is hoping he doesn't get a basket with no bottom."

"Frederich, is this you talking or the fever?"

"I am trying to tell you something about—my country, Caroline," he answered impatiently, because he was losing the struggle to subdue the pain.

"Ah. Then do proceed."

"I think you are not—interested."

"Well, you think wrong. Tell me. Please," she added when he didn't immediately continue.

"There are symbols—so no one has to *hear* their feelings being—hurt, you see?"

"I... think so. The bottomless basket is a 'no.'"

"Yes."

"It's a 'yes'?"

"Yes, it is a no!"

"All right! And then what?" she asked him.

"Then there are the—gifts."

"For her?"

"Yes, for her—who else would get gifts?"

"I don't know, Frederich, that's why I asked. Go on."

"In olden times it would be—a yoke of oxen, and a horse—with bells and ornaments all over the cloth skirt thing that covers the knight's horse—I don't know the word in English—and a shield and lance and spear."

"Why?"

"For their life together—for the wars and for the peace."

"If there is any."

"Yes. But now the man gives his intended gloves—engagement gloves. Then the wedding is on a Friday—"

"Always?"

"Or a Sunday—or Tuesday. Maybe a Thursday. Sometimes on Saturday..."

She was smiling.

"At noon," he told her.

"Or one o'clock?" she suggested.

"No. Never—never at one o'clock. If it is one o'clock, somebody sets—all the clock hands back to—noon."

"Of course," she said agreeably.

"But first the *Hochzeitslader* goes—door to door and invites everyone to the wedding—"

"Does he carry a sword, too?"

"No, he wears a big—hat with flowers and tall boots. He carries—a—long—a—long—stick...."

The intense pain in his leg and arm suddenly overwhelmed him and he turned his face away. He bit down hard to keep from crying aloud, but he couldn't keep from writhing in a vain attempt to escape. He could taste the blood on his lower lip.

"I'm sorry, Frederich," Caroline said, her face close. "There is nothing—no laudanum to be had. If the train stops long enough, I'll try to find some willow bark—"

"You promised—me—"

"I *will* get you home," she whispered.

She put her hand in his, and he clutched it hard.

Don't let me die, Caroline! Don't let me die!

"Johann and I—we couldn't find Avery," she said after a very long period of silence.

"You don't—worry about Avery," he said. "If he isn't—dead or in prison, he will be—somewhere with a woman—waiting on him."

"Sort of...like you?" she suggested, and in spite of the pain, he smiled.

But he didn't want to smile, and he began to take great pains to guard against it. He hurt too much, and he remembered all too well that she didn't want him or the marriage. For whatever reason, she had done as he asked and gotten him away from Eli's charity. He still desperately needed her help, but he could imagine himself severing all ties between them once and for all. It would be easy. He could do it with one small question:

When will you go to Eli?

The question sat there in his mind all the time—like some wild beast straining to be unloosed. And why not? When terrible things happened to him—when Anna died and when he was wounded—Eli was there in the midst of it. In his more lucid moments, he thought that word of the battle must have reached the Pennsylvania relatives, and then Eli must have taken it upon himself to come to Gettysburg to look for him. Eli had dragged him in the pouring rain all the way back to Virginia. He was alive because of Eli.

And he hated it.

Better to be dead than indebted to Eli! he thought wildly.

But it wasn't so. He was alive. Caroline was here. Perhaps he would even see his children.

"Where are we?" he abruptly asked.

"I don't know," Caroline said.

He could see how tired she was—exhausted—but he chose to be displeased anyway.

"Can you not *ask?*"

"Yes, I can *ask,*" she said. "But I think I'll be too busy throwing *you* off the train!"

There was a ripple of laughter from the stretchers around him, and after a moment, he himself smiled—in spite of his resolve.

He looked into her eyes until she smiled with him.

My Caroline, he thought. *My wife.*

Chapter Twenty-Two

"Frederich? Frederich! He can't hear me—!"

"Now, now—you don't fret. He is all right."

"But—"

"You don't worry yourself, Caroline. Come, Frederich!" John Steigermann said loudly, lifting him out of the back of the wagon. "Get the door, Caroline," he said, and she ran ahead of him to do as he asked.

"Why aren't Beata and the children here?" she said over her shoulder.

"They go to the church for prayers on Wednesday evenings. These are sad times. Everyone is there. We were very sorry to know about William."

Frederich moaned as John Steigermann jarred him up the steps.

"You think an old man like me cannot carry you?" he asked loudly, and whatever Frederich replied made Mr. Steigermann laugh.

"You see, Caroline? I tell you he is good and he is!"

"What did he say?" she asked, drawing an immediate protest from Frederich.

"He says you are not to know that, Caroline. Your ears are too delicate for such things."

"I am Avery Holt's sister. How could my ears be delicate?'' she answered, feeling hopeful suddenly. Perhaps everything would be all right after all.

She led the way up the stairs, hurrying down the hallway to open the door to the room where Frederich had always slept. The place was hot and stuffy, and she threw up the windows to let in some fresh air. The bed had been made. Thanks to Johann's telegram, Beata had known Frederich was coming, just as John Steigermann had. Caroline still couldn't believe Mr. Steigermann had been waiting for them at the train station—that he had gone to town a day early to make sure he didn't miss their arrival. When she stepped off the crowded train to search for someone to help her move Frederich, she had all but wailed like a lost-child-found at the very sight of him, her aging knight-in-shining-armor— again.

She could hear voices downstairs suddenly—a lot of voices.

"Go and see," John Steigermann said. "I will get Frederich settled. She did well, did she not, Frederich? To get you home."

She didn't wait to hear Frederich's answer, though some part of her would have dearly loved to hear just a small measure of praise and gratitude from him. She was exhausted—both of them were. It had been so long since she'd slept lying down or slept at all, for that matter.

She braced herself before she went down the steps. She hadn't forgotten that she was a pariah still, and that the women whose voices she could hear would not receive her kindly. Frederich was in good hands now. It was all she could do not to take the back stairs and flee them all.

But she could hear Mary Louise's voice—and Lise's. It was only that that kept her from bolting. She moved quickly down the steps. The noisy kitchen—full of women with offerings of food—fell silent the moment she appeared. She saw Beata first. Beata had a firm grip on Lise and Mary

Louise both, but her face was filled with worry for a change instead of her usual righteous indignation.

"I couldn't find Avery, Beata," Caroline said immediately. "He wasn't in any of the hospitals." She didn't know what else to say.

"Did you even look?" Beata said.

"Of course, I looked! Johann is still there—looking."

"Caroline!" Leah cried in a blatant attempt to intercede. She stepped forward and hugged Caroline hard. "We've had word of Kader," she said brightly. "He's been captured and sent north—to New York, they say. I believe he'll be all right there."

Caroline forced a smile. Of course he would be all right— because Leah Steigermann wanted it.

More and more of the women came forward.

"My boy, Conrad, Caroline? Did you see him—?"

"My brother, Caroline—"

"And mine—"

The room was a blur of faces suddenly; she had to bite her lip so as not to cry.

"No, I'm sorry," she said, her voice husky and strange sounding. "There was only Frederich. And William—"

She abruptly turned her attention to her nieces.

"Did you bring Papa?" Lise asked anxiously, trying to pull free of Beata's hold. "Did you?"

Mary Louise stood with her finger in her mouth, forgoing for once her usual role as the echo.

"Yes, my loves. He's upstairs—wait!" she said, grabbing both their dresses to keep them from breaking free of Beata and rushing off to see him. "Mr. Steigermann is with your papa now and he will say when you can come up." She ignored Beata and put her arms around them both. "Your papa has been hurt—in his arm and in his leg. So you can't jump on him or anything like that—"

"Can he play his fiddle?" Lise asked.

"No, Lise, he can't."

"That's all right. I can still have my birthday table without it."

"Yes, you can," Caroline said, looking past them because John Steigermann was standing at the top of the stairs. When he nodded, she sent them on, but, subdued now, they walked hand in hand slowly up the stairs.

"Caroline," Mr. Steigermann said, motioning for her to come, too. "Frederich worries when you are not near."

She frowned a bit, not knowing whether the remark was for her benefit or for the onlookers. But she went. For days now, her every waking moment had been filled with nothing but Frederich; she couldn't ignore him, even if she'd wanted to.

"I have a hurt and hungry man upstairs," Mr. Steigermann said to the women. "You will put together the dinner for him, yes? We will pray for him and then we will feed him and then we will let him rest."

Caroline followed Mr. Steigermann and the girls, but she stood well back to let Frederich have his reunion with his children alone. He spoke to them in German, loving, gentle words that made them bashful and made them laugh. When she finally stepped into the room, she could see that his pain was intense, and she took them in hand immediately, sending them downstairs to help fetch his supper.

"Are you all right?" she asked.

"Are—you?" he countered.

It was on the tip of her tongue to say of course, but it would have been a lie. Her encounter downstairs had taken more out of her than she would have anticipated. She felt so weak suddenly. She needed to do a hundred things—none of which she could bring to mind. She crossed her arms over her breasts as if she were cold. Indeed, she was shivering, in spite of the summer heat. She was so tired! She could feel her body sway, and she tried desperately to catch on to something.

"John!" Frederich called loudly, his voice penetrating the roaring in her ears, and the old man was there, catching her just as she would have hit the floor.

"Where to take her?" Mr. Steigermann said from somewhere very far off. She felt him lift her off her feet, and it was suddenly that other time, when Avery had realized she was illicitly pregnant.

William crying—

No, William is dead.

I'm all right. I can stand, she thought she said, but clearly she had not, because no one seemed to have heard her.

"Here—put her here by me," Frederich said. "She's shaking all over—there are quilts—in that chest."

"Be still, man," John Steigermann said. "You will open your wounds. I will take care of her."

She could hear them perfectly now—no roaring—and she tried to protest. She was quite fine—really. She just couldn't stop trembling.

She could feel herself being covered by a cedar-scented quilt and a hand stroking her face.

"Caroline—" Frederich's voice said very close.

"So... tired," she murmured.

"I know," he whispered. "Find her some—brandy, John. She's exhausted—I have seen soldiers in battle too long—shake like this."

"You are not far from that yourself, Frederich. I will bring Leah to put her to bed."

"No, I want her to—stay here. I want her to sleep—as long as she needs to. I don't want her where I can't hear—what Beata—will say to her."

"Yes," Steigermann said. "That is good. I will get the brandy. And I will get enough for you, too."

She tried to sit up, but she couldn't manage it. It felt so good to just lie there. And if she drank the brandy Frederich sent for, she didn't remember it. She only remembered

voices from far off—Lise and Mary Louise, Leah Steigermann, and yet another of Beata's eloquent sniffs.

Voices, she thought sleepily. *And birdsong.*

The sun was shining. The breakfast was cooking. A warm
body lay all along hers. Because she had shared a bed with
another human being only once in her adult life, she came
awake and upright at the same moment.

It was the same human being.

"*Mein Gott,* Caroline! You scared me half to death!"

"What are you doing here?"

"I am wounded," he reminded her, sinking back on the
pillows. "It is *my* bed—"

She licked her lips and stared at him. "Have I—hurt
you?"

"Yes," he said pointedly.

"I'm sorry," she whispered, sliding her feet to the floor.
"How long have I—"

"A *long* time," he assured her.

"I'm sorry," she said again.

"It's all right for you to be here, Caroline. We said the
words to the marriage ceremony—if little else."

Their eyes met, and she immediately looked elsewhere.

"Where are you going?" he asked when she turned away
and began looking for her shoes.

"I'm going home," she said. "Nothing has changed,
Frederich. I *have* done what you asked of me. I have
brought you back here. I'll come later to help Beata—if
she'll let me—but I told you before. I can't live here."

"Even if I—?"

She waited for him to go on, but he didn't. He looked at
her with a sadness she could hardly bear.

"Even if I—asked?" he said finally, and she shook her
head.

"I can't," she said, and she sounded determined, even to herself. But she couldn't keep from giving him one last look as she went out the door.

Nothing has changed.

Frederich in his helplessness wondered if she really believed that.

She kept her word on both accounts. She came back to help Beata as she said she would—every day—and she would not live in his house. She took great care of him; even the worst of her critics—Beata herself—could not find fault with that. He tried not to miss her when she was gone. He tried not to worry about her staying at the Holt place alone. He tried to grow stronger, to enjoy his children, to forget about Eli—but there were times when it was all he could do not to make a fool of himself and beg for what he wanted.

Stay with me, Caroline.

The truth of the matter was that he couldn't bear to have her out of his sight—and yet he did everything he could to drive her away. He lay now with his eyes closed as she bathed him, waiting for her to cause him pain so that he could complain.

But she was always gentle.

So...gentle...

"Where were you all those months?" she asked him. Her hands moved over him, soaping his body, his unwounded arm and hand, his shoulders and chest and belly. Her lingering touch was a long-desired thing he had never expected to know again, and he gave himself up to the memory. The cold attic room. The crackling of the cedar fire. And her hands moving over him.

"What—months?" he forced himself to ask.

"When the army took you away—and we couldn't find where you'd been taken."

"I was in Richmond. The prison—Castle Thunder. They were going to make an example of me," he said, his eyes still closed. "My commanding officer came and ordered me back to the regiment. He was very angry. He told them to make an example out of somebody who didn't know how to sergeant."

"You . . . never sent word."

"No," he said. "I never did."

"Frederich—"

"You say my name wrong, did you know that?" he asked with his eyes still closed—because he still needed to find fault. "'Frederich.'"

"Do you want me to say it the German way?"

"No. The German way is dying here. I will be like *John* Steigermann. He changes the *Hans*. I will change the *Frie-drich.*'"

She leaned across him to dry his shoulder; he opened his eyes. Their faces were inches apart, but she was too intent upon her task to notice. He wanted to kiss her mouth. Now. Perhaps she would even stand still and let him do it.

As she straightened, their eyes met.

"Do you think about us at all?" he asked quietly, because truly he felt that if he said such a thing too loud she would run from him. "Do you think about what it was like with us? Or do you only think about him—?"

"Oh, don't!" Caroline said, her eyes locked with his. "I can't bear it! If you say anything to me about Eli, I will go out of this house and I won't come back."

He believed her. He had already guessed as much—that any insinuation about her and Eli on his part would be unforgivable, regardless of how guilty she might be. All he had to do was make the unsubtle remark, ask the accusatory question, and she would be gone. She would endure everything else about him—his bad temper and his fevers and his wounds—but not that.

"I don't know why you are here at all!" he said.

"It doesn't matter."

"It matters to me!"

"All right! You took care of me when I was so ill—when it was of no importance to me if I lived or died. I am repaying that charity—"

"I never held that up to you!"

"No. But I feel obligated anyway. Just as I feel obligated to do penance for Ann."

He stared at her.

Penance for Ann.

He had heard that before.

Penance for . . . Anna . . .

She tried to move away from him, but he held on to her, his eyes searching hers. "Is that all there is between us? Debts to be paid? Is it? Is it?"

She suddenly bowed her head.

"Caroline," he whispered, straining upward so that he could get closer to her. She held herself rigid, unyielding. "Caroline—"

Their faces touched, and she made a soft, yielding sound, clinging to him for a moment before she pushed herself away.

She slipped from his grasp and stumbled toward the door.

"Caroline, I want to know what is between you and Eli!"

"There is nothing! How many times do I have to tell you? I see how much you want to forgive me. I know all I have to do is ask. But it's Ann who needs it. I will *not* be forgiven for something I haven't done!"

Chapter Twenty-Three

Nothing has changed. I will never understand these people!

But she did understand. She understood how proud Frederich was. She understood that, because of Ann, he believed the worst of her, even after she'd dragged him more dead than alive all the way back from Richmond. She understood that on some level he needed her, was grateful to her, regardless of the fact that he'd left it unsaid.

But she was proud as well, and she couldn't change that any more than he could. She had but one recourse—to stay away from him—for both their sakes—as he himself had once told her to do. She would take things to the house for him—what food she could spare, honey for his wounds, but she wouldn't sit in constant attendance. Beata or one of the other German women could do that for him. And she would see the children until he forbade it.

She heard a horse and buggy approaching, and she stepped outside, relieved that the army wasn't foraging again. She recognized the somber black clerical garb immediately. She had heard from Leah Steigermann that Johann had at last returned and that he hadn't found Avery or any of the others. She was glad to see him, even if he was likely here to chastise her for her abandoning her husband. She walked out into the yard to meet him.

He got down from the buggy and took off his hat and began to fan himself vigorously. "Weather's abominably hot today," he said as if it hadn't been weeks since they'd last talked—as if he weren't here for a purpose.

"Is there any news about Avery?" she asked immediately, even if that was not the foremost thing on her mind.

"No. Nor any of the others. My friends in Richmond will continue to look—so we mustn't give up hope."

"You have been to see Frederich today?" she said, asking what she really wanted to know.

"Yes," he said.

"How is he?"

"He's...the same," he said, and she earnestly believed it. Frederich never changed. Well or wounded, he still thought she had betrayed him.

'You know that I've come to talk," he said, sitting down on the edge of the porch.

"There is nothing to talk about—"

"Please!" he said, holding up his hand. "I am hot. I am tired. And I want you to start at the beginning."

"There is no 'beginning.' Why don't you go and ask Frederich if you want revelations?"

"I did. It didn't do any good. He is no more forthcoming than you are. If I am to give my counsel—"

"Johann, I haven't asked for your counsel."

"Well, I intend to give it. I have to. It's what I *do.*"

She paced around the yard for a moment, then turned over a pebble with the toe of her shoe. "Frederich asked me about Eli," she said abruptly. She glanced at him, but for once his face told her nothing.

"Did you expect that he would not? You are his wife. It's a matter of his pride—a personal attribute you know well, if you will pardon my bluntness. And he's not a saint."

"He did it after I told him to do so...would drive me from his house."

"And?"

"And . . ." She gave an offhand shrug "I'm . . . here."

"Which accomplishes nothing—except your mutual misery, as far as I can see. You think he asked the question unjustly, then."

"Yes," she said evenly.

"He thinks he has the right to know."

"There is nothing to know! He can ask all he wants!"

"There *is* the money Eli sent you," he reminded her.

She sighed.

"Does Frederich know you used it to bring him home?"

"No," she said.

"It's just as well. He wouldn't be happy to find out he's even more indebted to Eli than he realized."

"What do you mean?"

"I mean that Eli is the one who carried him from the battlefield and then stole a wagon to get him to Richmond—he brought Frederich and William both, and he was paying the German woman for Frederich's care. That is the reason Frederich was so desperate to be away from there."

"How do you know that?"

"Eli told me."

"Eli—?"

"He's here, Caroline. He came back yesterday. He came to make sure Frederich had survived the journey. And to work the land until Frederich can do it. He did make a promise to Ann, and he is determined to keep it."

"Frederich must be—"

"Exactly," Johann said.

She pushed the pebble around with her shoe again.

"Eli wants to talk to you, Caroline," he said, and she looked at him.

"I want to talk to him," she said quietly.

"When?"

"Now. Before he disappears again."

"You'll come back to the house with me?"

"Yes," she said, understanding now the purpose of this visit. "I just wish..." She abruptly stopped and looked off in the direction of the Graeber place. But she couldn't see anything of the house in full summer with the leaves on the trees.

"What? What do you wish?"

She looked at him. "I wish that, just once, Frederich had seen *me*."

"He sees you, Caroline."

"Then why don't I feel it? Why can't I tell that I matter to him? I don't know what to do, Johann. I just know I can't live in Ann's shadow."

"Caroline, Caroline," Johann said with a sigh. "You and Frederich both keep backing yourselves into corners without the slightest idea how to get out—when it's perfectly obvious to me."

"Is it?" she said, very close to becoming annoyed.

"Of course, it is. The past cannot be changed. It cannot be forgotten. But it can be forgiven. One forgives and one moves on. You see?"

"No," she said, and he smiled.

"I am not the one who needs to be forgiven, Johann. I am not Ann."

"Yes, well," he said. "I suppose it's all up to Frederich then, isn't it?"

"Does he know you came for me?"

"He knows."

She sighed again. "Then I believe we had best be on our way."

Frederich sat propped up in bed, straining to hear the voices downstairs—Johann and the children, and a lengthy protest of some kind from Beata.

Had Caroline come?

He couldn't hear her or Eli—but she must have come or Beata wouldn't be arguing about leaving the house with the children. He lay there looking at the ceiling, unsettled and helpless. The room was hot. His wounds throbbed and burned.

Caroline.

How could he feel so many things for one person? She infuriated him more times than not, and yet he had trusted her with his life and he had not been disappointed. He was about to do the same again, but this time he had no hope. None.

He looked around sharply at the sound of footsteps, and he thought for a moment that she had come to him. But it was Leah Steigermann.

"Good afternoon, Frederich," she said with the considerable charm she had at her disposal.

He didn't answer her. She was not deterred.

"I've come to keep you occupied for a time—Johann seems to think you need company."

"I don't."

"That is what I told him, but you know Johann. He says you want to behave well while Caroline and Eli have their tête-à-tête—but you might not unless someone helps you." She brought a bottle of his own plum brandy out from behind her skirts. *"This,"* she said, "was my idea. Now. In answer to your questions—"

"I haven't asked any—"

"In answer to your questions," she interrupted pointedly. "Yes, Caroline has come to talk with Eli. Yes, both she and Eli are downstairs now—she is sitting at the kitchen table—he is pacing. He apparently has things he wants to say to her, but no, he hasn't said what they might be. And whatever they are, Johann is on hand to translate so there will be no misunderstanding. Does that about cover it?"

"Yes," he said, reaching for the bottle. He was reasonably certain that Leah knew about Ann and Eli, and she had been kind to Caroline. He supposed that if he must be plagued by a keeper, it might as well be she. "I only have the one cup," he said.

"None for me. It won't do for both of us to get tipsy."

"You shouldn't be up here at all."

"Why?"

"It doesn't look—"

"No, it doesn't, does it? But if my father, the Reverend Rial *and* your wife have no objections, who am I to argue? Shall I pour that or can you do it one-handed?"

It was on the tip of his tongue to ask what her fiancé might think about her being here, but he didn't. And he didn't intend to pour. He drank the brandy straight from the bottle.

He turned his head sharply at the sound of someone—Eli—talking.

"So," Leah said. "It begins."

He took another drink. It came to him suddenly that he was afraid. He was as afraid as he had ever been before a battle—perhaps more so, because there was nothing he could do. Nothing.

He stirred restlessly. He could hear Johann now, and a softer murmur that must be Caroline.

"Shall I read to you?" Leah asked.

"No—" he said impatiently, still trying to hear. "What does he want?" he said, more to himself than to her.

"He wants to make things right," Leah said.

"It's too late for that."

"He is very...changed."

"So are we all—particularly Anna."

He glanced at her. She was looking at him thoughtfully.

"Say it," he said. "And be done with it."

"All right. Caroline told me once that you had no affection, no regard, for Ann. If she felt that—as an outsider—then how must Ann herself have felt? Perhaps she even said as much to Caroline—I don't know. But you must understand this small thing about us women. We don't need *things*

to make us happy, Frederich. We need to know that we
matter, that our simply *being* is important to the man we
marry—apart from the things we do for him and the things
we bring him as dowry. Perhaps Ann felt her lack of importance—whether you intended it or not—it was a very sad
time for you then, yes? And Beata would have surely helped
foster such a notion—"

"Leah—"

"Wait—there's more. The thing I really want to say is that
perhaps you are making the same mistake again—with
Caroline. I think I know her as well as anyone, and I am
telling you this. If she is important to you, you had better
swallow your pride and let her know it—in no uncertain
terms. You won't have her otherwise—"

It's too late, he was about to say, but a sound came from
downstairs and they both looked toward the door. Someone crying—sobbing. It grew louder. Frederich forced himself upward, trying to slide his good leg to the floor, the
effort it took making him cry out in pain.

"Wait!" Leah cried, catching him by the shoulders to
keep him from falling. "Wait—! It's not her, Frederich. It's
Eli."

It seemed a long while before the downstairs grew quiet
again. Then he could hear Caroline's voice, speaking quietly, on and on. He lay there, imagining her comforting Eli.
Perhaps she had her arms around him—perhaps she would
agree to go with him.

He gave a shuddering sigh.

"Someone's coming," Leah said. She stood up so that she
could see out the door. "It's Eli. I'll go now. You remember what I've said—"

"Leah—" he protested, because now he wanted her here.
He was not ready to listen to Eli!

But she slipped out and left them staring at each other. Eli
came farther into the room without asking and he closed the
door behind him. He looked haggard, exhausted, his eyes

red-rimmed from weeping. Frederich searched deep, but he could find no compassion for him, because of the way he did *not* look—guilty.

"I have something to say to you—" Eli began.

"I don't want to hear it," Frederich said listlessly. He turned his face away as if that would be some kind of deterrent. He could feel Eli waiting, and his own impatience began to get the best of him. After a long moment, he asked the only thing he really wanted to know.

"Caroline is . . . all right?"

"She is very sad," Eli said, taking the chair Leah had vacated—again without his leave. "We have talked about William. Don't worry—" he said when Frederich was about to protest. "I guessed that for her sake you said the boy died easy. I didn't tell her otherwise. But now I have something I want to tell you." He stopped, waiting until Frederich looked at him. "It's over, Frederich. We are even—"

"What do you mean?"

He held up his hand. "Johann says you accused Caroline wrongly—because of the money and the letter I sent. I regret that, but I had to do it. I had to keep my promise to Anna to take care of the people she loved. Beata wrote to me—"

"No one knew where you were!"

"She did. I told her where I was going the morning I left. And she wrote to me about how badly you treated Caroline—she was proud of you for doing it—proud that you would be so cruel to Anna's sister, because they both deserved it."

Frederich stared at him. He and Caroline had had their differences, and more than one clash of wills, but he had never been cruel. Had he? How could he have been? He had loved Caroline Holt—even then.

"You . . . believed Beata?"

"Why would I not believe her? I knew how much you hated me—and Anna. But she was dead, and Caroline was in your house and already suffering. She didn't deserve to suffer for *our* sin as well. I thought all the time about how uneasy Anna must rest knowing what was happening to Caroline and about how I had made the promise to her—"

"You had no right to promise her anything!"

"I loved her!"

"You killed her!"

Now, Frederich thought. *Now he looks guilty.*

Eli took a wavering breath. "What happened between Anna and me happened—and none of us are blameless. But what you say is true. I had no right to make promises. Even so, I gave my word to her, and then, instead of keeping it, I ran away. In doing so, I made what I felt for her—what we felt for each other—worthless. So I asked our cousin to write the letter in English for me and I sent Caroline a way to escape—only Beata got the letter and gave it to you and she kept the page where I wrote the *why* of it and her part in it—"

"I want to know what you meant about us being 'even.'"

"What? Do you still think that Caroline and I were lovers? If you do, I feel sorry for you. I meant, Frederich, that I don't have to beg your forgiveness anymore. I meant that my debt to you has been paid. When I found you on the battlefield and brought you out, I gave you back your life. And I gave you another chance—with Caroline. What I took away from you by loving Anna, I have given you back again. You can make use of it or you can throw it away—but I am free."

Frederich clenched his fist, struggling for control. "I don't want anything—!"

Eli abruptly stood up. "I told you before. It doesn't matter what you want. I will stay here for a while—until you are more able. Then I will go back to Pennsylvania. And once again, it doesn't matter what you want. I own half the farm, and I won't see Anna's children go hungry.

"This country—this land here means nothing to me—except for the fact that *she* sleeps in it. I feel the same about it as you do about the sea. It's her grave and I don't want to be anywhere near it. Someday you can buy my share from me. This war won't last forever. What I saw at Gettysburg tells me that. If I were you, I would get well enough to push a plow, but not to carry a gun. Then, when you can pay, you write to the Pennsylvania relatives. We will negotiate."

"Where is Caroline?"

"Still here—or gone. I don't know. Wherever she is, know this, Frederich. I will still keep my promise to Anna. If Caroline is done with you, if she thinks there is no hope for her marriage to you and she will be better away from here, I will help her go."

Frederich closed his eyes. He wanted to rail and to accuse, to throw things with his one good hand, to do everything that his fierce pride demanded. But he was so tired. He had questions still—about Eli's being in the church with Caroline, about his promise to Ann. He heard Eli cross the room and open the door, but he said nothing.

Caroline's face rose in his mind. What was it she had told him?

I'm worth having.

And so she was—except he had never told her. He wanted her here—now—always. And he had ruined his only chance. He hadn't believed her. She would never forgive him for that.

He put his hand over his eyes for a moment and drew a deep breath, struggling not to lose what little control he had. Suddenly, it was William's voice he remembered, in those first days after the marriage.

You be good to Caroline. I mean it, Frederich. I don't care what she's done—she's my sister. I stood by and let Avery hurt her, but I won't let nobody do that again. I want your word—man to man. You be good to her or you answer to me.

And when William was dying...

You said you'd take care of her. You—didn't do it, Frederich! I told you and told you how worried—she is about you. You don't do nothing! She's all by herself—people won't even talk to her. Look at me. I can't watch out for her no more. How am I going to do it now? I'm all...

He looked toward the door. Someone was coming down the hall. Johann—worried.

"I came to see if you're...all right," he said, watching him closely.

"Oh, yes," Frederich said sarcastically. "I am just fine."

Johann smiled. "Good. I thought you might be feeling sorry for yourself. What can I do for you?"

"Give me your hand," he said, straining upward.

"What?"

"Give me your hand, Johann. I want to sit on the side of the bed. I've had enough of being an invalid."

Johann looked doubtful, but he offered his hand, pulling hard until Frederich was able to hang both legs off the side. The pain was excruciating.

"Now what?" Johann said, anxious and hovering.

"Now—Johann—I have to find the way to bring home—my wife."

Chapter Twenty-Four

"What are those?" Johann asked.

"Swords," Frederich said, without looking up. "Made out of wood," he added unnecessarily, because he was obviously hard at work sanding one of them until it was as smooth as the other.

"You made them?"

"John Steigermann made them. I can't cut wood—I can only sand it."

"I see. But aren't they a bit small?"

"They are for my children."

"Ah! And all this time I could have sworn your children were girls."

"Not today, Johann. Today, Lise is my *Degensmann*. Mary Louise is my *Degensmann*. You see?"

"No, I don't think so—unless—are you going to see Caroline?"

"I am."

"Well! Going to see Caroline with a *Degensmann*. Well!"

"Two of them, Johann," Frederich said, still sanding.

"Even better! I suppose she knows you are coming?"

"No."

"No?"

Frederich looked at him, but didn't reply.

"Shouldn't you—"

"Yes, I should, Johann, but I can't. I can't get around all that well yet. I can't waste my strength on skirmishes. I have to save it for the big campaign. Besides that, forewarned is forearmed. I learned that in the army."

"But what good will this—campaign—do, if she has—what is that term you rebel soldiers use—skedaddled?"

"She hasn't skedaddled. My oldest *Degensmann* has her cornered. We three will rendezvous in the hickory woods this afternoon and we will then complete our plan."

"Which is?"

"None of your business."

Johann grinned. "This isn't like you, you know. This isn't like you *at all.*"

"It used to be like me, Johann. You didn't know me then."

"I told you I could have carried letters for you."

"And I told you I don't write in English," Frederich said, the translated letter Eli had written her coming immediately to mind. "Ever. What I have to say to Caroline, *I* will say. I want no one in the middle."

"Then I will pray for a great victory."

"You do that, Johann."

"Does . . . Beata know what is afoot?"

"She does."

"In that case, I will pray harder. But first I would like to offer a small suggestion. You could stand a good barbering, Frederich—but never fear, I am willing to offer you *my* services."

"I think I would be better off letting a *Degensmann* do it," Frederich said, glancing at Johann's hit-and-miss look.

"Not at all! I really don't think their swords will cut cleanly, do you?"

"Do you *know* how to barber?"

"Of course—and any skill I may lack, the Lord will provide."

* * *

Caroline abruptly stopped and listened. She looked toward the open back door.

Whispering?

Yes, she thought. Had Lise forgotten something and come back? What in the world could she be doing?

She stepped around the kitchen table. At least it wasn't the army. They were never quiet when they came. The whispering suddenly ended, but it was followed by a clearing of the throat and a chopped-off, half-smothered giggle. Caroline put down the egg she was about to crack and walked to the back door.

Lise and Mary Louise stood on the porch. They were both wearing their Sunday dresses and bonnets and, incredibly, small wooden swords tied around their waists with gold braid. She tried not to smile, because in spite of the game they were obviously playing, they were both most serious—and because Beata would likely turn them into frogs if she discovered they were out and about in their good clothes.

"Good afternoon," Lise said solemnly.

"Good afternoon," Mary Louise added with her finger in her mouth. Lise reached over and pulled it out.

"Good afternoon," Caroline responded. "To what do I owe the pleasure of this visit?"

It immediately set them to conferring.

"She wasn't supposed to say *that,*" Mary Louise whispered.

"It's all right, Mary Louise," Lise assured her. "It fits."

"It does?"

"Yes! It's your turn to say—"

"I can do it! I am the *Degensmann* of Friedrich Gustav Graeber," she said, still whispering.

"Out loud!"

"I am the *Degensmann* of Friedrich Gustav Graeber!" Mary Louise responded loudly.

"I, too, am the *Degensmann* of Friedrich Gustav Graeber," Lise said, for once the echo.

They both gave smart bows, bending at the waist, their right hands on the wooden hilts of their swords. Then they parted and turned to face the yard.

Caroline gave a soft "oh" sound. Frederich stood a few yards away—*stood*—a few yards away. She took a step forward, but his nearest *Degensmann* caught her skirt.

"No, Aunt Caroline," Lise whispered. "You have to let him walk here. It's important—"

Yes, she thought. She could see that by the determined look on his face. He stood for a moment longer, swaying slightly, then slowly, painfully, he began to make his way in her direction. She waited, trying not to cry.

Look at you! she thought. *Oh, look at you!*

When he neared the porch, she could stand it no longer and she hurried down the steps to help him. He put his arm around her shoulders and leaning heavily on her, made his way to the shaded edge to sit down—in much the same place where he'd been tied the day the army took him away.

"I can't—manage steps very well—yet," he said, clearly winded by the effort.

It took every ounce of strength she had not to fuss over him, not to chastise him for taxing himself so.

She wiped furtively at her eyes with her fingertips and tried to smile. Then she took several deep breaths. "I knew you were getting up now—but I never dreamed—" She had to stop or cry.

"Practice makes perfect, they say," he answered. He gave a small crooked smile. "I still have a lot of practice to go."

She stared at him. He was so thin—and so handsome. He had had his hair cut and his beard trimmed. And the blue of his eyes took her breath away.

He seemed to grow uneasy under her scrutiny, and he turned to nod to his ambassadors. They both trotted around to the side of the house and shortly returned with a big bouquet of yellow and white wildflowers that must have been stashed there during all the whispering. They sol-

emnly gave the bouquet to their father, then came to stand
at his side.

Lise whispered something into his ear, and he nodded
again.

"I am here on behalf of Friedrich Gustav Graeber—who
asks you to please be his wife," she said, and Caroline
looked sharply away. When she looked back, Frederich was
holding the flowers out to her. She looked down at them,
and then at both children, and then into his eyes.

"There is no bottomless basket here for you to give me,
Caroline. I won't make it easy for you to say no. You will
have to say it to my face."

She took a deep breath, but she still didn't take the flowers.

"Each *Degensmann* will stand away now," he said, patting his daughters on the cheek. "There—and over there.
And you will keep watch for me, yes?"

They nodded dutifully and went to stand where he indicated.

"I should have told you this long ago," he said when they
were out of earshot. "I was afraid for you to know. I am still
afraid, but I will say the words, if you will listen."

He waited, and after a moment she nodded.

"You, Caroline Holt Graeber, are more to me than I can
ever say. I tried hard not to let it happen—this love I feel for
you. I think you know that is true. But it is here—in my
heart—in spite of everything I could do. In spite of everything that has happened. I ask you now to forgive me for the
hurt I caused you in the struggle. I ask you now to be my
wife. If you want, we will say the words again in front of
Johann. In front of everybody. Caroline—"

She averted her eyes, turning her attention to where the
children were standing, their faces worried, hopeful.

"No," he said. "Don't do it for them. Do it only if you
love me, too."

She looked at him then, her mind full of images. She saw him grim-faced and unhappy when they said their marriage vows. She saw him kind and gentle at her baby's grave. She saw him passionate in his need of her on their belated wedding night. She saw him betrayed—wounded—suffering. And she saw him now. The man she had come to love with all her heart.

"Caroline, is there nothing about me that pleases you?" he asked quietly.

"Quite a lot, Herr Graeber," she answered, staring into his beautiful, sad, eyes. "You are no ordinary man."

She reached for the flowers then, and for him, careful of his wounds but clinging to him hard.

"Forgive me," he whispered against her ear.

"I love you, Frederich," she told him fiercely.

His swordsmen were there suddenly, covering them both in hugs and kisses. She leaned back to see their faces.

"Are you coming home?" Lise asked, delighted and afraid, as Caroline was herself. "Are you?"

She looked into Frederich's eyes and took Mary Louise onto her lap. "Yes, my loves. I'm coming home."

Epilogue

July 4, 1865

The sudden burst of male voices startled her.

> So flaxen were her ring-a-lets!
> Her eyebrows of a darker hue!
> Bewitchingly! O'er archingly!
> Two laughing eyes of lovely blue!

Robert Burns? she thought. Why would the men be reciting Robert Burns?

> Like harmony her motion!
> Her pretty ankle is a spy!
> Betraying fair proportion!
> Would make a saint forget the sky!

She moved to stand at the kitchen door, and she smiled at the wild cheer that punctuated the end of the recitation. For days, she and Frederich had been preparing for their neighbors to come and help cut the winter supply of wood, trying to put together enough food and drink to feed them all and to honor Private William T. Holt not quite in the way he'd wanted.

But how William would have loved this gathering of his friends and family and his old comrades. Johann had just opened another keg of cider and she doubted if any of them would be able to find their way home.

So few of them left, she thought sadly. Soldiers were still straggling back from the hospitals and from the prisons in the North—Leah had hope yet that one of them might be Kader, and Beata was relentlessly expecting Avery.

Avery. Caroline wondered just how changed he would be. Johann's inquires had finally resulted in a letter from a prison surgeon at Fort McHenry in Maryland, one that curtly assured her that her brother was recovering and that he would be able to travel south soon. She had no doubt that Avery *had* changed. For one thing, the old philandering Avery would have never looked twice at Beata Graeber, who had neither the land nor the looks to interest him. This new and apparently needy one wrote letters to Beata faithfully, letters that sent her rummaging in her hope chest to inventory her yellowed bridal linens, letters that made her object vehemently to today's festivities because ''her'' Avery hadn't yet arrived.

But Frederich hadn't wanted to wait any longer for William's *Leichenbier*. The war was over, and whether Beata's marriage prospect had returned or not, it was time for him to keep his word.

The Robert Burns began again, this time to the accompaniment of sawing and chopping. Caroline smiled to herself, both at the recitation and at the notion that Beata might soon be Avery's wife. Poor Avery—and poor Beata, too. How suited they were for each other. She must remind herself not to enjoy their comeuppance so.

She shifted little William Gustav on her shoulder. He was fed and fast asleep and she needed some place to put him down. She could see Frederich coming with another log, skillfully cajoling old Koenig along as he had always been able to do. He limped still, but there was no doubt that he made her heart flutter. She watched him fondly, smiling a bit when John Steigermann suddenly intercepted him, patting him heartily on the back and shaking his hand. Johann and several of the others followed suit—veterans of Company 'K'' and the 5th North Carolina Regiment. Jacob Goodman brought him a dipperful of cider and cheered him while he drained it.

Frederich saw her then and began to walk toward her, smiling broadly at whatever they called after him and boldly kissing her and the baby when he reached her—in spite of the crowd.

"What was that all about?" she asked, because the men were still looking in their direction and they all grinned and waved.

"Company 'K' has always enjoyed its cider," he said, kissing her again.

"And Robert Burns," she said, a bit taken aback by his display of affection. Frederich Graeber was a private man—except today. Today, he was feeling their great good fortune, she suddenly realized. He had survived, and so had their precarious love for each other. They had only to look around them to know how truly blessed they were.

He looked at her blankly.

"The poem—it's Robert Burns," she said.

"Robert Burns to you—a way to keep a bunch of German plowboys with two left feet in step to me."

"You drilled them to Robert Burns?"

"All the time. It was something Avery started—to annoy Gerhardt, I think. It worked very well—I'm just glad 'The Lass Who Made the Bed to Me' hasn't come to mind—Beata will be out here cracking heads with her broom. You should have seen William when we marked cadence to that one—his ears would turn a fiery red. Where are the girls?"

"Helping Beata in the kitchen—they must be doing well. I don't think she's thrown things a single time. We'll be ready to eat soon...." She stopped because he wasn't lis-

tening. He was grinning over his shoulder again at the sti‌
laughing John Steigermann and the others.

"What is so funny?" she said.

"Nothing," her much too innocent husband informe‌
her.

"Frederich, why are they staring like that? I want to kno‌
what is going on?"

"It's nothing—"

"It *is* something—"

"John Steigermann just noticed you were carrying again‌
that's all."

"Well, there is nothing funny in that," she assured him‌

"He gave me his congratulations—because here you hav‌
one on your hip and one coming, and he just wondered if‌
had any idea what was causing all these babes."

"And you said?"

"Nothing much—"

"Frederich, what? What did you say!"

He grinned from ear to ear. "Oh, I said *I* knew what wa‌
causing them—but *you* didn't!"

* * * * *

I also used material... plan... a manuscript original, simply
the original manuscript... of Kurt Brandt's bar... they
sa... for Cochran... poem "Jack Frost in... an... as
a short story... Two by Two," which Charlotte Park...
for... the August... editions of... Family... magazine.

Author Note

Like *The Prisoner,* this novel is based upon an obscure bit of local history, one especially interesting to me because it occurred in the community of my mother's German forebears, who had emigrated into Piedmont, North Carolina from the Palatinate of Germany via Pennsylvania in the 1700s.

This particular incident came to light as a result of a high school class assignment that required each of us to search old church records for the "human element." The terse account was simply this: At the end of a Sunday service, a man publicly and inexplicably withdrew his pledge of marriage to a woman of the congregation. The pastor then asked if someone else would be willing to marry her. Another man stood and said, "I will."

Now what in the world was that all about? I wondered. I was hopelessly intrigued, and nothing would do but that I eventually create my own version of the occurrence, the "before" and the "after." The fact that two of the old German churches and several of the early houses still exist in the area brought about an acute sense of place. My choice of a time for all this to happen was sparked by my empathy for my own great-great-grandmother, Catherine, who made the frantic trip to Richmond in 1864 to be with her wounded soldier husband, but who arrived too late.

I also used music to enhance a nineteenth-century mind-set—the original soundtrack of Ken Burns's *The Civil War* and *Rivers of Delight: American Folk Hymns of the Sacred Harp Tradition* by the Word of Mouth Chorus, particularly the poignant rendition of "Parting Friends."

Coming in July from

DARLING
JACK
by
MARY
McBRIDE

He was the country's number-one Pinkerton
operative...she was his pretend wife.

"I can hardly wait for her next one! She's great!"
—*Affaire de Couer*

Available wherever Harlequin books are sold.

Look us up on-line at: http://www.romance.net

BIGB96-5

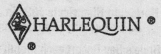

BRIDE'S
BAY RESORT

UNLOCK THE DOOR TO GREAT ROMANCE
AT BRIDE'S BAY RESORT

Join Harlequin's new across-the-lines series, set
in an exclusive hotel on an island off the coast of
South Carolina.

Seven of your favorite authors will bring you exciting stories
about fascinating heroes and heroines discovering love at
Bride's Bay Resort.

Look for these fabulous stories coming to a store near you
beginning in January 1996.

Harlequin American Romance #613 in January
Matchmaking Baby by Cathy Gillen Thacker

Harlequin Presents #1794 in February
Indiscretions by Robyn Donald

Harlequin Intrigue #362 in March
Love and Lies by Dawn Stewardson

Harlequin Romance #3404 in April
Make Believe Engagement by Day Leclaire

Harlequin Temptation #588 in May
Stranger in the Night by Roseanne Williams

Harlequin Superromance #695 in June
Married to a Stranger by Connie Bennett

Harlequin Historicals #324 in July
Dulcie's Gift by Ruth Langan

Visit Bride's Bay Resort each month wherever
Harlequin books are sold.

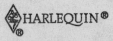 HARLEQUIN ®

BBAYG

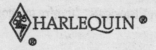